PRAISE FOR DIANNE DUVALL'S BOOKS

Aldebarian Alliance Books

"Intense, addictive and brilliant... I want more!"

—Caffeinated Reviewer

"Full of adventures, sizzling passion, romance, and yes kick-ass fighting."

—Book Dragon

"An action-packed, hair-raising, and heart-rending journey."

—Reading Between the Wines Book Club

"A fascinating world filled with danger, romance, humour, and wonderful discoveries."

—Totally Addicted to Reading

"An Epic Adventure!"

—EnjoyMeSomeBooks

Immortal Guardians Books

"Crackles with energy, originality, and a memorable take-no-prisoners heroine."

—Publishers Weekly

"Fans of terrific paranormal romance have hit the jackpot with Duvall and her electrifying series."

—*RT Book Reviews*

"Each of these stories... has been heart-stopping, intense, humorous and powerfully romantic."

—*Reading Between the Wines Book Club*

"My favorite series, hands down. Every character is beloved. Every story is intense, funny, romantic, and exciting."

—*eBookObsessed*

"Full of awesome characters, snappy dialogue, exciting action, steamy sex, sneaky shudder-worthy villains, and delightful humor."

—*I'm a Voracious Reader*

The Gifted Ones Books

"Full of danger, intrigue, and passion... I'm hooked!"

—*Reading in Pajamas*

"Dianne Duvall has delivered a gripping storyline with characters that stuck with me throughout the day... A must-read!"

—*Reading Between the Wines Book Club*

"Addictive, funny, and wrapped in swoons, you won't be able to set these audios down."

—*Caffeinated Book Reviewer*

"Medieval times, a kick-ass heroine, a protective hero, magic, and a dash of mayhem."

—*The Romance Reviews*

TITLES BY DIANNE DUVALL

THE
RENEGADE
AKSELI CYBORG

ALDEBARIAN ALLIANCE

NEW YORK TIMES BESTSELLING AUTHOR

DIANNE
DUVALL

For my family

ACKNOWLEDGEMENTS

As always, I'd like to thank Crystal. You're such a pleasure to work with. I don't know what I (or members of the street team and books group) would do without you. I also want to send love, hugs, and a huge thank you to my awesome Street Team. You're the *best*! I hope you know how much your support means to me. I appreciate it so much. Another big thank you goes to the members of Dianne Duvall's Network Headquarters, my books group on Facebook. I have so much fun in there with you. If you haven't joined yet and enjoy my books, we'd love to meet you. We always keep things positive in there, so feel free to jump in.

Thank you, Kirsten Potter, for your stellar narration. You have a true gift for giving characters unique and entertaining voices that continue to delight listeners. I always enjoy working with you.

And, of course, I want to thank the wonderful readers who have purchased copies of my books or audiobooks. You've made living my dream possible. I wish you all the best.

PROLOGUE

R ACHEL STRODE DOWN A long corridor, so distracted that she nearly bumped into a Lasaran woman who walked in the opposite direction. This corridor was one of Rachel's favorites because it boasted windows constructed of unbreakable *stovicun* crystal that gave passersby a stunning view.

Or perhaps it only stunned *her* and the rest of the "Earthling" contingent.

Her lips twitched. Even after four months aboard the Lasaran warship *Kandovar*, being called Earthling made her fight the urge to laugh. The term simply resurrected too many memories of sci-fi movies in which aliens with robotic voices said, "Greetings, Earthlings. We come in peace." But out here in space, people tended to identify each other by their planet of origin.

Rachel shook her head. *Out here in space.* Life could take some odd turns. And this was one of the oddest and most momentous she had ever experienced in her long life.

The first had struck during the era historians often referred to as the Dark Ages. Rachel hadn't been as lucky as some of her Immortal Guardian brethren who were born into the aristocracy. Her parents had been poor. Hunger had haunted every waking moment. Only two of her siblings had lived past the age of three. And because all of them had been born with unique gifts that other people lacked, danger had stalked them.

Viking attacks in Britania had made life even more perilous, as she had learned to her detriment when she was slain during one.

Or *nearly* slain.

She *would've* been slain if a vampire hadn't found her before an axe could. Vampires relished chaos and destruction. They flocked

1

to it like flies to corpses, eager to feast upon the weak and wounded. To this day, Rachel didn't know why the vampire who found her as she fled had transformed her instead of killing her. She had no memory of him, only of the terror he'd instilled. The fear that the shadowy figure pursuing her was one of the Viking marauders who had slain everyone she loved.

Perhaps the vampire had not yet succumbed to madness.

Immortal Guardians now knew that vampirism resulted from a very rare virus that behaved more like a symbiotic organism. An alien race—the Gathendiens—created it in a lab and released it on Earth long ago, intending to render humanity extinct without war so the evil bastards could claim the planet, its many resources, and whatever technology remained in the aftermath. All humans infected with the virus swiftly succumbed to insanity and became vampires, having no natural defense against the progressive brain damage it spawned. But those like Rachel were spared that fate. The advanced DNA *gifted ones* were born with not only granted them special abilities, but also protected them from the more corrosive aspects of the virus. Hence, they became immortal, receiving the enhanced strength, speed, heightened senses, and regenerative abilities associated with vampires without the madness that would drive them to tear each other apart.

Had the vampire who transformed Rachel still been sane enough to desire a companion? Or had one of the Vikings stumbled upon the vampire who turned her, killed him, and left her for dead?

She would never know. Fortunately, Seth—the immensely powerful leader of the Immortal Guardians—had sensed Rachel's transformation in that odd way of his, found her, and taken her under his wing. He'd trained her. Given her a purpose. Provided all the food she could eat, she thought with a fond smile. And she'd spent almost every night of the ensuing centuries hunting and slaying psychotic vampires to keep them from wiping out humanity.

Definitely an odd turn of fate.

Pausing, Rachel stared through one of the windows. Bright light streaked past, the pulsing colors almost hypnotic. Sometimes she thought waking up and discovering she had gained preternatural strength and speed had been a lot less shocking than Seth sitting her, four fellow Immortal Guardians, and ten *gifted ones* down and asking them if they would like to travel across the galaxy in an alien spaceship... *after* informing them that his adopted daughter, Amiriska—whom Rachel had thought a *gifted one*—was an extraterrestrial from the planet Lasara.

An *extraterrestrial*.

Absolutely amazing. As was the sight beyond the window.

The *Kandovar* currently barreled through a *qhov'rum*, which created a lovely light show. She had no idea how *qhov'rums* worked but understood them to be like the wormholes scientists on Earth discussed. Instead of bending space, however, a *qhov'rum* provided ships with a safe path free of debris and catapulted them forward at speeds even the most advanced ships couldn't hope to reach, enabling them to cross vast distances in far less time.

Footsteps approached.

Shaking herself out of her reverie, Rachel continued up the corridor.

Two Lasaran males walked toward her, garbed in the uniforms of soldiers.

She smiled. "Hello."

Returning her smile, they dipped their chins in a nod. "*Ni'má.*"

With a barely noticeable delay, the translator in her right ear said, "Miss."

The Lasarans had encouraged her to wear a translator in both ears, but Rachel opted to use one instead, hoping it would help her learn the language faster. The mortal *gifted ones* in their group all bore permanent translator implants, the lucky ducks. Rachel had wanted one of those, too. Alas, the symbiotic virus that set itself up as her immune system had rejected it and forced it out again within minutes of the implantation.

Both soldiers took pains to avoid brushing her arm as they passed. Such always amused her. Lasarans had stringent rules that forbade unmarried men and women from touching. They had enacted the laws long ago to ease overpopulation. The life span of Lasarans greatly exceeded that of humans. Some lived up to a thousand years. So, even with the social restrictions, terraforming two of Lasara's moons had become necessary.

Rachel couldn't wait to see them.

A Yona warrior approached her. Though he resembled a muscular human or Lasaran, his skin held a grayish tint that made him look a little like a photograph desaturated by editing software.

"Hi, Ari'k."

He nodded. Unlike the other soldiers she had passed, Ari'k didn't smile, not that she expected him to. Yona warriors harbored no emotion. Their inability to feel fear, fury, or panic lent them such an advantage in battle that the Lasarans often supplemented their army with Yona. The stoic warriors' complete lack of envy, jealousy, hate, and greed also made them the perfect choice to serve as royal guards. Like Ari'k. He and a few others protected Prince Taelon, his Earthling wife, Lisa, and their adorable baby, Abby.

Recalling a conversation she'd had earlier with a fellow Immortal Guardian, Rachel stepped into Ari'k's path. "Why did the medical officer lose her temper?" she asked.

He halted. "A medical officer lost her temper?"

"No. Let me rephrase that." Though her empathic immortal friend Simone insisted she felt no emotion around the Yona, Eliana believed the stalwart warriors might not be as emotion-free as Lasarans thought. Rachel was still undecided on the matter. "Why *might* a medical officer lose her temper?"

"The possibilities are numerous."

"Try one."

"Because a subordinate disobeyed her orders."

She grinned. "No. Because she had no *patients*."

He stared at her, his expression utterly impassive.

"Get it? Patients? Patience? It's a joke."

Nothing.

She eyed him thoughtfully, detecting neither a twitch of his lips nor a roll of his dark eyes. "Perhaps it lost something in the translation."

"It did," he confirmed stoically, luring a laugh from her. "But that doesn't signify. I believe you are attempting to make me laugh. And I am incapable of feeling emotion."

Smiling, she patted his brawny shoulder. "Apparently so. You may go."

As he left, she headed for a door a few strides away. When she stopped in front of it, it slid up.

Darkness lay within.

Rachel frowned. Smaller than others on the ship, Engine Room 9 boasted a staff of half a dozen men and women. Lively conversation usually filled the large room, drowning out the barely discernible hum of the engines. On any other day, bright lights would illuminate the faces of the industrious men and women as they grinned and called out greetings when Rachel entered.

The hairs on the back of her neck stood up. Now, the only light originated from small monitors on the machines. Even the Lasaran version of laptops, computers, and tablets were dark. Though Rachel's enhanced vision enabled her to see in almost complete darkness, she glimpsed no engineers. Her ears, however, detected several heartbeats within.

"Sinsta?" she called.

Her Lasaran friend didn't answer.

"Endon?"

No answer.

Her eyes narrowed. Reaching over her shoulder, she slid a katana from its sheath.

A faint moan carried to her ears.

Her gaze slid in the direction from which it had come and landed upon nothing but machinery. When she drew in a deep breath, the acrid scent of smoke and burnt electrical components tickled her nose.

Had there been an accident?

Her heartbeat picked up as she strode inside. "Sinsta?" There *must* have been an accident. Lights in every engineering room came on automatically whenever someone entered and didn't turn off until no one remained inside.

An unseen force suddenly yanked the katana from her grasp. Sucking in a breath, Rachel drew the other one and used her excessive strength to hold on to it when the same force tried to take that one, too.

Something shoved her from behind.

Bracing her feet, Rachel spun around in a blur of motion and found nothing.

A foot scuffed behind her. Rachel whirled around again... and gawked.

A hulking figure lunged from the darkness. At least ten feet tall, it looked like a Sasquatch with mange and huge teeth!

"Oh shit!" She dove out of its path.

Roaring, the creature turned and charged again.

Rachel swung her katana.

It passed right through it! "What the hell?"

Her sword leapt from her fingers and clattered to the floor on the far side of the room.

Rachel drew a dagger.

Something swept her feet out from under her. Instinct drove her to tuck her chin and protect her head a split second before her back hit the hard floor. "Oomph!" Bright light banished the darkness and pierced her eyes. Squinting, Rachel started to rise but couldn't. Some unseen weight pressed down upon her as six figures encircled her, each aiming a *tronium* blaster at her head and chest.

Silence reigned.

With her enhanced strength and speed, Rachel could gain her feet and either disarm them or seek shelter before they even realized she had moved. It would be a struggle. But she could do it.

Instead, she grinned. "That was *brilliant!*"

Smiling, Sinsta lowered her weapon. "It was?"

"Absolutely."

Endon and the other engineers all lowered their weapons, too.

Rachel extended a hand to Sinsta. "Help me up, will you?" She didn't need it but knew it would bolster Sinsta and the others' confidence even more if they thought she did.

Sinsta clasped Rachel's forearm and tugged. "Are you okay? You didn't hit your head, did you?"

"No, I'm fine. And very impressed." Giving each of them a proud smile, she brushed off her pants. "You've come a long way."

Endon's smile morphed into a puzzled frown. "No. We were just hidden on the other side of the room."

Rachel chuckled. The Lasarans' translator could be amusingly literal sometimes. "It's an Earth saying. It means you've improved. A *lot*."

"Oh." Face reddening, he grinned back and gave her a slight bow. "Thank you, Rachel."

"It's a compliment you've earned. *All* of you. I didn't know what the hell was happening." She sniffed the air. "What is the smoke from?"

"I believe Earthlings call it incense," Sinsta said.

Temera, one of the other engineers, grinned. "I thought of it."

"Very clever," Rachel praised. "I might've caught on sooner that this was an exercise had you not employed it. Once I smelled it, I worried there had been an accident and dropped my guard."

Two of the engineers returned her katanas.

Thanking them, Rachel slid both into the sheaths on her back with practiced ease.

"I nearly cut myself when I caught it," one admitted sheepishly.

She smiled. "But you didn't. That's what's important. And you worked together with great efficiency. I'm proud of you."

All beamed.

Rachel had spent so many centuries hunting and slaying psychotic vampires that she'd desperately needed a respite from battle. Like her fellow immortals, she'd viewed this adventure in space as a chance for a fresh start. Lasara sounded like a utopia. There was no war. No strife. No famine. No crime. (Since Lasarans were all telepathic, Rachel assumed it would be impossible to get away with crime on their planet if one tried.) And because they were members of the Aldebarian Alliance and valued their many allies, Lasarans didn't hate those who differed from them.

Hate had dogged Rachel's footsteps all her life. For centuries, she'd had to hide who and what she was to keep others from hunting her and wanting to kill her because they believed her unique abilities had been demon-spawned. Or because they thought she was a vampire and steeped in evil. Or, more recently, because they wanted to force her to use her gifts to help them gain power and wealth.

Well, no more. The Lasarans treated her the same way they treated each other. They didn't even care that she had to transfuse herself with blood periodically. It was wonderful.

But a few weeks into her journey to Lasara, Rachel had begun to worry about what her place would be on the alien planet. The *gifted ones* in their group already knew what theirs would be. They would integrate into society and see if they could find love with a Lasaran male. That was the basis for the treaty Seth had negotiated with Ami's people. Gathendiens had also released a virus on Lasara. One that had rendered almost the entire female population infertile. The few who could conceive had great difficulty carrying their babies to term. Consequently, the Lasaran birth rate had plummeted.

If Lasarans had the same life span as humans, their race would be nearly extinct.

Fortunately, Ami and Taelon had both found love on Earth and proven that humans were reproductively compatible. Shortly thereafter, Seth had asked the *gifted ones* if they would be interested in traveling to Lasara and starting a new life. All voluntary. No pressure. No forced marriage or mating. Nothing of that nature. In return, the *gifted ones* would live the rest of their lives on a planet where they would no longer have to hide their differences from the rest of the world.

Seth had also asked Immortal Guardians Rachel, Eliana, Simone, Dani, and Michaela if they would like to accompany the *gifted ones* and guard them to ensure the Lasarans treated them well. But Ami had promised nothing nefarious would happen to the women. And Seth trusted Ami implicitly.

Rather than expressing an overabundance of caution, had he perhaps wanted the Immortal Guardian women to make a fresh start, too? After all, it didn't sound like there would be anything on Lasara that the *gifted ones* would need protection from.

The more she thought about it, the more Rachel had feared she would become obsolete once they reached Lasara, her services no longer needed. Where would that leave her? What would she do?

When she had met Sinsta, an idea had arisen. A solution she found far more palatable than simply becoming a soldier in another army.

Sinsta had envied Rachel's fighting skills after watching her spar with her fellow immortals. "I wish our ship were run more like Segonian warships," the younger woman had admitted wistfully. "All personnel on those ships—even engineers—undergo rigorous training so they can help defend the ship if enemies ever manage to board it." Glancing around furtively, she'd leaned in closer and whispered, "If I had your skills, I might even find the courage to visit Promeii 7."

Promeii 7 was apparently the Las Vegas of the galaxy. What happened there stayed there. Rachel had lost count of the times she'd heard someone snort with laughter and say, "What *doesn't* happen on Promeii 7?"

"Perhaps we could help each other," Rachel had suggested. "If you teach me engineering, I'll teach you how to fight like a pro." Unlike her fellow Immortal Guardians, she had always been curious about new technology. And the tech aboard the *Kandovar* fascinated her.

Sinsta had jumped at the opportunity. And both the number of pupils Rachel trained *and* her knowledge of Lasaran engineering had grown in the months since.

Sinsta drew Rachel into an exuberant hug. "Thank you. I didn't believe we could defend ourselves without weapons." Only soldiers and the Immortal Guardians carried weapons on the *Kandovar*.

"As you just proved, you can if you work together. Which one of you made me see the beast?" In addition to telepathy, each Lasaran was born with one or two abilities that varied as much as those of the *gifted ones* on Earth.

Endon's hand shot up. "I did."

"Who swept my feet out from under me?"

An alarm blared.

Rachel winced as it pierced her sensitive ears. Pointing at the ceiling, she called over the noise, "Who's fabricating the alarm?"

The engineers lost their smiles and exchanged looks.

"None of us," Endon blurted.

Her expression pensive, Sinsta shook her head. "We're not doing this."

Rachel frowned.

"All crew members to battle stations," a male called over the ship-wide speakers. "Repeat—all crew members to battle stations. We are under attack."

A second alarm sounded in the room, not as loud and carrying a different cadence. Everyone but Sinsta ran to their stations.

"You should go," Sinsta said, backing toward her console.

"This isn't another illusion?" Rachel had encouraged them to practice creating those to confuse any enemy who might breach the engineering room and seek to harm them.

"No!" Sinsta ran the last few steps. Her face paled when she viewed the screen. "Find the other Earthlings. Prepare them for the pods."

The escape pods?

Boom. Boom. Boom.

The floor shook beneath their feet.

Oh hell. The ship *was* under attack! While Lasarans like Endon and Prince Taelon could make Rachel *see* and *hear* things that weren't there, they couldn't make the entire ship quake!

Endon swore and raced for the back of the room.

Rachel hated to abandon her new friends, but protecting the *gifted ones* was her top priority. "Do you need me? Should I—?"

"We've got this." Sinsta met her gaze, her eyes full of fear. "Just get your friends to the pods!"

Nodding, Rachel backed into the doorway. "What should I do once they're safe?" Should she return? She could move fast enough that the human eye would only catch a blur of motion. There must be something more she could do.

"Help the pilots!" Temera called as she took off after Endon.

Rachel nodded. "I will! Stay safe!" Her anxiety hitting twenty on a scale of one to ten, she shot away. As Rachel swept through one corridor after another, she encountered none of the pandemonium she expected. Everyone in the hallways ran, ducking and dodging each other. But each clearly had a destination in mind and knew their duty in a crisis. Whenever Rachel encountered pilots, she asked them what bay they needed to reach, hefted them over her shoulders, and got them there in seconds.

She reached the Earthling quarters at the same time fellow immortals Dani and Eliana did.

Four *gifted ones*—Allison, Madeline, Charlie, and Liz—stood in the doorways of their quarters, looking terrified. Each held a go bag. All staggered as another barrage of explosions rocked the ship.

"Ava, Natalie, Mia, Michelle, Sam, and Emily are at the pods," Eliana shouted over the noise. Had she already gotten them there by herself? That only left the four. "Simone is helping them."

Dani nodded. "I'll take Allison and Charlie."

Rachel motioned to the last two *gifted ones*. "I'll take Liz and Madeline."

"Shield integrity compromised," the ship's computer announced in a pleasant female voice. "Shields at seventy-nine percent."

More booms rocked the ship.

The scent of smoke reached them.

Eliana turned to Rachel and Dani with wide eyes. "Go. I'll help the Lasarans get to the pods."

She shot away as Dani headed for Allison and Charlie.

Rachel motioned for Madeline and Liz to stand closer together. As soon as they complied, she bent, folded them over her shoulders, and raced down the corridors so quickly that everyone they passed only felt a breeze. The women's go bags floated behind her like heavy parachutes as she ran, the *gifted ones* clinging to them with desperation.

Rachel halted before a bank of escape pods. Simone finished fastening a harness around Mia in one as Rachel lowered Liz and Madeline to their feet. Dani urged Allison and Charlie into their respective pods. Michaela—the fifth Immortal Guardian—skidded to a halt beside them, conducted a quick head count, then zipped away again.

"Get inside and buckle up," Rachel ordered. More booms rocked the ship as she, Simone, and Dani secured them in pods.

Eliana and Michaela zipped past regularly, conveying Lasarans to other escape pods.

Once the *gifted ones* were settled, Simone closed the hatches. "I'm going to help Eliana and Michaela evacuate the Lasarans."

Rachel nodded. "We will, too."

"Be safe!" Dani called before they each took off in a different direction.

Rachel raced toward the closest Medical Bay.

The alarm continued to blare. Explosions rocked the ship on a near-constant basis. She stopped half a dozen more times to help crew members reach escape pods before she flew through Med Bay's open doors.

Medical officers shouted orders as they tended to injured men and women.

Was incoming weapons fire already penetrating the *Kandovar*'s shield in places? Or were these wounded pilots who had made it back on board?

Lights in the apparatus above every exam bed flickered while the machines conducted scans and delivered pain medication. The smell of blood, sweat, and fear hung heavily in the room as Rachel paused.

"Shields at fifty-four percent," the computer reported placidly.

Several Lasarans spat swears.

Rachel circumvented the large emergency room and headed for the back.

One of the medical officers she'd befriended trotted toward her, arms full of supplies. When her eyes met Rachel's, they conveyed fear and resignation.

"You aren't going to evacuate?" Rachel asked.

Halia shook her head. "I can't. They need me. But you should go." Abandoning the no-touch rule, she caught the arm of a male medic as he passed and thrust the supplies into his hold. "Get these to seven." Grabbing Rachel, she tried to shove her back the way she'd come. "Go. Get your people off the ship while you can."

Rachel dug in her heels. "They're already in pods. And I need blood. Any you can spare."

Nodding, Halia reversed course and ran to the last room.

Rachel followed on her heels and stopped short inside. She'd expected to end up in a supply closet. This room had no shelves or drawers. Only tiled walls.

Halia touched one tile. It lit up, turned opaque, and opened. Inside lay bags of blood that looked remarkably similar to the ones the network used to keep Immortal Guardians supplied with blood back on Earth. "This is all Segonian blood," she said. Immortal Guardians couldn't transfuse themselves with Lasaran blood. It would kill the virus that infected them and leave them with no viable immune system. But Segonian blood was safe. "Med bag, Evie!"

The computer opened a slot in the ceiling.

When a med bag dropped out, Rachel hastily caught it. "How much can I take?"

"Shields at thirty-two percent," the computer announced calmly. *Boom. Boom. Boom.*

"Take whatever you need," Halia replied, her expression grim.

Because she thought they all were going to die?

Well, not if Rachel could help it. "Go," she ordered. "I'll do whatever I can to try to halt the attack."

"Just get to safety!" Halia reiterated and darted away.

It took Rachel mere seconds to fill the med bag with blood. As soon as she sealed it, she looped the strap over her shoulder and sped to her assigned escape pod.

"Evie," she commanded, throwing herself into the pod's only seat, "launch the pod." The Lasarans had named the computer after the engineer who had designed and installed it, but Rachel could never remember if it was Evie or E.V.

"Emergency launches have not yet been initiated," the computer informed her calmly.

"I don't care." She withdrew a bag of blood. "Do it. Now."

"Affirmative. Commencing launch."

A rumble arose. Rachel sank her fangs into the first bag and rapidly infused herself, drawing the blood directly into her veins.

"Please fasten your harness to prevent injury," the computer requested.

"Just go!" Rachel roared and reached for another blood bag. "As soon as we're clear, head straight for the ship that's attacking the *Kandovar*."

"Such would endanger you and defeat the purpose of seeking safety in an escape pod."

"I'm aware. Do it anyway."

"Affirmative."

Pressure shoved Rachel back against the seat. Light flickered on and off behind the impenetrable crystal window as the escape pod shot down the launch tube. Then black space surrounded her, interrupted by bright explosions.

Glutted by the blood infusions, Rachel lunged toward the pod's window.

A small gray craft shot past, followed closely by a sleek black fighter. Light flashed as the black Lasaran craft fired its weapons, striking the gray craft. As the latter exploded, two more gray craft moved into position behind the black one.

Rachel reached toward the first gray craft. Focusing her telekinetic energy, she swung her hand to the right.

The first gray craft veered away and crashed into the second. A spectacular explosion destroyed both craft.

Rachel focused on another gray craft and flung it into its companion. Another explosion heralded their destruction. "Yes!" she cried.

Rachel, was that you? Michaela asked telepathically.

Yes. Where are you?

Heading toward the Gathendien ship. It's behind the Kandovar.

Gathendiens are attacking?

Yes.

Those assholes! Rachel clenched her teeth when a black craft exploded not far away. The battle was fast and intense, like something you'd find in a freaking Star Wars movie.

Concentrating on the gray craft that blew up the black one, she pushed it into the path of another Gathendien fighter. A head-on collision decimated both.

Her excess energy waned.

Rachel persevered and took out two more enemy craft.

The exterior of the *Kandovar* lit up in multiple places as the pod passed close to it. How much of a barrage could a ship that size take?

"Evie, how's the *Kandovar*?" Rachel asked.

"Shields at thirty-two percent."

She swore.

So did Michaela, who heard the response telepathically. *How are you on energy?*

Already running low. Moving something the size of a fighter craft was like pushing a damn F-16 across a landing strip. *But I brought blood with me.*

Like minds. Let's see if we can stop this.

As weakness spread inside, Rachel lunged for the med bag and infused herself with more blood. She'd need as much strength as she could muster to halt the Gathendien ship that launched this attack.

How do you want to do this? Michaela asked.

Rachel started to reply, but her first glimpse of the Gathendien warship left her speechless. Like the *Kandovar*, it was huge. Yet it bore none of the cool sleekness of the former. Rather, it looked as if someone had constructed it with parts scavenged from a junkyard.

Are you shitting me? Michaela blurted. *We can't stop that!*

Rachel had hoped for something smaller, too.

Bright blasts shot from the *Kandovar*'s rear e-cannons and bombarded the Gathendien ship. The latter's transparent shields lit up with each strike but seemed to hold.

Can we board it? Michaela asked.

Two Immortal Guardians tearing through the Gathendien ship could definitely turn the tide of this battle. *I doubt it. Not without being hit by friendly fire.* "Evie," Rachel said aloud, "can you avoid the *Kandovar*'s fire and land this pod inside one of the Gathendien ship's bays?"

"Negative. There is a one hundred percent chance the warship's shields will only allow Gathendien craft with clearance codes to depart and enter."

We'll just have to take out as many of their fighter craft as we can, Rachel declared.

Okay, Michaela agreed. *Be safe!*

You, too!

"*Kandovar* shields at twenty percent," Evie announced placidly.

Swearing, Rachel peered through the window. "Head to the front of the ship." She didn't want to get caught in the nearly constant weapons fire passing between the massive ships.

As the pod raced along the side of the *Kandovar*, Rachel braced her feet and extended her hands in front of her. Although she moved objects with her mind—not her fingers—she had always found it easier to focus her telekinetic ability when she pointed or reached toward the object she wanted to move and mimicked the action she wished it to take.

Familiar heat rushed through her as she targeted another gray craft.

The escape pod shifted suddenly, knocking her off balance and sending her to the floor.

"Damn it." Leaping to her feet, she returned to the window. "Keep the pod steady!" Rachel targeted another Gathendien craft but failed to wreck it before it blew up a black fighter craft. Swearing, she sent the gray craft veering into one of its comrades. Both exploded. She did the same again. And again.

Her heart ached for every Lasaran and Yona she couldn't protect. They were excellent pilots, but the sheer number of Gathendien craft, coupled with the suddenness of the attack, was overwhelming them. And they had little room to maneuver inside the *qhov'rum*. Even as she watched, a black craft flew too close to the *qhov'rum*'s walls and vanished in a bright flare of light.

She swallowed. Had it exploded?

"*Kandovar* shields at thirteen percent," Evie announced.

Panic rose as Rachel gave one gray craft after another a hard telekinetic push. If the *Kandovar*'s shields failed...

She swore when she barely nudged the next craft.

Bending, she grabbed two more bags of blood. The pod jerked sharply. Rachel dropped the bags and cried out as she flew up and struck the pod's metal ceiling. Pain shot through her head. More erupted in her knees when she slammed to the floor. During the next several seconds, she lost sight of up and down as she was tossed about like a gerbil in an exercise ball.

What the hell was happening? Was Evie dodging fire or something?

Bright light poured through the window, blinding Rachel. A screeching, grinding noise filled the pod, piercing her sensitive ears. She crashed into the cramped lav. Bone snapped in one arm. Something hard hit her head.

She slumped to the floor.

Darkness.

CHAPTER ONE

THE VICIOUS POUNDING IN her head roused Rachel.

Grimacing, she hissed in a pained breath. Immortal Guardians didn't get headaches like this one unless they were concussed. Cautiously, she combed her fingers through her hair, traced her scalp, and found wet, matted locks over two lumps. "What the hell?"

"Greetings, Rachel," a woman said.

Jumping, she opened her eyes and moaned. *Everything* hurt. Light illuminated what appeared to be the interior of an escape pod. An open med bag lay on the floor not far away. Blood bags—some full, some empty—littered the rest of the area.

Memory rushed back in an instant and stole her breath.

Oh shit. The battle. A Gathendien ship had attacked the *Kandovar*!

Heart racing, Rachel swiftly pushed herself up. Agony cut through one arm like a knife. Crying out, she cradled it to her chest and glanced down at it.

Bone protruded from the skin in a grisly display.

Well, she'd have to deal with that later after the... battle.

Everything within Rachel went still as she noticed the silence and darkness that reigned outside the pod.

Scrambling to her feet, she raced to the window.

Beyond it, where the bright lights of the *qhov'rum*'s walls should streak past, endless darkness stretched instead, interrupted only by distant stars. No small gray Gathendien craft or sleek black Lasaran fighter craft zipped back and forth as they engaged in brutal battle. No massive warships loomed in the background.

Pressing her nose to the glass, Rachel looked left, right, up, down, and could spy no other craft at all. "Where's the ship?" Panic rose as she strained to see more. "Where the hell is the ship?"

"Which ship do you seek?" Evie asked politely.

"The *Kandovar*," Rachel snapped. Shouldn't that be obvious?

"The *Kandovar* has been destroyed."

Rachel's knees weakened. Staggering backward, she reached out with her good hand and gripped the back of the pod's only seat to steady herself. "What?"

"The *Kandovar* has been destroyed. The explosion its destruction produced propelled this escape pod through the walls of the *qhov'rum*."

Tears blurred Rachel's vision. Her throat thickened. It couldn't be true. "Hail the ship."

"The ship no longer exists," Evie stated. "Any attempt to hail it would be futile."

"Try anyway." The *Kandovar* was huge. Maybe only part of it had exploded and the rest remained intact.

"Attempting to hail the *Kandovar*." A moment passed. "Unable to make contact."

Rachel closed her eyes. Tears slipped over her lashes and trailed down her cheeks. Was it really gone? "Maybe their communications array was damaged. Can you pilot us back to the *Kandovar*'s last location?"

"Negative. Such would require us to re-enter the *qhov'rum*. This pod's engine cannot generate the propulsion required to penetrate the walls."

Which lent more credibility to the explosion-hurtling-them-through-it theory.

Rachel didn't want to believe it. All those people... Sinsta, Temera, Endon, and her other friends in engineering. Halia in Med Bay. "How many people were still aboard when the ship exploded?" Loyal to their last breath, any Lasaran crew members needed to keep the ship going would've remained at their posts as long as they could.

"Unknown," the computer responded.

The Yona would've remained aboard, too. They felt no emotion, no fear. Only duty and obligation. And the *gifted ones*...

"Did the other escape pods launch?"

"According to my last contact with the *Kandovar*, many escape pods launched successfully prior to the ship's destruction."

The *gifted ones* should've gotten away safely then. But what of Eliana and the other immortals? Rachel knew from her brief telepathic conversation with Michaela that *she* had made it into a pod. But the last time she'd seen the others, they had been rushing around the ship's corridors, trying to help Lasarans evacuate.

Eliana! she called telepathically.

Nothing.

Simone!

Silence.

Dani! Mikaela!

Only the faint hum of the pod's engine reached her.

Opening her eyes, she struggled to hold back more tears and called out to the *gifted ones*.

None responded.

"Would you hail the other escape pods, please, Evie?"

"Hailing escape pods now."

She glanced around. How sturdy *were* these pods? Could the blast waves of the *Kandovar*'s explosion rip one apart? Or colliding with a fighter craft?

"All attempts to hail other escape pods have failed," Evie announced.

"Why?"

"None are within range."

Rachel shook her head. "How is that possible? If the explosion forced other escape pods out of the *qhov'rum*, they should be all around us." Returning to the window, she peered outside.

"No escape pods are within range," the computer repeated.

"Then where are they?"

"I cannot say with certainty."

"Then guess and give me the most likely possibilities."

"Processing request. Some escape pods may still be traveling through the *qhov'rum* if it remains functional. If it does not, they may be trapped inside it."

That didn't sound good.

"The Gathendien ship that attacked the *Kandovar* may have retrieved others."

That was even worse.

"Many were likely thrust through the walls of the *qhov'rum* by the explosion."

Rachel didn't want to ask her next question but forced it past tight lips. "Could the Gathendiens have destroyed the other escape pods?" She wouldn't put it past them.

"That is another possibility," Evie acknowledged. "The weaponry used to pierce the *Kandovar*'s shields could easily destroy an escape pod."

Rachel swore.

"However, my last examination of the battle indicated that Gathendiens were not targeting escape pods."

Only the black fighter craft.

Hope rose. "What about the Lasaran fighter craft? Can you hail them?" The Gathendiens would've probably blown up any left behind after the *Kandovar*'s destruction. But maybe the explosion forced some fighters out of the *qhov'rum* like her.

"Attempting to hail Lasaran fighter craft." Pause. "Attempts failed."

"Damn it! They can't all be dead! Why aren't any of them responding to your hails?"

"The range of this pod's communications system is limited. Any escape pods or fighter craft that remain intact may have already traveled beyond its reach."

"How? If they were shoved outside the *qhov'rum* the same time this pod was, shouldn't I be able to see them and contact them?"

"Negative. The *qhov'rum* propels craft forward at speeds that even the fastest engines cannot replicate. A minute's distance apart *within* the *qhov'rum* represents a distance *outside* it that would take this pod with its weaker engine many months to traverse. Because each pod exited the *qhov'rum* at a different point, they are likely scattered across vast sectors of space. The Lasaran fighter craft as well. My inability to contact them supports this conjecture."

So Rachel was alone out here in an escape pod with only two months of life support?

She thought furiously. "What about the Gathendien ship?" She still had enough blood from Med Bay to bolster her strength and mend her arm. She'd rather let the Gathendiens nab her and then do her damnedest to kill them all and commandeer their ship than sit here and wait for her oxygen supply to run out. "Did *it* exit the *qhov'rum*?"

"Affirmative."

A hint of relief eased the tightness in her chest. That meant it wasn't inside, trying to pick off survivors. "Where is it?" A huge, putrid yellow ship wouldn't fade into the dark background of space.

"I am unable to locate it."

"Then how do you know it's out here somewhere?"

"I noted its departure shortly before this escape pod exited the *qhov'rum*."

"And now it's too far away for you to even determine what direction it took?"

"Affirmative."

So much for hitching a ride. "How far away is Lasara?"

"It would take this pod many years to reach the Lasaran home-world."

"And I only have two months of food and life support?"

"Correct."

The pain in her arm hindered her ability to think straight. Kneeling, Rachel grabbed a bag of blood. As soon as her fangs descended, she sank them into the bag and siphoned the ruby liquid into her veins.

Silence threatened to smother her. Rachel had never in her life experienced this level of quiet. Her heightened sense of hearing could perceive a sneeze five miles away. And her telepathy had always led the thoughts of others within the same radius to bombard her on a near-constant basis.

The longer the quiet lasted, the more it amplified her grief and sense of utter isolation.

She lowered the empty bag.

Almost immediately, the virus within her went to work, repairing the damage wrought by being flung around the pod. It focused on her arm first. Rachel gritted her teeth as the broken bone reset itself and began to mend.

"Are any Aldebarian Alliance ships within range?" Multiple alien races composed the alliance. Lasarans. Segonians. Yona. Secta. Rachel hadn't memorized the names of them all, but Evie could tell her who was whom.

"Negative. I detect no ships in good standing with the Aldebarian Alliance nearby."

"What about ships that *aren't* in good standing with the alliance?"

"Negative."

"Any space stations or spaceports? Friendly *or* hostile?" She'd take anything she could get.

"Negative."

"What about planets? Are there any inhabited planets within range?"

"Negative."

"Any planets that aren't inhabited?"

"None that provide the atmosphere you require."

Well, crap. "Are any planets within reach currently being terraformed?"

"Negative."

"Do members of the Aldebarian Alliance ever set up outposts on planets that lack a habitable environment and atmosphere without terraforming them?"

"Affirmative. Alliance members sometimes construct communications arrays on such planets."

"Locate any planets within a two-month travel distance from us that could support such an array."

"Processing request."

The pain in Rachel's arm eased a bit. She studied it while she waited.

The torn flesh where the bone had protruded had drawn together. A dark, grisly bruise covered most of her forearm. Over the next few hours, a scar would form and gradually fade away. The bruise would also disappear as the healing continued. Though another blood infusion would eradicate the rest of her aches and pains, she should probably hoard the remainder of her supply, just in case.

"I have located one system within reach. It includes five planets and forty-three moons that revolve around a single sun. Only one planet exists in what the Aldebarian Alliance deems the habitable zone. However, all investigations of the planet have yielded the same conclusion—that it is incapable of supporting life and lacks any desirable resources."

"Do you detect any communication signals coming from that system?"

"Negative."

"Is there anything else we can reach in two months?"

"Negative."

"If I reduce the oxygen concentration in the pod, limit my energy usage, and ration food and water, can I survive longer than two months?"

"Affirmative. However, lower oxygen levels may cause headaches, dizziness, nausea, fatigue, and shortness of breath."

"I'm okay with that." She could withstand far more damage than an ordinary human.

"Oxygen deprivation may also cause fluid to build up in your brain or lungs, resulting in serious, life-threatening—"

"I got it." Maybe she could stave that off with the supply of oxygenated blood she'd brought with her. "Is there a refrigerated compartment in this pod? I need to store this blood and keep it from spoiling. Preferably somewhere that won't increase the pod's energy consumption."

"Affirmative. There are two compartments adjacent to the battery housing unit that remain cold enough to keep the blood viable. No additional energy usage will be necessary."

"Excellent." Rachel finished gathering the blood bags and returned them to the med bag.

"If I can last four months instead of two, could we make it to *any* place that's inhabited?"

"Searching for inhabited destinations within the new range." Pause. "Negative."

"Does this pod have a homing beacon?"

"Please submit inquiry using alternate terms."

"Is there an emergency signal or distress beacon this pod can send out for a long time after landing? Something that ships coming close enough might pick up and wish to investigate?"

"Affirmative. If this pod lands on a planet whose surface receives sunlight, it can transmit such a signal indefinitely using energy derived from the sun."

"Can it produce oxygen in the same manner?"

"Negative. Oxygen stored on this escape pod is limited."

Oh well. It was worth a shot. "Let's head for that solar system you mentioned."

"Setting course for designated system now."

If worse came to worst and no knight-in-shining-armored spaceship showed up to rescue her, she could land on the hostile planet, force herself to go into stasis—a creepy form of dormancy or hibernation Immortal Guardians could succumb to in dire circumstances—and last for decades, if not centuries, on whatever oxygen remained. One of her Immortal Guardian brethren back on Earth had lived for two years, buried alive with only a miniscule pocket of air, after slipping into stasis.

Rachel shuddered at the thought of it.

Hopefully, it wouldn't come to that.

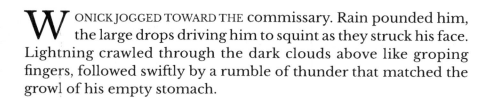

WONICK JOGGED TOWARD THE commissary. Rain pounded him, the large drops driving him to squint as they struck his face. Lightning crawled through the dark clouds above like groping fingers, followed swiftly by a rumble of thunder that matched the growl of his empty stomach.

Thrilled by the return of the rainy season, *duwens* of various hues and sizes filled the air with croaks, peeps, and twangs. All but one leapt out of his path. The remaining *duwen* refused to move and evinced no fear as the cyborg warrior splashed toward it. Its body the size of Wonick's head, the creature boasted long back legs that could take it high into a tree's limbs with a single jump. It also bowed to no one, since the toxin it released when threatened could kill almost anything within minutes. The cyborgs had come *vuan* close to losing one of their men who had thought to cook one their first night on the planet.

If a *duwen* could be arrogant, this one certainly was.

Smiling, Wonick shook his head as he veered around it. Upon reaching the entrance to the commissary, he paused beneath the awning, drew a hand over his face and closely cropped hair, and shook his clothes to remove some of the moisture before entering.

This time of evening, cyborg warriors usually occupied every table, their conversations producing a steady hum. Tonight, however, most chairs were empty. Abandoned plates with partially eaten food covered every table's surface.

He glanced to one side where his brethren clustered together.

Savaas, the leader of the cyborgs, noted his appearance and waved him over.

"Has something happened?" Wonick asked as he joined them.

"A small craft is approaching our system," their leader responded.

Wonick frowned. "What kind of craft?" One of this planet's most desirable features was its distance from Aldebarian Alliance-occupied space. Few travelers ventured this far. And the cyborgs had filled the galactic network with false information to discourage any who might brave the trip anyway in search of undiscovered resources and riches.

"We don't know yet. It's too far away."

"She said it's a Lasaran escape pod," Jovan blurted.

Wonick studied him. "Who did?"

"The female in the craft. She's broadcasting on all channels. I was on communications duty and caught her signal. She claims she's a survivor of the *Kandovar*'s destruction."

Wonick met Savaas's gaze. "Is she?"

"We can't confirm that with certainty until the craft is closer." And the cyborgs didn't want *any* craft coming near their new homeworld. "Nor is there any way to confirm that the occupant is female. It could be pirates using a voice modifier."

Such wouldn't be the first time. Most pirates lacked honor and would use any means necessary to lure unsuspecting ships into traps.

Wonick performed a quick calculation. "If it *is* a Lasaran escape pod, it was ejected from the *Kandovar* and the *qhov'rum* long enough ago that the occupant will soon run out of resources." Not just food and water, but breathable air.

Savaas shook his head. "That's not our concern."

Jovan glanced at the others. "What if it *is* a female?"

"That doesn't signify," Savaas said.

Jovan pursed his lips. "It signifies a little. Doesn't it? If it's a woman—"

Savaas's expression chilled as he pinned the younger warrior with a glare. "The Akseli soldiers who hunted and slew our cyborg brothers by the hundreds weren't all male. There were females among the ranks. Would you have spared their lives?"

Jovan dropped his gaze. "No."

Savaas swept the group with a hard gaze. "We'll monitor the situation and—as we always have in the past—take whatever actions we must to protect our world. Dismissed."

As the other soldiers trailed away and returned to their cooling meals, Savaas left the commissary. Wonick followed, knowing without being told that Savaas wished it. The two friends had been through much together and didn't always require verbal communication.

They walked some distance in the rain and entered dense forest. A well-worn path allowed them passage.

"Will those actions include blowing up the escape pod?" Wonick asked at length, already knowing the answer.

"If necessary," Savaas replied with no discernible hint of unease. He could be utterly ruthless when it came to keeping his fellow cyborgs safe.

Wonick could, too, he reluctantly acknowledged, and *had* been on multiple occasions.

The memories of it still haunted him. But when he and Savaas had tried to do the right thing and refused a direct order issued by Chancellor Astennuh, leader of Aksel, to execute two young men who were clearly innocent of the charges laid against them...

Astennuh had deemed all cyborgs a threat to his newly found-ed dictatorship, filled the Akseli airwaves with propaganda that labeled cyborgs as malfunctioning robotic mass murderers, and called for them to be *decommissioned* immediately. Since he could no longer control them, he'd wanted them all dead.

That order had instead driven Savaas and Wonick to launch a rebellion. The two of them had placed honor above all and lost far more cyborg lives in the ensuing battles than they'd saved. Those they managed to get off-planet, they considered family. The two eldest cyborgs would now sacrifice whatever they must in order to keep this settlement a secret and keep their brothers safe.

Even honor.

Wonick was less willing to sacrifice that than Savaas. Honor had set them on this path. If they abandoned it now, what had it all been for? And yet, like Savaas, he couldn't bear to suffer any more losses.

Savaas was inherently a good man. Wonick deferred to him as their leader for just that reason. *And* because Savaas was less tortured by making the hard decisions... like allowing a female to die inside an escape pod in order to ensure the continued safety of his flock.

If it *was* an escape pod.

The two warriors' stroll through the forest led them to the primary communications monitoring station. Trees that seemed tall enough to pierce the clouds concealed the building from above with a thick canopy that remained green throughout the planet's changing seasons. They did not, however, disrupt the station's ability to scan for nearby signals.

When Savaas and Wonick entered, strange music filled the room. The two cyborgs manning the station glanced up. One hastily tapped the console's surface to silence the sounds.

"Leave us," Savaas commanded.

Rising, they left without a word.

Once the door slid closed, Savaas crossed to the console and tapped it.

The odd music resumed, a steady thrumming beat with a howling instrument Wonick couldn't identify. He'd heard nothing quite like it before.

Two women suddenly began to sing, inviting anyone listening to watch them fly.

Wonick's eyes slid to Savaas, who showed no reaction as the music continued a little longer.

"And that, my friends," one of the women announced when the music ended, "was 'Set it All Free' performed by Scarlett Johansson and accompanied by yours truly."

"That isn't Lasaran," Wonick pointed out.

"No."

"It's Earth English."

"Yes."

"It sounds as if there may be *two* women in the pod."

"Yes."

Again the woman spoke. "For those who are tuning in to the Galactic Music Hour for the first time, my name is Rachel. I was recently aboard the Lasaran warship *Kandovar* when Gathendiens attacked and destroyed it. I am now drifting through space—alone in an escape pod—and would greatly appreciate it if some knight in shining armor would ride to my rescue."

She had a lovely voice. One that appealed to him and made him want to listen more. Yet it failed to distract him from the significance of her speech. "The only Earthling travelers in the galaxy were aboard the *Kandovar*." Earth's civilization had not yet advanced enough to venture into deep space.

"And we have confirmed that Gathendiens destroyed the *Kandovar*," Savaas said.

"Then this woman must indeed be in a Lasaran escape pod."

"Unless she is a pirate, luring members of the search and rescue mission into a trap," his friend countered.

Lasarans weren't the only ones searching for survivors. All member nations of the Aldebarian Alliance had sent ships to locate as many as possible. And the smaller the craft, the greater the lure for pirates.

"Pirates wouldn't have access to Earth music," Wonick pointed out. "Nor would they know her language." Most language translators did not yet include those from Earth. Even Wonick and Savaas wouldn't know Earth's languages if they hadn't stumbled upon them in a Gathendien database they'd infiltrated.

"If pirates confiscated a Lasaran escape pod," Savaas pointed out, "and enslaved the inhabitant, they could easily use her as bait... if she still lives. They could've also forced her to make a recording, then slain her."

Wonick bit back a curse, unable to refute the possibility. "And if they didn't? If this *is* an Earthling, alive in a pod and in need of assistance?"

Music resumed, the woman now singing with a man. Something about still standing.

She must be singing along to recordings. Three people wouldn't have survived this long in an escape pod meant for one.

Savaas raised his head and met Wonick's gaze. "It isn't our concern."

And yet, Wonick remained troubled by the notion of letting her perish. "We could send an anonymous tip to the Lasarans and let them know where to find her. Since they can't break our encryption, we would risk nothing."

"Lasaran ships couldn't make it out this far in time to rescue her."

"One of their allies might. The Segonians have a base on Mila 9. If their fastest ship heads for the pod and they tell her how to alter the pod's trajectory to meet them..."

Savaas shook his head. "Aldebarian Alliance ships have never ventured this close to us. Do you really want them to now?"

"Rescue ships would only see what we let them see, like the pirates who happen by." The cybernetic implants embedded in cyborgs' brains allowed them to gain as much knowledge as an unbridled AI. And they had used that knowledge to create a shield that encircled the entire planet, one that—as he'd pointed out—only showed passersby what the cyborgs *wanted* them to see. "None would even attempt to land."

"Are you sure? Pirate ships usually boast outdated, scrapped-together technology. Any Aldebarian Alliance ships that take part in the search will have updated systems."

"Their scans still couldn't penetrate the shield we've erected."

"But their ships can. If they encounter any difficulties and require repairs, they may brave the apparently hostile atmosphere here to land. Or they may simply take this opportunity to discover if the rumors are true and explore our system, since few alliance ships venture this far. Other unwise travelers and explorers have in the past."

True. A few *had* ventured close enough to investigate whether the rumors were true, hoping the planet's hostile surface might conceal a treasure trove of resources they could exploit.

The cyborgs destroyed any craft that breached their atmosphere.

"If a rescue ship decided to land here," Savaas continued, "instead of allowing one to perish to ensure our existence remains a secret we would have to slay many. You know how much the Lasarans and other members of the Aldebarian Alliance disapprove of advanced AI creations."

"We aren't AI."

"No. We're Akseli warriors with multiple enhancements and cybernetic implants that make our bodies harder to destroy and enable our brains to function like computers. Most beings believe we're more machine than man now. To them, we are as artificial and great a threat to their existence as T."

The cyborgs had created T, an artificial intelligence, for their only ally—Janwar, a notoriously dangerous Akseli pirate. Janwar had gained his violent and merciless reputation in part by aiding the cyborg rebellion. Bounty hunters throughout the galaxy were as eager to capture and kill him as they would be to capture and kill cyborgs if they knew Wonick and the others still lived. The price on Janwar's head by far exceeded that of other known targets. And his retaliations in the past had instilled enough fear in bounty hunters to grant him safe passage now.

Most days.

Janwar was the only being Savaas and Wonick trusted, because he and his cousin were the young men Chancellor Astennuh had sent the cyborgs to execute all those years ago. Janwar owed his life and Krigara's to Savaas and Wonick. And the cyborgs on this planet owed the contentment they'd found in the years since the rebellion to Janwar and the rest of the *Tangata* crew.

A heavy sigh escaped Savaas, the only sign that he regretted the decision he must make. "Akseli civilians weren't the only ones who looked the other way and refused to help us. Few nations objected when Astennuh ordered our extermination."

Wonick couldn't refute that. The Aldebarian Alliance may have expelled Aksel from its member nations. But it hadn't stepped in to aid the cyborgs, unwilling to embroil their worlds in galactic war to save a few artificially enhanced beings that rumor labeled emotionless killing machines. "We could contact Janwar," he suggested. Janwar visited their planet regularly, bringing supplies they requested. He also had the fastest ship in the galaxy, courtesy of the cyborgs.

Savaas shook his head. "He's too far away to render aid. When we last spoke with him, he was ferrying Prince Taelon, his Earthling lifemate, and their heir to Lasara."

Even the *Tangata* couldn't cross such a vast distance in time to save the woman.

Savaas rested a big hand on Wonick's shoulder. "I'm not without sympathy for the female. That we must make such regrettable decisions angers me. But Astennuh has forced our hands, and decisions like these enable us to live another day."

"It angers me as well," Wonick admitted. "Callous disregard for life is what sparked our rebellion. Engaging in the same feels dishonorable."

Savaas's grip tightened as anger darkened his features. "Do *not* compare the two. Astennuh sacrificed hundreds of thousands to hide his perfidy and increase his own wealth and power. And billions suffer beneath his rule. *We* must sacrifice *one* to ensure the safety of our entire settlement."

Weary of it all, Wonick shook his head. "One feels like too many."

"Agreed." Releasing him, Savaas looked toward the console when silence fell. A moment later, music poured over the speakers once more. "If we were considered equals in the Aldebarian Alliance, we could join the search and rescue mission." A muscle twitched in his jaw. "But we are not. Alliance members made that clear when—instead of defending us or offering us asylum—they sat back and watched us fall, one by one." Fury burned in the eyes Savaas turned upon him. "If they ever learn of our existence, we will never know peace again."

Wonick had concluded the same during the early years of their newfound freedom when hunger and hardship had made contacting the alliance tempting.

Savaas strode past him to the door. "I want *you* to monitor the communications. If any relief teams express doubt about my stance, replace them."

Wonick could only issue an abrupt nod as his friend left, fearing others would find the stance as distasteful as he did.

The woman happily advising him through song not to worry about a thing merely increased his misgivings.

CHAPTER TWO

Pain woke Rachel. It began as mild heat along her right side. Sluggish from the long slumber, she rolled onto her back.

Brightness flared behind her closed lids. "Lower lights," she mumbled.

"Lights are off," Evie replied cordially.

Rachel frowned. Was Evie malfunctioning? The lights were *not* off. But they *should* be. She had ordered Evie to shut down everything possible to preserve power and resources while Rachel sank into the deepest sleep she could, short of succumbing to stasis. As far as she knew, *that* state could only be achieved through extreme blood loss, which she'd prefer to avoid if possible.

The skin on her face, arms, and hands tingled uncomfortably.

Rachel opened her eyes. The ceiling of the escape pod greeted her, no darkness in sight despite the lack of artificial light. Sitting up on the seat she'd reclined to form a bed, she reeled drunkenly. Everything around her spun in dizzying circles. Her head pounded. Her stomach roiled. Her skin burned.

"You appear to be in distress," Evie pointed out. "Do you wish me to return oxygen levels to normal?"

Oxygen levels?

Oh. Right. She'd told Evie to reduce those, too. "Yes. Please restore normal oxygen levels."

A hiss sounded. Rachel's head gradually ceased pounding. Her stomach stopped threatening to heave as the interior of the pod ceased spinning. Her face and hands, however, merely hurt more.

Rachel stared down at them, uncomprehending. "Why are my arms pink?" And was it her imagination, or were they thinner?

"Unknown."

"Is it from the low oxygen levels?"

"Negative. The skin discoloration caused by low oxygen levels is blue, not pink," Evie replied.

"Then what...?" Her eyes widened as realization dawned.

Swearing, Rachel scrambled off the bed, turned it back into a chair, and ducked behind it. "Evie, is that sunlight pouring through the window?"

"Yes."

"Can you shield me from the ultraviolet rays?"

"Affirmative."

Silence fell.

"Well?" Rachel asked. "Did you do it?" The light inside the pod hadn't dimmed.

"Affirmative."

Hesitantly, Rachel raised a hand.

Sunlight illuminated it, but the sunburn she'd suffered didn't worsen.

She raised her other hand.

Her skin didn't blister.

Only then did she rise and let light bathe the rest of her.

It wasn't as bright as it had seemed when she'd first awakened. She hadn't transfused herself with blood since her first day in the pod, opting to keep it for an emergency. That must have caused the virus-induced photosensitivity to kick in faster than usual.

Cautiously, Rachel moved to the window. "Wow," she breathed.

Until now, her trek through the galaxy had shown her only dark space filled with stars and the bright inner walls of the *qhov'rum*. Now a sun shone in the distance, far enough away that the light reaching her was about the equivalent of what she would've experienced on Earth at sunset.

"Is that where we're going?" she asked.

"Affirmative."

"Can you enhance the visuals or zoom in or whatever?"

A clear screen slid down in front of the window. "Enhancing visuals."

Rachel gasped as the sun abruptly raced toward her. Stumbling back a step, she stared, wide-eyed, as additional details took shape.

"Oh wow," she repeated. The pod's camera had one heck of an impressive lens. It now displayed not only the planets circling the sun but also the moons revolving around the planets. Evie even displayed each body's elliptical orbit. "That's amazing."

Unlike Earth's solar system, the planets revolved around the sun vertically instead of horizontally.

Or was the pod tilted sideways, altering her perspective? Since Lasaran escape pods generated artificial gravity, she supposed it could be either.

In the early days of her expulsion from the *qhov'rum*, she had asked Evie to turn off the artificial gravity, hoping that would both conserve power *and* help her stave off anxiety and boredom. The pod may be small, but there was still enough room to bounce from one wall to the other and do some flips.

Alas, Evie had refused, her protocols preventing her from overriding the safeguard. Evidently, Lasarans, Sectas, and some of the other more advanced Aldebarian nations had learned during the early years of their space exploration that long-term exposure to no gravity weakened the crew's muscles and bones. It also shrank crew members' hearts by as much as twenty percent each year they spent in space, resulting in needless suffering and death before they found a way to generate artificial gravity.

Rachel stared at the planets. The camera failed to zoom in enough to show details of the planets' surfaces. They were just balls of various sizes and colors, circling the sun. None, however, bore the vibrant blue and green of Earth when viewed from space, something that seemed to confirm Evie's conviction that they couldn't support life.

"Have you picked up any communications coming from that system?" she asked.

"Negative."

"If the planet we're heading toward had a communications array, would you pick it up? Or are we still too far away?"

"Any communications array erected by a member of the Aldebarian Alliance would reach us without difficulty. However, if a less developed nation or someone with limited resources erected a more primitive array on the planet, it may not be capable of covering this great a distance yet."

"Someone with limited resources?"

"Criminals or pirates who must avoid alliance spaceports and planets would have limited resources."

"Great. Anyone else?"

"If any undiscovered, fledgling civilizations exist in nearby unexplored systems, they may be new to space travel and have limited resources. However, such a civilization would likely lack the technology needed to erect *any* structures on a hostile world."

Honestly, Rachel would prefer the former. She could always defeat pirates, steal their ship, and have Evie guide her to the nearest Aldebarian Alliance station or planet. Someone who could barely make it from one system to the next likely couldn't help her with that.

"No one has responded to the distress calls or honed in on the beacon?"

"Correct."

"Have you been playing the recordings I made?" She had recorded a day's worth before shutting down as much as she could and sinking into a deep sleep.

"Affirmative," Evie replied. "I have broadcast one every day for one hour, as you instructed."

"On every channel?"

"Correct."

"How many are left?"

"I have broadcast twenty-one recordings twice and three recordings once."

Rachel quickly did the math in her head. "So I've been asleep for forty-five days?"

"Affirmative."

No wonder she was so out of it. And parched. And hungry. She must've come close to achieving stasis *without* blood loss, otherwise she would've lost more weight. "No nibbles yet?"

"Please repeat inquiry."

"Has anyone responded?"

"Negative. A response would've prompted me to wake you as instructed."

That sucked. "Have you broadcast today?"

"Negative. It is not yet time."

"Then we'll broadcast live as soon as I've bathed and eaten something."

If only she *could* bathe. All the little pod offered was a goodly supply of cleansing wipes and a clothing sanitizer. Though she was clean when she finished, Rachel found it far less satisfying than a warm shower or bath.

It didn't take long to prepare dinner afterward. The MREs in the pod were surprisingly tasty. Rachel hadn't devoured this much in one sitting since Seth had taken her under his wing shortly after her transformation. It had been the first time in her life that she had consumed three full meals a day.

"Okay." She dropped the tray in the pod's sanitizer. "Let's do this."

Taking out her phone, she accessed her music and scrolled through her playlists. "All I have to do is press play, right?"

"Correct. I have remotely interfaced with your device."

"Excellent. Record these while you broadcast them in case I end up stranded on that planet." Hopefully, someone would pick up her broadcast before that.

If they didn't, she'd have to slip into stasis and have Evie broadcast once a day until the pod ran out of energy.

"Affirmative."

"Ready to broadcast?"

"Affirmative. You may begin."

Rachel returned to the window and stared at the planets in the distance. "Good morning, good afternoon, or good evening," she said as if she were a radio announcer. "If you've been tuning in, you already know my name. For those who are new to the Galactic Music Hour, I'm Rachel. I was recently traveling aboard the *Kandovar*, a Lasaran warship that Gathendiens destroyed, and am now drifting through space, alone, in an escape pod. Would anyone care to come to my rescue?"

Silence.

"No?"

More silence. "Perhaps you're shy. If that's the case, settle back, and I'll help you get to know me better by sharing some music from my homeworld. Let's start with... 'Sunroof,' performed by Nicky Youre and accompanied by yours truly." Hitting play, she began to sing along with the la's and da's. Rachel thought it particularly appropriate since she was staring at a brilliant sun, was blasting music, and had one thing on her mind. Not what the singer did, of course. She just wanted to be rescued. To hear another person's voice and know she wasn't all alone out here.

She followed that song up with Evie Irie's "Hello World."

"Come on, mates," she cajoled when the song ended. "Take the plunge and talk to me. Or better yet, head my way so we can meet face-to-face. Don't you want to be a hero and rush to my rescue?" She sang along with Stephanie Kirkham's "Best Time Ever" next.

Perhaps she should try a different tactic. "Anyone out there as lonely as I am?" Rachel played DJ Snake's "Let Me Love You." Next, she channeled the Hollywood bombshells of yesteryear and manifested a breathy voice. "I've been out here on my own for an awfully long time and sure could use some... company." She cringed a little. Never in her long life had she attempted to use her feminine wiles—as some would say—to get something she wanted. It was so demeaning. But friendly recordings weren't getting the job done.

She tilted her head to one side.

Hmm. Perhaps spouting niceties wasn't the way to go here. If only pirates ventured out this far...

"Hey. Are there any pirates out there?" she asked shrewdly. "Any bounty hunters, perhaps?" Back on Earth, greed always seemed to supersede goodwill. "Have I mentioned that there's a price on my head?" She named an exorbitant amount of credits. "I wasn't really a passenger on the *Kandovar*. I was a prisoner. Now they're after my ass. Which one of you has the ballocks to come collect?" Maybe she could get some greedy bastard to pick her up. "It'll be fun," she taunted. "However many of *you* pitted against little old *me*. Anyone up for the challenge?"

She played Demi Lovato's "Confident" next. "Come and get me, boys," she singsonged when the music ended.

"You shouldn't do that," a deep voice spoke.

Gasping, Rachel nearly fell out of her seat. "Evie, was that you?" If so, something was seriously wrong with her voice modulator.

"Negative," Evie replied. "Incoming communication."

Excitement struck. "Incoming from where?"

"Origin unknown."

Rachel lunged for the window and peered out, hoping to find a big ship parked outside.

Only space and the distant solar system met her gaze.

"Hello?" she called.

Silence.

"Hello?"

Still nothing.

"Come on. I haven't been out here long enough to lose my mind. *Yet*. Who said that?"

Silence.

Whoever had spoken had warned her to stop trying to lure pirates and bounty hunters, so... "Victim here! Victim here!" she cried. "Calling all pirates, bounty hunters, and other ne'er-do-wells! Come and get me, baby!"

"Cease!" the deep voice thundered.

Rachel's heart slammed against her ribs. "Why?"

"You do *not* wish to attract pirates or bounty hunters."

She loved his voice. It was deep and smooth, rumbling through the cramped escape pod. "Hey, if that's all I can get, I'm going for it."

"You have a death wish?"

"No. That's why I'm offering to take on all comers. If I don't find help soon, I'll die."

"Oxygen deprivation will grant you a far kinder death than pirates will."

"Pirates won't deliver death at all."

"What makes you think they'll spare you once they're through with you?"

She grimaced at the activities *that* brought to mind. "They can't kill me if I kill them first."

Silence.

"Hello?"

Panic crept in when no response came. "Are you still there?" *Please, don't let him cut communications.*

"Yes."

Relief suffused her. "Then why aren't you saying anything?"

"I was questioning the validity of your statement."

"Which one?"

"The claim that you haven't been out here long enough to lose your mind."

She laughed. "Yeah. I guess I sound pretty crazy, don't I? I can't help it. You're the first person I've spoken to in over forty days. What's your name?"

Silence.

"Not ready to give me that, huh? Okay. I can understand that, what with you believing me insane and all. Why don't I call you... Handsome? Thank you for responding to my transmission, Handsome."

"Handsome is a term used for those you find appealing?"

"Yes."

"Are you mocking me?"

Oh crap. Had she struck a nerve? Did he bear features he deemed unappealing? "No. I meant no offense. Honestly, you just have a very appealing voice."

He grunted.

She grinned. "Even when you grunt." He didn't dignify that with a response. "Where are you? You must be close if you're picking up my transmission."

More of that aggravating silence.

"Not willing to impart that either?" She bit her lip. That didn't bode well. If he wouldn't tell her where he was, she doubted he intended to lend her a hand. "I'm not really crazy, if that's what you're worried about."

"It isn't."

Which implied something *did* worry him. "Are you a pirate? Or someone with a bounty on your head? Is that it? Because I'm not a bounty hunter."

"I deducted as much."

So formal.

She pursed her lips. "Is it the killing thing?"

"What killing thing?"

"You know, me saying that pirates can't kill me if I kill them first. I mean, it's not like that's why I'm out here. I'm not actively hunting pirates or anything." She frowned. "Is that even something people do? Hunt pirates?"

"If they've committed crimes against any Aldebarian Alliance station or settlement, yes."

"Well, that's not my goal."

"Does that mean that if I'm a pirate, you'll vow not to kill me?"

She opened her mouth to agree, then hesitated. "Hmm. I may have backed myself into a corner there," she muttered.

A low chuckle carried over the speakers.

Nice. "How about," she proposed, "I won't kill you as long as you don't attempt to harm me. Or any of my friends. Or my acquaintances."

"Would you like to add pets to your list?" he drawled.

Rachel laughed. "If I had one, yes."

Another chuckle was her reward.

"So," she began tentatively.

"So?"

"Will you help me?" All serious now, she swallowed. "Please?"

More of that unnerving silence fell, as did her hopes.

She closed her eyes. "Why?"

After a long pause, he said softly, "I cannot." And she didn't think she misread the regret in his voice.

"You can't or you won't?"

"I... cannot abandon my post."

She stared at the solar system Evie continued to display. "Are you on a ship, a planet, or a space station?"

"I can't disclose that information. I shouldn't even be speaking with you."

That sounded as if he risked something by communicating with her. "Is it an employment thing? Your boss doesn't want you to waste time chatting with—"

"No."

If it wasn't a job-related risk, was he being held somewhere against his will? The Aldebarian Alliance forbade slavery. But that didn't mean other nations didn't engage in it, especially way out here where few policed their actions.

Could he be in as great a bind as she was?

If so, she may have found an ally after all.

W ONICK HADN'T MEANT TO answer so abruptly. But he hadn't lied. He shouldn't be speaking with her.

"Are you...?" Rachel's lovely voice conveyed concern. "Are you being held somewhere against your will? Is someone forcing your hand?"

He wasn't being held against his will, but Savaas *was*—in a manner of speaking—forcing his hand.

When he didn't answer, she continued. "If so, perhaps I can help you."

Unbelievable.

"If you're close enough to hear my communications," she continued, "you may be close enough for me to reach. If you tell me where you are, who's holding you, and why... maybe I can get you out of there."

Wonick stared at the blank console screen.

"Wait." Her voice changed, darkening with anger. "Is it Gathendiens? Are *they* the ones holding you?" she asked. "If so, it will take me longer to rescue you because I'll have to kill them all first."

His jaw dropped.

"If it's anyone else, I'll probably incapacitate as few as possible and try to get you out without seriously injuring anyone. No offense, but I don't really know you and would rather not kill someone I may later discover didn't deserve it."

Wonick could find no response to that.

"Hello? You got quiet again."

"Because I am once more questioning your belief that you haven't lost your mind." Did she truly believe she could kill an entire regiment of Gathendien warriors by herself? This was her first trip into space. She probably didn't even fully understand the weaponry they possessed.

She laughed. "Why? Is that too bloodthirsty for you? Well, too bad. Gathendiens tried to eradicate all people on my homeworld *and* on Lasara. And now they've blown up the *Kandovar* and may have killed all my friends." Her breath caught on the last words as if she fought sudden tears.

If the latest reports were any indication, she likely *had* lost some of her friends. And time was running out for anyone still in an escape pod. "Apologies," he offered softly. He knew what it was like to lose many you cared about.

A sniff carried over the com. "You'd better not be apologizing because you're a Gathendien."

"*Srul* no!" he blurted. "I merely wished to express sympathy."

"Oh." Her voice was softer now, as if grief and concern had robbed her of some of her vibrancy. "Will you tell me where you are?"

"No. *My* safety isn't all that imparting my location would threaten."

"Can you explain why? I mean, I really want to understand what your situation is."

"I cannot."

"You mean you *will* not."

"Would you disclose information about your friends if you feared it would place them in danger?"

She sighed. "No. Are you on one of the planets in... what's that solar system called, Evie?"

"System 61-75948."

"Are you on a planet in that solar system? Or maybe one of the moons?" she pressed.

"According to all records, none of the planets or moons in that system are habitable."

"That's what Evie keeps telling me. But it's looking more and more like I'm going to have to land there."

"You should not. The reports also state that none who have attempted to land there in the past survived."

"Yep. Evie told me that, too."

"You should heed the warnings."

"You seem to know a lot about that system."

"I know a lot about many systems."

"Can you tell me where you're from? Do you still live on your homeworld? Or did—"

"Where are *you* from?" he asked, hoping to slow the tide of questions he couldn't answer.

How would she respond? The Aldebarian Alliance had concluded that Gathendiens had attacked the *Kandovar* purely to acquire Earthlings. Since she'd had no contact with anyone since the assault, Rachel had no way of knowing that. But might she have guessed it?

A long pause ensued. "Far away," she finally responded, her voice tinged with sadness. "I'm from far, far away."

"What system?"

"I don't know what it's called out here."

"What planet or station?" Some beings weren't born on a planet or moon. Some were born on ships or space stations.

She grumbled something under her breath.

"I didn't hear that. What?"

She loosed what could only be described as a frustrated growl. "Okay. I get it. There are some things *you* can't tell me and others that *I* can't tell you. Not without endangering my friends."

Apparently, she *had* guessed. "Then you *do* understand."

"Well..." More than a hint of despondence now infused her words.

A twinge of guilt struck.

"If you can't help me, would you at least stay on the line?"

He frowned. "Stay on the line?"

"Keep talking to me. Keep the channel open or however you put it out here." She really was new to space travel. "It's... unnerving."

His frown deepened. "What is?"

"The quiet. Usually, I'm bombarded with sound. The conversations of anyone nearby. Their movements. The music or entertainment vids they're listening to or viewing. Their thoughts."

"You're telepathic?"

She hesitated. "I guess I probably shouldn't have let that slip."

"All Lasarans are telepathic," he pointed out. Perhaps she would feel more comfortable talking about herself if she believed he thought she was Lasaran.

"Are there other telepathic beings?" she asked, curiosity lightening her voice.

"Yes. Purvelis are telepathic."

"Oh. I haven't heard much about them."

Had she heard *anything* about them? Since Purvel wasn't a member of the Aldebarian Alliance, he doubted Lasarans mentioned them often. "Their planet has much more water than land. And their unique biology enables them to spend hours or even days at a time underwater."

"That is awesome," she said, sounding a little cheerier. "I guess they would *have* to be telepathic in order to communicate underwater."

"It would be convenient."

She chuckled. And Wonick found his lips curling up with pleasure at the sound.

Silence descended.

"I don't think I've ever experienced this kind of quiet before," she mused. "My hearing is exceptional. Back on my homeworld, I lived way out in the country. No other homes or businesses around for miles. Only forest and fields with a long enough drive from the major thoroughfares to keep traffic noise from reaching me. But I'd hear the animals foraging in the wild. Birds chirping. Insects buzzing. My Second puttering around the house and taking care of business."

"Your second what?"

She laughed. "My Second, as in—I don't know—second-in-command, I suppose. That's the name given to the woman who served as my guard."

Surprise coursed through him. "Are you royalty?"

She snorted. "No. On my homeworld, you don't need to be royalty to require extra protection. But Amara was more than a guard to me. She was my friend. She *is* my friend. I love her like a sister. My family died a long time ago. And she and my brethren now fill that gap."

"Ah."

"Do *you* have family?" she asked. "Brothers? Sisters? Parents who might be worried about you?"

As always, thoughts of his family saddened him. They had protested with many others when Chancellor Astennuh ordered all cyborgs to be *decommissioned*, a term the *grunark* had intentionally used to advance the belief that cyborgs were inhuman. Instead of rethinking his position, Astennuh did the same thing that worked well for him when Janwar's parents and others had protested his assuming total power over the planet: He lied, deemed the pro-testers terrorists, and told the military to fire upon them. Wonick's family had been among the lucky few who'd fled without being identified and never protested again. Not because they didn't care. But because his parents had been too afraid to risk losing the rest of their children.

"Handsome?"

The word jolted him from his thoughts. He'd forgotten the name she had bestowed upon him. "I lost my family long ago." None of them even knew he still lived.

"I'm sorry," she said softly.

Old emotion rising, he nodded before remembering she couldn't see him. "I am, too."

The quiet that encompassed them was one of commiseration and carried no awkwardness. Much to his surprise, Wonick found comfort in it.

"Do you have no one?" she asked tentatively.

"I have friends I consider brothers."

"Good. On my world, we call that a *found family*. I've been very fortunate to amass a rather large one," she said.

"As have I," he admitted.

"Then we have something else in common." The smile returned to Rachel's voice. "We're both in a bind. And we're both fortunate

47

enough to have found new families after losing the ones we loved." A teasing note entered her voice. "Careful there. If we find anything more we have in common, you might have to consider me a friend and add me to that family of yours."

A possibility he couldn't let himself imagine. It was far too appealing.

When he noted the time on the console, regret filled him. "I must end communications. My shift will end soon." Since her broadcasts usually only lasted an hour, Savaas had relented and allowed Jovan to monitor comms for brief periods.

"Oh." She didn't even try to hide her disappointment. "Will you speak with me again tomorrow?" she asked hopefully.

"Only if you refrain from mentioning it if you continue to broadcast after I go."

"Would mentioning it get you in trouble?"

So much trouble. Savaas would be furious. "Yes."

"Then I'll say goodbye and sign off after one last song."

"As you wish. Until tomorrow."

"Until tomorrow." There was a momentary pause before she spoke again. "And now, ladies and gentlemen," she said as though addressing a wide audience, "for your listening pleasure, I present a song I'd like to dedicate to Handsome—'Lean on Me,' performed by Bill Withers and accompanied by yours truly."

Music carried over the comm. And soon Rachel began to sing alongside a man with a pleasant voice. As Wonick listened to the lyrics, his lips stretched into a smile that soon blossomed into a full-blown grin as he shook his head.

Clever female.

If only they *could* lean on each other.

CHAPTER THREE

Rachel leaned back in her seat and propped her boots on one corner of the console. "You know what keeps running through my mind?" She had spoken to Handsome every day for almost a week. Some of his somber mien had melted away, as had his reticence, revealing a very appealing personality. She now considered him a friend and looked forward to their daily chats.

He must feel the same way because he no longer restricted the length of their chats. Sometimes they talked for hours. "What?" he responded.

"Why would Gathendiens attack a Lasaran warship?" The action baffled her. "And not *any* Lasaran warship, but one belonging to a Lasaran prince? I mean, does that make sense to you?"

"The Gathendiens' past overflows with irrational behavior," he replied, seeming unsurprised. Perhaps because he knew more about the reptilian aliens than she did.

"But this went *beyond* irrational. This was just plain stupid."

"And yet, the attack was a success," he reluctantly pointed out.

"I know." That both baffled *and* infuriated her. "What did they get from it, though? How did they benefit? After the Gathendiens feigned friendship then released the virus on Lasara that rendered most of the women infertile, the Lasarans kicked their asses. And the rest of the Aldebarian Alliance helped them. That's the whole point of having allies. Allies can be a far greater deterrent to attacks than weapons simply because everyone in the galaxy is aware of what enemies will face if they harm a member nation. Not only retaliation by the one they harmed—"

"But retaliation by the military might of every member of the alliance."

49

"Exactly. And who can stand against that?"

"No one thus far."

"So why would the Gathendiens attack Prince Taelon's ship after the alliance had already kicked their asses to such an extent that—by all accounts—they're still limping?" she asked.

He must not have an answer, for silence descended.

"They must have wanted something," she murmured. "Risking the wrath of the Aldebarian Alliance and retaliation by their massive fleets for shits and giggles would be stupid, as I said. And Gathendiens aren't stupid. Greedy? Yes. Devious? Yes. But stupid? No. Their scientists and strategists are so sharp that they've already come close to eradicating *two* civilizations." She stared at the blank vertical console, wishing she could see his face instead. Alas, he either couldn't or wouldn't initiate video contact. "The more I think about it, the more convinced I become that they were after something. At first, I thought they wanted Prince Taelon or maybe wanted to get their hands on—" She broke off.

Few knew the *Kandovar* had been carrying one of only two babies born of the Lasaran royal line in decades. The other—Adira, daughter of Princess Amiriska and her lifemate Marcus, an Immortal Guardian—resided on Earth with her parents and remained a closely guarded secret of the royal family. The Lasaran monarchs had not even shared news of Amiriska's daughter with the rest of Lasara, fearing it would spread to nefarious individuals who might wish to kidnap the Lasaran heir from Earth and hold her for ransom.

"On?" Handsome prodded.

"On something that belongs to him," she finished carefully.

"A logical conclusion," he murmured.

"Not really. Wouldn't that spark the same counteroffensive that blowing up the ship for fun or as some kind of vendetta would?"

"Yes."

Which only left one suspicion that had grown stronger every time she pondered it.

"Rachel?" he queried when she hesitated to voice it.

"I know this may sound incredibly narcissistic, but..." she began uncertainly.

"That didn't translate."

"Self-centered or self-absorbed? Having an excessive interest in oneself or believing the world revolves around you?"

"Ah. Continue."

"I think the Gathendiens were after us," she admitted, troubled by the notion. "I think they were after me and my friends."

"For what purpose?"

"Is this a secure line?"

"I don't understand."

"Can anyone else listen to our conversation?"

"No. It's encrypted." And he'd insisted that Evie refrain from recording or broadcasting their conversations on other channels.

Rachel drew in a deep breath. "A long time ago, Gathendiens released a virus on my homeworld that was supposed to kill us all off. I think my planet is their Plan B."

"I don't think that translated correctly."

Her lips twitched. They'd encountered some amusing translation mistakes during their conversations. "What did it say Plan B means?"

"Machinations that involve Earth pollinators."

She laughed. "B, as in the second letter in our alphabet, not the pollinator bee."

"Ah."

"Plan B would be the Gathendiens' backup plan, or their *if all else fails and we can't conquer alliance-occupied space, we can always settle far enough away that they'll forget about us* plan."

He grunted. "Such would not surprise me."

"But the virus didn't succeed. And I don't think they like to lose, or for anyone to disrupt their plans."

"They don't."

"So they're cheesed off that they didn't succeed in exterminating what they likely view as my more primitive race and, thus, want to get their hands on me and my friends to find out why their laboratory-grown virus failed to get the job done." But how had they known the Earthlings on the *Kandovar* were the key to their discovering why the virus had failed? How could they have guessed that Rachel and her friends differed from most Earthlings?

"You mentioned coming from far away," he said. "If you were their target, stealing you from the *Kandovar* would spare them a very long trip, particularly since the Sectas haven't given Gathendiens access to the *qhov'rums*. The Aldebarian Alliance is probably still trying to figure out how the *grunarks* managed to get inside one."

What if they *hadn't* known Rachel and her friends were different? Could Gathendiens want them for another reason? Perhaps to prevent Lasarans from finding a race that could help them increase their numbers and ensure the continuation of the Lasaran species? That was why the *gifted ones* were traveling to Lasara, after all. Immortal Guardians like Rachel couldn't help with that. They'd yet to find a way to conceive children without infecting the baby with the vampiric virus in utero. And they didn't know what the virus would do to a fetus or an infant. Or to a child.

"Are Lasarans reproductively compatible with other species out here?" The Yona hadn't seemed all that different from Lasarans, aside from their coloring and lack of emotion. She'd often wondered why the Lasarans weren't reproducing with *them* or with others close by.

"Though many alien species in the galaxy bear strong similarities in appearance, they often can't reproduce together," he said. "Purvelis, for example, differ too much from Lasarans genetically to reproduce without risking fatal abnormalities in their offspring. Segonians *never* reproduce with other races unless those races commit to permanently settling on Segonia. Rakessians scorn anyone on their planet who lacks the traditional markings most are born with. Therefore any offspring produced by a Rakessian–Lasaran bonding would be treated harshly by its Rakessian parent."

"Really? Its mom or dad would do that? Rakessians sound like assholes."

He laughed. "Lasarans *have* reproduced with other species. But as is often the case when two different species bond, the offspring were almost always sterile."

"Oh. Right." Her Second had once shown her a picture of a zebroid—which resulted from breeding a zebra with a horse or other equine—and mentioned that such hybrids were usually sterile.

"Sterile offspring," he concluded, "won't help the Lasarans secure the continuation of their civilization."

Seth had used his healing ability to determine that both Adira and Abby would have no reproductive issues. So, Earthlings could very well be the Lasarans' last hope.

Which meant the Gathendiens had *two* reasons for getting their hands on Rachel and her friends.

"That sucks."

"I don't think that translated correctly."

"That blows?" she suggested.

"Now I'm even more confused," he muttered

She laughed. "'That sucks' and 'that blows' are slang on my world. It's like saying that's *drekked* up."

"Ah. Yes, it is."

Quiet descended.

"All those people on the *Kandovar*..." she whispered. "They died because of us, because of me and my friends."

"They died because Gathendiens destroyed the ship. *Not* that they all died," he hastened to add. "I'm sure the escape pods launched successfully and the Aldebarian Alliance is rescuing as many as they can."

"I hope so." A long sigh escaped her. "You know, this was supposed to be a fresh start for me. The launch of a new life. No more hiding what I am. No more hunting every night."

"You hunt your food?"

"No. I hunt vampires, people who have been driven insane by the virus Gathendiens released on our planet. My brethren and I hunt them to protect innocents from being killed and to ensure the continuity of our species. If we didn't keep vampire numbers in check, Earthlings would've long since gone extinct."

"And this was your profession? Hunting vampires?"

"Yes."

"It was a noble one."

"Yes. Most people on my planet don't know about it, though."

"I don't understand."

"Most Earthlings don't know vampires exist," she explained. "They think they're merely myths and legends. Stories passed down from generation to generation. The subject of scary entertainment vids. And we work hard to keep it that way."

"Why? Would it not be better if they were aware of the threat?"

"No. Because that would make them aware of *us*—me and my brethren—and *our* differences. Then they'd want to kill or capture us as well."

"That isn't logical."

"No, it isn't. Our differences enable us to protect them. But that's my world. And I thought I'd left all that behind. Now this." She sighed, her spirits darkening. "It's exhausting, you know? Having to hide what you are. Worrying about slipping and someone finding out you're different, because chances are excellent that once they do they'll try to kill you or capture you and profit from exploiting you."

A long moment passed before a heavy sigh carried over comms. "Such has been my experience."

Was he different, too? Is that what landed him in whatever untenable position he was in now? "I'm sorry."

"I am, too."

"You know, I was sent out here to guard my friends and ensure the Lasarans welcome them, as promised. But since Prince Taelon assured us that all would be well, I figured my friends wouldn't really need guarding and I might find something new to do with my life." She huffed a laugh fraught with disappointment. "So much for that idea."

"Starting anew doesn't always go as we hope," he offered in commiseration.

"Did *you* try to make a fresh start?"

"Yes."

"And?"

"Many deaths ensued." The simple statement conveyed the same weariness that afflicted her.

"That sucks."

"Yes, it does."

"And now here we are."

"Here we are."

"I suppose that makes us kindred spirits."

He frowned in puzzlement. "I don't think that translated correctly."

Amusement rose, banishing some of the disappointment that had settled upon her. "What did your translator say this time?"

"That it makes us familial... ghosts? Hauntings?"

She laughed. "By kindred spirits, I mean we're similar."

"Despite our different origins?"

"Yes."

"I'm beginning to agree."

"Does that mean you'll help me?" she asked hopefully.

A heavy pause ensued. "Is that why you're befriending me? To coax me into ignoring the risks such would entail?"

She sighed. "No. I'm befriending you because you seem nice and we're a lot alike. I just thought I would ask in case you were refusing to help out of an overabundance of caution."

"The risks remain," he replied apologetically. "If they didn't, I would do whatever I could to reach you."

"Well... thank you for that. It means a lot. It really does." She glanced at the time code on the console. "Your shift ends soon, doesn't it?" They had talked often enough that she had learned his work schedule.

"Yes."

"Then I'll leave you with this."

As she had each day she'd spoken with him, she signed off by playing and singing along to "Lean on Me."

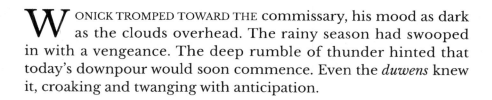

WONICK TROMPED TOWARD THE commissary, his mood as dark as the clouds overhead. The rainy season had swooped in with a vengeance. The deep rumble of thunder hinted that today's downpour would soon commence. Even the *duwens* knew it, croaking and twanging with anticipation.

But Wonick didn't care.

Or perhaps the problem was he *did* care. Too much. For Rachel. And he grew increasingly frustrated by his inability to race to her aid.

Hence, his dark mood.

When he swung around the corner of the commissary, he stopped short. Savaas, Benwa, and Retsa stood, talking, where the path to the commissary met the path to the radar monitoring station.

Schooling his features into a blank mask, Wonick called a greeting and joined them.

"There's been a development," Savaas announced before Wonick could speak.

"What kind?"

Savaas glanced over at Ruska. "Tell him."

Ruska, who kept them apprised of any and all activity near their sector of space, faced Wonick. "A Gathendien warship appeared on long-range scans an hour ago."

He frowned. "Where?"

"Near the Nikassi System."

That was only four systems away. Not good. "Are they headed to Promeii 7?" he asked hopefully. The *grunarks* visited the planet regularly, probably to sell captured beings to Pulcra—owner of the galaxy's most notorious fighting arena—in exchange for parts for their scrapped-together ships.

Ruska shook his head. "No. If they maintain their current course—"

"They're headed here," Savaas announced. "They're coming for the escape pod."

Wonick's frown deepened. "They don't even know it's nearby. The pod's communications won't reach that far."

"But the beacon might."

That gave him pause. "Beacons in Lasaran escape pods have a limited range."

"The beacon's range is broader than their comms."

"Not broad enough to reach *that* far."

"Well, they must have updated it. If the Gathendien ship were headed to Promeii 7, their trajectory would take them on an alternate path."

Wonick wanted to suggest it was coincidence but knew what a laughable proposal that would be.

Savaas crossed his arms over his chest. "We'll have to do something about the pod." His grim expression suggested that whatever he proposed would not sit well with Wonick.

Before his friend could say anything more, Wonick issued a decisive nod. "I'll infiltrate the pod's system remotely and disable the beacon."

"That won't stop the Gathendiens from continuing on to the pod's last position."

"Neither will destroying it," Wonick countered, guessing where Savaas's mind had gone. "The error was mine. I didn't think the beacon's signal would carry that distance."

Ruska grunted. "I didn't think a Gathendien ship would stray this far. Shouldn't they be slinking back to whatever base they've set up before Alliance ships catch sight of them? They must be aware of the search and rescue mission."

Benwa nodded. "They caught the *Kandovar* crew off guard in the *qhov'rum*. They won't survive a battle with a warship that's actively hunting them in open space."

Savaas arched a brow. "So you want to wait and see what happens? Give the Gathendiens time to broadcast their location to the rest of their ilk, if they haven't already, and lure more of them near our homeworld?"

Wonick shook his head. "The commander of that ship won't want others to take credit for capturing the Earthling. They probably haven't even notified anyone of their find." Gathendiens were greedy *grunarks* who would do anything to be the first to gain their ruthless emperor's favor, including withholding information that might benefit others of their ilk.

"*If* they've found her." Benwa shook his head. "They may refrain from notifying others of the Earthling if they capture her. But that doesn't mean they won't keep the rest of the fleet apprised of their location."

Hoshaan swept them all with a glance. "Why don't we take the *Shagosa* up in stealth mode and destroy the Gathendien ship?"

Wonick and his brothers had painstakingly designed and built the *Shagosa*. It was the most technologically advanced ship in the galaxy, with the possible exception of Secta ships. Sectas were the oldest species in the galaxy and so advanced that they had designed and built the *qhov'rums*, a feat other engineers still couldn't explain.

Only one other ship like the *Shagosa* existed: the *Tangata*, which they had constructed and given to Janwar as thanks for all he'd done for them.

Savaas looked at Benwa. "You don't think the Gathendiens will want to know who destroyed it?"

Benwa shrugged. "We can put the word out that pirates did it."

Even Wonick had to shake his head. "Most pirates lack the power and weaponry needed to take out a warship. I'll disable the beacon in the pod, and we'll see what happens. We don't know with certainty that the Earth female is the reason Gathendiens are nearby." When Savaas opened his mouth to speak, Wonick quickly jumped in again. "The Gathendiens may already have an Earthling or two in custody and simply have opted to take a circuitous route back to their base to avoid detection by search and rescue ships or travelers to Promeii 7."

Savaas's look turned thoughtful. "I hadn't considered that."

Hoshaan grunted. "Or perhaps they're looking for a place to construct a new base."

Benwa grimaced. "I hope not. I would hate to have those *grunarks* for neighbors."

All offered grumbles of agreement.

Savaas studied Wonick. "Disable the beacon and have Jovan monitor every communication sent or received by the Gathendien ship. Find out what they're doing out here." He swept the others with a glance. "Dismissed."

Everyone except Wonick left, many heading for the commissary. Speculation abounded in every conversation that carried to him.

Savaas caught Wonick's eye. "You're only delaying the inevitable."

So many words wanted to pour forth, all almost certain to launch an argument. Instead, Wonick shook his head. "Can you blame me?"

His brow furrowing, Savaas looked away. "No." He sighed. "You should take your meal to the comm station. Jovan is there now, monitoring the escape pod. He's shown more sympathy for the female than some of the others. I worry he may try to warn her about the Gathendien ship and reveal our position."

Guilt suffused Wonick because *he* intended to do just that.

As though sensing it, Savaas scrutinized him. "How are *you* doing?"

"What do you mean?"

"You've been working double shifts, monitoring the pod for long hours. Are you getting enough rest?"

The query merely enhanced the guilt that pecked at him. "Yes."

"Good." Savaas clapped him on the back.

Wonick followed him into the commissary, claimed his meal, and hurried away through the forest. Had his tray not sported a cover, he likely would have spilled most of the food in his rush. But the rapid trek uphill didn't leave him breathless the way it would've others, thanks to his augmentations.

Eager to contact Rachel, he activated the comm station door.

Jovan spun toward him and leapt to his feet. Alarm painted the younger man's features.

Wonick frowned. "What is it?"

"She knows about the ship."

Drek. Wonick crossed to the console and set his tray on the table beside it. "The Gathendien ship?"

"Yes."

"You told her?" Savaas would be furious. But Wonick couldn't fault the younger cyborg for doing something *he* had planned to do.

Jovan shook his head. "The pod's AI detected it and informed her."

"When?"

"About ten minutes ago."

"What was her reaction?"

Jovan tapped the console, activated the volume control, and slid his finger along the smooth surface.

Music thundered through the small room. A man alternated between speaking to the beat and singing. Rachel accompanied him, taunting Danger to come for her.

Oh, drek.

Jovan looked as distressed as Wonick felt. "She keeps playing it over and over again. And when it ends..."

"You hear that, Gathendiens?" Rachel demanded as the music ceased. "I know you're there. And I'm right here within your reach. You want an Earthling? Come and get me, you spineless bastards."

———◆◇◆———

PROGRAMMED TO REPEAT, BLACKWAY & Black Caviar's "What's Up Danger" filled the pod again. Every time it played, fury burned inside her, swiftly coalescing into a raging inferno. Those Gathendien bastards had possibly killed her friends, had likely killed at least *some* of her new Lasaran friends, and had *definitely* killed *all* of her Yona friends. Now they were *here*?

Full of restless energy, she drew a dagger and fought imaginary opponents in the limited space the pod provided as she belted out the lyrics. She would've loved to use her katanas but lacked the room.

"Cease!" a deep voice thundered.

Caught off guard, Rachel accidentally stabbed the seat. *Oops.*

Swearing, she yanked the blade out and leaned over the console to shut off the music. "Handsome?"

"Yes. Close all other channels."

"Do it, Evie," Rachel ordered.

"All other communication channels closed," Evie announced.

"What the *drek* are you doing?" he demanded.

Dropping into the seat, Rachel eagerly relayed her news. "A Gathendien warship showed up on Evie's long-range radar or whatever. Isn't that great?"

"*No*, it isn't great," he nearly shouted.

"Yes, it is. All I have to do is lure them to me—"

"Get captured and die," he finished for her.

She snorted. "Yeah. That's not how it's going to go, honey."

"If you believe that, you *have* succumbed to insanity. And why did you call me a sticky substance made by pollinating insects on Earth?"

She laughed. "It's a term of endearment."

"It is?" Surprise wiped all anger from his voice.

"Yes. I know it may be hard for you to believe, but I can do this," Rachel promised.

"By *this*," he began, the anger returning to his voice, "I assume you mean lure the Gathendiens into bringing your escape pod on board? Then what? You'll defeat them all? By yourself? Gathendiens lost most of their ships during the War of Retribution. You probably won't just face one contingent. You'll face as many soldiers as they could cram onto the *drekking* ship."

"And they'll be expecting a meek, frightened little Earthling who will cower in fear. *Not* a warrior who can kick ass."

"Ass. Not *asses*."

She laughed. "Oh. I've kicked many asses during my long life. And by that, I mean multiple asses at once. Do you have any idea how many vampires I've come up against while hunting alone? Their numbers have exploded in recent years. And don't get me started on mercenaries."

"Were you in an enclosed space when you fought those vampires and soldiers for hire? Were you in a transport bay with limited maneuvering room between craft?"

"No." An overwhelming majority of her battles had taken place outside in open areas that provided plenty of space for her to swing her katanas and dodge the blades or bullets of her opponents. "But—"

"A bay with dozens of soldiers lined up, waiting for their turn to attack you?"

"That doesn't concern me. I can take them."

"A bay with a sealed door requiring a Gathendien passcode that would prevent you from making it farther into the ship?"

"No, but I could always force a Gathendien to—"

"A sealed door that would enable those on the other side to vent the oxygen from the room if the battle didn't go their way?"

That gave her pause.

"A bay with AB devices and other tools lying around that could—"

"What are AB devices?"

"Handheld acquisition beam devices used to load freight and other heavy objects. They displace the gravity around an object so it will float and can easily be moved."

Rachel pondered that a moment. "*Any* objects?"

"Yes. If they locked a beam on you, you would rise off the floor and have no way of keeping them from floating you right into a cell."

She frowned. That would be a problem. A *huge* problem. Her shoulders drooped as she slumped back in her seat. "Well, that sucks."

His sigh conveyed both sympathy and relief.

Rachel's mind raced as she sought ways to counter every issue he'd mentioned. "I could feign weakness and compliance until they get me past the bay door thing and *then* go medieval on their asses," she proposed thoughtfully.

"And while you fought the many warriors who converged upon you, all they would have to do to disable you is toss a stun grenade in your midst."

Her frown deepened. She wasn't sure if a stun grenade would take down an Immortal Guardian. She could take a lot of damage. But she'd never been electrocuted and didn't know what to expect.

Rachel had done her best to familiarize herself with the weapons she would face out here. But they deviated enough from weapons on Earth that she really wasn't certain how much damage they could do. When she'd asked some Lasaran soldiers to shoot her, wanting to gauge the effect, the soldiers had looked so appalled that she had opted not to ask again.

Simone wanted to talk a Yona warrior into doing it but—as far as Rachel knew—still hadn't succeeded before the Gathendiens attacked.

Would a stun grenade incapacitate her the way it would most beings out here? Or would it simply hurt like a bitch and be easy to shake off?

She couldn't afford to let the Gathendiens get their hands on her. If they did, a close examination of her blood and tissue would reveal how different she was from other Earthlings and might provide the bastards with the information they needed to find a virus that would succeed where the other had failed.

"Thaaat's a thinker," she muttered irritably. "I guess not ordering Evie to alter our course was a good call."

"You were going to alter your course?" he asked, perking up a little. "To elude the Gathendiens?"

"No. I was going to head straight for them."

He swore.

Rachel grinned. He was even appealing when he was grumpy. "I thought that might spoil the whole *helpless victim* façade and changed my mind. Now it looks like I need to formulate a new plan."

"Warning," Evie stated suddenly, her voice as calm as usual. "Distress beacon has ceased functioning."

Rachel straightened. "What?"

"The distress beacon is longer functioning."

"What the hell? Why?"

"Unknown."

Other than shutting off the music, she hadn't touched anything. "Wait. Is this because I stabbed the seat?"

"You stabbed the seat?" Handsome asked.

"Yes. It was an accident. You startled me when you bellowed at me to stop singing."

"It was... more of a request," he said, a wince in his tone.

"It was a bellow. Are the distress beacons located in the seat?" That seemed weird.

"Negative," Evie responded at the same time Handsome said, "No."

Rachel threw up her hands. "So it just stopped working? What kind of crap is that?"

"Please repeat inquiry," Evie responded.

Handsome laughed.

Again, it made Rachel smile. "You see what I've been dealing with."

"Yes."

Aggravated, she looked around. "I guess it shouldn't surprise me. My Second was always complaining about software glitches and computer malfunctions. The *Kandovar* was stuck out in the boonies by my homeworld for three years or thereabouts. If they only perform routine maintenance on escape pods when they're on Lasara, this one is overdue for a tune-up." The significance of that made her stomach sink. "Evie, is everything else still functioning?"

"Affirmative. All other systems are functioning as intended."

"Good."

Silence fell.

"Handsome?" she asked when it stretched. "Are you still there?"

"Yes."

"You went quiet. What's on your mind?"

"I was secretly hoping the Gathendien ship would veer away and head for Promeii 7."

A spark of hope flared to life. "Is Promeii 7 nearby?"

"No."

"But you said you hoped the Gathendiens would head for it."

"There's little else this far from alliance-occupied space. Unless they're pursuing you, I see no other reason for them to be in your area."

"Is Promeii 7 near enough for me to reach?"

"No."

"Bollocks," Rachel muttered.

A long moment passed. "I'm sorry," Handsome offered somberly.

"It's not *your* fault." Rachel sank down into the seat once more. "Too bad I *didn't* end up near Promeii 7. I hear all sorts of nefarious characters and adventure seekers gather there. I'm sure I would've had better luck coaxing someone into coming and rescuing me if I had."

"Anyone from Promeii 7 would more likely capture you and sell you to Pulcra."

"Who is Pulcra?"

"The wealthiest man on Promeii 7. He owns the most notorious colosseum, in which warriors battle—often to the death—in front of large audiences."

"Sheesh. Do you know how disappointing it is that people who have advanced enough scientifically to travel through space are still barbaric enough socially to get off on that shit?"

He paused. "Yes?"

She laughed before returning her attention to her situation and how the beacon failing had altered it. "I suppose I may as well head toward the Gathendien ship."

"What? Why? I thought you decided not to."

"That was before the distress beacon stopped working. I don't really have any choice now. Without that beacon, no one else will know I'm here."

"Except for me."

"Yes," she said gently. "But you've already said you can't help me." If racing to her aid would endanger his friends, she understood and didn't hold it against him. "And you won't tell me where you are so I can try to help you."

His silence confirmed it.

"Evie," she ordered resolutely, "set course for the Gathendien ship."

"Setting course for the Gathendien ship," Evie responded.

"Rachel," he nearly growled, "don't do this."

"I have no choice."

"You already admitted that battling the Gathendiens on their ship would have a bad outcome for you."

"Definitely a possibility, which is why I have no intention of battling them on their ship."

"You're going to surrender and let them capture you?" he asked in astonishment.

"Hell no. I have a *new* plan. I'll head toward them until I'm sure I've snared their attention. Then I'll lead them to one of the planets in System 61-75948 and fight them there. Evie can land the pod for me—"

"All records show that none of those planets have a breathable atmosphere. The moons don't either."

"I know. But I found a space suit in one of the compartments." She glanced toward it. "Evie said all escape pods are equipped with one. It's too big and awkward. But I can still kick ass in it."

"Even in low gravity?"

That *would* make things more difficult. "Hmm. Evie, do any of those planets or moons have a gravitational force similar to Lasara's?" Ami and Taelon had both said they'd noticed little difference between Lasara and Earth's gravitational pulls.

"Searching. Two planets and one moon possess a comparable gravitational force."

That was promising. "Do any of them have a breathable atmosphere?"

"Negative."

Rachel had already known that but had to ask anyway. "What are the surfaces like?"

"The moon is covered in ice, as is one of the planets."

"Any mountains on either of them?"

"Negative."

"Hills?"

"Negative. Their surfaces are uniformly smooth with a few shallow craters on the moon."

So she'd have nothing to hide behind while she hunted the Gathendiens after drawing them out of their ship. "What about the other planet? Tell me about it." It would be nice if she could find one that boasted the equivalent of a rainforest. Lots of life and other heat signatures to confuse her prey, along with a multitude of plants she could lurk behind.

"A dust storm constantly sweeps the surface with high winds."

"Would the winds be too strong for me to remain upright in?"

"Maintaining your footing would be a challenge in these winds," Evie confirmed.

A challenge. Not impossible. Especially since she had incredible strength, and the boots attached to the space suit had soles that could produce the equivalent of cleats. "Would there be low visibility?"

"Affirmative."

"Any physical structures I can duck behind?"

"Records suggest the presence of mountains, but I cannot confirm it with scans."

"So I may find some cover. What about the temperature?"

"Records suggest surface temperatures are much higher than on Lasara."

"High enough to melt my suit or weapons?" She didn't have many. Only her swords, a couple of daggers she still carried out of habit, and a blaster that every pod came equipped with.

"Negative."

"Good. Then I can survive it in the suit. And the temperatures should make it harder for the Gathendiens to scan for heat signatures. Okay." Rachel nodded. "That's the one we'll head for as soon as I snag the Gathendiens' attention. What do you think, Handsome? Sound like a decent plan?"

Quiet fell in the wake of her announcement.

"Handsome? Are you there?"

Silence.

Evie spoke. "We have lost Handsome's communication."

CHAPTER FOUR

W ONICK PACED THE SMALL comm station. As soon as he cut comms, Rachel returned to broadcasting her music and taunting the Gathendiens.

Anxiety tore through him, as did guilt over remotely disabling the pod's distress beacon. But he'd been trying to keep her safe, *vuan* it! And as Rachel would say, boy had that bit him in the ass. Rachel's Plan B would lure the Gathendiens right to the cyborgs' homeworld.

Once Savaas found out, he would order the escape pod destroyed to prevent the Gathendiens from finding their settlement.

Wonick swore. He didn't want Rachel to die. Not by Gathendien hands. And certainly not by cyborg hands.

Long minutes passed as he struggled to find a solution, a way to help her and still maintain the cyborgs' anonymity. Halting, he swore again and dropped into one of the seats before the large console.

His fingers flew over the surface while he opened another highly encrypted communication and sent it with the following heading:

Code 39712

Designation: Urgent

Moments later, one of the screens above the console lit up, and a familiar face stared back at him. The man's features were Akseli. But unlike Wonick and his cyborg brothers, this man's dark hair was long. Drawn back from his face in braids to the crown of his head, it then dangled down his back past his shoulders in a combination of braids adorned with beads and loose locks that were mussed enough to reveal he had been sleeping when the comm reached him.

As if to punctuate the thought, the man yawned and squinted auburn eyes.

His skin bore the same bronze, faintly reddish hue as Wonick's. Although a significant amount of time had passed since Chancellor Astennuh had sent Wonick and Savaas to execute Janwar, the young man who had grown into one of the galaxy's most feared pirates had aged well.

"Wonick?" Janwar asked. "What's up?"

Wonick glanced toward the comm station's closed door. His sharp hearing confirmed that no one approached it from the outside.

Facing forward once more, he blurted, "You told us to monitor every communication that passes through our sector and keep an ear out for any mention of Earthlings."

Janwar's expression lit with interest as he leaned forward. "Did you find something?"

"Yes. An Earth female in a Lasaran escape pod is headed our way." Wonick quickly filled him in on the situation. But Janwar proved to be annoyingly unhelpful. It would seem he had been on quite an adventure recently, aiding the alliance search and rescue mission, attacking Gathendiens ships and bases.

Shock struck. Janwar had only ever allowed crew members and cyborgs on his ship. Yet now he'd not only docked with a Segonian warship and allowed the commander to board the *Tangata* but also had Earth females on his ship?

What the *srul* had been happening out there?

Halfway through their communication, in which Janwar repeatedly urged Wonick to brush off Savaas's concerns and go rescue his new *best buddy*, the pirate broke off and looked to one side. His face brightened with a smile, the likes of which Wonick had never seen grace his friend's face. Was that... affection?

"Hi, babe," a female spoke. "What are you doing?"

Wonick sat up straighter. That was Earth English.

Janwar hesitated only a second before announcing, "Another Earthling has been located."

Drek! What was he doing? Who was he talking to?

"What?" A figure moved between Janwar and his desk, momentarily blocking Wonick's view, before a female plopped down on his lap and peered at the screen. "When? Where'd you find her? Who is it? How is she? Is she okay? Is she hurt? Are you the one who rescued her? Is she safe?"

Wonick froze and could only gape in utter astonishment.

Janwar really *did* have a female on board the *Tangata*. And he must trust her. Otherwise, he would've dumped her off his lap, something rumor claimed he did whenever pleasure workers refused to take no for an answer.

The woman frowned. "What's wrong?" She leaned closer to the screen. "Did we lose the connection?"

When she reached toward the console, Janwar hastily grabbed her hands.

"You didn't lose the connection," Wonick told her.

"And you're back!" she exclaimed brightly, throwing her arms up in celebration. "Hi. I didn't introduce myself. I'm sorry. That was rude of me. I'm Simone. It's nice to meet you."

Again, Wonick stared.

What was happening? Janwar was as reluctant to trust as Savaas and the rest of the cyborgs. Who *was* this female?

Her brow furrowed. "Damn it. He froze again. What's happening? Is it buffering? Because if it is, I have to tell you my admiration for alien technology just took a nosedive."

Janwar leaned to one side, so he could see Wonick better, and smiled. "It isn't buffering. He's just shocked."

"By what? My appearance?" Glancing down, she tugged at the shirt she wore, trying to get it to cover more, he supposed, even though the viewscreen only showed her from the waist up. The garment was far too large for her and threatened to slip off one delicate shoulder.

Was it Janwar's? Such hinted at an intimate relationship... as did her position on Janwar's lap.

"Well," Simone said, "if I'd known you were video conferencing, I would've donned something more appropriate." She combed her fingers through her hair.

"It isn't that," Janwar said. "He's never seen an Earthling before."

Wonick studied her with avid curiosity. Was she really an Earth-ling? "You look Lasaran."

She smiled. "So I've been told. But I don't think a Lasaran woman would walk the *Tangata*'s hallways garbed only in a man's shirt."

His eyes narrowed. Good point. Lasarans—be they male or fe-male—always wore clothing that covered them from their necks to their wrists and ankles. But her words carried an accent that Rachel's lacked. "You're too small and pale to be a Segonian. But you could be a Segonian/Lasaran half-breed." Those were rare and only lived on Segonia.

She wrinkled her nose. "Really? Half-breed? Is that term still used out here?"

"Wonick has trust issues," Janwar inserted. "He's doubting you're an Earthling."

Simone rolled her eyes. "Oh, brother. Is he your friend? Do you trust him to keep a confidence?"

"Entirely."

She turned back to the screen. "Then Wonick, can Lasarans or Segonians do this?" Her big brown eyes flashed bright amber. Then she bared her teeth in a silent snarl.

Wonick's jaw nearly hit the floor when pointy fangs descended from her gums, looking as dangerous as those of the large jungle predators on Aksel.

Even Janwar looked surprised. His eyebrows flew up. "You have fangs?"

Eyes widening, she clamped a hand over her mouth and turned sideways on his lap to face him. "Yes," she said hesitantly behind her fingers. "Retractable ones. I didn't think to tell you because... well, I forgot. I haven't had to use them since coming aboard the *Tangata*. If I need a transfusion, I just get one from the Med Bay thingy."

It was difficult to see from this angle, but when she lowered her hand, Wonick thought the fangs were gone. The glow in her eyes remained.

"There *have* been a few distractions." He rubbed her back sooth-ingly. "You use them to infuse yourself when you need blood?"

She nibbled her lower lip. "Yes."

71

"Why do you look so worried?" Janwar asked gently. "You think I'm going to love you less now that I know your teeth are different?"

Janwar *loved* her?

That stunned Wonick even more than the fangs had.

"No." She smiled sheepishly. "Sorry. Force of habit. The fangs never went over well on Earth."

"Then you *are* an Earthling?" Wonick leaned forward. Her slender build lent her a delicate appearance, and she was small compared to Janwar. Her paler skin looked soft, providing a vivid contrast to her long dark hair. Wonick couldn't deny the appeal of her features. She was lovely. "Do all Earthlings look like you?" Did Rachel?

"Do all..." She glanced at Janwar. "What is he?"

"Cyborg."

Wonick sucked in a shocked breath.

She swung back to Wonick. "Do all cyborgs look like you?"

Betrayal struck like a blow to the chest. Janwar had done the unthinkable. Without even hesitating, he had revealed Wonick's origins, something he *knew* would endanger not only Wonick's life but the lives of all remaining cyborgs. How could he have done that?

Wonick shot Janwar an accusatory glare.

Simone's eyes widened. "Wait. You're a cyborg?"

Guilt darkened his friend's expression.

But Simone didn't seem to notice. Nearly bouncing with excitement, she studied Wonick. "It's so nice to meet you," she gushed. "Are you *the* cyborg? The one who was supposed to execute Janwar but didn't?"

"One of them," Wonick growled, now questioning that decision. How could Janwar betray them like this?

"Oh, my goodness!" she exclaimed with a huge smile. "Then it's doubly nice to meet you. Thank you so much for saving his life. I owe you a great debt."

Wonick stared at her.

"What?" Janwar asked, seeming as confused at Wonick.

"If you hadn't saved him," she continued, "I would never have met him. He wouldn't have saved my life. The damned Gathendiens would've succeeded in killing me. And I wouldn't have fallen head over heels in love with him. If you knew how long I've waited for the last, you'd understand how much that means to me. And now you've found one of my friends? I can't thank you enough."

Wonick shifted uncomfortably. She was thanking him for saving Janwar because it had enabled her to fall in love with him? *And* thanking him for finding Rachel, whom he had done nothing to aid? How the *srul* was he supposed to respond to that?

His gaze slid to Janwar.

Smiling, Janwar arched a brow, the smug *grunark*. He almost looked as if he were enjoying Wonick's discomfort.

"Who is it?" Simone asked. "Did she give you her name?"

"Rachel."

Her eyes welled with tears and began to glow again. "Is she okay? What kind of condition was she in when you rescued her?" She seemed to care about Rachel deeply.

"I haven't exactly rescued her. I just... located her."

"Is she okay?"

"Yes. She's still in the Lasaran escape pod and said she is unharmed."

Her brow puckered with worry. "She must nearly be out of oxygen. How soon can you reach her?"

Again, Wonick shifted. "I am unable to leave the planet at this time."

"Unable," Janwar prodded, "or unwilling?"

Wonick shot him another glare.

"I don't understand." Simone's gaze darted back and forth between them. "You don't have a ship? Can *she* reach *you* then?"

Wonick looked everywhere but at Simone while he searched for a response.

Janwar cleared his throat. "It took the remaining cyborgs a long time to find a planet they could call home. They're fiercely protective of it and can't let anyone know its location."

"Rachel won't tell anyone." Shaking her head, she addressed Wonick. "Why would she? Do you know how many people have tried to kill me and my friends in the past because we're different? How many have hated us? Feared us? Called us evil? Dangerous?

Wanted to eradicate us? How many have tried to capture us and force us to use our special gifts to help them gain power and wealth or harm others?"

Rachel had told him the same.

"That's why we left Earth," she continued. "To get away from that bullshit. If you save Rachel and don't mistreat her, you will have a friend and ally for life. Should anyone approach her in the future and ask if she's ever seen a cyborg, she will laugh it off. If they persist, she'll tell them to go *drek* themselves. And if someone ever locates you through other means—because they sure as hell won't find you through us—and harms you?" A grim smile curled her lips. "She will hunt them down and ensure they can never hurt you or anyone else again. And I'll help her. We've been in your position. Had to hide our existence. We know how crappy that is. And we're loyal to our friends. Save my friend's life," she vowed, "and if yours is ever threatened, I will risk my own to aid you."

The pledge floored him.

"I will, too," Janwar added, clarifying that his loyalty to the cyborgs remained unaltered.

He seemed certain that aiding Rachel would not endanger the cyborgs.

Wonick's shoulders slumped in defeat. "You won't be *able* to aid me because Savaas will kill me for this."

Grinning, Simone punched the air with a fist. "Yes!"

Wonick gaped at her again. She wanted him dead? She'd just claimed she would defend him!

She laughed. "Not *yes*, Savaas will kill you. I meant *yes*, you're going to save Rachel. Keep Savaas at bay until we get there. I'll deal with him myself."

She'd *deal* with him? When she looked as fragile and in need of protection as Princess Amiriska?

Wonick caught Janwar's gaze and shook his head in bafflement. "Who *are* these females?"

Wrapping his arms around Simone, Janwar cradled her close. "Worthy allies and true treasures."

"Awwww." Cupping his jaw in one hand, Simone brushed a kiss across his friend's lips. "You say the sweetest things."

The love the two shared was unmistakable.

Longing struck as Wonick's thoughts turned to Rachel. Shaking his head, he muttered, "I am so dead," and cut the connection.

The door to the comm center slid up.

Startled, Wonick leapt to his feet and spun around, expecting Savaas to fill the doorway.

Instead, Jovan stared at him with wide eyes.

Frowning, Wonick took a step toward him. "What is it?"

"You need to come to the commissary. Now."

"Why? What—?"

"The escape pod has changed course. It's headed straight toward the Gathendien ship."

Wonick already knew that.

"Or it *was*," Jovan continued breathlessly. Had he run here at full speed? "But as soon as the Gathendien ship increased its speed and started heading toward it, the pod changed course again and is now headed here."

Already? Reaching out, Wonick touched the console and raised the volume of Rachel's transmissions. Once more, she was playing the song she'd used to taunt the Gathendiens earlier and daring them to *come and get her*.

It looked like the escape pod had also increased its speed. At the rate it now traveled, it would enter the solar system and breach his planet's atmosphere by sunset tomorrow.

Swearing, Wonick strode toward the open doorway.

Jovan ducked out of his way to allow him to leave then kept pace with him as he entered the forest. "Savaas is talking about remotely diverting the pod enough to make it crash into one of Dynestra's moons."

Wonick ground his teeth.

"Do you think he'll do it? Do you think he'll kill Rachel?"

Wonick stopped short and studied the younger cyborg. "You don't think he should?"

Jovan clamped his lips shut. A muscle in his jaw twitched. "No."

"Why?"

He shook his head. "She isn't a pirate. Or a bounty hunter. Or a member of the Aldebarian Alliance that did nothing to halt our decommissioning. She hasn't wronged us in any way. She's merely trying to survive. Like us. Killing her would be wrong."

Wonick clapped a hand on Jovan's shoulder. "Agreed. Now, we must convince Savaas and the others."

INSIDE THE COMMISSARY, THE cyborgs all clustered around Savaas.

"There's been another development with the pod," Savaas informed him as he and Jovan pushed through the throng.

Wonick joined him in the center. "Jovan told me. He also said you want to crash the pod."

Savaas regarded him with a grim expression. "I don't *want* to. But the Gathendiens will have no reason to linger in our system if the pod *attempts to land* and instead crashes. It would also spare the female the torturous end she would meet as the subject of their lab experiments."

All eyes focused on Wonick, awaiting his response. And there were enough furrowed brows to lend him hope.

Crossing his arms over his chest, Wonick said, "I say we let her land."

Savaas's eyebrows flew up. "On the moon? The Gathendiens will capture her if she does. A quick death would be far kinder."

"No. I meant let her continue on her current course and land here."

Savaas's green eyes widened before darkening with anger. "What?"

"What you've suggested would be the equivalent of slaying her. We aren't killers."

"Aren't we?" Savaas quickly countered. "How many pirates have we slain? How many bounty hunters have we killed? All to keep ourselves and our new home safe."

"Those *grunarks* would've sold their own offspring for a profit. They posed a serious threat to our existence. Rachel does not."

"Rachel?" someone murmured.

Wonick glanced at the crowd. "That's the female's name."

Savaas's eyes narrowed. "You don't know that she poses no threat."

"I *do* know it. You would, too, if you'd listened to her transmissions."

Jovan nodded. "I don't think she poses a threat either."

"She's bound for Lasara," Savaas reminded them, "a nation that did nothing to prevent our kind from being hunted and slain like animals. A nation known for its disapproval of sentient AI. And she hails from Earth, a planet that Sectas claim is a primitive nation ruled by hatred and greed."

Wonick couldn't deny any of that. Rachel had repeatedly mentioned wanting to escape the hate and told him Earthlings had hunted her because they wanted to profit off her differences. "She isn't like that."

"And you're drawing that conclusion based on what? The music she sings?"

Here it came. "No. I've spoken with her."

Utter silence fell.

"What?" Savaas demanded.

"I've spoken with her," Wonick repeated, addressing the group as a whole.

Even Jovan looked shocked at that.

"She left Earth because she's different from other Earthlings. And like us, she was hated and hunted because of it. She hoped to make a fresh start on Lasara. Princess Amiriska vowed that she and her friends would not be treated unkindly there and would find acceptance."

Nebet snorted. "They didn't accept *us.*"

"Princess Amiriska did," he reminded them. "Or she would have. Even though she was new to her diplomatic position, she lobbied hard for the Alliance to offer us asylum, but her hands were tied by the holdouts."

Savaas's lips curled in a sneer. "The alliance acts unanimously, or it doesn't act at all."

"A faulty system," Wonick agreed. "But my point is—Rachel will not view us the way others do. She'll accept us."

If anything, Savaas's expression darkened further. "Did you tell her about us?"

"No. I only contacted her to warn her not to dare every *grunark* in the galaxy to *come and get her*."

Benwa laughed. "She actually did that?"

"Yes." Wonick found no humor in it. "She knows her oxygen and other supplies are running low and believes she can fight her way out of their custody. She's desperate."

The men exchanged looks.

Savaas grunted. "Desperate people will say whatever they have to in order to save themselves."

Wonick shook his head and met as many gazes as he could. "The men we've killed since settling here were the scourge of the galaxy, no better than the Gathendiens. No better than Astennuh. Rachel isn't like that. I trust her. And so does Janwar."

Shocked murmurs erupted.

Jovan's face lit with hope. "You contacted Janwar?"

"Yes. I hoped he'd be near enough by now to rescue her. But he isn't." He addressed the group. "You know Janwar rescued Prince Taeon, his Earthling lifemate, and their infant daughter, as well as their Yona guard. But you *don't* know that he has since rescued three more Earthlings. And he trusts them as much as he trusts us. I think he's even taken one as his lifemate. They appear to love each other deeply."

Jaws dropped.

"So his perception has been compromised," Savaas pointed out.

Again, Wonick shook his head. "I don't think it has. I spoke with her—Janwar's lifemate, Simone. Without any prompting, she told me the same thing Rachel did. That she and her friends differ from other Earthlings and suffered because of it. Like us. Simone understands our situation and empathizes with us. She has vowed not only to keep our existence a secret but also to come to our aid if anyone else ever exposes us and puts us in danger. Janwar did, too."

Savaas's fury erupted in a shout. "She knows cyborgs still live? Who told that female what you are?"

"Janwar did to demonstrate the trust he places in her."

"Did he learn nothing from Krigara nearly dying at the hands of a woman?"

Frustration battered Wonick, swiftly morphing into anger. "I told you. Simone isn't like that. Janwar wouldn't be with her if she were. And neither is Rachel."

"You don't know that!"

"Not with absolute certainty, *vuan* it," he conceded, his voice rising. "I need more time for that. Time she doesn't have. But I trust Janwar. And I trust my instincts. And my instincts tell me we should help her!"

"You'd risk so much for a woman you don't even know?" Savaas bellowed.

Wonick shouted back, "I'd risk my life for her!" And he was as stunned by the words he'd blurted as the others. Because he realized he meant them.

Several heartbeats passed as Savaas glowered at him, unwilling to bend. "Would you risk the lives of your brothers?" A valid question, because that was what this would entail.

Turning in a slow circle, Wonick studied the men around him. "Is *this* what we rebelled for? So we can do the very thing that launched our rebellion in the first place? Kill an innocent?"

"*We* didn't put her in that pod," Savaas reminded him.

"But we can rescue her. Isn't sitting back and watching her die the same thing as killing her? Crashing her pod sure as *srul* is."

"You've forgotten," Savaas ground out, "that allowing her to land here will bring the Gathendien warship directly to the home we struggled for years to create *and* conceal. You know those *grunarks* will delight in discovering a planet with this many resources and so few inhabitants to conquer. Especially when they realize those inhabitants are cyborgs Astennuh will pay them handsomely to kill!"

Wonick threw up his hands. "Have we grown so weak and complacent that we can't defeat a ship full of Gathendiens?"

"You're assuming they'll be the only ones we'll face. Once they inform their emperor of their find, he'll salivate over the haven this planet could offer them and send more ships."

"They *can't* inform their emperor. I've already infiltrated their communications array and blocked all incoming and outgoing messages."

A long moment passed as the significance of *that* settled in. It didn't just reveal the depth of his determination to save Rachel. It proved he'd thought this through and already enacted measures to ensure their safety and continued anonymity.

"Once that Gathendien ship lands, all we have to do is make sure it can't leave," Wonick told them. "The barrier we created around the planet ensures that no signals other than our own can leave it. No scans can pierce it. As long as we treat this like a standard hostile force incursion, it will not threaten our ongoing safety. We'll divide into units. One will retrieve Rachel. A second will infiltrate the system of whatever dropship they send and disable their launch capabilities. A third will focus on sealing their bay doors to prevent them from utilizing smaller craft when the *grunarks* realize someone's killing them off. That will ground them all and leave them at our mercy. When the Gathendiens scatter to search for Rachel, a fourth unit can infiltrate their ship and ensure no Earthlings are being held captive. After we've dispatched all the Gathendiens here, we'll head up to the warship, defeat the rest, and end up with a new ship, multiple shuttles and fighter craft, and a wealth of Gathendien data to use however we will."

Everyone stared at him.

He shrugged. "I'm up for a fight. Aren't any of you?"

They glanced at each other.

"I say we save Rachel," Jovan said.

When Savaas opened his mouth to protest again, Wonick raised a hand. "Once she's here, you can decide for yourself whether you think we can trust her. But don't do to her what the Akseli people and the Aldebarian Alliance did to us. Don't assume that she means us harm and look the other way while she's killed."

More murmurs arose.

Shaking his head, Savaas addressed the whole. "We'll put it to a vote. Who's in favor of rescuing the female and bringing the Gathendiens down on our heads?"

A roar of *I*'s filled the commissary.

Relief brought a smile to Wonick's lips as he looked at Savaas. "I don't think you need to ask who isn't."

Savaas shook his head. "All right. The escape pod will likely breach our atmosphere tomorrow evening, followed quickly by the Gathendiens." He glanced at Nebet for confirmation.

Nebet nodded. "The Gathendien ship is approaching fast enough that it will almost be close enough to the pod to lock an acquisition beam on it when the pod breaches our atmosphere."

"Then mealtime is over." Savaas motioned to the room. "You know the drill. Time to strategize."

The crowd quickly dispersed, cyborgs heading for tables and repositioning them to form a large rectangle that would allow them to face one another while they plotted and planned.

Savaas caught Wonick's gaze. "I hope you're right, brother."

"I am. You'll see."

"If you aren't, that female won't leave this planet. And you will have condemned her to a very lonely life. I won't have her disrupting the peace it has taken us so long to cultivate." Crossing his arms over his chest, he watched the other cyborgs work. "If she can't accept us, she's not welcome here. We'll build her a home on the other side of the planet and provide her with quarterly provisions. But if she ever tries to harm any of us..."

"She won't." At least he hoped she wouldn't.

If she tried to harm *anyone*, he suspected it would be him.

How would she react when she realized Wonick had deceived her, that he could have lured her here to safety all along and hadn't?

His stomach burned at the thought of it.

CHAPTER FIVE

Restless energy ricocheted through Rachel like an electrical current. The Gathendien ship approached far faster than she'd anticipated.

"Are you sure we can make it to the planet before they catch us?" she asked for the dozenth time.

"Affirmative," Evie replied patiently. "Once this pod breaches the planet's atmosphere, the Gathendien ship will not be able to lock an acquisition beam on it."

"Are sandstorms still raging down there?" The more cover she'd have, the better the outcome would be.

"Unknown. I cannot scan the planet's surface from space. And reports speculate that fluctuating magnetic fields on the planet's surface interfere with many ship functions, including communications and scans that are needed to determine location, map topography, and more."

Here's hoping the reports are right, Rachel thought. "Okay. Remember the plan. As soon as we push through the atmosphere, start looking for a place to land that will provide me with some cover. Mountains. Rock formations. Valleys. Anything I can disappear into."

"If I cannot scan topography—"

"Then eyeball it."

"Please repeat using alternate terms."

"Use every means at your disposal to see what's down on the ground. Or show *me* what's below us." How dense were the sandstorms? "I mean, if all else fails, this pod has proximity sensors. Use those to create a rudimentary map of formations around us as we go."

"Affirmative. Approaching atmosphere."

Rachel's heart began to beat faster. "Anything from Handsome?"

She'd heard nothing from him since she'd revealed her plan... which she wasn't even sure he'd heard in its entirety. Had whatever disrupted scanners near the planet also disrupted communications with him? Or had he cut communications himself?

If *he* had cut them, why had he done it? Did he not agree with her? Or had something happened? Had his superiors or captors caught on that he'd been communicating with her and removed him from his post? Had they punished him?

She hoped not. Despite his reticence, Rachel liked him and enjoyed making him laugh, coaxing him into loosening up, and bantering with him. "Open the communications channel with Handsome. Keep all others closed."

"Opening channel."

"You there, Handsome?" Rachel called.

Silence.

She sighed. "I wish I could speak to you one last time. We're about to punch through the planet's atmosphere. I don't know how this is going to go. I just wanted to thank you for talking to me this past week. It's been fun and really nice to know I'm not all alone out here."

No response.

"If all goes well, I may soon be the proud new owner of a certain warship with enough oxygen and provisions to keep me alive for quite a long time." No one could ration supplies like an Immortal Guardian could. Her biggest challenge would be finding the blood she'd need in order to avoid slipping into stasis. Lasarans had mentioned that synthetic blood may suffice but had refused to test it until they reached Lasara and could have the royal family's medics on hand. Evidently, they were the best of the best. "I have no idea how to fly a ship like that. Or even if one person *can* fly it alone. But I'm going to try." She stared at the planet ahead, seeing nothing but a round reddish blur, which she supposed resulted from the sand blowing around. "If you use this channel to convey your location, I'll do my best to find you. To free you from whatever bad situation you're in." And maybe the friends he wished to protect, if he turned out to be the good guy he seemed.

"If I *can't* fly it..." A daunting prospect. She'd be stranded, with only two choices. One, live as long as she could on the Gathendiens' rations, struggling to learn how to read Gathendien and figure out their communications system, and let death claim her if she failed. Or two, slip into stasis, spend however many decades or centuries the odd state of hibernation would allow her to survive on the ship's oxygen supply, and hope someone would eventually find her.would probably have to slip into stasis and spend however many decades or centuries the odd state of hibernation allowed her to survive on the Gathendien ship's oxygen supply hoping someone would eventually find her.

That was about as grim as it got. "If you ever find your way to freedom..." She swallowed hard. "Would you come find me? Please?" It was a lot to ask. For all she knew, he might be hunted forever if he escaped his current circumstances. "You're the only one who knows I'm here." Even though he would never see it, she forced a smile. "And I would very much like to meet you in person."

Silence.

"If you can't, please send a message to Lasara, letting them know where I am. It may seem useless if years pass, but my friends will want to know what happened to me." And would come for her, hoping stasis would keep her alive long enough for them to reach her.

Moisture filled Rachel's eyes when no replay came. She really wished she could hear his voice one more time. "Don't forget to send me your location. I'll take the pod with me if I get off the planet and have Evie check messages regularly. You'll have to include enough information for me to identify you and track you down. Until then... or until you find me..." Her throat thickened. "Goodbye, Handsome."

She closed her eyes. Why did saying goodbye make her want to ball her eyes out? She had only known him a week.

"We have lost communication capability," Evie announced.

"Did you send my message?"

"Affirmative. Please fasten your harness to prevent injury."

Rachel shook off the sadness, pushed aside the fear of possibly spending the rest of her life alone on an uninhabitable planet, and focused on the job at hand: find a place to land that was obvious enough to enable the Gathendiens to find her, abandon the pod, lure as many warriors as she could into the sandstorm, pick them off one by one, then sneak onto their ship and kill whoever was left.

She would keep a handful alive to run the ship but had zero faith that they wouldn't try to kill her at every opportunity. So the manuals Evie offered to translate would have to suffice.

"Entering atmosphere," Evie announced placidly.

The pod began to shake. A rumble arose next, like thunder that wouldn't cease. Everything in the pod's compartments began to rattle.

Rachel tensed and curled her hands over the seat's armrests, gripping them tightly. The world outside the pod's unbreakable *stovicun* crystal window darkened as the sun that had grown brighter and brighter as they entered the solar system was obscured by—

"Is that fire?" Rachel blurted, panic rising when a blur of orange and yellow blocked everything else out.

"Negative."

"Are you sure? Because it's getting hotter in here."

"A rise in heat is standard for planetary entries," Evie informed her.

Seconds later, bright light flooded the pod.

Rachel raised a hand to shield her eyes.

The light began to dim and flare minutely.

Cautiously, she lowered her hand and peered through the window.

"Holy hell," she breathed.

Fumbling with her harness, she unlatched it and lunged toward the view.

"Please return to your seat and refasten your harness to ensure your safety."

So flummoxed she couldn't speak, Rachel flattened both hands on the crystal glass and pressed her nose to the window like a child hoping for a glimpse of Santa Claus on Christmas Eve.

The light outside flickered because they were passing in and out of fluffy white clouds. Once they descended beneath them...

She stared. No sandstorm scoured a barren surface. Instead, the air was clear, the sky a pale blue in one direction and tinged with a faint rosy glow from the setting sun in the other. Vast, dark blue ocean stretched beneath her, the same color as those on Earth. And beyond it lay a tropical paradise.

"It's beautiful," she whispered.

Where the ocean became shallower as it approached land, the water was clear enough for Rachel to see the bottom between the waves. A picturesque beach with white sands formed a bridge between the water and a wall of lush vegetation.

"It looks like a rainforest," she murmured, marveling over its magnificence. Trees reached toward the sun, so high they rivaled Earth's tallest skyscrapers. Their canopy wove together so densely that her eyes couldn't penetrate it, creating a thick green blanket of foliage that stretched over hills and climbed the sides of majestic mountains, broken only by a few meadows here and there.

Movement above the snow-capped mountain peaks drew her attention.

"Birds!" she exclaimed. A whole flock of them left their perches in the canopy, perhaps startled by the sudden appearance of the pod. "There's life on this planet!"

"Affirmative," Evie stated. "Though many of our scanners are malfunctioning, I detect motion in the air around us."

Rachel peered down at the ocean. Her breath caught. Several sea creatures the size of whales skimmed through the water.

Hope rose. She could survive here. Hunting and eluding the Gathendiens in that forest would be a breeze. Afterward, she could find plants and game to sustain her while she learned how to pilot the Gathendien ship or waited to be rescued. She might even find a mammal with blood of sufficient quality to pacify her need for infusions. She'd never used animal blood before and shuddered at the thought of it. But if it worked and this planet had the right atmosphere...

Her heart began to beat faster with excitement. She could conceivably live here for hundreds of years! Surely *someone* would come along and find her.

This planet had water, plants, and animal life like Earth. Wouldn't that require a comparable atmosphere? Didn't the blue sky and rosy sunset suggest the air was of a similar composition to Earth's?

"I mean, it would be a different color if it had a different chemical makeup, wouldn't it?" she murmured.

"Please repeat inquiry," Evie responded.

"Can you tell me if the atmosphere is breathable?"

"Negative. All scans appear to be malfunctioning."

Alarm rose. "You can still land the pod, right?"

"Affirmative."

"Good. Land it on the beach, in that stretch there where it's widest."

"Such would put the escape pod at risk of being swept away with the tide if this planet's tidal forces are strong."

"Oh." Well, she didn't want that to happen. "Then land in the closest clearing. Right in the center. I don't want the Gathendiens to have any trouble finding me."

"Altering trajectory. Please be seated and fasten your harness to ensure your safety."

Though Rachel hated to abandon the view, she returned to her seat and strapped in. This was better than anything she had hoped for. It was almost too good to be true.

Alarm surfaced. Wait. *Was* it too good to be true?

"Evie, how are the oxygen levels inside the pod?" Punching through the atmosphere hadn't damaged anything, had it?

"Oxygen levels are normal."

Good. For a second there, she'd feared she was hallucinating.

"Reducing speed," Evie announced as a plethora of green whipped past the window. "Prepare for landing."

Nearly bursting with excitement, Rachel said, "I'm ready." She'd spent hundreds of years tracking and killing vampires through forests on Earth. As long as this planet had a friendly atmosphere, picking off the Gathendiens would be child's play.

She grinned. "Come and get me, boys."

"YOU AREN'T WEARING EXO-ARMOR?" Jovan asked.

Wonick shook his head, opting for a lighter-weight armor than the others. He had insisted on leading the team that would locate Rachel and didn't want to alarm her by showing up in full exo-armor or carrying multiple weapons. Jovan and four others would accompany him. When choosing his team, Wonick had carefully selected those who had expressed the most unease at the thought of letting Rachel die.

Jovan volunteered to wear the lighter-weight armor, too. But Wonick told him to stick with the exo-armor. The Gathendien warship would likely remain in orbit outside the planet's atmosphere, unwilling to risk their instruments failing under the influence of whatever kept interfering with their scans. Instead, they would send a dropship full of soldiers to investigate and hunt down the missing Earthling. Wonick didn't know yet how many Gathendien warriors that would entail and didn't want to risk any of his men falling to heavy fire.

As he armed himself, Wonick had to admit that—without the camouflage activated—his brothers *did* look more machine than man when geared up for battle. Metal plating covered them from their necks to their fingers and toes, lending them greater bulk. A helmet with a clear faceplate that also served as a data screen shielded their heads and concealed their faces. Though their armor boasted a number of deadly built-in weapons, most of his brothers carried O-rifles and more.

It was an intimidating sight that had—in the past—led enemies to erupt into panicked flight. Especially after seeing the speed and strength the cyborgs demonstrated before they even raised a weapon. Cyborgs were incredibly strong and fast *without* the armor. *With* it, they could race a hoverbike and win.

Though the armor Wonick chose to wear was more subtle than the other, resembling black pants and a long-sleeved shirt that was standard military issue, it could nevertheless protect him from a few hits from an O-rifle. Anything more than a few and he'd be in trouble. Especially since he'd forgone wearing a helmet and opted for only a clear visor that would display the information his helmet otherwise would have.

The escape pod has landed, Savaas announced via the private comm channel the Akseli military had embedded in every cyborg's brain. It operated much like the Lasarans' telepathy, enabling the cyborgs to communicate with each other on the battlefield without the enemy's knowledge. *It's in the meadow at the base of Mount Shojaa.*

The tallest mountain on the planet's only continent, Mount Shojaa allowed anyone in the watchtower they had constructed in its peak to see clearly in all directions. Savaas and his team currently perched up there, ready to launch heavy artillery if this situation got out of control.

Wonick led his crew from the armory. *And the Gathendien ship?*

Stationary outside our atmosphere. But they launched a G-27 dropship that followed the escape pod.

Boom.

Birds burst from the trees and fluttered away.

It just cleared a large enough swath of forest to land near the pod.

Frowning, Wonick hit the forest at a jog and increased his pace. G-27 dropships were the transports often deployed in war. In addition to soldiers, they carried multiple land and air vehicles for surveillance and to get soldiers where they needed to go in hostile environments. Either the Gathendiens believed Rachel posed a genuine threat or they worried that traditional troop transports wouldn't fare well in the raging sandstorm the cyborgs showed them from space.

Why didn't they land in the clearing? Wonick asked. There should be room enough for both craft.

Because the pod rests in the center of it.

The dropship's scans wouldn't function long enough to determine whether Rachel still inhabited the pod, thanks to the cyborgs' interference. Since the Gathendiens wanted to take her alive, they must have opted not to land on top of it and risk crushing her.

Activating the cybernetic implants in his head, Wonick projected a translucent map on his visor and began searching for heat signatures.

The female left the pod, Benwa announced. Wonick and Savaas had positioned a team near every large clearing that would be visible from the projected atmospheric entry point of Rachel's escape pod. Benwa and his team were dug in at the base of Mount Shojaa. *She looks Lasaran*, he said, curiosity tingeing his mental voice. A snort of laughter carried across comms. *She just made a gesture toward the Gathendien craft that I'm certain must be obscene on her planet and took off.*

Wonick nearly laughed and wished he could've seen it.

What the srul? Benwa continued. *You have to hear this.*

Moments later, a female voice carried over the channel. "What's taking you so bloody long? Come and get me, mother*drekkers*!"

Laughter erupted on the channel.

Her heat signature appeared on Wonick's map, a small red splotch that stood out starkly against the cool jungle she ran through.

He frowned. Her gait was odd. She didn't run like he and his men did, with smooth precision. She ran with her arms straight out to the sides and seemed to drag her feet.

Why is she running like that? Jovan asked.

Unknown, Wonick answered. *Stay focused.* Rachel headed toward a much smaller clearing a third of the way to the cyborg settlement. He veered in that direction to intercept her.

Gathendiens have powered down engines, Benwa told them. *The first unit is disembarking.*

How many? Wonick asked.

Twenty. And two sedapas.

Swears erupted.

Sedapas were vicious reptiles with two spiked tails, multiple rows of sharp teeth, and an incredible sense of smell. They would have to be dealt with swiftly to keep the Gathendiens from locating the cyborg settlement.

Unit Four, progress report, Savaas said.

Hoshaan responded. *We've scrambled their scanners and external monitors and are now approaching the rear of the dropship in full camouflage.*

Unbeknownst to the rest of the galaxy, the camouflage cyborgs had added to their newly designed exo-armor rivaled that of the Segonians. Millions of color generators embedded in the metal shielding reflected the scenery on the opposite side of their armor. Once they activated it, the cyborgs blended in perfectly with their surroundings no matter what angle one viewed them from.

Hoshaan and his unit faced the most dangerous task today. They had to use *kadas*, or hoverboards, to carry them up the dropship's exterior and attach welding cables along the outer edges of the bay doors. Once activated, a chemical reaction would heat the cables up in an instant, melt them, and weld the doors shut while the team descended to the ground and disappeared into the forest, leaving the Gathendiens with no way to launch surveillance drones or use swift land or air vehicles to hunt Rachel. Even though the camouflaged cyborg warriors themselves would be difficult to differentiate from the ship's battered exterior, the hoverboards and cable would not, hence the risk. Any Gathendiens sent out to guard the ship would know something was wrong if they simply looked up.

Have they posted guards? Wonick asked.

Not yet, Hoshaan and Benwa replied simultaneously.

Good. Wonick's heartbeat picked up. Not from running at such high speeds. His augmented heart could easily sustain such for hours. But because he was nearing Rachel's position and would finally see her for the first time.

He and his brothers arrived at the clearing seconds before she did. *Stay back,* he ordered and strode forward a few paces to stand in front of them. He didn't want her first glimpse to be of armored warriors bearing weapons. He wanted her to see an apparently unarmed male.

With that in mind, he adjusted the strap of his O-rifle, ensuring the long weapon dangled down his back, out of sight.

"*Woooooooohooo!*" Rachel cried.

He winced at that and at the sound of her clomping through the forest. What was she doing? Did she know nothing of stealth? If she didn't—

"I'm *waaai*-ting!" she called merrily.

Seconds later, a figure burst from the trees.

He gawked. She ran with both arms extended, a long sword clutched in each hand, cutting a swathe through the foliage that even a complete imbecile could follow. And she was *intentionally* scuffing her feet!

"Come and get me, boy—oh *shit*!"

Skidding to a halt, she regarded them with astonishment.

Wonick thought his heart would pound right out of his chest. This was Rachel?

Like Janwar's lifemate, she had a slender build and was small enough that he didn't think her head would even reach his shoulder. Her skin was paler than his and lacked the ruddy bronze hues common among Akselis. Her long dark hair was drawn back from her face in a wavy bunch that fell to her waist. And perhaps most surprising, her clothing closely mirrored his own: black pants with many pockets, a long-sleeved black shirt that hugged a narrow waist and full breasts, and sturdy-looking black boots.

She was absolutely beautiful.

"There are people on this planet?" she blurted. Before he could untie his tongue and find his voice, her eyes widened. "Oh no." Sheathing her swords, she strode toward them. Her brown eyes locked with his. "I am *so* sorry. I didn't know anyone lived here." She jerked a thumb over her shoulder. "There are some really bad aliens after me, and they'll be here any moment. You need to go. Now." Grabbing his arm, she spun him around and gave him a push toward the others. "Run. Find somewhere to hide. I'll lead them away from you. And once I've dealt with them, I'll return and let you know it's safe."

Wonick dug in his heels, finding it surprisingly hard to keep her from pushing him farther.

His men stared at them with flabbergasted expressions behind their helmets' visors.

She stopped suddenly.

Turning, Wonick glanced down.

She had noticed the armored warriors. "Wait, are you soldiers?" Raising her hands in the air, she backed away. "It's okay. I'm a friend. *Friennnd.*" Brow furrowing, she muttered under her breath, "What's the Alliance Common word for friend? Dor-something? *Dorwenzi*? Right!" She patted her chest above her breasts. "*Dorwenzi. Dorwenzi.* I mean you no harm." She glanced over her shoulder. "But *those* assholes *will* if they see you." Frustration filled her features as she faced them. "Okay. I hope you have translators because I don't have time to explain it. I'll lead the Gathendiens away. Please don't shoot me in the back."

When she started to leave, Wonick held up a hand to stop her. "Rachel, wait."

She sucked in a breath and froze mid-turn. Swiveling back, she gazed up at him in shock. "Handsome?" she asked softly.

Nodding, he took a step toward her.

Handsome? Nebet repeated in his head and laughed.

Wonick ignored him. "Yes. It's me."

She shook her head even as her features lit with cautious joy. Joy at seeing *him*. "What are you doing here?" She smiled. "Did you receive my message? How did you get here so fast?" If anything, her eyes widened even more as her smile vanished. "Wait. Did you escape from whoever was holding you?" Her gaze shifted to the armored cyborgs behind him and narrowed. "Did they send these guys after you?" Her voice deepened and turned more ominous with every question. "Are they trying to take you back?" Her brown eyes began to glow with amber light.

Utterly fascinating.

Her lips tightened. "Well, *drek* that."

She extended a hand toward his brothers, clenched it into a fist, and mimicked throwing a ball.

Every cyborg's weapon broke free of its harness, flew out of their hands, and soared into the forest behind them. Every *tronium* blaster jerked out of its holster and followed.

Exclamations of shock filled the air. When the cyborgs automatically activated their armor's defenses and weapons popped up on their shoulders, Rachel repeated the gesture.

This time, the cyborgs themselves lifted off the ground, flew backward into the trees, and crashed into the foliage quite a distance away.

Wonick's jaw dropped. "What the *srul* are you doing?"

"Oops." She shrugged a little. "I didn't know those weapons were attached." Grinning, she hurried forward and grabbed his arm. "Let's go before they get up."

Wonick! Savaas called over the comm channel. *What's happening?*

Nothing. I have it under control. Wonick covered Rachel's hand on his arm and again dug in his heels. This was not at all how he had imagined this going. "Rachel, stop."

She shook her head. "We need to leave before they return."

"No, we don't. Those are my brothers."

She quit tugging and stared up at him. As he had suspected, the top of her head didn't reach his shoulder. "What?"

"The warriors you hurled into the forest." She must have incredibly strong telekinetic abilities. "Those are my brothers."

Dismay rippled across her pretty features as she looked toward the trees. "They are?"

Jovan was the first to emerge, weapons back in place. The others followed.

Rachel threw up her hands again. "I'm sorry. I didn't know you were family. I thought you were trying to arrest Handsome and take him back."

"His name is Wonick, not Handsome," Nebet grumbled.

Rachel returned her attention to Wonick, her lips curling up in a faint smile. "Your name is Wonick?"

"Yes."

"I like it." She glanced toward the path she'd cut into the forest. "Okay. You can tell me all about how you escaped later. The Gathendiens will be here soon, and you all need to skedaddle so I can ambush them." She gestured with her hands the way someone might if they were trying to shoo away an animal.

Wonick stared at her. "You intend to fight them by yourself?"

"Yes."

"There are twenty of them."

"I know."

"You do?"

"Yes."

"And two *sedapas*."

"I don't know what that is."

"Four-legged reptiles about your size, perhaps twice your weight, with multiple rows of sharp teeth, poisonous venom, two spiked tails, and an exceptional sense of smell that allows them to hunt and easily find prey."

"They won't need to use that sense of smell to find me. I left a path even a toddler could follow."

"You did that on purpose, knowing there were twenty of them?" he nearly shouted.

"Yes."

"And you intended to fight them all yourself?"

"Yes. Why? Is someone else coming? Whoever was holding you maybe? Are they hunting you like the Gathendiens are hunting me? Because maybe we can pit them against each other, then pick off whoever's left standing. That might actually be pretty entertaining."

Wonick could only stare at her.

"No one is hunting him," Jovan said, cautiously easing closer. "Or *us*. No one's hunting us."

"Jovan," Wonick warned.

"This is our homeworld," the youngest cyborg told her, gazing at her in fascination.

Confusion shadowed Rachel's features as her gaze bounced back and forth between Jovan and Wonick. "What?"

He sighed. There was never going to be an easy way to tell her this. "This is our homeworld."

Shaking her head, she backed away a step. "I don't understand. You live here?"

"Yes."

"No one is forcing you to or..."

"No."

She backed away another step and again shook her head. "I don't understand."

Wonick held his hands out in both a calming gesture and one that pled for understanding. "There are those who would hunt us—my brothers and I—as determinedly as the Gathendiens now hunt you. Of necessity, our presence on this planet is a closely guarded secret. Only six people in the entire galaxy know we live here." Janwar and the crew of the *Tangata*.

Now Simone knew, too.

The amber glow in Rachel's eyes brightened. "You've been here... on this planet... this whole time?"

The hurt that darkened her features and tightened her jaw as the depth of his betrayal sank in made his chest tighten. "Yes. I wanted to tell you, but—"

"While we talked and—I *thought*—became friends, you were here?" She shook her head. "You *knew* my situation. You *knew* how desperate I was. I practically *begged* you to help me. And you refused. You did nothing."

"Rachel—"

"You let me believe I was going to die out there, alone. You told me you couldn't help me when all you had to do was tell me to come here. To your *home*."

"I couldn't do that."

"Why?"

"As I said, this planet is a closely guarded secret. If anyone found out about it—about us—we would be more hunted than you are."

"I wouldn't have told anyone!"

Jovan shifted. "We didn't know that. We couldn't be sure."

Anger darkening her features, she studied them all. "So you would rather watch me die... just in case? It never even occurred to you that I may be trustworthy? That I would've gladly kept your secret and never told a soul? That I even would have defended you if someone found out?" Her luminous gaze pierced Wonick like a knife. "I shared my history with you. I told you! I've been hunted! I—" Breaking off she waved a hand. "You know what? None of that even matters. If you didn't trust me, you could've contacted the Aldebarian Alliance and let them know where I was. I would've left this system and headed for whomever they sent to get me. And you would've never had to meet me face-to-face."

96

"We couldn't do that," Wonick told her. "We couldn't risk them tracing the comm signal's origins."

She cut a hand through the air like a knife, her face flushing with fury. "Bollocks! You've kept this planet a closely guarded secret for how long?"

Nebet shook his head. "Don't answer that."

She didn't give Wonick time to. "Evie could find no records in *any* galaxy database that claimed this was a habitable planet. *Every* mention declared it a toxic wasteland with *no* resources... and it's a tropical paradise! A virtual utopia!" she shouted. "You've even made it appear an unwelcoming wasteland from space! And kept any travelers from scanning the surface and discovering the *bounty* that exists down here. I assume you're the reason no scans work?"

"Yes."

She loosed a fury-filled laugh. "And you want me to believe that you can do all that but you can't send an untraceable, anonymous message that an Earthling from the *Kandovar* is stranded out here in need of aid?"

He ground his teeth. "None of them could've made it here in time."

"How would *you* know?" she bellowed. "There could've been someone close enough to reach me."

"There wasn't. We monitor everything within fifty *prets* of our homeworld and track every craft that wanders nearby."

She threw up her hands and made a scoffing sound. "Then you knew about the Gathendien ship, too!"

"Yes. I was hoping it was taking a circuitous route around Promeii 7."

"Then why didn't...? If you didn't want me to come here, you should've told me to head toward Promeii 7 instead of convincing me not to!"

"You wouldn't have made it," he countered, voice rising, frustration building.

"You don't know that!" She pointed back the way she had come. "If you enter that escape pod right now and ask Evie to list all resources currently available, she'll tell you that I have almost two months left. Oxygen. Food. Water. And I can extend it even further if I have to. *Much* further," she ground out. "Because I am *not. Like. A Lasaran.* I'm not even like other Earthlings! I'm *different!*"

She had already told him as much.

Guilt flayed Wonick as she visibly struggled to bring her anger under control.

The look of disgust in the glowing eyes she focused on him made him feel lower than *tinklun bura.* "I can't believe you did that," she said softly, shaking her head. "I can't believe—" Her voice broke. Straightening her shoulders, she began to slowly back away. "I can't believe I thought you were my friend." A lone tear trailed down one cheek as her lips curled up in a cold smile. "You sure put one over on me, didn't you?"

Wonick took another step toward her. "Rachel, please. If you'll let me explain—"

"No." Tight smile still in place, she impatiently swiped the moisture from her cheek. "I think you've explained it quite well. I'm not welcome here. I imagine the Gathendiens I've brought to your doorstep after you *refused to help me* are not welcome either. Well... don't worry. I'll take care of them for you and be on my merry fucking way."

Alarm rose. "You can't defeat them all—"

"Oh," she interrupted with a dark laugh. "You don't know what I can or can't do." Reaching over her shoulders, she drew the two long swords. "I am capable of far more than you can imagine. So you might just want to keep your distance from me." Every step carried her closer to the trees behind her.

She raked a scathing glance down his form and nodded as she gave one sword a twirl. "Yeah. You keep your bloody distance." Spinning around, she took off into the forest.

CHAPTER SIX

Rachel fought back tears as she raced through the forest, her heart weighed down by Handsome's—no, by *Wonick's*—betrayal.

She remembered the last message she sent him, urging him to let her know his location, promising to help him if she could. All this time, he'd been lying to her. He had let her believe they were both stuck in bad situations, that his hands were tied and some threat kept him shackled—either figuratively or literally—preventing him from coming to her aid.

Instead, he lived in a tropical paradise and simply didn't want anyone learning about his secret retreat.

Her throat thickened as new tears threatened. What a fool she had been.

Refusing to weep, she resolutely channeled the pain of betrayal into anger.

Rage burned through her as she headed straight for the Gathendiens.

She had originally intended to lead them to the other clearing she'd spotted as the pod landed, then dart in and out of the shadowy forest and pick them off one or two at a time. The sun was setting, the tall trees blocking the brightest light and protecting her photosensitive skin. The dimmer the light, the more confident she became that she could slay them with ease because she could see as clearly as a cat in almost complete darkness, and their heat signature scanners were probably wonky. But now...

All she wanted to do was loose the fury that seared her insides. To hurt. To punish. And these Gathendien bastards were aching for punishment. They killed all those people on the *Kandovar*, trying to get their hands on Rachel and her friends. *Well, now they'll get me,* she thought with malice.

The Gathendiens' stench reached her before she spotted them. Dank and unpleasant, it reminded her of stagnant water and would've clogged her nostrils if her nose weren't starting to run from the tears she fought.

"Idiot," she muttered.

The first Gathendiens she spotted were big. At least as tall as the warriors she'd left back in the clearing, they wore no armor. Rachel had never seen any beings who appeared this alien before. Lasarans resembled Earth men and women closely enough that most couldn't tell the difference simply by looking at them. They even had similar variations in skin tone, hair color, and facial features. Yona were a little different. Their skin held a noticeable grayish hue, and their eyes had larger irises. But their features, like those of Lasarans, looked human.

It shouldn't surprise her. If the planets had similar atmospheres and life arose from the same six basic elements as Earth's, why wouldn't they have developed similar life forms? But these guys...

She leapt up to a sturdy branch in one of the towering trees and paused to study the two who led the charge. No hair graced their forms. Both were bald with yellowish skin resembling leathery hide that coated their faces, necks, and chests. Vests like those the Yona wore protected their chests. Though the material looked thin, she knew from conversations with Ari'k that it was more like Kevlar and could sustain several O-rifle blasts, offering lightweight protection. Pants of the same material covered their legs. Unlike Wonick's brothers, the Gathendiens didn't seem to boast any other armor aside from silvery spikes attached to their long, thick tails.

Their facial features lent them a reptilian look. Thin lips. Eyes with slitted pupils. No eyebrows. A flattish nose. No ears. Only holes that she assumed enabled them to hear. The skin on the back of their heads and on the outside of their arms, shoulders, backs, and tails was a dark green and looked as thick as alligator hide. It also bore thick ridges and a rough texture that might make it difficult to pierce with a blade.

The two lead warriors gripped leashes.

She dropped her gaze.

The creatures at the ends of those leashes reminded her of Komodo dragons and powered forward with such strength that the Gathendien warriors had to lean back to maintain control and keep the *sedapas* from dragging them forward on their bellies. There were some important differences from the giant lizards on Earth, though—namely, two spiked tails and the multiple rows of teeth Wonick had mentioned.

They seemed *keen* to get those teeth on her.

Rachel didn't give them the chance to.

Catching her scent, the beasts stopped short—forked tongues flicking—and hissed.

Dropping from her perch in the tree, Rachel swung her katanas. The heads of both *sedapas* tumbled to the ground before their handlers even knew an enemy had landed in their midst. As the Gathendiens opened their mouths to either yelp or call for help, she spun and swept their heads from their shoulders, too.

That hide *was* hard to pierce. Fortunately, she had preternatural strength.

Fury driving her, Rachel continued onward, found the larger group, and swiftly cut a swathe through the rest of the reptilian warriors, dodging O-rifle fire and felling every warrior without sustaining a single injury.

Did it help that the bastards wanted to take her alive and couldn't risk fatally wounding her? Absolutely. But even if they'd been set on killing her...

Rachel had slain powerful, exceptionally fast, psychotic vampires almost every night for centuries. And her recent clashes with mercenaries had taught her well how to dodge rifle fire.

Every warrior was down within minutes.

Her breath coming quickly, she caught the sounds of approaching bodies. Not from the direction of the Gathendien ship but from the clearing she had just left.

Dragging an arm across her face to wipe away some of the blood that had spattered her (apparently Gathendiens bled red, too), she looked down at her last opponent. Eyes with slitted pupils stared blankly at the foliage above. Bracing a boot on the Gathendien's belly, she clasped the hilt of her katana and tugged the blade from his chest.

Wonick and his buddies burst upon the scene, weapons drawn. All eyes widened and several men spewed stunned curses as they surveyed the carnage she had wrought in the scant minutes it had taken them to catch up with her.

Keeping her expression impassive, she bent and drew the flat of her blade across the dead enemy's pants, flipped the weapon over, and did it again to remove most of the blood. By the time she straightened, her breathing had returned to normal. "Are you going to try to kill me now?" Giving both swords a little twirl, she arched a brow. "Notice I said *try*. You won't succeed, of course. But I suppose you feel you have to do what you have to do to ensure I won't share your little secret once I off the rest of these bastards and steal their ship."

Wonick's brows drew down in a scowl. "No. We—"

"Then stay out of my way." Spinning on her heels, she sheathed her weapons and marched through the trees toward the ship. If there weren't any more Gathendiens searching for her, she would lure the rest out. Rachel wanted to finish this as quickly as possible.

When footsteps followed, she ignored them. *Bloody bastards will alert everyone within a five-mile radius of my approach.*

"Rachel." Wonick spoke right behind her. "You can't defeat them all by yourself."

Stopping short, she spun around, jabbed a finger into his chest hard enough to spark a wince, and snarled again, "You have *no* idea what I can and can't do."

He grabbed her wrist, drew her closer, and dipped his head until mere inches separated their faces. "And *you* have no idea how much I regret deceiving you." His voice rang with sincerity. His gaze conveyed both sorrow and shame. But she refused to let it sway her.

Yanking her arm free, she placed some distance between them and kept careful track of the positions of his brothers as they moved to stand nearby. "You'd like me to believe that, wouldn't you? But you're just playing nice to keep me from broadcasting your location to all and sundry once I get that piece of crap ship off this planet." She shook her head. "Well, you've no worries there. You want this planet to yourselves? Enjoy it. Because I intend to forget you ever existed as soon as I break atmosphere."

Something flickered in his expression, a microchange—there and gone in an instant—that seemed to reflect... hurt? As if she'd struck a blow.

Then his frown deepened. "I can't explain it now. There isn't time. But if you'll—"

"Nothing you say will excuse what you did." Hardening her heart, she glared up at him. "So save your breath."

Wonick swore foully. "Doesn't anything about my appearance strike you as odd?" he demanded.

Confused, she looked him up and down. "No." He was handsome as hell. Tall—several inches over six feet—with broad shoulders, a muscled chest, a narrow waist, and thick thighs. He'd shorn his raven hair close to his head in almost a buzz cut. And the skin covering his ruggedly handsome face boasted a five-o'clock shadow marred by a few scars on one side near his ear. "Looks like I was more accurate than I knew in naming you Handsome." She offered him a tight smile. "But I know from past experience, most recently confirmed by you, that deception can come in very pretty packages."

Growling in apparent frustration, he turned to his brothers.

Rachel tensed, hoping she wouldn't have to fight them. While Wonick had pissed her off, she couldn't stomach the notion of killing him.

"Raise your faceplates," he ordered.

The other warriors' faceplates rose, revealing their full faces.

Wonick gestured toward them and eyed her expectantly. "*Now* do you notice anything different?"

Rachel frowned as she studied them. "No."

"You don't think it odd that we all bear scars on the same side of our faces?"

Sure enough, they did. Some of the scars were thicker and created a different pattern than the others. But they all appeared in the same general location.

She shrugged. "No. I figure it's a cultural thing." A coming-of-age ceremony, perhaps. Cutting, tattooing, and more were common components of rituals back on Earth. She even recalled a time when children used to cut their palms and press them together to seal vows of friendship.

Lips tight, Wonick reached behind his back and drew a dagger.

Rachel swiftly drew a dagger of her own. Placing more distance between them, she turned slightly to one side and assumed a fighting stance.

The action seemed to anger him, drawing his brows down into a deeper scowl. Rather than attacking her, however, he began to roll his left sleeve up past a metal wristband.

"Wonick," one warrior said, his voice carrying a warning. He and the others exchanged troubled glances.

Rachel frowned. What did they think was about to happen?

"Watch," Wonick ordered her shortly.

Dragging her gaze back to him, she sucked in a shocked breath as he clenched his left hand into a fist and—with his right—drew the blade across one side of his forearm, cutting deeply. Red blood poured forth while he wiped the blade on his shirt and tucked it back into its sheath.

Her heartbeat quickened. *What the hell?*

"Look," he ground out. Extending his wounded arm, he pressed his fingers against the edges of the wound and parted them.

Rachel couldn't prevent her feet from carrying her forward. Peering down at the wound, she tried to see past the blood and flesh to whatever he wanted her to—

She gasped. The blade had cut all the way to the bone. But pale bone wasn't what he'd revealed. *Metal* gleamed beneath the copious red liquid and damaged tissue.

As though wanting to ensure she didn't miss it, he swept one finger through the wound, gritting his teeth against the pain, and left no doubt that metal resided where bone should have.

Rachel's heart beat faster as she looked up at him. "What...?"

His reddish-brown eyes met and held hers. "You aren't the only one who's different."

She shook her head. "What are you?"

A muscle twitched in his cheek beneath the scars. "We're cyborgs."

Rachel could not have been more shocked.

Sinsta and Rachel's other Lasaran friends on the *Kandovar*'s engineering team had told her about the cyborgs. For years, they had led the Akseli military to victory after victory, trouncing every opponent, until they had malfunctioned and become rabid killing machines.

At least, that's what the Akseli chancellor had claimed. But Sinsta had expressed doubt. Apparently, a pirate named Janwar had gained at least part of his ruthless reputation by aiding in a subsequent cyborg rebellion. But Janwar and Prince Taelon were good friends. And Sinsta, who secretly harbored quite a crush on Prince Taelon, didn't think Taelon would've befriended someone of poor character.

The Akseli government had long ago announced that all cyborgs had been *decommissioned*. Every cyborg should be dead.

And yet, one stood before Rachel.

She glanced at his brothers.

No, *five* stood before her. Five cyborgs who really *would* be hunted more vigorously than she would if knowledge leaked that they still lived.

All anger drained from her as she met Wonick's gaze. "Holy hell."

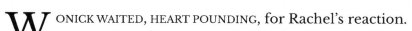

W ONICK WAITED, HEART POUNDING, for Rachel's reaction.

It was not what he expected.

After sheathing her dagger, she grabbed the fabric of her shirt at one shoulder and tugged. The sleeve tore away at the seam with a loud rip.

His gaze immediately went to the slender arm revealed. Rachel may appear delicate, but the alluring curves of lean muscle rippled beneath her pale skin as she moved.

Stepping closer, she took his wounded arm and started wrapping the cloth around and around the wound in a makeshift bandage.

"Are you insane?" she asked, head down, as she focused on her task. "You couldn't have found a less detrimental way to tell me that?"

Pain shot up his arm as she tied the ends of the fabric in a tight knot. "You seemed disinclined to listen and likely wouldn't have believed me."

Her full lips pursed. "True. My head can be very hard at times. And..." Glancing up at him, she admitted in a whisper, "I was hurt." The honesty and vulnerability of the admission tugged at him.

Wonick swallowed. "I know. I wanted to tell you the truth when we communicated but was bound by loyalty and concern for my brothers. I hope you can forgive me."

Those tempting lips turned up at the corners as she gave his chest a little pat. "As long as you entrust me with the truth from this point on, all is forgiven. On Earth, I had to keep a similar secret that I couldn't even share with people I came to care for because it wasn't solely my secret to share. And because I wouldn't be the only one to suffer if my trust ended up being misplaced." The entrancing amber light in her eyes faded to a deep brown as she glanced at his brothers. "My brethren would've suffered as well." Finished with her ministrations, she took his hand between both of hers and gave it a squeeze. "Shall we start again?"

Pulse picking up, he nodded.

Rachel smiled up at him, lovely even with speckles and streaks of blood on her face. "It's good to finally meet you in person, Wonick."

Warmth fluttered through his chest. "It's good to meet you, too, Rachel."

Releasing him, she backed away. Her smile stretched into a grin that flashed straight white teeth. "You're bigger than I thought you would be. For some reason, I pictured you as a pale, skinny fellow stuck in a tiny, dimly lit room for days on end with too little food."

He smiled back. "And you're smaller."

"Don't let my size fool you. As my friend Eliana is fond of saying, dynamite comes in small packages."

"My translation matrix tells me dynamite is an explosive substance on Earth that's capable of causing substantial damage."

"Yes, it is."

He laughed, as did his brothers, and they glanced at the downed warriors around them. "Clearly true."

She motioned to his arm. "Do we need to get you back to your home base or wherever you live and seek medical attention for that? It's a deep cut."

"No. We heal at an accelerated rate."

Do you intend to share all *our secrets with her?* Savaas growled in Wonick's head.

No, Wonick responded. *Only most of them.*

Curses flowed over the line.

She smiled. "Good."

Wonick's visor flashed a warning that the dropship was trying to broadcast a signal to the hunting unit, one they blocked.

Rachel tilted her head as though listening to something. Glancing down at one of the Gathendiens, she pointed. "I think someone on the smaller ship is trying to contact that one. I heard a burst of static."

She did? Her hearing must be incredibly acute. Without the cybernetic enhancements in his ears, Wonick wouldn't have heard anything broadcast through the receiver hidden inside the Gathendien's ear canal.

He waved Nebet forward.

Rachel granted the warrior a bright smile. "Hi. I'm Rachel." She thrust out a hand.

Eyebrows flying up, Nebet clasped her forearm. "Nebet."

"Good to meet you, Nebet. I love your armor. Very sleek."

He glanced at Wonick, then back. "Thank you?"

Grinning, she released him.

Wonick raised his left wrist, equipped with a high-tech gauntlet, and nodded to Nebet.

Nebet positioned his gauntlet beside it. Once he tapped in a command, it began to produce a static sound.

Wonick looked at Rachel. "Remain quiet, please."

Nodding, she watched them curiously.

Dipping his chin closer to his wrist unit, he used his cybernetics to tap into the Gathendien communication channel and temporarily unscramble it. While Nebet raised and lowered the volume of the static, Wonick spoke several gruff words with odd gaps and pauses in between.

Once done, he swiftly scrambled the channel again and closed communications.

Nebet discontinued the static.

Rachel grinned at them. "Well done. I assume you pretended to be one of the Gathendien hunting party?"

Wonick nodded.

"It totally sounded like static was interfering with your connection. What did you tell them?"

"That the *sedapas* had your scent. But you're faster than you look, and we haven't yet reached you."

She delivered a light punch to his shoulder. "Clever boy."

Wonick arched a brow. "I'm fully grown."

She gave his form a quick assessing sweep. "Oh, I already knew that." Did that look indicate... attraction? "On my planet, adults who are well acquainted sometimes address each other as boy or girl."

"We do the same." He smiled. "However, since species age at various rates out here, I just thought you should know."

She winked. "Duly noted."

"I'm fully grown," Jovan blurted, stepping forward. The smallest cyborg in their settlement, he was also the most innocent and naïve, appearing barely old enough to grow a beard.

"So I see," Rachel said without missing a beat and extended her hand. "I'm Rachel."

"My name's Jovan."

"It's a pleasure to meet you, Jovan."

The young male flushed and offered a quick dip of his head as he clasped her forearm.

Rachel introduced herself to Sonjin and Taaduro next then faced them all with a smile. "Now, I have quite a few Gathendiens left to kill. I'm not sure how long it will take. But I would love to meet you afterward. Shall we arrange a time and place?"

All stared at her blankly.

Is she serious? Nebet asked.

Peering at them curiously, she waved her hands in front of them. "Are you all doing that thing cyborgs in movies do where they don't appear to be aware of their surroundings while they run a bunch of code or information through their cybernetic brains, analyzing data at an astonishing rate?"

Jovan blinked. "What's a movie?"

She grinned. "And you're back! Movies are entertainment vids on Earth."

Wonick shook his head. "We weren't analyzing data. We were trying to decide if you were jesting."

"About meeting you when I'm done? No. I would really love to get to know you better and—"

"About killing the rest of the Gathendiens yourself."

"Oh, that?" She waved a hand. "No, I wasn't kidding." Eyes narrowing, she crossed her arms over her chest. "Why? You aren't questioning my fighting skills because I'm a woman, are you?" Her tone left no doubt that she wouldn't appreciate it.

Jovan looked at the others, then at Rachel. "Maybe," he answered innocently.

Wonick jumped in quickly. "It isn't because you're a woman." Female Akseli and Segonian soldiers were as fierce as their male counterparts. "It's because you're one against many. And you may not be familiar with all the weapons Gathendiens wield."

Her eyes lit with amusement. "Good save. And I appreciate your concern. But I have a good idea of what I'll face."

"You're still one against many," he pointed out again.

"True. And normally I wouldn't turn down the help. Going up against that many on my own, I'm bound to incur injuries." She motioned to Wonick. "But you aren't supposed to exist. Fighting by my side would be counterproductive. So I'll fight them myself. All they know right now is that this planet isn't as crappy as they thought. They don't know that it's inhabited by cyborgs, and we want to keep it that way. Since *I'm* the one who put you and your brothers at risk by leading them here, *I'll* be the one to clean up the mess." Glancing at the downed warriors littering the ground, she wrinkled her nose. "Figuratively," she added. "I'll clean it up *figuratively*. Once I'm done, I wouldn't mind you guys helping me clean up the literal mess."

Who is *this female?* Sonjin asked.

Wonick shook his head. "You would risk your life and fight the Gathendiens alone to keep our secret?"

"Of course. That's what friends do." Her voice rang with sincerity.

Did you all get that? he asked across the mental comm channel, knowing his brothers were listening.

A chorus of affirmative answers swelled.

Savaas?

A long moment of silence fell. *We'll see,* the stubborn cyborg leader answered.

Hoshaan, Benwa suddenly said over comms, *you almost done?*

No. We've attached the welding cables to three sides. But I want to do the fourth to make sure it holds. Why?

You're about to have company. Guards are exiting the ship in pairs and are spreading out to guard the perimeter.

Hoshaan swore.

So did Wonick and the others.

"What's wrong?" Rachel asked.

"The Gathendiens are about to discover the team we sent to weld the dropship's bay doors closed and keep them from launching any smaller craft."

All the cyborgs readied their O-rifles.

"Will having the Gathendiens look in this direction help?" she asked before they could move forward.

"Yes."

Tucking two fingers between her lips, Rachel let out an ear-piercing whistle that echoed throughout the forest.

Wonick winced.

All animal and insect sounds ceased.

Tilting her head back, Rachel bellowed up to the sky, *"Is that all you've got? Twenty puny soldiers and two tame* sedapas? *Come and get me, you wankers!"* A smile toying with the edges of her lips, Rachel studied him. "What's happening now?"

Wonick sent the cyborg comm chatter to his gauntlet and swiftly programmed it to transform the cyborgs' thoughts into speech.

"Hold position, Unit Four," Benwa murmured.

"What do you see?" Hoshaan asked softly.

"The warriors have returned to the base of the ramp and are clustered together, gesturing toward the forest."

Rachel again tilted her head back and belted out, "I'm *waaaai*-ting!"

Wonick arched a brow. "Do you have a plan beyond getting their attention?"

She drew one of her swords. "Yes. The plan is *one*, lure them here. Then *two*, kick their asses."

Multiple chuckles carried over the comm.

"Sounds like one of *your* plans, *Savaas*," someone muttered.

"Unit Four," Benwa said, "you're clear to continue welding, but finish it fast. Unit Two, you've got twenty more Gathendiens headed your way."

"We're Unit Two," Wonick told Rachel.

"Okay." She nodded at his gauntlet. "Can you by any chance use that to show me where they are?"

He sent several mental commands to the gauntlet through his cybernetic link and extended his arm. A holomap rose above it, displaying the terrain between them and the Gathendien dropship. Tiny red figures lit up, forging a path toward them.

"Cool." She shifted until she stood right in front of him. Her slender back nearly touched his chest, and her hair tickled his chin as she stared through the holomap into the forest.

Again he marveled over her diminutive size. She wasn't even half his weight... and stood so close.

"Okay. Got it." She moved away. "You should go. I'll head them off before they get this far. But in case a few slip past me, I don't want them catching sight of you and the others."

"We're going with you," he informed her.

"Wonick—"

"They won't identify us." He nodded toward his brothers. "Show her."

The other warriors lowered their face shields and engaged their camouflage. Their forms seemed to disappear as their armor swiftly took on the coloring of the foliage behind them.

Rachel's eyes widened as a wide smile lit her pretty features. "That is freaking awesome!" She turned back to Wonick. "How long will that last?"

"Until the armor sustains sufficient damage to reduce power or render some of the sensors inoperable."

"Okay. But won't the Gathendiens still know you're cyborgs underneath? If they've seen your armor—"

"The camouflage feature isn't standard for cyborg armor."

"It isn't?"

He shook his head. "We designed new armor after we went into hiding."

"Well, you did a smashing job of it." She motioned to him. "What about you?"

"I opted not to wear my exo-armor. I worried it might make you uneasy."

She stared up at him. "You knew you would probably fight Gathendien soldiers today and took the risk of not wearing heavier armor because you didn't want to scare me?"

He couldn't tell how she felt about that. "Yes."

Something new entered her expression, something softer. "That's so sweet." His treacherous heartbeat quickened again when she rested a small hand on the center of his chest. "But without the armor, won't they identify you?"

Despite the curious scrutiny of his brothers, Wonick covered her hand with his. "The scars cover my cyborg ident bars."

Her brown-eyed gaze went to the scarring on his cheek. He watched carefully for any sign that she found the disfiguration unpleasant but read only curiosity in her gaze.

"With the shorter hair," he continued, surreptitiously drawing his thumb across her soft skin, "at a glance, I can pass for a Segonian. Akseli warriors all wear their hair long and adorn it with war beads, one for every enemy they defeat." Once the rebellion ended, he and his brothers shaved their heads and burned the beads they'd earned while obeying Aksel's leadership, calling into question every attack that had been ordered. "Segonians keep their hair short."

Her fingers moved beneath his, shifting back and forth over the fabric above his heart as she dropped her gaze to study their clasped hands. "This feels like lightweight armor. Will it offer you enough protection? Once I start tearing through their ranks, the Gathendiens may fire wildly. I don't want you to get hurt."

"I'm a more-than-capable warrior, Rachel, with or without armor."

"I meant no insult," she quickly clarified. "I just don't want to lose any more friends."

He studied her. "You still consider me a friend?"

"Yes." Her lips stretched in a grin as mischief brightened those brown eyes. "As long as you help me clean up the mess I'm about to make."

He laughed. "The mess *we* are about to make."

"Right." Withdrawing her hand, she stepped back. "So how do you want to do this?" She glanced around. "The light is fading pretty quickly. Can you all see in the dark?"

"Yes." He motioned to his visor. "These provide adequate night vision and enable us to track heat signatures."

"So you block everyone else's signals but can still use your own?"

"Yes."

"You guys are brilliant."

"I like this female," Benwa announced over the comm.

Rachel laughed.

"What about you?" Wonick asked. "How is your night vision?" He didn't want encroaching darkness to hinder or endanger her.

"It's excellent." She drew her other sword, now holding one in each hand as she looked around. "The Gathendiens on the way here have no idea what they're up against. But seeing this will certainly tip them off. What direction is your base or town or whatever?"

"Don't answer that," Savaas ordered.

Rachel frowned at Wonick's gauntlet. "Who was that?"

"Savaas," Wonick told her. "Our leader."

She spoke to his gauntlet. "Well, Savaas, the smartest play here is to lead the Gathendiens *away* from your base and keep them from inadvertently stumbling upon it while looking for *me*. If we're

113

going to do that, I need to know which direction I should *not* herd them in."

Silence.

When she looked at Wonick, he jerked a thumb over his shoulder. "We should avoid that direction.

Savaas swore.

"Unit Four reporting," Hoshaan interrupted. "Welding cable in place. We're making our way into the forest. Welding will commence in five, four, three, two, one." A pause ensued. "Bay doors successfully sealed."

Rachel looked at Wonick. "So the Gathendiens can't send any shuttles or fighter craft out after me?"

"Correct."

"Excellent. How about you boys head toward the beach, blend into the foliage along the edges of the forest, and I'll lure the Gathendiens after you."

"Rachel..."

"Don't worry. I'll lead them past you and wait until they hit the sand before I attack." She grinned. "Be ready for all hell to break loose."

CHAPTER SEVEN

T HE LOOK OF CONCERN on Wonick's face as Rachel backed away was so sweet that she wanted to hug him. And maybe she would. Later. Right now, they had work to do.

Rachel wanted to catch the Gathendiens unawares without doubling back and leading them to their dead comrades. Sheathing her swords, she turned to the nearest tree. It reminded her of the primary-growth forests she'd explored in her youth. These trees, like those, seemed to go on forever and provided a network of branches thick enough to hold her weight. The dense canopy far above them allowed so little sunlight to filter down that foliage on the ground grew in sparse clusters, resembling ferns and other shade lovers back home. As the sun set, nocturnal bioluminescent insects began their nightly forays, their lights twinkling amid the leaves.

The lowest tree branch was a good twenty feet up. Biting her lip, Rachel glanced at Wonick and the others, who stood watching her. She rarely demonstrated her unique abilities to others. But the cyborgs had ultimately trusted her with their secret. *And* they'd already seen how fast she was. Not much to lose in terms of showing them more.

Bending her knees, Rachel pushed off with the enhanced strength the odd symbiotic virus gave her, soaring through the air like a rocket, and alighted upon a branch.

Gasps and mutters erupted below.

Then a heavy weight landed a foot away on the same branch, startling her so badly that she almost lost her balance.

Hastily reaching toward the trunk, Rachel steadied herself and gaped at Wonick. How the hell had he done that? Did cyborgs have greater strength, too? She'd thought most of their enhancements were technology-oriented, their strength stemming from their fancy exo-armor.

When she kept staring at him, he arched a brow. "I go where you go."

Her lips tightened. "Because you don't trust me?" That would hurt.

His eyes never left hers. "Because that's what friends do."

Damned if that didn't make her heart go pitter-patter. Smiling, she nodded. "Okay. Let's do this."

Together they trod across stout branches and leapt from tree to tree, making their way back toward the Gathendien ship. Thank goodness she wasn't afraid of heights. Not anymore anyway. She *had* been as a girl. But once she'd gained the incredible regenerative ability the vampiric virus bestowed upon immortals and discovered that she could jump off four- and five-story buildings without suffering any harm, that fear had vanished.

Perhaps Wonick healed as quickly as she did, because he evinced no fear or uneasiness either. He also moved quietly. The big cyborg warrior barely made a sound, reminding her of her brethren back home.

Rachel had hunted with many immortal males over the centuries. All had respected both her intelligence and her skills. And all had treated her like one of the guys. Hunting with Wonick should've felt the same. Yet, his presence proved far more distracting. The way he touched her arm to steady her when a breeze set the trees to swaying. The tingling awareness that seeped through her when his arm brushed hers or when their positions required him to crowd her. And his scent...

Rachel drew in a surreptitious breath.

She loved his scent. It was as fresh as the foliage around them and did funny things to her insides.

Until the Gathendiens' stench reached her.

Grimacing, she pointed toward them.

Wonick raised his gauntlet. That fascinating holomap appeared above it, clearly delineating twenty Gathendiens.

She wouldn't have thought one Earth woman would warrant such a large hunting party. From what she'd learned, Gathendiens believed humans were a weak, inferior species. One they thought they had easily conquered with the release of a bioengineered virus.

They must have taken her taunts seriously.

No *sedapas* accompanied the second pack of Gathendiens. Leaning forward, she whispered in Wonick's ear, "I'm going to drop down and get them to chase me. You bring up the rear and help the others ambush them. They'll be so busy looking at me that they won't even know you're there."

In return, Wonick pressed his lips to her ear. "If they see you, they'll stun you."

A delightful shiver rippled through her as his warm breath tickled her. Her eyes met his, which were a pretty auburn color. "That isn't going to happen." She rested a palm against his stubbled cheek. "Be safe."

Fighting a surprising desire to kiss him, she stepped off the limb.

A thud sounded as she landed in a neat crouch on the ground below. Kinda hard to jump from those heights *without* making noise. But she'd wanted to get the Gathendiens' attention and give them a little something to make them nervous and twitchy.

Quiet as a mouse, Rachel crept toward the interlopers' last position.

The reptilian warriors did nothing to hide their approach, making as much noise as she had when she'd raced through the trees earlier with her swords held out to the sides.

She glanced behind her to make ensure Wonick hadn't followed. Nope.

The Gathendiens would march into sight any minute now.

Rachel ducked behind a tree trunk thick enough to carve a house out of.

Twenty pairs of boots tromped past, the bastards completely unaware of her presence as they grumbled to each other and tried to get their scanners to work.

Grinning, she stepped out from behind the tree. She didn't scuff her feet this time as she followed them, curious to learn how much time would pass before they realized they were no longer alone.

Quite a bit, as it turned out, perhaps because she was downwind. Her patience waned. Rachel needed them to swerve off their current course and head away from the cyborgs' home.

Wonick's brothers should've made it to the beach by now. And *still* the Gathendiens didn't look back.

Rolling her eyes, she palmed a couple of daggers and deliberately stepped on a branch.

Snap!

They swung around.

"Finally!" Rocketing forward, she burst through the middle of the group, drawing blood as she went, swerved left, and headed for the beach.

Shouts erupted behind her. The bright blasts of O-rifles struck tree trunks as she passed. Bark pelted her. Dirt and detritus flew up in explosive plumes like charges in an action movie when blasts hit the ground. *Ha!* They couldn't risk a kill shot and must be trying to scare her into stopping.

You won't get me that easily, she crowed mentally.

When a stun grenade bounced off a tree trunk to her right, Rachel quickened her pace and raced forward so fast she blurred, ensuring she was well past it before it exploded.

Her sudden burst of speed coupled with the bright flash of light made it seem as if she had disappeared, throwing her pursuers into confusion while Rachel powered forward.

The trees thinned moments before she hit a sandy, picturesque beach. She had reached such speeds by then that she was waist-deep in the ocean before she managed to stop. The sun had set, leaving only the faint remnants of a distant glow on the horizon. It was both beautiful and convenient. Now she wouldn't have to deal with sunburning and blistering while she fought.

A full moon had already risen, gracing the ocean with enchanting bluish light.

Spinning around, she waded back to wet, packed sand.

It would take the Gathendiens a few minutes to reach her. To pass the time, she studied the forest's edge. Foliage was thicker there, the tree trunks not as broad. Perhaps hurricanes—or this planet's equivalent of the powerful storms—had knocked down old growth and allowed newer trees to replace them. Quite a few were about the size of fifty- or sixty-year-old oaks on Earth. And somewhere among them...

There. A faint deviation in color on the rough bark of a tree. Something ordinary human vision likely wouldn't detect. Except the slight deviation wasn't in the bark itself. It was in the armor of the cyborg who stood in front of it.

"You go high. I'll go low," she whispered, hoping their cyborg ears were as sharp as hers.

As the Gathendiens crashed through the sparse underbrush, growing ever closer, she picked out the other cyborgs and marked their positions to reduce the risk of accidentally impaling them with a dagger or a swing of her sword when she engaged the enemy. She failed to locate Wonick up in the branches and assumed he was doing as she'd suggested—closing in on the Gathendiens from behind.

Lumbering figures emerged from the deepening shadows, plowing toward her, their green hide helping them blend in with their surroundings. A small silver ball flew through the air. Quick as a blink, Rachel used telekinesis to redirect the grenade and sent it flying out over the ocean.

It exploded in a burst of blue crackling light she hoped wouldn't harm any marine creatures before plopping into the water.

Erupting into action, she scooped two fistfuls of loose sand and let it fly. The cyborgs' faceplates would protect them from any that reached them. But the Gathendiens lacked those and howled as sand found their eyes and tiny shells that she'd inadvertently included with it hit them with the force of buckshot.

Rachel drew her swords and raced forward. The Gathendiens in front were easy pickings. Grains of sand hampering their vision, they frantically blinked and rubbed their eyes. The warriors behind them snarled and pushed forward to meet her, ready to fight. Rachel stayed low as she'd promised, ducking and dodging Gathendiens' weapons while she inflicted fatal wounds. Their bellies and throats were the best targets. The ridged hide that coated the rest of them like armor was so thick that she couldn't have pierced it if she were human. Nor would she have been quick enough to avoid their swinging tails.

Because the vampires she'd spent centuries fighting had lacked those, she had to adjust her usual battle techniques on the fly to account for them. The heavy tails extended a good five or six feet and could easily sweep her off her feet. They also bore silvery spikes that looked sharp enough to lodge themselves in deep like a dagger.

Blaster fire erupted around her, accompanied by O-rifle fire. Very different from the bullets back home, they lit the darkening night like fireworks.

Two Gathendiens fell beneath the cyborgs' sudden assault. The rest panicked when confronted by a new threat they couldn't see and fought more fiercely.

Something sharp cut across Rachel's thigh.

Swearing, she swung a blade at the source.

A Gathendien howled and grabbed his tail, now two feet shorter than it had been.

Enraged by the wound, Rachel forgot to stay low and straightened long enough to sweep his head from his shoulders. Blasterfire grazed her shoulder.

Oops. Well, it was kinda hard to stay low when most of the Gathendiens were targeting the only opponent they could see. Or *one* of them. Rachel glimpsed Wonick kicking ass on the far side of the throng.

A blade buried itself in her left side.

Swearing, she dropped a katana enough to reach down and pull the dagger out.

Nope. Not a dagger. Another tail spike.

Rachel retrieved her sword and cut said tail off with one swipe. A swing of her other sword ended the life of the tail's owner. The tail sagged, its weight tugging at her wound. A flurry of O-rifle fire bought her enough time to pry the damn spikes out of her side and drop the twitching tail to the sand.

Creepy.

She swiveled to face her next opponent.

No others remained standing.

Well, one did. But Wonick took care of him in the next breath and let the body drop to the sand.

Breathing hard, Rachel glanced around.

All the Gathendiens were down.

She gave Wonick a quick visual inspection. No wounds. Good. Clenching her teeth against the pain radiating from her thigh, side, and shoulder, she wished she could say the same.

The other cyborgs disabled their camouflage, flickering into view and sliding up their face shields.

"Good job," she praised them.

Wonick scowled. "You're wounded."

"Yeah." Glancing down, she took in the blood that coated her side and thigh. "I'm not used to fighting anything with a tail. That will take some getting used to." She sheathed the right katana easily. When she tried to do the same with the other, she stopped with a grunt as fire raced up her side into her shoulder.

Wonick stepped over the bodies of their downed adversaries and approached her. Holstering his weapon, he gently took the sword from her fingers, wiped the blade clean, and slid it into its sheath on her back.

Rachel smiled wearily. "Thank you." Even though she had tanked up on blood before leaving the escape pod, fatigue hit her like a sledgehammer. She'd expended a lot of energy in the past hour, and now the virus worked frantically to heal her wounds.

Jovan stepped over bodies and joined them, his eyes wide. "Apologies. I shot you." Even though he appeared fully grown, something about him screamed innocent youth.

Rachel shook her head. "No apologies necessary. You didn't shoot me. I was cheesed off and forgot to stay low. Thanks for looking out for me."

He practically melted with relief and ducked his chin in a nod.

Wonick frowned. Glancing down at his gauntlet, he tapped it. "Repeat."

"Wonick, report," Savaas commanded.

"All hostiles are down," Wonick informed him.

Rachel appreciated him letting her listen in. Though she had telepathic abilities, the mental means that cyborgs used to communicate stemmed from technology and didn't register as thoughts for her.

Surprise gripped her when she realized she couldn't read their organic thoughts either. The cybernetic implants must interfere with them.

"Any hostile survivors?" Savaas asked.

"None."

"Did Unit Two incur any injuries?"

"Rachel did."

She smiled, happy to be included in their unit.

"How seriously?"

She was surprised he'd even asked. He wasn't exactly her number-one fan and probably thought they'd all be better off if she'd died in battle.

"Unknown." Clasping her shoulders, Wonick gently turned her away and reached for her shirt.

A metal gadget the size of a marble slid from the side of Jovan's helmet and directed a bright beam of light onto her side.

She met his gaze over her shoulder. "Cool."

He forced a smile but looked worried as Wonick tugged her shirt out of her cargo pants and carefully raised it.

Rachel clenched her teeth as it pulled ragged pieces of torn fabric out of the wound.

Wonick swore.

Nebet joined them while Sonjin and Taaduro kept watch.

Nebet swore, too.

Raising her arm, Rachel glanced down and grimaced. Tail spikes left larger entrance wounds than flat blades did. And there were two instead of one. "Yeah," she muttered, "he got me good. But I'm stronger than I look and heal quickly."

His handsome face grim, Wonick reached into one of his pants pockets and withdrew a palm-sized metal canister that reminded her of a miniature can of WD-40. "Send a transport to our position," he muttered.

"Sending transport now," Savaas replied.

Rachel tried to catch Wonick's gaze, but he focused on her wound. "I'm okay," she assured him. "I've received far worse than this in the past." Did it hurt like hell? Yes. But Immortal Guardians healed quickly.

Her words didn't seem to relieve his mind at all. Shaking his head, he positioned the sprayer a couple of inches from the wound and pressed the top. "The wound doesn't concern me as much as what it may contain." Cool liquid hit her, a startling contrast to the balmy heat surrounding them.

Rachel stared at him, a little spark of alarm striking. *Something it may contain?* Like what? Gathendien blood? She didn't think any had gotten into the wound, but enough of it had splattered her during the battle that it wasn't out of the question.

Was Gathendien blood dangerous? Did it carry freaky alien parasites?

Or was it like Lasaran blood?

Ami and Seth had warned her before she'd embarked upon this journey not to infuse herself with Lasaran blood. Lasarans bore incredible regenerative capabilities, healing from wounds as swiftly as Immortal Guardians did and aging so slowly that their hair didn't even begin to gray until they were four or five hundred years old.

Melanie, the top viral researcher at network headquarters, believed Lasarans might also have a natural immunity to the virus since Ami had borne her Immortal Guardian husband, Marcus, a child without being infected. And both Melanie and Seth worried that a Lasaran blood transfusion might actually destroy the virus, leaving Rachel with no viable immune system.

Would Gathendien blood do the same?

"What do you mean?" she asked.

"Gathendiens have begun to lace their spikes and bladed weapons with *bosregi*, a poison that can cause illness in most inhabitants of the galaxy."

"Life-threatening illness?" she asked, feeling a little better about it. Immortal Guardians were immune to all poisons and toxins on Earth.

"Usually, no." He met her gaze as the liquid he'd coated her wound with swelled into white foam that turned pink as it mingled with her blood. "But *bosregi* can be fatal when administered to Earthlings."

She stared at him, staggered by the revelation. "How do you know that?" Lasarans hadn't mentioned it. She was sure they would have told her if they'd known.

And how would Wonick know *anything* about Earthlings' health?

Opting not to answer, he drew a package and another canister out of his pocket. Tearing open the package, he pulled out a sterile white bandage.

The foam had dissolved, leaving her wound clean.

She winced when Wonick added the bandage and used the canister to coat it with a clear, shiny substance that seemed to vacuum-seal the bandage to the wound and hold it in place without tape.

A faint hum, barely detectible even with her sharp hearing, arose behind her.

When Rachel glanced at the ocean, the sky above it seemed to ripple slightly as if it were painted on a flag the wind had set into motion.

"The transport's here," Wonick announced.

Seconds later, the sky dissolved into a hovering craft.

Her jaw dropped as the side opened, revealing a brightly lit interior. A ramp extended down toward them and sank into the sand at her feet. "Can Lasaran craft disappear like that?" If so, why hadn't the *Kandovar* activated the camouflage as soon as the Gathendiens struck?

Not that she supposed it would've helped much. By the time the attack commenced, both ships were crammed inside the *qhov'rum*. Even firing blindly straight ahead would've enabled the Gathendiens to hit them.

"No," Wonick murmured.

When the pain in her side eased, she glanced down. "What did you spray that with? It isn't hurting as much now."

"*Imashuu*. It cleans and disinfects wounds while numbing the pain."

"Thank you."

"We need to get you to home base and determine if the wound was tainted by *bosregi*. Time is short." Curling a big hand around her biceps, he urged her toward the ramp.

"What do you mean time is short?" Rachel's boots made squishy sounds as she trod up the ramp beside him. Both were full of water thanks to her unintended foray into the ocean.

"*Bosregi* is fast-acting. If you've been exposed, we need to administer the antidote as quickly as possible to ensure a positive outcome."

A positive outcome? What constituted a negative one?

The interior of the small cyborg transport was utilitarian in nature. Just a row of seats straight ahead and more on either side of the door hatch. A gear and weapons locker covered a wall on the left with a door beside it. On the right, two cyborgs manned what she thought of as the cockpit. Both swung around to look at her as she and Wonick entered.

Smiling, she offered them a little wave. "Hello. I'm Rachel. Thank you for coming to our aid."

Their eyebrows flew up. Sliding each other a glance, they issued abrupt nods and turned back to the controls.

Boots clomped up the ramp behind her.

Wonick guided Rachel to one of the seats and urged her to sit. As soon as she did, he fastened her harness for her and knelt at her feet.

Jovan sank into the seat beside her. Nebet, Sonjin, and Taaduro claimed those on the other side of him.

As the ramp closed, droplets of water trailed down the inside—likely deposited there by her boots—and puddled at its base. Then the transport rose and left the beach behind them.

Wow. These vehicles made almost no sound when they moved.

A tug on her pants drew her attention away from the cockpit.

Wonick tore the fabric to expose another wound in her thigh. His brow furrowed with concern as he tended to it the same way he had the one on her side.

Rachel wasn't used to anyone fussing over her. Even Amara, her Second back on Earth, hadn't fussed over her. With Rachel's rapid healing, it seemed unnecessary and tended to make her cranky. But with Wonick?

Her lips formed a faint smile.

Wonick's fussing didn't make her cranky at all.

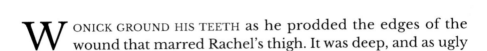

WONICK GROUND HIS TEETH as he prodded the edges of the wound that marred Rachel's thigh. It was deep, and as ugly as the Gathendien who had inflicted it.

She winced and nodded at it. "That's my only pair of pants, you know."

"I'll replace them," he mumbled.

That brought a smile to her lips. "With what?" She motioned to his large form. "I'm pretty sure your clothes would swallow me."

If he weren't worried about her, the thought of her garbed in his clothing would've made him smile, too. The shirt's sleeves would dangle well beneath her fingertips. The hem would fall to her knees. And she probably would have no hope at all of keeping his pants up.

Wonick sprayed the ragged wound with *imashuu*. "It's a simple matter of reprogramming the clothing printer."

Her features alight with curiosity. "You print your clothing?"

"Yes." He cast her a glance. "Why? How is clothing made on Earth?"

"With needle and thread. People use sewing machines to make the work go faster."

He nodded. "Most Aldebarian Alliance member nations only produce printed clothing for their military. They insist individuals sew the rest to provide adequate occupational opportunities for their populace."

"But you use clothing printers?"

He sent her a sheepish smile. "Yes. None of us know how to sew."

She laughed as he moved to sit beside her. "And have no interest in learning. You guys are brilliant. I'm sure you could figure it out if you wanted to."

Hard not to puff up a little at the compliment. "It's more a lack of time than a lack of interest." By necessity, they designed and built every structure on their planet themselves. They also planted and harvested most of their food, creating complex irrigation systems that carried fresh snowmelt to the plants and provided the settlement with potable water.

He tore her shirt sleeve at the shoulder and examined her blaster wound.

"It just grazed me," she said.

A quick inspection confirmed it. Though the wound was minor, he sprayed it with *imashuu* to reduce the pain.

Some of the tightness in her expression eased. "Were *you* injured?" She gave him a quick visual inspection.

Warmed by her concern, he shook his head. "My armor protected me." Though lighter weight than that of his brothers, it could shield him from everything but stun grenades as long as the battle was brief.

"Good."

"How are you feeling?"

She shrugged. "Tired, but otherwise fine. That *imashuu* stuff is awesome. My wounds barely hurt at all."

He thought that an exaggeration. Rachel had been ready to continue fighting after yanking the tail spike out of her side, something that demonstrated a high tolerance for pain. Those spikes hurt a *lot*. He'd been impaled by them twice when Gathendien bounty hunters had caught him off-world years ago after desperation had driven him to risk a run to Promeii 7 for supplies.

As slender as she was, he wondered if the strike might've broken some of Rachel's ribs.

He peered down at her. Her breathing didn't sound impaired. But the possible *bosregi* poisoning concerned him. "We'll reach our settlement soon."

"Okay." Sighing, she closed her eyes and leaned her head against his shoulder. Perhaps she *wasn't* feeling any pain, because she looked like she was settling in for a nap.

Or was *bosregi* already working its way through her system and sapping her strength?

Wonick ignored the curious stares of his brothers and anxiously counted the minutes it took the transport to fly them home.

"Are you angry?" Jovan asked suddenly.

Wonick glanced at him. "At the Gathendiens? *Srul* yes."

Anxiety darkened the younger cyborg's features. "No. At me."

He frowned. "For what?"

Shame lowered his eyes. "I shot her."

"Nope," Rachel murmured without opening her eyes. "I jumped into your line of fire. Stop beating yourself up about it, Jovan. That was *my* mistake, not yours. I told you to go high while I went low. Then I let anger get the best of me and screwed up. You did well."

Pleased by her defense of the boy, Wonick nodded. "You did well."

Smiling, Jovan slumped back in his seat.

Wonick fought a sudden urge to wrap an arm around Rachel, both in support and in gratitude for alleviating Jovan's concern. Cybernetic uplinks enabled him to monitor the progress of the transport. Relief filled him when they reached the landing site.

"Rachel?"

Her eyes opened. "What?"

"We're here."

The transport door opened. Nebet rose and activated the ramp.

"Oh. That was fast." Rising, she covered her mouth with one hand to hide a yawn. "I don't know why I'm so tired," she muttered. "I shouldn't be. Not after such brief battles."

If the speed and strength she'd repeatedly exhibited didn't usually fatigue her, she must have as much or more stamina than a cyborg. "Let's get you to the infirmary."

"Okay." Her quick acquiescence merely increased his concern.

Blindfold her, Savaas commanded over internal comms.

I'm not going to blindfold her, Wonick snarled back.

You would risk her reporting every detail of our settlement to—

She won't report it to anyone, Savaas. You heard her. She's sympathetic to our plight.

Or she may be lying to get us to drop our guard.

And the kindness she offered Jovan? Do you think that was a lie, too?

Possibly.

He ground his teeth.

"You look irritated," Rachel mentioned. "What's going on?"

"Nothing."

"Let me guess. Savaas is bitching over your secret cyborg comms about you bringing me here because he doesn't want me to see your home and report back to whomever he thinks I may tattle to."

Wonick didn't know what *bitching* or *tattle* meant but could guess from the context. "Something like that."

"Well, kindly point out to Savaas that a visit to your infirmary will equip *you* with information about *me* that Gathendiens would pay dearly for. Information that would enable them to kill every man, woman, and child on Earth. Trust goes both ways, asshole."

He blinked.

"I was calling *him* an asshole," she added hastily, "not you."

The other cyborgs laughed.

Smiling, Wonick took her uninjured arm. "Let's go."

The others stood back to let them exit first.

He watched Rachel from the corner of his eye for signs of pain as they trod down the ramp. But all he could discern was a slight slumping of her shoulders.

Her pretty face lit with curiosity as she looked around.

After the first hastily constructed temporary shelters they'd fashioned, the cyborgs had put a lot of thought and planning into the construction of their new home. Military men to their core, all had agreed that the first transport landing site should be close to the infirmary. Wonick and his brothers had no knowledge of this planet when Janwar brought them here. They'd had to learn through trial and error which plants were edible and which would spawn illness. They also tangled with some of the planet's larger natural predators after inadvertently encroaching upon their territory, sustaining impressive injuries before finding ways to strike a careful balance. Having quick access to medical care had saved quite a few lives in the early years.

Rachel studied the building they approached. "Is this the infirmary?"

"Yes."

"It's covered in plants."

He nodded. "Those on the roof prevent aerial surveys from distinguishing it from the ground."

"And the plants growing on its sides?"

"They provide camouflage, too, but are also medicinal."

"That's awesome. But what about the transport? Wouldn't it stand out like a sore thumb if someone flew overhead?"

Wonick ignored the reference to a sore thumb, unsure what an injured digit had to do with it, and answered the other question. "Look."

Pausing, she glanced back as a whirring sound disrupted the quiet.

A wall of interwoven vines on one side of the landing pad leaned over, providing a living umbrella above the craft.

Rachel smiled. "Very cool." When she turned back and started forward once more, her injured leg buckled.

Wonick tightened his hold on her arm as she stumbled and threw the other out to catch her if she fell.

"I'm okay," she said, finding her balance once more. "Just weirdly tired. Sorry about that."

Frowning, Wonick hurried her into the building.

Taavion awaited them in the emergency bay.

Rachel offered him a smile and thrust out her hand. "Hi. I'm Rachel."

Eyebrows rising, Taavion clasped her forearm. "Taavion. Chief Medic."

"Nice to meet you."

"Wonick wishes me to examine your injuries."

"Okay. They should be fine, though. I heal quickly, like a Lasaran."

"Understood." He motioned to a medbed. "Please allow me to scan you."

Wonick guided her to the bed. Designed for taller cyborgs, it was high enough off the ground that she would have to jump up to sit on it, something that would aggravate her injuries. He reached out to grasp her waist and aid her but paused upon realizing that he couldn't lift her without risking further damage to the wound in her side.

Rachel smiled up at him. "It's okay. I can do it." Turning her back to the bed, she jumped up and back, landing on her bottom with her feet dangling well above the floor.

He didn't miss the wince she attempted to hide.

Nor did Taavion. Frowning, he drew a handheld datapad from his pocket. "Lie on your back," he ordered absently.

Wonick moved closer and gently eased her legs onto the bed to spare her more pain.

Again she smiled. "Thank you."

Nodding, he eased back.

As Taavion tapped a series of commands into his datapad, a wand descended from the ceiling above the bed and began a slow sweep over her.

"This is so weird," Rachel mumbled.

"Being scanned?" Wonick asked.

"Being fussed over. I really do heal quickly. I should be fine in a few hours."

He hoped she was right.

"Burns detected on right shoulder," a tranquil female voice announced. Wonick didn't know how he'd done it, but Janwar had obtained this Lasaran-designed scanner for them shortly after Jovan nearly died of blood poisoning the first year they were here.

"Minor damage to right deltoid detected," the scanner told them

"That'll heal," Rachel mumbled as the scanning light passed down her form.

"Puncture wound detected in left side. Oblique nondisplaced fractures detected in the ninth and tenth ribs. Kidney damage detected. Internal bruising detected. "

She slid Wonick a glance, seeming more concerned about his reaction than the litany of damage itself.

"Laceration detected on right thigh. Damage to quadriceps detected. Oblique nondisplaced fracture detected in right femur."

Wonick stared at her. She hadn't even limped!

"It's not that bad," Rachel assured him.

"Depleted blood volume detected."

She frowned. "What?"

A mechanical arm lowered from the ceiling.

Rachel warily eyed the needle at its tip. "Um... what's happening?"

Taavion answered without looking away from his tablet. "I need to collect a blood sample to scan you for *bosregi* poisoning."

She jumped a little when the mechanical arm sprayed the bend of her arm. A second later, the needle unerringly found her vein. Red blood slithered up a tube into the apparatus in the ceiling.

The scanning wand announced no more injuries before it folded back into the ceiling.

Rachel glanced at Wonick. "My blood volume shouldn't be low."

Shouldn't it? "You bled when you were injured. That's normal."

She opened her mouth to speak but seemed to reconsider and sealed her lips.

"Cellular anomalies detected," the scanner announced.

Taavion frowned as he perused the data constantly streaming from the scanner to his tablet. "Your genetic composition deviates from that on file for other Earthlings."

She sent the medic an uneasy look. "As I told Wonick, I'm different from most Earthlings."

"Warning," the scanner said, voice still calm. "Virus detected. Possible contagion. Recommend isolating patient and all who have been in contact with her."

Wonick stilled.

Rachel grimaced. "Yeah. That would be the virus the Gathendiens released on my planet. Don't worry," she added hastily. "It isn't contagious. It's blood-borne and poses no threat to you or others unless you transfuse yourself with a significant amount of my blood. Four of my friends carry it, too. The Lasarans never would've let us aboard the *Kandovar* if they thought it could spread or viewed it as a threat."

Taavion didn't look convinced. *All cyborgs who came into contact with the Earthling, report to the infirmary immediately.*

Taavion, report, Savaas commanded.

The Earthling carries a virus. We should quarantine everyone who had contact with her, including the transport pilots, until I confirm it isn't contagious.

Do it.

Rachel's gaze darted between them both. "What's up? I'm telepathic. I know the signs of silent communication."

She was telepathic? Wonick fought a groan. Savaas would be doubly suspicious of her now.

Taavion tilted his head to one side. "If you're telepathic, don't you already know? Didn't you read it in our thoughts?"

"No." She shrugged. "For some reason, I can't read you guys. I figure your cybernetic... implants or whatever... have altered your mental pathways enough to interfere with ordinary telepathy." She smiled. "It's actually kind of nice. Earthlings don't have as much control over our telepathy as Lasarans do, so the thoughts of others constantly bombard us. The mental quiet I experience around you all is refreshing. I'm enjoying it. But it *does* put me at a disadvantage. I know you're silently communicating with each other. What's happening?"

Wonick stepped closer to the bed. "Taavion is quarantining us."

Her brows drew down in a scowl. Covering the wound in her side with one hand, she grimaced and sat up. "You know, the whole doubting every word that comes out of my mouth thing is really starting to annoy me."

Wonick shook his head. "I don't doubt you, Rachel. It's merely a precaution. *Any* virus we've had no contact with in the past would spark the same action."

"Oh," she grumbled grudgingly. "I guess I can understand that."

The pilots entered. "Savaas told us to report for quarantine."

Taavion tapped several commands into his datapad. "Initiating quarantine protocols now." A crystal door slid down to seal the emergency bay and separate this portion of the infirmary from the rest.

When Rachel swiveled to sit with her legs hanging over the side of the bed, she winced and covered the wound in her side again.

Wonick frowned. "Is the *imashuu* wearing off already?" It shouldn't have.

"I guess so."

Taavion moved closer and set his datapad on the bed. "Let me examine it."

She lifted the hem of her shirt enough to bare the bandage Wonick had applied.

Reaching up, Taavion selected a tube from the tools overhead and used it to spray the wound. The *kesaadi* that sealed the bandage to the wound dissolved, allowing him to remove it.

Rachel's brow furrowed as she stared at the wound. "What the hell?"

CHAPTER EIGHT

THE WOUND IN RACHEL'S side *should* have been healing. She'd known she would be fighting the Gathendiens for quite a while, so Rachel had consumed enough calories to get her through countless bursts of preternatural energy *and* had tanked up on blood.

Even though the tail spikes had created larger entrance wounds, the edges should already be drawing together. In another half hour, they should seal and form a scar that would melt away by the time she woke up tomorrow.

Instead, the size of the wound had not altered. At all.

And the edges were turning black.

"Ew! Gross! That is *nasty*," she blurted in dismay. "What *is* that?"

"*Bosregi* poisoning," Wonick and Taavion replied together.

"Warning," the computer announced placidly. "*Bosregi* poisoning detected."

Rachel responded with a humorless laugh. "Yeah, no shit." Her gaze bounced between the two men. "Poisons don't affect me."

"This one does," Wonick told her, stating the obvious.

Taavion crossed to a door in the wall opposite the entrance and disappeared down a hallway.

"But how? What does it do?"

"In most species, it causes brief illness—nausea, vomiting, dizziness, fatigue—that can last for a period ranging from a few hours to a few days. Nothing life-threatening unless one's health is already compromised."

"Okay. That doesn't sound too bad." So why did he look as if someone had died?

"For Earthlings," he began hesitantly, "it poses a greater threat."

"How do you even know that? We're the first Earthlings to venture into deep space. I assumed we'd be a total enigma to everyone out here."

"To many, you will be. But we have an ally off-world."

An ally who knew about Earthlings? Her brows drew down. "Who?"

"Janwar."

The same Janwar Sinsta and some of the other Lasarans had spoken of in whispers? "The *pirate* Janwar?"

Surprise lit his features. "Yes. You know him?"

Rachel shook her head. "I know *of* him. I think one of my Lasaran friends has a thing for bad boys." Her stomach soured. Or Sinsta *used* to. The last time Rachel had seen her, the engineer had been valiantly trying to keep engines and weapons running as long as possible.

Had she even made it to an escape pod before the ship exploded?

Tears burned the backs of her eyes.

Wonick took a step closer to her. "Rachel?" he asked softly.

She shook her head. "You were going to tell me something about the pirate."

Though he looked uncertain, he nodded. "Janwar is Akseli. And like us, he's wanted by the government."

"Well," she said, "he *is* a pirate." Pirates on Earth were despicable villains.

But Rachel had spent four months getting to know Prince Taelon on the *Kandovar* and—like Sinsta—had found him to be a great guy. Taelon didn't have a dishonorable bone in his body. How bad could this Janwar fellow be if Taelon considered him a friend?

"Despite his vicious reputation, Janwar is a good male," Wonick stated.

"Not so vicious then?" she asked.

Wonick smirked. "Oh, he can be utterly ruthless when circumstances require it."

"And yet you trust him."

"Implicitly." He motioned to the room they and the other cyborgs occupied. "He's the one who found this planet and helped us make it our home. He also feeds the rumors that it's an inhospitable wasteland."

No wonder they trusted him.

"And he's the reason we know *bosregi* is dangerous for Earthlings."

"How would *he* know?"

"He bonded with an Earthling who was poisoned with it."

Utter shock swept through Rachel. For a moment, her heart seemed to stop beating. When it kick-started again, it pounded in her chest like a bass drum. "What?" She wasn't the first Earthling Wonick had heard about?

"Janwar has bonded with—"

"Bonded as in *married*?" Taelon often described his relationship with Lisa as a bonding and referred to her as his lifemate.

"I believe so. He hasn't confirmed it. But they clearly share an intimate relationship."

One of her friends had hooked up with a space pirate? That was utterly mind-blowing! "Who?" she demanded. Surely not one of the *gifted ones*. It had to be a fellow immortal.

"Simone."

Tears filled Rachel's eyes when he spoke her French friend's name. "Simone survived?"

"Yes. But she was—" He broke off when Rachel's breath hitched in a sob.

It was the first confirmation she'd received that any of them still lived. Simone had made it. She was alive!

Another sob slipped out. Rachel covered her mouth in an attempt to hold the rest in. But tears filled her eyes and streamed down her cheeks.

Everyone in the room froze and stared at her with dismay. Clearly, they hadn't expected that reaction and didn't how to react.

Brow furrowing, Wonick inched closer. "Rachel?"

Shaking her head, unable to speak past the lump in her throat, she grabbed a fistful of his shirt and yanked him close enough to bury her face in his chest. She'd tried very hard to remain positive, to stay strong and hold on to hope, afraid that even *thinking* she might have lost her friends would somehow make it a reality. But that fear had formed an icy knot in her stomach that had grown bigger every day.

After a moment's pause, Wonick closed his arms around her and patted her back. It was so adorably awkward that it almost sparked a laugh as she wrapped her arms around his waist and hugged him tight.

"Your friend is well now," he assured her.

She sniffed. "Now?" That implied she hadn't been before.

"Simone battled Gathendiens, too. The *bosregi* on their tail spikes poisoned her."

No wonder they knew it could harm them. "I assume she kicked ass?"

He chuckled. "Yes."

Though she craved the comfort he offered, Rachel released him and swiped at her tears. "The *bosregi* made her feel sick?"

Taavion reentered the room. "It did more than that. It nearly killed her."

Stepping back, Wonick shot him a dark look. "Why did you tell her that?"

The medic shrugged. "So she won't object when I offer her the antidote." Stopping beside them, he held up a handgun-shaped tool with a vial attached and arched a brow.

She glanced up at Wonick. "Is this really necessary?"

"If you don't take the antidote," he told her, his expression earnest, "the black along the edges of the wound will spread across your skin like the branches of a tree."

"Well, that's creepy." She fought a shudder. "Okay. Go ahead and administer it."

Taavion pressed the barrel to her neck. A *psst* sound accompanied a tiny prick.

"That's it?" she asked in surprise when he stepped back. It hadn't even hurt.

"That's it," Taavion confirmed.

"Now what?"

Taavion motioned to her. "I'll monitor your condition over the next few hours. Because you received the antidote much sooner than Simone did, I don't expect you to become ill."

"I feel tired," she mentioned.

He nodded. "You may rest as soon as you go through decontamination."

"I feel more tired than I should," she elaborated. If fatigue was a symptom of the poisoning, she thought it pertinent enough to mention.

Wonick touched her arm. "You've fought two battles today. That's to be expected."

"I engaged in battle on a nightly basis for years, Wonick. I know the level of fatigue I should feel right now." She met Taavion's gaze. "And this exceeds that."

No unease touched the medic's features. "That's probably because the peculiar symbiotic virus you harbor is expending energy to keep the poison from spreading. Simone and Eliana both lost consciousness and descended into what I believe Earthlings may call a coma while their bodies fought the poison."

She bit her lip. "You, uh... you already knew about the virus? Because you seemed surprised earlier when..." Her eyes widened as the rest of his words registered. "Wait. Eliana made it, too?"

"Yes," Taavion said.

She looked at Wonick.

He nodded.

Joy rose inside her. Letting out a loud "Woohoo!" she thrust a triumphant fist toward the ceiling. Pain shot through her side, burning like a welding torch. "Ouch!" She hastily dropped her arm with a laugh. "Maybe I shouldn't have done that."

Excitement filled her. *Two* of her friends had survived. Surely that meant more could have. Slipping off the bed, she drew Wonick into another hug. "Simone and Eliana survived!"

Wonick wrapped his arms around her, less awkward this time. "According to the records Janwar sent us, they aren't the only ones."

She looked up at him. "They aren't?"

"Lisa, Ava, Allison, and Liz survived as well."

That was even better! "What about Taelon? And Abby."

"Prince Taelon, Lisa, and their daughter Abby are all safe on Lasara."

Including Rachel, that meant at least six of the fifteen women who had accompanied Lisa and her new family on the *Kandovar* were safe, which reignited hope for the rest.

Despite the pain, Rachel started jumping up and down. "This is the best day of my life!" she shouted.

Loosing a startled laugh, Wonick held on tight as she took him with her, lifting his toes off the floor with every exuberant leap. "You were injured and have been poisoned. How can this be the best day of your life? Stop jumping!" he ordered on another laugh.

Relenting, Rachel ceased and looked up at him. "But I'll recover." She patted his chest with a smile. "*You* ended up not being an untrustworthy asshole and are once more my friend. Together, we killed at least *forty* Gathendien warriors intent on committing genocide. And *six* of my friends I worried were dead are actually alive. What's not to celebrate?"

He seemed to be struck speechless. Why? Because she was suddenly full of energy and optimism? Or because she'd demonstrated that she was strong enough to lift him without effort?

Who cared? Rachel took his hand and twined her fingers through his. "Let's hurry up and go through decontamination. I want you to tell me *everything* you know about my friends." She glanced at Taavion. "Which way?"

Eyes bright with mirth, the medic pointed.

Rachel took off down the hallway, tugging Wonick after her. "What exactly does decontamination entail?"

"I believe you would call it a shower."

She stopped short and grunted when Wonick bumped into her.

"Apologies." Releasing her hand, he gripped her shoulders to steady her.

"We're going to shower together?" Why did the thought of that make her mind swerve in a direction it shouldn't?

He hesitated. "I assumed you'd wish to shower alone."

"Oh." A blush crept up her cheeks.

He shifted his weight from one foot to the other. "Did you *want* to shower with me?"

She certainly wouldn't mind it. Wonick was her only friend on this planet. She kinda didn't want to let him out of her sight.

Plus, it would mean she would get to see all of those glorious muscles that rippled beneath his shirt and pants.

Jovan entered, his armor gone, replaced by a shirt and pants that reminded her of standard military fatigues. "Are you headed to decon?"

"Yes," they answered.

"Me, too. See you there." He strolled away.

Rachel turned back to Wonick. "Why do the others have to go through decontamination? They were wearing armor. Shouldn't that have protected them?"

"They raised their faceplates at my request."

"Oh. Right." She pursed her lips. "So this showering... Does it involve getting naked?"

"Yes."

"Uh huh. Uh huh. Then yeah, that's going to be a hard no for me."

"What?"

"I'm not going to get naked and shower with your whole team."

He arched a brow. "Am I wrong in believing you were considering getting naked and showering with *me* before Jovan interrupted us?" That was very direct and to the point, but not in an obnoxious way. Rather than flirting, he seemed puzzled.

"No," she admitted, opting for honesty. "I *was* considering it."

"Why?"

Yep. He definitely seemed puzzled. "Why wouldn't I?"

He opened his mouth to reply, closed it, opened it, and closed it again.

"Wonick?" she prompted.

"You know what I am," he said gravely.

"A cyborg. Yes."

He shifted restively. "You're not... repulsed by that? By my... augmentations?"

Wow. This man really knew how to tug at her heartstrings.

Smiling, Rachel reached up and rested a palm against his stubbled cheek. "We are two peas in a pod, aren't we?"

"I don't understand that analogy. My translation matrix said it refers to legumes on your planet."

"It means we're the same," she informed him softly. "I harbor a virus genetically engineered by the most despicable beings in the galaxy. One that led fellow Earthlings to hunt me all of my life and to kill some of the Seconds who tried to protect me over the years. And since you aren't Lasaran, I'm guessing I'm a lot older than you." Oddly, the last concerned her more than anything else. "Are you repulsed by what I am?"

His Adam's apple bobbed in a swallow. "No. You fascinate me."

"Ditto."

"I don't know what that means."

"It means you fascinate me, too." Her smile widened. "But I think we should have separate showers. I want to hear more about my friends." She let her gaze rove his big body. "And something tells me that showering together would distract us from that."

He nodded somberly. "It really would."

Grinning, she took his hand again and started up the hallway. "Then let's get this over with, shall we? Where *is* this decon thing?"

"The next door on the right." He opened it with a quick mental command.

Rachel stepped inside... and stopped short. Wonick managed not to bump into her this time, but she barely noticed. On the other side of a glass wall, half a dozen cyborgs stood beneath a liquid spray that seemed to come from all directions at once.

Half a dozen bare-ass naked cyborgs, some of whom were bent over, tugging their boots off to add to the sodden piles of clothing at their feet.

Heat filling her face, she spun around and gave them her back. "Okay. That was a *lot* more than I needed to see." When a deep chuckle rumbled from Wonick's chest, she tilted her head back and shot him a narrow-eyed look. "Why didn't you warn me?"

He grinned, exposing straight white teeth. And what a magical transformation the action wrought. He looked so young and care-free when he smiled, his auburn eyes sparkling with boyish mischief that made her pulse leap. "You knew they were showering," he said. "What did you expect?"

She motioned behind her. "Not a big glass wall that would let any perve watch!"

"Is a perv a sexual deviant?"

"Yes."

He loosed a full-blown laugh at that. "The glass allows Taavion and his team to monitor any who may be ill and ensure they don't lose consciousness during decontamination."

"Oh."

He backed into the hallway, giving her enough room to exit. The door slid down. "If you'll wait here, I'll shower and let you know when the others have finished."

She grabbed his shirt. "Wait."

"Yes?"

Rachel mentally cursed and called herself a wus. "I'm guessing big, bad Savaas is probably heading this way. I'd rather be with *you* when he finds me."

Wonick frowned and touched her arm. "He won't hurt you, Rachel."

"*You* I trust. *Him*, not so much." The cyborg leader had wanted to let her die at the hands of Gathendiens. Knowing that made it a little difficult to expect good things from him. "Can we wait and take turns showering after the others finish? I promise not to peek." It would be awfully tempting, though.

"Of course."

Minutes ticked past as they waited quietly in the pristine white hallway.

Rachel glanced at him from the corner of her eye. "Aren't *you* going to promise not to peek?"

His lips twitched. "I was hoping you hadn't caught that."

She grinned. "Oh, I caught it."

"I promise not to peek."

"Thank you."

A teasing glint entered his eyes. "*Nensu* hinderer."

She blinked. "What?"

"It's a phrase we use when others seek to prevent us from engaging in an activity we believe we would enjoy."

Nensu hinderer? Because she'd asked him not to peek at her while she was in the—"*Ohhhhh.*" She grinned as his meaning sank in. "On Earth, we call it a spoilsport."

143

Again, he sent her that utterly charming, mischievous smile. "I promise not to peek... spoilsport."

Rachel laughed. She *really* liked this cyborg.

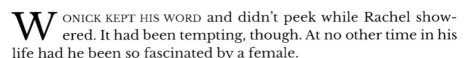

W ONICK KEPT HIS WORD and didn't peek while Rachel showered. It had been tempting, though. At no other time in his life had he been so fascinated by a female.

Rachel's reluctance to forgo his company pleased him. He knew it mostly stemmed from a desire for self-preservation. Savaas could be damned intimidating, and she knew the cyborg leader didn't trust her. But Wonick appreciated the extra time it gave him with her.

Taavion didn't hesitate to approve the two of them staying in the same quarantine room. "You've had the most contact with her, Wonick. If anyone has become infected with the virus she carries, it will be you."

The medic's words, of course, had frustrated Rachel, who continued to insist she wasn't contagious.

Now they sat cross-legged atop narrow beds located on opposite sides of a tiny white room that boasted a glass wall through which Taavion could observe them. The rest of his team shared similar quarters—with Taavion's work station in the center—and directed frequent looks their way.

Rachel pointed to the plate on the mattress before her. "I don't know what this is, but it's delicious."

He smiled. Her appetite rivaled his own. "It's *daehedi* with *drosden*."

She had already devoured at least two-thirds of the meal. A military man to his core, Wonick finished his within minutes and contented himself with observing her while she ate heartily and pelted him with questions.

The only patient clothing in the infirmary was designed for cyborgs. The smallest size fit Jovan, who was a little shorter than the others with a slimmer build. Wonick had chosen those for Rachel.

He fought a smile.

Rachel said the sleeveless shirt reminded her of something called a tank top on Earth. This one was so large on her that she had to tie the narrow shoulders into knots to keep the neckline and armholes from dipping low enough to show her breasts.

Her full, unbound breasts that moved enticingly whenever she shifted position.

Though the length of the shirt had shortened once she knotted the shoulders, the hem still reached her thighs. Beneath it, she wore shorts that had fallen to her ankles every time she stood up until Taavion fetched her a belt. Now they covered her to her knees.

Wonick studied the legs she'd crossed. They were much thinner than his own. But like her arms, they bore the alluring curves of lean muscle.

"I don't understand," she said after swallowing another mouthful. "You said you only spoke to Janwar briefly. How do you know so much about my friends?"

He considered his answer carefully. "May I share a confidence?"

"Of course. If you don't want me to mention the information to anyone, I won't."

He believed her. "The implants in our brains enable us to process information faster."

"Cool. I can read really fast, thanks to the virus. But sometimes it takes my mind a while to catch up."

"We lack such issues."

"Even cooler."

"The Akseli military wanted us to cull data faster than our adversaries to help us strategize better and win battles. However, they failed to consider that our ability to acquire and process information at such speeds would also enable us to learn and progress faster, eventually attaining more knowledge than their top scientists and engineers."

She swallowed the latest bite and considered him for a moment. "Are you talking about evolution? You're evolving faster?"

"Only in terms of our mental acuity and technological innovation."

"So you're smarter than other Akselis?"

"We're smarter than most races now, surpassed only by the Sectas."

"I'm guessing that's one of the reasons many view you as a threat."

He nodded. "We've developed technological innovations that members of the Aldebarian Alliance are generations away from achieving. And we used those to build a ship."

"What kind of ship?"

"One that's faster than any other in the galaxy, boasts more deadly weaponry and more efficient stealth technology, and can generate energy and sustain life within it indefinitely."

She stared at him. "That sounds amazing."

"We're very proud of our creation."

"Where is it?"

"We gave it to Janwar."

"To thank him for helping you?" She ate another mouthful.

"Yes. But I admit not all of our motives were altruistic. We didn't just want to thank him for all he risked and continues to risk for us. We still need the supplies Janwar brings, which gives us even more reason to keep him safe than just fear of losing our only friend."

She smiled. "He's not your only friend anymore. Now you have me."

That odd warmth settled in his chest again. "Here's the part I would rather you not share with others."

"Okay."

"Janwar doesn't know that the ship we gave him provides us with a back door into the mainframe on which he stores every piece of information he gathers." Or perhaps he did and simply didn't care because he trusted them. "When I talked Savaas into allowing you to land here, he insisted we use that back door to collect every bit of information we could arm ourselves with to determine your level of trustworthiness and find weaknesses we could exploit if..."

She arched a brow. "If I turned out to be an asshole?"

He smiled. "Yes."

"And you perused that information?"

Shrugging, he dropped his gaze to his discarded tray and, with one finger, realigned it so it lay perfectly parallel to the mattress edge. "I was... curious after our communications."

"I was, too," she confessed.

"I also thought you might wish to know what happened to your friends." He risked a glance up at her and found no condemnation.

"My mind is blown by everything you've told me."

"Does your mind being blown mean you're shocked?"

"*Very* shocked."

"I am as well. I didn't have time to finish processing all the information before your arrival but have been sifting through it in the background throughout the evening.

"Really? You can do that? Even while fighting Gathendiens?"

"Yes. We have a remarkable ability for multitasking."

"I wish I could say the same." She finished the rest of her meal. "I still can't believe all that's happened while I was stuck inside the pod. Simone hooked up with the galaxy's most notorious pirate. Ava fell in love with a Purveli. Eliana has taken a Segonian commander as her lifemate. And they've *all* been kicking Gathendien ass, even the *gifted ones*."

He smiled. "You Earthlings are a force to be reckoned with. Is that the correct usage of that Earth saying?"

She laughed. "It is. And we are." Setting her plate aside, she leaned forward and rested her elbows on her knees. "Hey, do you think I could talk to them when we get out of here? My friends?"

"I have no problem with comming Janwar and Simone."

"And Liz. She's still with them on the *Tangata*, right?"

"Yes."

"But you'd rather I not contact Eliana and Allie on the *Ranasura*? Or Lisa on Lasara?"

He nodded reluctantly. "We don't want the Segonians and Lasarans to know about us."

A moment passed before she nodded. "I guess I can understand that."

Taavion entered the room. After glancing at her empty tray, he arched a brow. "I see the *bosregi* poison hasn't affected your appetite."

Smiling, Rachel rose and lifted the hem of her shirt so the medic could examine her wound.

Wonick leaned forward to peer at it, too.

On one of his earlier inspections, Taavion had left the bandage off and covered the wound with clear *kasaadi*.

"Good," Taavion murmured. "The black is receding." Only a little bit tinged the edges now.

Rachel studied it. "So the antidote is working?"

"Yes. How is the fatigue?"

"Still there."

"Any worse?"

She slid Wonick a glance. "Yes."

Concern resurfaced.

"I'd take another blood sample to check your viral count," Taavion said as he knelt to examine the cut on her leg, "but your volume is already low, and I have not yet determined if it's safe to transfuse you with ours."

Wonick watched them. "What about synthetic blood?"

Taavion shook his head. "Another unknown. I divided the small blood sample I took earlier and added synthetic blood to one and ours to the other to test their effects. The viral count in both samples has dropped. But I can't determine with certainty whether it's because of the poison that had infiltrated her bloodstream or the blood I added." He rose.

Rachel dropped the shirt hem back into place. "Have you confirmed that the virus I carry isn't a danger to your men?"

"As you said, it doesn't appear to be airborne, but more time is needed to be certain." Without another word, he gathered their trays and left the room.

The door slid shut behind him.

Rachel threw up her hands in frustration. "How much more time does he need? It's been hours."

"Standard quarantine can last up to sixty standard alliance hours," Wonick informed her.

"Sixty!" She began to pace.

"That distresses you?"

"Yes."

"Why?" Was his company already a source of strain? Wonick hadn't spent this much time alone with a woman in...

Even with his impressive implants, it took him a minute to realize it had been twenty-seven years. And the last experience had not been a good one. He'd discovered, much to his disappointment and disgust, that the woman had only tried to seduce him because she wanted to find out what copulating with a machine was like.

"I'm worried the Gathendiens will get bored, looking for me," Rachel said. "Either that or freak out when they find what's left of their colleagues. We can't let them return to the warship, Wonick. They'll blab to the rest of their comrades. Then Gathendiens will add this planet to the list they want to conquer."

He shook his head. "My brothers are taking care of them."

Frowning, she stopped pacing and sat beside him on his bunk. "Taking care of them how?"

"They're moving in on the dropship," he murmured, distracted by her nearness.

"Really?"

"Yes."

"How do you know?"

"I'm monitoring their progress remotely." He forced his gaze away from the glimpse of cleavage his greater height afforded him.

She stared at him. "You mean they're doing it right now?"

He nodded. "We expected the Gathendiens to remain in the dropship overnight and send another hunting party out at daybreak to locate their men when the other units failed to return. Striking now, while the rest of them are all in one place, seemed the smartest option."

"How's that going?"

"My brothers have eliminated the guards and are now infiltrating the ship in full camo."

She slumped against the wall. "I feel bad."

Worry resurfacing, he studied her closely. "You are unwell?" Taavion had listed nausea as a symptom of *bosregi* poisoning. Had her meal—?

"No. I meant I feel guilty. I'm the one who brought the Gathendien mess to your doorstep. You shouldn't have to clean it up."

When Wonick leaned back against the wall, his arm brushed her bare shoulder. Aside from tending her wounds, briefly holding her hand, and Rachel touching his face, it was the first flesh-to-flesh contact he'd had with her and—after such a long dearth of physical intimacy—sped his heart rate. "The Gathendiens wouldn't have found you if we had guided you here as soon as we heard your communications. The mess is more ours than yours."

Rachel hid a yawn behind her hand.

"You need rest."

"I guess so." She leaned her head against his shoulder, further quickening his pulse. "Once your guys take out the Gathendiens, would you ask them to drop by the escape pod? There's some bagged Segonian blood in the cold compartment by the battery housing. I'm going to need that if Akseli and synthetic blood end up being bad for me."

"I'll tell them now." *Hoshaan.*

Yes?

Once you've finished eliminating all threats, search Rachel's escape pod. You should find bagged blood in the cooling compartment located beside the battery housing. Bring it to the infirmary.

Affirmative.

"It's done," he assured her.

Rachel stifled another yawn. "Thank you." More of her weight settled against his side as a comfortable silence blanketed them. Soon slumber claimed her.

Wonick glanced at the glass wall. Taavion stood before a console, muttering to himself while he analyzed in microseconds whatever data scrolled before him. Bright light illuminated his spotless lab.

The quarantine room Jovan occupied on the other side was dark, but ambient light from the lab enabled Wonick to see without his night-vision implants. The youngest cyborg lay sprawled on his bunk, sleeping with one leg dangling off the side.

Sonjin and Taaduro remained awake in another room, heads bent over a game of *Ori*.

Wonick glanced at the next room and stiffened.

Nebet sat on his bunk with his back resting against the wall, legs stretched out in front of him, arms crossed over his chest. His eyes met Wonick's, dropped to the Earthling who slept trustfully at his side, then returned. He arched a brow.

Had he just been sitting there, watching them?

Scowling, Wonick activated the implant that enabled him to interface remotely with all electronics in their settlement and accessed the controls of the glass wall. Nebet's face lit with amusement as the glass darkened and became opaque, affording them privacy.

Accessing more controls, he lowered the lighting in the room until it matched that of a night illuminated only by a pale sliver of a moon. Speakers ushered in nocturnal sounds from the forests outside. Cyborgs had spent so many years in infirmaries, recovering from excruciatingly painful surgeries and injuries, that all loathed the places now. When Taavion had refused to treat them in their homes, they had made this compromise to make any time spent here more bearable. The regular recovery rooms and treatment rooms went even further with at least one wall displaying the forest outside.

Now insects chirped. Amphibians croaked and twanged. Nocturnal birds sang.

The pleasure Wonick took in it paled in comparison to that he found in Rachel's presence. Her form was warm against his, the pressure soothing.

Memories of his boyhood surfaced. He could recall his parents sitting like this after a long day spent working the family farm while he and his brothers wrestled and played on the floor in front of them. Hands linked, they would speak in low tones and share weary but loving smiles the boys paid little attention to.

Wonick glanced down.

One of Rachel's hands rested on the mattress beside her. The other hand lay in her lap, palm up, fingers curled as though waiting to hold something.

In painstakingly slow increments, Wonick reached over and gently clasped that hand.

His eyes shot to her face.

Still sleeping.

Splaying her hand on his, he studied it. Soft, pale skin covered faint blue veins. Her slender fingers ended in short, rounded nails. In comparison, his hand was tanned from years spent working in the sun with the reddish hue characteristic of Akselis and a network of fine scars. It was also so much larger than hers that, when he lined up the base of their hands, her fingertips barely extended beyond his palm.

Wonick traced her fingers, one by one. They seemed alarmingly fragile, easily broken compared to his, which were thicker and reinforced with *alavinin*. Yet when she had poked him in the chest during their initial confrontation, it had felt as though she were stabbing him with a dull blade and had nearly made him stumble back a step.

Finished with his curious examination, he twined his long fingers through hers and settled their hands on his thigh, mimicking the pose of his father and mother.

Wondrous peace suffused him as he rested his head against the wall behind them and imagined ending every evening in such a way.

Was this what Janwar had found with Simone? This tantalizing contentment that seemed to fill all the hollow spaces spawned by years of isolation?

If so, Wonick couldn't blame his friend for succumbing to the allure.

A sigh replete with pleasure escaped him as he closed his eyes. Then he, too, let sleep claim him.

CHAPTER NINE

"**R**ACHEL."

A deep voice penetrated sleep.

What had she been dreaming about? Something about a baby?

Babies in dreams often represented new ventures. What new ventures?

"Wake up."

Torn between wanting to continue sleeping and wanting to discover the source of that lovely voice, she settled for the first and sighed with contentment as she snuggled into the blankets.

"Rachel?" Something shook her.

Frowning, she grumbled, "What?"

"Are you well?"

Was she well?

As the last vestiges of sleep fell away, her senses kicked into gear. Light shone behind closed lids. An antiseptic smell made her nose tingle. Turning her face away from both, she buried it in warm fabric. *Oooh. Much better*. It was darker now, and she liked this scent. It reminded her of skin warmed by sunshine.

Smiling, Rachel tightened her hold on the pillow she hugged to her chest.

Wait. Frowning, she slid her hand up and down the surface.

That didn't feel like a pillow. It felt like hard muscle.

Her eyes flew open.

At some point, she and Wonick must have fallen asleep. They now lay on their sides, facing each other. His big biceps pillowed her head, and her face nuzzled a muscled chest. Dark hair peeked from the top of his tank top, tickling her nose. Their legs were intertwined like lovers', their hips aligned, and...

153

She bit her lip. Well, she now had the answer to Curious Question #47. Cyborgs could definitely become aroused.

Tilting her head back, she looked up.

Passion didn't darken Wonick's eyes. Instead, his brow crinkled with concern.

She smiled to allay it. "Hi, there."

"Hello. I had difficulty waking you. Are you well?"

"I think so." Rachel took quick stock of her body, noting only a rapid pulse that resulted from waking up in Wonick's arms. (She really wished she could enjoy that a little longer.) "I'm not in pain or anything."

"I had difficulty waking you. I called your name several times and had to shake you."

She wrinkled her nose. "Sorry about that. I tend to sleep deeply when I'm injured and didn't think to warn you."

"Such leaves you vulnerable."

"Yes, it does. That's why I always had a Second, or guard, back on Earth." Her Seconds had ensured that no one who suspected she may be something more than an ordinary human could sneak in during the day while she slept and take her by surprise. When she was unharmed, Rachel slept lightly enough for her heightened senses to alert her to danger. But if she sank deep into a healing sleep, someone could easily get the drop on her.

"May I check your wounds?" he asked.

"Sure." A flush heated her cheeks as she slid her arm from around his waist and eased her knee from between his.

Was she mistaken, or did *his* cheeks darken with a flush, too? That would be too adorable and merely increase her attraction to him.

Sitting up, she cleared her throat. "Sorry about that. I seem to have fallen asleep on you."

He shifted to sit beside her and lowered his feet to the floor. Dark hair dusted muscled legs that held the same bronze, ruddy hue as the rest of him and took up quite a bit more space than her pale, slender ones. Though scars marred his knees, both looked healthy. His feet bore a network of fine scars and looked twice the size of hers, which couldn't even reach the floor.

Why did seeing his bare feet and legs feel... intimate? Her last male Second had often worn shorts at home and walked around barefoot. Seeing *him* in shorts had never affected her. But Wonick made her want to uncover more.

Glancing up, she caught him staring at her. "What?" Had he noticed her ogling his legs? He didn't think she had a foot fetish now, did he?

"Would it offend you if I admitted I wasn't sorry?" he asked.

It took her a minute to catch his meaning. "About me falling asleep on you?"

"Yes."

She smiled, charmed by his honesty. He didn't ask it as a sleazy come-on. He just seemed curious about her reaction to their sleep-induced clench. "No. I was only sorry because I have no knowledge of Akseli social etiquette. I spent four months aboard a ship full of Lasaran males who looked scandalized anytime I accidentally brushed against them in the hallway or forgot and touched their arms while chatting with them. I actually thought this was a great way to wake up but wasn't sure if I had crossed a line."

"Savaas may think you did," he admitted. "Or rather, he may think me mad for trusting you enough to sleep beside you." He gave her a slow smile rife with mischief. "But I enjoyed waking up this way, too."

"Yet another thing we have in common," she said with a wink before turning her attention to the wound on her thigh. "This one looks good. It's closed." She prodded the clear, rubbery *kesaadi* covering it. "Normally, the scar would've already faded. But that probably won't happen until I get a transfusion."

"What of the other?"

She tugged the oversized tank top up enough to reveal her side. The puncture wound no longer bore black edges. But the virus that now served as Rachel's immune system must've focused almost entirely on fighting the poison until the antidote could kick in, because it hadn't shrunk much.

"It looks better," he murmured, gently touching the area around it. "Does it hurt?"

"A little."

He yanked his hand back. "Apologies."

Smiling, she lowered her shirt. "No apology necessary." When he seemed unconvinced, she took his hand. "I'm a warrior, Wonick. I'm accustomed to such wounds." She'd suffered worse than this in the past. Just nothing as freaky as that poison.

His gaze dropped to his hand, now sandwiched between hers.

Rachel glanced down. It was big. Not surprising. He was a big guy. As she studied it, though, she noticed fine-line scars—like those on his feet—that traveled up the center of each finger and intersected on the back of his hand before continuing to his wrist and stopping. She turned his hand over. A thicker scar began on the inside of his wrist and traveled all the way up his inner arm.

She traced the thinner scars on his fingers. "What are these?"

"The scientists that headed the Akseli cyborg program reinforced all of my bones with *alavinin*."

She looked at him in surprise. "That's one of the metals that can repel blasterfire, isn't it?"

"Correct."

"I don't understand. *Alavinin* is solid. How could they coat all of your bones with—?"

"They heated it to its boiling point and applied it while it was molten."

She stared at him. "How did they keep surrounding tissue from being damaged?" Muscle? Tendons? Nerves? Arteries?

His lips tightened. "You don't want the details."

Maybe she didn't. She frowned. "Don't bones need a healthy blood supply? Wouldn't coating them in metal deny them that?"

"Over time, the scientists developed polymers they could add to the *alavinin* to make it porous without reducing strength, enabling the bones to access my blood supply and rid themselves of metabolic waste as usual."

The scientific advancement that would require blew her mind. But Akseli scientists sounded like butchers who didn't care about the men they experimented on.

They sounded like Gathendiens.

"Were you conscious when they did it?"

156

He shook his head. "They kept me sedated through most of it."

"Most? Not all?" she pressed, appalled. She couldn't even imagine the pain he must've experienced.

He shrugged. "When they reconnected the nerves, they needed me conscious."

"Reconnected? That makes it sound as if they took you apart and put you back together again." That was barbaric!

"Something like that."

Realizing she was staring, Rachel dropped her gaze to his legs. "Why don't you have scars on your thighs?"

"I do. They went in from the back on those." He gave her a tight smile. "Less muscle tissue to cut through."

The thought sickened her. "I don't know how you survived it." She smoothed a hand across the back of his hand as if the tender touch could somehow erase the pain he'd suffered.

"Many didn't."

The gruff response drew her attention back to his face.

His fingers curled around hers. "Early efforts to create cyborgs failed." His Adam's apple rose and fell. "Savaas and I were the first they considered a success."

Her heart went out to him. "Were you forced to become a cyborg? I mean, were you conscripted or something?"

He dropped his gaze. "No. It was voluntary. When they launched the program and encouraged soldiers to sign up, they withheld crucial details. We knew little more than we would become a new branch of the military. Stronger. Faster. Heroes of the Akseli tetrad. Most of us believed it would include more advanced armor and the installation of processing matrices in our brains that would pose no greater risk than the translation matrices already installed."

That was messed up.

"The military showed their appreciation for every soldier who signed up by rewarding us with more credits than we could earn in a lifetime for joining the program and promising an ongoing salary that would ensure our families would never go hungry again."

Realization dawned. "You did it for your family?"

"Yes."

Something heavy settled in her stomach. "You were bonded?"

"No. I've never had a lifemate. I did it for my parents and siblings." He stared, unseeing, across the small room. "We were farmers. Drought had plagued our quadrant for several years, something made worse by a neighboring quadrant damming a river we needed to irrigate our fields. The pay I earned as a soldier in the standard military helped feed my younger siblings. But my parents grew thinner and thinner as the drought continued."

Rachel had seen the same with her own family. "Your parents went without so your younger siblings would have more food?"

He nodded. "Forecasts predicted the drought would worsen. And my parents had difficulty finding alternate employment as more and more farmers and fishermen flooded the workforce."

"Fishermen were struggling, too?"

"Yes. When the river slowed to a trickle, most of the fish died. Livestock farms struggled as well because the grass that fed the herds died."

"So you signed up to become a cyborg."

"Yes."

Twining her fingers through his, she held it tight and reached up with her free hand to cup his jaw. Dark stubble coated it and abraded her palm in an appealing way. She was surprised his face wasn't riddled with scarring, too. The scientists must've thought that undisguisable evidence would prove too much for the Akseli populace. "Does your family know what you suffered to support them?" She didn't think any parent willing to go hungry in order to feed their children would've sanctioned that.

"No. Nor did they ask me to enlist in the new program. I only told them after I deposited the signing bonus in their account. I had to explain where the credits had come from and why I would be leaving."

"How did they react?"

"My mother wept and clung to me as though I'd announced I had a fatal illness. My father was furious and shouted a lot. Both had tried to dissuade me from joining the military in *any* capacity. They thought the ruling tetrad showed an appalling lack of concern for soldiers once those soldiers served their purpose.

But when three years passed and I seemed to thrive in my new role, they came to accept it... as well as my help in supporting my siblings." Glancing down at their clasped hands, he smoothed his thumb over her skin in a gentle caress. "The military didn't call it a cyborg program then. But rumors abounded. My parents feared the officials had held back enough details to keep me from knowing what I was getting into." A humorless laugh escaped him. "They were right. While the scientists warned us we could have no contact with our loved ones until after the surgeries were completed, they failed to mention that those surgeries and the lengthy recovery times between each would encompass three years."

Horror filled her. "Three years?" He couldn't contact his family for that long? While suffering surgery after surgery? His parents must've been frantic with worry. "How old were you?"

"I was twenty-one solar cycles when I entered the program."

Twenty-one years old. Kids that age on Earth often lived with their parents or in college dorms, partied with their friends, spent hours on their phones, worked transient jobs, and tried to decide what they wanted to do with their lives. "You still lived at home?"

He nodded. "And worked the farm with my parents whenever I was planet-side."

Rachel let it all sink in. "Do your parents know you're still alive?"

Sadness filled his dark eyes. "No. They believe I was slain during the rebellion. I wanted to contact them and let them know I'd survived, but it would've put them at risk. As long as the Akseli government believes they mourn my death, they'll remain safe."

"And you didn't want them to worry about you?"

He nodded.

Sliding her hand around his neck, she drew him into a hug. "I'm sorry, Wonick."

He wrapped his strong arms around her and rested his chin atop her head. "At least they're all well."

"Your family?"

His chin ruffled her hair as he nodded. "I routinely scour the Galactic network for information on them. While other farmers suffered as the drought continued, my parents used the credits I gave them to launch a new business that has thrived over the years.

My siblings didn't go hungry. They were all well educated and now live comfortable lives. It was worth the sacrifice."

Rachel would've done the same for her family.

She hugged him tighter. What a great guy.

Bright light flooded the room.

Wonick abruptly released her and stood with a scowl.

Rising beside him, Rachel followed his gaze to the formerly opaque wall that was now transparent.

Taavion, Nebet, Jovan, Sonjin, Taaduro, and a handful of other cyborgs stood on the other side of the glass. The tallest among them crossed his arms over a beefy chest and scowled menacingly. The rest gaped.

No one spoke.

Rachel glanced at Wonick. Judging by the way his hands curled into fists and a muscle in his jaw ticked, he appreciated neither the interruption nor the prolonged scrutiny.

She doubted the disapproval emanating from the tallest one helped matters.

When the others didn't move and kept watching them as though glued to a television screen, eager to see what would happen next, Rachel figured she'd give them a show. Break the tension a little.

Shrugging, she stepped forward and started to sing Soul to Soul's "Back to Life." Music filled her head as she coaxed the stoic cyborgs—through song—to tell her what they wanted from her and suggested she could be there for them. Swinging her hips, she tried to keep a straight face as she belted out the lyrics. She really did. But she couldn't help grinning when their eyes widened and all looked at her as if she had lost her mind.

"Rachel?" Wonick asked behind her.

Twirling around, she continued dancing to the music in her head. "Yes?"

"What the *drek* are you doing?"

Halting, she grinned up at him and jerked a thumb over her shoulder. "Since they kept staring without speaking, I figured I'd put on a show. A little something special for my fans. They've probably all heard my Galactic Music Hour communications, right?"

Deep laughter filled the room. Not Wonick's. He just stood there, looking enchantingly perplexed as she resumed singing and dancing.

When she twirled around again, the glass wall had risen up and disappeared into the ceiling.

Jovan grinned from ear to ear as he watched her, bobbing his head to the song. Nebet laughed heartily. Not at *her*. At the others. Even Sonjin and Taaduro looked as if they wanted to guffaw.

Rachel halted and stopped singing.

Nobody moved or spoke.

Shifting to stand beside Wonick, she rested a hand on his broad shoulder, acted as if she were casually leaning on him, and motioned to the two of them. "Why don't you make a holovid? It'll last longer."

Nebet eyed the others and laughed again.

"Seriously," Rachel said, "how do you want us to pose?" Stepping in front of Wonick, she drew his arms around her waist, tilted her head to one side, and smiled as if they were a happy couple on the cover of a rom-com novel. Seconds later, she swiveled to the side and leaned back. Wonick hastily locked his fingers together to keep her from falling as she assumed a deep dip position and brought the back of a hand to her forehead as if she were fainting.

When she straightened and glanced at their audience, all now grinned except for the tallest one.

Her smile still in place, Rachel approached him. "No sense of humor, huh? You must be Savaas." She thrust out a hand. "It's nice to meet you."

He studied her for so long that she began to think he wouldn't deign to respond. Then he grudgingly clasped her forearm. "I can't say yet whether it's nice to meet you."

Unoffended, she nodded and backed away a step. "I get it. You're worried about the possible threat I pose to you and your brothers. I would be, too, in your position. I'm just as protective of my brethren back home. *And* out here. Thank you for letting your guys help me take care of the Gathendiens who followed me here." She patted her side. "And for patching me up after I was injured. I appreciate it and hope that, in time, you'll come to realize that I have no interest at all in harming you. I've been in your position. I've had to hide my existence from most of Earth society for pretty much my entire life. It sucks. It's wrong. But apparently things aren't much different out here, so I'm hoping we can be allies."

"Allies in what war?"

She pursed her lips. "The war against assholes?"

The other men laughed.

Savaas's lips twitched the tiniest bit.

Rachel glanced at Taavion. "I take it you've determined I'm not contagious."

"I have." His gaze slid to Wonick. "Although I have not yet determined the ease or extent of transmission that takes place through the exchange of bodily fluids."

Was that a blush heating her cheeks? "We were just hugging!" she blurted. "No fluids were exchanged. Sheesh. Did you think we were in here humping like rabbits with all of you out here, possibly listening in?"

More snickers and stifled laughter.

"And did you forget I'm injured?"

Savaas nodded toward her side. "How is your wound?"

"Better, but not yet healed."

He made a motion with one hand.

Another cyborg moved forward. "I'm Hoshaan."

Rachel smiled. "Nice to meet you, Hoshaan."

After drawing a duffle off his shoulder, he tucked a hand in it and drew out a bag of blood. "We retrieved this from the pod."

Relief suffused her. "Oh wow. Thank you. That's Segonian blood. It will really help speed my healing."

Taavion reached for it. "I will arrange a transfusion—"

Rachel took the proffered blood bag before he could touch it. "That won't be necessary. I can do it myself."

The medic frowned. "You don't have access to our system."

"I don't need it." Unease rising, she backed away until she once more stood beside Wonick. Her grip on the bag tightened as all watched her.

A warm hand tentatively touched her back. "Rachel?"

She looked up.

Wonick studied her, his concern evident. "You need the transfusion."

"I know. But..." She glanced at the others. While they waited in silence, she shifted her weight from foot to foot. "This is hard for me, okay?"

"What is?" Wonick asked softly.

"The Gathendien virus changed me in ways that..." Rachel released a frustrated growl as she struggled to find the words. "Ways that made people on Earth view me as a monster. A threat. Something to hunt and kill. Or something to dissect and study to discover how it all works and how to use it to their advantage." She met his gaze. "I've had to hide those changes for so long that it's not easy for me to put them out there now."

"You don't have to—"

"Yes, I do. Because it's the only way to make some of you"—she cut Savaas a squinty-eyed glance—"understand that we aren't so very dissimilar and that you can trust me."

"I trust you," Wonick professed.

"I know. And I believe you. But..." Rachel shrugged miserably. "I like you," she admitted softly, "and I worry that this will make you view me in a negative light. I don't want you to think me a monster, too."

His hand slid up and down on her back in a comforting caress. "I won't."

She wasn't as sure. But—tamping down the vulnerability that gripped her—she stood taller and angled her body to enable everyone present to see her. "This is why I don't need access to your system to get a transfusion. The changes wrought by the virus enable me to do it myself." Parting her lips, she let her fangs descend.

All gaped as she sank her teeth into the bag and rapidly siphoned the blood into her veins.

◆●◆

W ONICK DID HIS BEST to keep his expression impassive as he watched Rachel empty the blood bag. The retractable fangs didn't surprise him. Simone had displayed fangs when he had commed Janwar. But the blood...

Did Rachel consume it?

He couldn't imagine doing so but refused to grimace at the thought. Though she stood with her shoulders back and her chin raised in defiance, Rachel's eyes shouted vulnerability and the same fear of rejection that every cyborg here had experienced countless times in the past.

Srul, some of them had even been rejected by their own families when their loved ones learned that their son, brother, or lifemate had internally become—in their minds, at least—more machine than man.

Rachel lowered the bag. As her fangs retracted, she drew a pink tongue across her lips.

Silence reigned.

Her brown eyes acquired an amber glow as she darted them all looks, not holding eye contact for more than a millisecond. "If it helps, I don't drink it," she murmured. "My fangs behave like needles and carry the blood directly to my veins."

Taavion stepped forward, his face alight with curiosity. "Fascinating. Did you have the fangs before you were infected with the virus?"

"No. They grew during my transformation."

"According to the data mined from the *Tanagata,* most Earthlings lack your speed and strength."

"That's correct. The transformation increased both exponentially. I also didn't heal as quickly before and aged normally."

"What is the common life span of Earthlings?"

"It varies according to where and how they live. But the average life span in the country I inhabited before venturing into space used to be about seventy-nine years. That decreased recently, though, to seventy-six."

"Seventy-six?" Wonick repeated. Were Earth years exceptionally long? "How many days compose one Earth year?"

"Three hundred and sixty-five."

He glanced at Taavion. "I can think of no nations in the Aldebarian Alliance that suffer such short life spans."

Taavion nodded. "Even Akselis live one hundred and fifty years or more."

Rachel shrugged. "It is what it is."

The medic took another step closer. "And the virus altered that life span?"

"For some of us. I was... atypical even before the virus. My DNA was more advanced."

"Deoxyribonucleic acid," Taavion recited.

She nodded. "The basic building blocks of my genetic makeup. I'm sorry I can't share why mine deviates from that of most Earthlings other than to say I was born this way. There aren't many of us. But our variances mutated the virus in ways we're still trying to understand. Now, as long as I have access to blood, I can live indefinitely. Some of my brethren are thousands of years old."

That even exceeded Lasaran life spans!

"And you?" Taavion pressed. "How long have you lived?"

She cast Wonick an uncertain look, before responding. "Centuries."

Wonick stared at her. "You've had to hide what you are for hundreds of years?"

Pain shone in her eyes when they met his. "Yes. It's why I embarked upon this journey. I hoped things would be different out here."

Wonick studied his brothers as chatter erupted on their mental comms.

Other Earthlings view her as a monster?

The way Akselis and the Aldebarian Alliance view cyborgs.

We've only had to hide what we are for a couple of decades.

She's hid it for centuries.

She really is like us, Jovan said with awe.

Agreed. Her alterations were just biological instead of mechanical.

If she's telling the truth, Savaas inserted.

Wonick glared at him. *Look at her! Her unease is unfeigned.*

It doesn't make sense, their leader insisted before addressing Rachel. "Why would the Gathendiens loose a virus on your planet that would make your people stronger if they wished to eradicate you and claim Earth for themselves?"

"There were fewer Earthlings like me back then. *Very* few. Too few to accidentally get scooped up with whatever group the Gathendiens abducted to study and test their viruses on. The advanced DNA *gifted ones* carry protects us from the more corrosive aspects of the virus. But in an overwhelming majority of Earthlings, the virus doesn't only make them stronger and faster and give them a need for blood. It also causes progressive brain damage that drives them insane and ramps up violent impulses. If my brethren and I hadn't banded together to hunt vampires—what we call ordinary Earthlings infected with the virus—humanity would've long since killed itself off."

"Brilliant," Taavion murmured.

Wonick worried the praise would infuriate Rachel, but she merely rolled her eyes as though she would've expected no other reaction from a medic.

I believe her, Nebet announced over mental comms. *Her history is so similar to ours that she may as well be one of us. We should trust her.*

Wonick added, *I already do.*

"Can anything kill you?" Savaas asked.

Wonick took a furious step forward. "Savaas—"

Rachel grabbed his arm and held him back. "Yes. Decapitation will kill me." Her expression turned ominous. "Many have tried in the past." Her full lips turned up in a dark smile. "All failed."

When everyone but Savaas eyed her with approval and appreciation, Wonick had to fight the urge to curl a possessive arm around her shoulders. The impulse was new and nearly impossible to deny, an indication that he was coming to care for her more than he should.

Savaas delivered a decisive nod. "I hope they will continue to."

She arched a brow. "Continue to try?"

The leader's lips twitched. "Continue to fail."

Some of the tension in her posture eased. "Oh, they will."

He smiled outright. "I have no doubt after my men's descriptions of your battles with the Gathendiens."

"Yes. I'm sorry I brought those *grunarks* to your doorstep." She glanced at Wonick. "Is that the right term? *Grunarks*? Similar to assholes or bastards?"

He chuckled "Yes."

Smiling, she turned back to Savaas. "I still have a few left to kill."

"Already done. There are no more Gathendiens on the planet."

Her eyebrows flew up with surprise. "Really? Good job," she praised.

"Taavion tells me you both slept through first meal." He slid Wonick a mocking glance before motioning to the doorway that led to the rest of the infirmary. "You must be hungry. Would you like to join the rest of us in the commissary for mid meal?"

Wonick couldn't tell if Rachel's cheeks pinkened because Savaas referenced them sleeping together or because her stomach chose that moment to growl.

"That would be a yes," she said with a smile.

Several men laughed as they filed through the doorway. When only Savaas, Taavion, Wonick, and Rachel remained, Savaas issued a warning, albeit in less ominous tones than expected. "Though I worry Wonick's motivations may be compromised..."

Wonick frowned.

"If he trusts you, *we* will trust you. As long as you honor that trust, we will consider you a friend and one of us. Abuse that trust, and we will hunt you to the ends of the galaxy."

Rachel thrust out a hand. "I vow the same. Deal honestly with me, and I'll be a friend for life. Deceive me or my friends, and I will succeed where all those who have hunted you in the past have failed. Do we have an accord?"

Shaking his head, Savaas clasped her forearm. "We have an accord."

Wonick caught his friend's eye. "We'll join you once we change our clothes."

Nodding, Savaas left.

Taavion handed Rachel a neatly folded pile of clothing. "These are clean and dry but have not been mended. Jovan scanned them with our clothing generator. We should be able to print more for you later today."

167

Rachel smiled and took the clothes. "Thank you."

He handed Wonick another pile.

The two of them ducked into separate rooms. After Wonick exchanged his med bay garments for the standard pants and shirt he usually wore, he headed for the infirmary's entrance. Rachel seemed relieved to be back in familiar clothing despite the tears it sported when she joined him.

Balmy air greeted them as they left, as did the sounds of the jungle, which was alive with birdsong.

They settled into a slow stroll.

"Wow." Rachel gazed at the structures they passed. "You've really built yourself a paradise here."

He nodded. "Janwar helped us a great deal, obtaining the supplies we needed."

"Piracy must be a very lucrative business. I'm sure all of this cost a *lot* of credits."

Amusement danced through him. "Janwar didn't purchase the materials. He… liberated them from Akseli government shipments."

She laughed in delight. "He stole it from the bastards who want you dead? That's poetic justice there."

"They want him dead, too," he reminded her. "So he finds thwarting them particularly satisfying."

She motioned to one of the buildings they passed. "I love the design you've chosen. The way you've incorporated plants into the structures themselves."

Wonick tried to see his home through her eyes.

The tallest building encompassed a mere three levels. Live plants covered all external walls and roofs. Stout evergreen trees grew beside each dwelling, thickening the canopy above and hiding both the buildings and the stone pathways between them from aircraft. The trees also afforded the cyborgs much-appreciated shade during the warmest months.

"That was my idea," he told her with a sense of pride. "Before we created the shield that prevents ships from seeing the planet's surface and dissuades them from visiting, we needed to ensure that anyone who flew overhead wouldn't locate our settlement."

"I'm guessing your work on the family farm came in handy."

"It did. And information gleaned from our ability to infiltrate almost any database in the galaxy helped us design a building surface that plants could cling to without their roots compromising the integrity of the structure."

"By infiltrate, do you mean hack?"

"Yes."

"Very cool. I'm impressed." She smiled at the homes they passed. "It's like living in a fairy garden."

Wonick didn't know what that meant, but Rachel seemed pleased.

"Are these mansions?"

According to his translator, mansions were exorbitantly large homes built by wealthy individuals. "No. They're multifamily homes. Many of us miss our loved ones and regret our inability to start families of our own the way we would have if we hadn't entered the cyborg program." He studied the world they had built themselves. "We enjoy camaraderie and brotherhood while working together during the day but quickly discovered that retiring to an empty home in the evening bred loneliness that threatened to consume us."

She nodded, her face sobering. "It was the same for us, for Immortal Guardians. That's one of the reasons Seth—our leader—started assigning us Seconds, or mortal guards. He didn't just want us to have added protection. He wanted us to have someone to come home to who would alleviate that loneliness." And it had helped. A lot.

"We concluded the same and converted the first few single homes we built into storage facilities and armories." He motioned to the surrounding structures. "These larger dwellings can house up to eighteen men, with six individual bedrooms and a shared living space on each floor."

She smiled. "I like it. Which one do you live in?"

He pointed to a building up ahead with two levels. "That one. The other cyborgs thought Savaas and I—as the leaders of the rebellion—should have special quarters. I wasn't as certain, but it helped set us apart as authority figures and made it easier to maintain order and settle disputes that arose while we forged new lives here."

"So it's just you two in that one?"

He shook his head. "Savaas lives on the second level. I reside on the first with Jovan."

She cast him a curious look and seemed to want to say something but didn't.

"What?" he asked. "You may speak freely, Rachel. We're friends."

Her expression warmed as she sent him a smile that made his stomach tingle. "Yes, we are." She glanced around, then lowered her voice. "I sense that Jovan is... unique."

An astute observation. "He is. He was an experimental model." His lips tightened. Fury always filled him when he thought of everything Jovan had suffered. "The rest of us were all over twenty solar cycles and fully grown when we joined the program. We didn't learn until we rebelled and delved into millions of classified documents that the government had launched a secondary cyborg program they hid from society."

"I'm afraid to ask."

"They were turning children into cyborgs."

Her mouth fell open. "What?"

"They conscripted the children of protesters slain by the government and subjected them to the same surgeries we endured."

"How young were they?"

"Some had barely seen five solar cycles. Jovan was six when they took him."

Fury darkened her features. "That's horrific!"

"Agreed. But the government was enthralled by the idea of cyborg soldiers that *no one* would suspect were a danger. When soldiers saw *us*—my brothers and I—on the battlefield, they knew they faced annihilation. When Jovan walked into their midst, they saw only a helpless child and had no idea he'd been cybernetically enhanced and conditioned to kill. Though much smaller and more innocent, he was as lethal in battle as we were."

Her pretty features filled with a combination of disgust and sadness. "I'd say that doesn't happen on Earth, but it does. Children have been forced to take up arms for as long as I can remember." She shook her head. "How did they even survive the surgeries?"

"They didn't. Jovan is the only one we found alive. The others..." He ground his teeth as he recalled the medical files he'd pored over. "When their bones were coated in *alavinin*, it hindered their growth and..." He swallowed, haunted by the results.

Rachel slipped her hand into his. "It's okay. You don't have to tell me."

"We were fortunate to have Taavion among our ranks. He's an accomplished medic and saved Jovan by performing a series of surgeries every year to accommodate natural growth spurts. But the implants in Jovan's brain affected his emotional development."

"I would imagine having to endure such agonizing surgeries every year would, too."

He nodded. "Though he's the youngest in our midst, he should've attained a greater height and maturity by now. Instead, he remains like a boy on the cusp of manhood."

"A teenager," she murmured.

He examined the translation. "Yes."

"Is that why he lives with you?"

Wonick nodded. "He views me as a father figure. And I find comfort in the role."

"Is he happy?"

"Yes. Much more now that he's stopped growing and no longer has to endure the surgeries."

Smiling, she slipped her small hand into his. "You're a good man, Wonick."

His pulse picked up at the simple contact. "I try to be."

She gave his hand a squeeze. "So."

"So?"

"Savaas seems to think your judgment is compromised when it comes to me. Any particular reason why?"

Caught off guard by the shift in subject, he floundered until he caught the mischievous glint in her brown eyes. Smiling back, he shook his head. "Perhaps because he knows me well enough to have recognized my fascination with you."

171

Curling her free hand around his biceps, she hugged his arm and dropped her voice to a whisper. "I'm glad you said that. Because I am utterly enthralled by you."

He stumbled to a stunned halt.

When he just stood there, staring at her, Rachel chuckled and tugged him toward the door to the commissary. "Come on, Handsome. Time to partake of whatever is creating the delicious aroma floating through those windows. I'm guessing that's the commissary?"

Feeling as light as air, Wonick nodded and followed her inside.

CHAPTER TEN

A LL CONVERSATION CEASED WHEN Rachel and Wonick entered the commissary.

Unsure of their numbers, she had expected a small cafeteria with a few tables. Instead, they entered a significantly larger room with dozens of long tables pushed together to form a huge square.

When she realized how many men occupied those tables, she couldn't keep her eyebrows from flying up in surprise. There must be well over a hundred, making her wonder how big the cyborg army had been to begin with since Wonick said few had survived.

With the exception of Jovan, all the men looked as though they were roughly thirty years old even though they must be in their forties or fifties by now. Every one of them was broad-shouldered and heavily muscled with a trim waist. Similar scarring adorned their faces, where they had burned or cut away what Wonick had called *ident bars* that labeled them Akseli cyborgs. And all wore their hair short.

Even without the similar clothing, they would resemble a tight military unit.

A few men looked more cyborgy than the others, if that was even a term. The glint of metal stood out in the form of... replacement limbs? Half of one man's face was covered with metal, much like the fellow in *Phantom of the Opera*.

As she stepped farther into the room, every man stood up.

Even that looked military, the way they all seemed to adopt a parade rest stance.

Rachel belatedly released Wonick's hand.

No one said a word as they stared at her.

"Well," she muttered in an aside to Wonick, "this isn't awkward at all, is it?"

Jovan and Nebet grinned.

Giving the room as a whole a friendly smile, she waved and said, "Hello. I'm Rachel. It's nice to meet you all."

"Hello," they replied in unison.

Unease trickling through her, she bit her lip. "Okay. I'm going to be honest with you. While I appreciate the greeting, that was a little creepy. Back on Earth, entertainers used to produce horror vids that featured evil alien invaders that had a hive mindset. All of you saying the same thing at the same time was a coincidence, right?"

They glanced at one another, then offered a jumble of responses.

Grinning, she pretended to wipe sweat off her brow. "Phew. Just checking. For the record, your being cyborgs doesn't bother me in the least. You all rather remind me of my brethren back home. But the hive mind thing would've freaked me out a little."

Several laughed. Others looked surprised.

Why? Had they thought she would fear them?

Jovan waved. "Hi, Rachel. Would you like to sit with me?" He pointed to a pair of empty chairs beside him.

"Thank you. I would love to... as soon as I discover what is producing that delicious aroma."

Wonick echoed her thanks as he steered her toward the other side of the commissary.

Three cyborgs stood shoulder to shoulder at the counter.

Wonick motioned to each in turn. "This is Ealis, Gauson, and Lenba."

She smiled and nodded. "Nice to meet you all."

"Nice to—" they began simultaneously. Breaking off, they looked at each other before offering a conglomeration of alternate greetings.

Rachel smiled when she realized they were trying not to sound as though they had the hive mindset she'd mentioned. "Uh-oh. Looks like I've started something. Don't worry about it, boys. Go ahead and speak as you normally would."

Wonick smiled. "These three have single-handedly kept us all from starving, providing us with satisfying meals even when times were lean."

"I can believe it." She drew in a deep breath. "What is that delectable aroma, and how much can I consume without you all thinking I'm a glutton?"

The cyborg chefs all laughed in delight.

"It's grilled *asaagi* with *mashu* sauce," Ealis responded. An air of authority declared him the head chef.

Gauson nodded. "With mixed *cadensu* on the side."

Rachel pursed her lips. "I don't know what any of that is."

"*Asaagi* is a freshwater fish," Lenba informed her. "*Mashu* is a sauce made from sea plants and spices native to the planet. And *cadensu* is a mixture of boiled vegetables we grow."

"Which only makes it sound more delicious. Will you please prepare me some? I would love to try it."

All smiles, they set about loading up a tray for her.

She glanced at Wonick and found him smiling at her. "What?"

He shook his head, opting not to comment.

The cooks returned with two heaping trays.

Rachel eagerly took one and brought it closer to her nose. Closing her eyes, she inhaled deeply. "Oh wow. If this tastes as good as it smells, you may have difficulty convincing me to leave."

The cyborg chefs grinned.

When Wonick took his tray and turned away, Rachel followed him to the seats Jovan had saved for them.

Rachel sat beside the younger cyborg with Wonick on her other side.

Silence fell, broken only by the *clicks* and *tinks* of flatware scraping trays as every man in the room ate quietly and watched her. Some eyed her surreptitiously. Others didn't even try to hide their curiosity.

Since no malice accompanied those looks, Rachel didn't find their scrutiny uncomfortable. Using a utensil that reminded her of a spork, she sectioned off a bite of *asaagi* and deposited it in her mouth. Flavor exploded on her tongue. Her eyes fluttered closed as she chewed. "Mmm. This is soooo good."

"You should eat in moderation," Taavion advised.

Opening her eyes, Rachel located him among the crowd. He must've arrived shortly after she and Wonick had, because he was seating himself across the way. "What?"

"Until we determine if any foods here will aggravate your digestive tract, you should eat in moderation."

"Not going to happen." She shoveled another sporkful in, chewed, and swallowed. "This is too damn good. If it makes me sick, it will have been worth it."

Deep chuckles rippled through the room.

Conversation gradually resumed.

Rachel spoke little as she devoured the delicious meal. She had gone quite a long time without eating in the escape pod. Though she had slept through most of the deprivation, hunger had made its presence known as soon as she had awakened and lingered even after she ate heartily. The calories she'd burned with her enhanced speed and strength while fighting the Gathendiens had merely made her hungrier. So she ate like someone who had been fasting for weeks.

Fortunately, it seemed to amuse the cyborgs rather than offend them the way the sight of a woman eating voraciously would've some on Earth.

Jovan peppered her with questions, his youthful curiosity both sweet and heartrending now that she knew his history.

When Wonick gently suggested Jovan give her a chance to finish her meal, Rachel waved off his concern. She didn't mind, preferring open curiosity to the silent suspicion her rarities usually sparked on Earth.

When Jovan reluctantly left to resume his duties in the communications tower, another cyborg took his seat.

This one was among the more cyborgy fellows present. The arm closest to Rachel was shiny silver. But it bore the same shape of a human arm, replicating muscle tone and everything. She could spot no overlapping of plates or mechanical joints, not even on his fingers, and wondered how the heck it worked.

He glanced at her from the corner of his eye and caught her staring.

Rachel figured she might as well be blunt. "Would it be rude to comment on your arm?"

He paused in his chewing, swallowed, and studied her impassively. "Depends on the comment."

She smiled. "I love your arm. It's beautiful."

His eyebrows rose as his gaze went over her head to meet Wonick's. "Thank you?"

"Am I right in assuming it's a prosthesis?"

"Yes. My arm was damaged beyond repair during the rebellion."

She nodded. "I lost my arm once. A vampire severed it right at the shoulder." She drew a line to represent where. "But Seth—our leader—reattached it. He has incredible healing abilities and found me in time. May I touch it?"

Again his chewing paused. "Yes."

She rested her fingers on his thick forearm. Her eyes widened. "It's warm!" She gave it a light squeeze. "And it gives. Like muscle."

He nodded. "Taavion has been experimenting with a new metal that, when combined with certain polymers, becomes more flexible and acquires the feel of human flesh."

"That's amazing. Can you feel me touching you?"

Another nod. "The limb is covered with sensors that communicate with my central nervous system the way organic nerves would. It feels very similar to my other arm."

"Is it stronger than your other arm?"

"Yes."

She grinned. "Could we arm wrestle later? I'd love to see how my strength compares to yours."

His eyebrows rose. "Arm wrestle?"

Pushing her nearly empty tray aside, she propped her elbow on the table and raised her hand in the arm wrestling position. "I hold my arm like this. You do the same with yours. Then we clasp hands and, on a count of three, see who can press the other's knuckles to the table first."

He studied her. "For what purpose? I would win."

"Not necessarily. I'm stronger than I look."

Wonick nodded. "She's faster, too. She killed twenty Gathendien warriors before the rest of us could even catch up with her.

Everyone stared at her.

"Truly?" The silver-armed cyborg asked.

She shrugged. "Yes."

He nodded. "I will arm wrestle with you."

"Good."

"Tonight," Savaas intoned. "After last meal. You have work to do, Foarek."

Chairs scraped flooring as dozens of cyborgs rose. After bussing their empty trays, all except Wonick, Savaas, and Taavion left.

Rachel glanced up at Wonick. "Apparently you guys eat with precision, too."

He smiled. "It isn't the hive mind you mentioned. Years of being soldiers and engaging in battle conditioned us to eat quickly. Even so, we don't usually all finish at once. The men simply lingered because they were curious about you. Now it's time for the afternoon shifts to begin."

"Do *you* have duties you need to attend to?"

"I reassigned them."

"When?"

"While we were eating." He tapped his temple.

"Oh. Right. You have an internal communications thing. That's pretty cool. It's like being telepathic."

He nodded. "It gave us yet another edge over our enemies in battle."

"I imagine it would." Reaching up, she drew a hand over his hair. He kept it short enough that she could easily run her fingertips along his scalp.

Wonick froze.

Like his hands and feet, his scalp bore a network of scars that his thick hair hid. "Did you know that whatever is up here prevents telepaths from reading your thoughts?"

"Yes." He glanced to the side, perhaps wondering what his friends thought of her touching him so freely.

Rachel couldn't care less. She liked touching him, and he seemed to enjoy it.

"You said you're telepathic," he murmured. Was it her imagination, or did his shoulders relax as she combed her fingers through his hair again?

"Yes. And I don't hear a thing when I'm around you." Dropping her hand to her lap, she smiled. "It's nice, not having to block out everyone's thoughts all the time. That can be exhausting. And we tend to lose that ability when we sleep. It isn't uncommon to end up in someone else's dreams."

"Did you enter my dreams last night?"

"No. I slept like a rock."

He smiled. "A peculiar saying."

She laughed. "It is. Hey, if you're taking the afternoon off, could we comm Simone and Janwar? I'd love to see her. Liz, too."

"Yes."

Across the room, Savaas rose. "I will be present when you do."

"Okay," Rachel said quickly when Wonick looked as if he wanted to object. She didn't want to be a source of strife between the two friends and had expected as much. "I have nothing to hide from you, Savaas, and am as dependable an ally as Janwar is. In time, you'll come to understand that."

If he gave her a chance to prove it. He was probably pretty keen on kicking her off the planet as quickly as possible.

Wonick rose. "Shall we do it now?"

Excitement struck. "Yes!" Rachel jumped up. "That would be great. Thank you."

Smiling, he bussed their trays and escorted her from the commissary.

The two of them kept up a steady stream of conversation as they left the settlement behind and followed a path through the forest. Most of it consisted of Rachel asking questions and Wonick answering them. Savaas remained quiet, walking slightly behind them and observing their every interaction.

"I'm glad the trees here and back in the settlement are so thick. Otherwise, I couldn't venture out here with you. Not until nightfall."

At last, Savaas spoke. "Taavion said the Gathendien virus causes photosensitivity."

She nodded. "It sucks. Sunlight won't kill me." At least, she didn't think it would. She had never stood in it long enough to find out. "But it hurts like hell." Glancing around, she spied a narrow strip of sunlight off the path and crossed to it. "I'm only going to give you a tiny demonstration because I have a limited supply of Segonian blood, but this is what would happen to every millimeter of exposed skin if I stepped into direct sunlight." She extended her forearm and moved it until a dappled drop of sunlight about the size of a quarter touched her wrist.

Wonick frowned as he and Savaas moved to stand in front of her. "You don't have to do this," he told her earnestly.

"I know."

The skin touched by sunlight began to tingle. As they all watched, it pinkened with a sunburn that swiftly worsened.

When blisters formed, Wonick grabbed her wrist and yanked her arm into the shade. "Enough." Frowning, he peered down at it. "Does it hurt?"

She grimaced. "Yes. It burns. But—"

Wonick tucked his free hand into one of his many pants pockets and drew out a small canister. The next thing she knew, the soothing foam of *imaashu* coated the burn, banishing the sting.

"Much better." Smiling, she motioned to the canister. "Do you always carry that around with you?"

He shook his head. "I wanted to keep it handy in case your wounds pained you. How is your side? Do you wish me to spray it?"

Rachel peeled up her slightly ragged shirt. "No. It's fine." Infusing herself with Segonian blood had done the trick. The edges of the wound had pulled together and sealed. A thick scar was already forming and would soon fade away.

Wonick brushed gentle fingers across it. "That's amazing."

"The burn will heal even faster since it's minor," she told him.

Straightening, Wonick sent her a frown. "You don't have to keep revealing vulnerabilities to us, Rachel. I already trust you. Savaas will, too, in time."

She arched a brow at the silent leader. "Care to confirm or deny that, big guy?"

"Not as yet, no."

She laughed. "I figured as much."

The three of them continued on until they reached what looked like a house carved out of the trunk of a massive tree, the tips of which seemed to pierce the clouds above.

Rachel stared at it in delight. "*This* is your comm station? That's amazing! How is the tree still living if you hollowed out the trunk?" She would've thought that would kill it.

"The base and center tower isn't actually a tree," Wonick said. "We just designed it to resemble the trunks of those around it, then planted saplings all the way up the exterior."

She'd seen nothing like it before. The closest comparisons she could think of were the tacky attempts by cellular companies on Earth to disguise their cell towers as trees by adding plastic foliage.

This looked far better.

Wonick activated the door and motioned for Rachel to enter first.

Jovan sat before a large console. As soon as they entered, he rose, his face lighting with a boyish smile. "Hi, Rachel."

How could she not love this guy? "Hi, Jovan." She motioned to the console. "What's the news?"

"The Gathendiens in orbit have realized that none of the communications they're sending to other ships are going through. They're arguing and fighting over possible causes. Most speculate that it's something to do with how our geomagnetic field interacts with solar winds. They tried retreating a bit but still received no responses from the comms they sent. Now they're disassembling their communications array in an attempt to locate the problem."

"Which I'm guessing is you guys?"

"Yes, *ni'má*," he confirmed with a proud grin.

She laughed. Rachel had learned on the *Tangata* that *ni'má* and *na'má* were the alliance common versions of miss and ma'am.

Wonick moved forward. "Have they mentioned anything about the hunting party?"

Jovan nodded. "Even though they allotted the hunters two days to locate and capture their quarry"—he shot Rachel an apologetic glance—"they're growing impatient. They thought the hunters would accomplish the task swiftly. And with no way to communicate with them, those on the ship are puzzling over the delay."

"Ha! *I'm* the delay," Rachel crowed and made the sign of the bull with one hand. "You mess with the bull, you get the horns, baby."

Jovan stared at her blankly. "What's a bull?"

"A large, incredibly strong mammal on Earth with two horns it uses to gore anything that provokes it."

Chuckling, Wonick motioned for Rachel to sit in one of the chairs available. "Jovan, take a brief break. We're going to contact Janwar."

Nodding, the younger cyborg left.

Rachel's heart began to beat faster as Wonick sat beside her.

Savaas opted to stand to one side, feet braced apart, arms crossed over his chest.

The chairs in here—like those in the commissary—suited larger men. She had to scoot forward to the edge of the seat and point her toes to touch the floor. Once she did, her knee bobbed up and down as butterflies invaded her stomach.

Wonick dropped his gaze to her bouncing knee. "Are you all right?" he asked softly.

"Yes. I'm just excited." She smoothed her palms up and down her thighs. "And maybe a little nervous," she confessed. "I know you told me they're okay. But after everything that's happened, part of me needs to *see* my friends in order to believe they're truly safe."

"Understood." He flattened a hand on the dark, glassy surface of the console. A clear panel rose and hovered above the station.

"Hello, Wonick," a cheerful male voice said, though the floating screen remained dark.

"Hello, T," Wonick said. "I have an urgent communication for Janwar, code 39712."

"Understood. One moment, please."

Silence fell.

"Who's T?" Rachel whispered. "One of Janwar's fellow pirates?"

"He's the AI that runs the *Tangata*," Wonick informed her.

"Cool."

"Thank you," T responded happily. "Simone has acquainted me with the Earth term. And I *am* cool. Simone also said I am a genius."

Rachel stared at the screen. "Shouldn't he be fetching Janwar and Simone?" she whispered in an aside.

"I have already notified them of the urgent incoming communication," T replied before Wonick could. "I am capable of performing multiple tasks simultaneously. Right now, I am—"

"That's all right, T," Wonick interrupted. "We don't require a list."

Rachel found a smile. T seemed like quite a character.

The screen in front of them abruptly lit up, displaying a generic office space and...

She stared at the man who seated himself in the lone chair behind the desk. He was incredibly attractive, with long black hair pulled back from his face in cornrows that ended at the crown. From there, the dark tresses flowed down his back in loose tendrils interspersed with braids that sported colorful beads. A short beard and mustache, coupled with a loose shirt, lent him a definite piratical air.

"Holy crap," she breathed. "It's Jack Sparrow."

His face creased with a pained expression. "I see you found the Earthling."

Feminine laughter carried over the comm seconds before a familiar figure plopped down in Janwar's lap.

"Simone!" Rachel's eyes filled with tears of joy at the sight of her friend. She looked good! Hale and hearty. Happy even.

"Rachel!" Simone's eyes lit with an amber glow as they filled with tears.

Both women burst into speech at the same time. Laughed. Burst into speech. Then laughed again.

Rachel reached out blindly and clasped Wonick's hand, her eyes glued to the screen. "You look good."

Smiling, Simone swiped at her tears. "I *am* good. Are you okay?"

"I'm fine."

"She was injured," Wonick inserted.

Rachel waved it off. "It was nothing."

"She was poisoned with *bosregi*," he refuted.

Simone's smile vanished. "You were? The Gathendiens caught up with you?"

"Yes. The bloody bastards followed me here, so I had to fight a few."

"Forty," Wonick corrected. "She fought forty."

"But only twenty at a time," Rachel said.

Janwar arched a brow.

Simone nodded. "I assume you kicked their asses?"

Rachel nodded. "With the help of my new friends, yes. But I had a bit of trouble dodging the bastards' tails."

"I know, right?" Simone commiserated. "They got me, too. That damn poison nearly killed me. Are you sure you're all right?"

"Yes. These guys were quick to administer the antidote. Where's Liz? Wonick said she's with you. Is she okay?"

Simone tilted her head back and spoke to the ceiling. "T, would you please ask Liz to join us?"

"Affirmative," T informed her cheerily.

Returning her gaze to the screen, Simone leaned closer and lowered her voice to a whisper. "Liz has been through a lot. She was captured by the Gathendiens and subjected to their torture."

Rachel's hand tightened around Wonick's. "What kind of torture?"

"They kept her in a cell that was so small that she can't stand to be in confined spaces now. And they took all kinds of samples from her. She was riddled with wounds when we found her."

Liz was a healer. Any wounds she received would've rapidly healed if she were in good health.

"She's also pretty emaciated," Simone continued. "Seeing her will be a shock. Try not to let it show. Allie was the same way."

"Oh no. The Gathendiens captured Allie, too?" Liz and Allison were *gifted ones*. They lacked the preternatural strength that enabled Rachel to easily defeat Gathendiens.

Simone nodded. "Those assholes actually took it a step further with Allie and experimented on her, performing exploratory surgeries and testing illnesses. She has nightmares about it and wakes up screaming every night."

Rachel's eyes filled with tears. "Is Allie there with you, too?"

"No. She joined Eliana and Ava on the *Ranasura*, a Segonian warship."

"What about Eliana and Ava? Were they...?"

"Eliana ended up floating through space in nothing but a space suit for an insanely long time."

"What?"

"But she's been kicking ass and taking names ever since Dagon found her."

"Who's Dagon?"

"Commander of the Segonian warship *Ranasura*." Simone grinned. "They're in love."

"Eliana and Dagon?" Wonick had told her as much, but it still stunned her.

"Yes." Simone leaned to one side and wrapped her arm around Janwar's shoulders. "And I've fallen hard for this handsome devil here."

Smiling, Janwar wrapped his arms around her waist.

"Full disclosure," Simone went on, "Ava fell in love with a Purveli she was incarcerated with on a Gathendien ship." Leaning forward again, she grinned in delight. "He has faint scales, slight webbing on his fingers, and can breathe underwater. It's freaking awesome."

Rachel gaped at her, tears drying on her cheeks.

Simone laughed. "I know. It's a lot to take in." Movement sounded in the background. Simone glanced to one side while pointing at the console. "Liz, look who it is."

The woman who moved to stand beside Simone had changed so dramatically that Rachel had to struggle to withhold a gasp of dismay. Liz had always been petite and slender. But now she looked downright gaunt. Her facial features were more angular. Her collarbones and the bones in her shoulders stood out prominently beneath the soft fabric of her shirt. And her arms looked almost skeletal.

But her precious face lit with a smile as she peered at the screen. "Rachel! Oh my gosh! Are you okay?" Her light brown eyes filled with tears of joy.

And Rachel wanted to sob. What had her friend suffered to look so lost and unwell? "I don't know," Rachel responded and forced a smile. "That depends. Is Simone sitting in Jack Sparrow's lap, or am I hallucinating?"

Liz laughed. "He *does* look like Jack Sparrow, doesn't he? We tease him about it all the time."

Janwar nodded with a long-suffering expression that sparked more laughter.

The women chatted a little longer before everyone got down to business.

"Now that we've undocked from the *Ranasura*," Janwar announced, "we can head your way."

"How long will it take you to get here?" Rachel asked.

"About two weeks."

She could be with her friends in two weeks! "Okay. I was going to kill off all the Gathendiens that are left, figure out how the hell their ship works, and take off looking for the rest of you. But I'll see if my new friends will let me hang around until you get here." She glanced at Wonick and raised her brows. "Would that be okay?"

He didn't hesitate. "Of course."

Leaning back, she consulted their silent observer. "Savaas?"

He hesitated. "That's acceptable." Not much enthusiasm there.

But it amused rather than annoyed Rachel as she faced the screen.

Simone's brow furrowed with worry. "Are you okay there, Rachel? Are they treating you well?"

"I'm fine. My wounds are healing. My belly is full. Wonick has been showing me around. And I think Savaas is warming up to me." She again glanced toward the cyborg leader. "Are you warming up to me, Savaas?"

"Undecided," he replied, deadpan. But she thought she caught a twinkle in his eye.

Amused, she smiled at Simone. "You see? We're good."

"If you say so," Simone said, clearly unconvinced. "But I'm just going to put this out there for anyone who's listening: Harm my friend and I will pulverize you when I get there. And by pulverize I mean there will be nothing left to bury once I'm finished with you."

Janwar murmured in her ear, loud enough for everyone to hear, "I don't think threatening them is the way to win them over, honey."

186

Rachel's lips twitched. The most feared pirate in the galaxy called Simone *honey*?

Too cute.

"Well, too bad," Simone countered. "We shouldn't *have* to win them over. We aren't their enemies. We've never wronged them or deceived them in any way and have no reason to dislike them or want them dead. *Yet*."

Liz crossed her arms over her chest and added a decisive nod.

"They won't harm me, Simone," Rachel assured them. "At most, they'll get tired of my incessant chatter and try to avoid me. So get here as soon as you can."

"We will," all promised.

Rachel's eyes filled with tears again as she smiled at them. "I love you."

"We love you, too!"

The screen went blank.

W ONICK WATCHED RACHEL.

The bright smile she'd kept through most of the brief conversation with her friends faltered. Ducking her head, she bit her lip.

"Rachel?" When a tear slipped down her cheek, his chest tightened.

"Did you see her?" she whispered brokenly.

"Liz?" he asked, recalling how skeletal and ill that friend had looked.

"Yes." At last, Rachel turned to him. Her eyes glowed bright amber and welled with more tears that spilled over spiked lashes. "They hurt her. Those bastards hurt her. And Allie. And Ava. They aren't like me, Wonick. They aren't like Simone and Eliana. They aren't infected with the virus. They don't have our strength and speed and fighting skills." Her breath hitched with a sob. "They wouldn't have been able to fight back."

Such despair and anger warred in those luminous eyes that Wonick couldn't take it. Acting on instinct—because he sure as *srul* had little experience—he reached over, picked her up, and settled her on his lap.

Instead of recoiling and asking him what the *srul* he was doing, Rachel threw her arms around him, buried her face in his neck, and wept.

Curling his arms around her, Wonick patted her back. It seemed woefully inadequate, but nothing he could say would erase what had happened to her friends, the pain and fear they had suffered at the hands of her enemies. Holding her and remaining quiet seemed the best option.

These Earthlings seem to inspire great trust in those they encounter, Savaas said over their private comm channel.

Yes.

And love.

Wonick opted not to comment on that.

I don't think I've ever seen Janwar so happy.

Wonick hadn't either.

Nor have I ever seen you so fascinated by a female. Savaas knew him better than anyone else.

She isn't staying, Wonick reminded his friend. And himself.

Yes. She'll leave soon. Opening the door, Savaas stepped outside. As the door slid closed behind him, he asked, *When she does, will you leave, too?*

The question stunned Wonick, not because of the uncertainty and dread it conveyed but because he didn't have an answer.

It should've been simple. A quick *Of course not. This is my home.* And yet the thought of saying goodbye to Rachel made him feel sick inside. He *was* fascinated by her and drawn to her. He'd smiled more since she'd come into his life than he had in a long time. She made him feel happier. At peace. As if there were no longer any missing pieces to his puzzle. As if he were whole again, the way he had been before he'd signed up for the *vuan* cyborg program.

Rachel made him wish for a future that entailed more than finding contentment and surviving. And yet, she *would* leave, either to launch her own search for friends still missing or to join those on the *Tanagata*. Then life here would return to normal, comfortable in its daily routines, something he used to find contentment with.

So why did dread slither through him at the thought?

CHAPTER ELEVEN

T HOUGH WONICK WOULD'VE BEEN content to hold Rachel longer, she shook off her tears in quick order. "Sorry about that." Rising, she abandoned his lap and swiped at her cheeks.

"No apology necessary," he insisted. "I wept, too, when I learned my family had not only survived the protests and rebellion but thrived in my absence."

Rachel shook her head, her nose a little pink from crying. "You make it sound as if your not being with them was a good thing. I bet they would gladly give up everything your sacrifice provided them with to have you back."

"They would." Smiling, he rose and held out his hand. "Come. I want to show you the armory."

Her face lit up. And she didn't hesitate to tuck her small hand in his. "Ooh. I love weapons."

He chuckled. "I suspected you might." But that wasn't his only motive in taking her. She would face Gathendiens in battle again soon. Wonick wanted her to be better prepared.

Upon reaching the armory, he introduced Rachel to Goaden, their primary armorer, who was as curious about her as the rest of his brethren.

While Rachel wandered the room, eagerly perusing the massive collection of weapons on display, Wonick ordered a suit of armor for her. "I want it to be lightweight, so it won't restrict her movements, but strong enough to keep a Gathendien tail spike from piercing it."

Goaden nodded. "You want a helmet, too?"

"Yes."

Rachel abruptly appeared at their sides. "Hi."

190

Both jumped, neither having heard her swift approach.

"What are you doing?" she asked.

"Ordering you some armor," Wonick replied.

"Thank you, but no. Armor will only get in my way."

"It won't be the bulkier exo-armor we wear in combat. Yours will be lightweight and move easily with you while affording protection against O-rifle fire and tail spikes."

She pursed her lips. "Are you sure it won't restrict my movements? You've seen how fast I can move."

"I'm sure."

"Okay. But forget the helmet. I don't want anything to hinder my vision or other senses."

"The helmet stays," he insisted. "It will protect you from weapons fire *and* from *tengonis* and other gasses the Gathendiens may deploy once you start tearing through them."

Goaden nodded. "It will also offer you an hour of atmospheric protection if you're unexpectedly sucked into space."

She nibbled her lower lip. "I didn't think about that. Okay, then. But will you please ensure that I have the broadest view possible?"

"Your helmet will be clear on all sides," the armorer vowed.

"Excellent. Will it hamper my breathing?"

"No."

"Will it fog up and cloud my view?"

"No."

She still seemed less than pleased when she glanced up at Wonick. "Isn't all of this moot?"

"What do you mean?"

"The Gathendiens expect their hunting party to return by tomorrow evening, so I'll have to get up there before the armor is ready."

He shook his head. "The armor will be ready tomorrow morning."

She cast Goaden a look of surprise. "Really?"

He nodded. "When I saw Wonick holding your hand earlier, I assumed he'd want to protect you. I got your measurements from Taavion and started working on the suit before mid meal."

Rachel's eyebrows rose as she slid Wonick an inscrutable glance. "Should I feel offended that he thinks I need protection?"

Wonick's lips twitched. "He didn't say you *need* it. He said he thought I'd *want* it. And since *we* will be much more heavily armored than you, who do you believe I think needs it more?"

She grinned. "Good point. And thank you, Goaden. I look forward to trying on my fancy new armor."

Wonick led her outside.

As they meandered away, she smiled up at him and slipped her hand into his once more. "Looks like holding your hand has more perks than speeding my pulse."

It sped his, too. If there weren't other cyborgs milling around, he would be tempted to do *more* than hold her hand. Alas, too many eyes followed their every movement. So Wonick contented himself with brushing his thumb across the back of her hand as he continued their tour of his new homeworld before returning to the commissary for last meal.

The tables remained in a large square, an arrangement usually reserved for meetings. It didn't surprise him. Everyone was intrigued by their petite visitor and wanted to observe her while they ate.

Rachel didn't seem to mind the attention and freely engaged in conversation with anyone who spoke to her. She even arm wrestled Foarek... and *tied*. Foarek's prosthetic arm could exert an incredible amount of pressure. And yet, to the astonishment of all, it couldn't exert enough to force Rachel's small fist down to the table. She had even come close to pressing Foarek's fist to the table before Savaas had declared the match a draw.

Benwa had asked to arm wrestle her next. Then Hoshaan. And Kendan. Nebet. And Jovan. She won the first four and tied the last, sparking shouts and cheers. When cyborgs began to line up to compete, Wonick called a halt to it, reminding everyone that she was still recovering from wounds and *bosregi* poisoning.

A smile hovered on Rachel's pretty face as they left the commissary and began a slow stroll toward the cyborg homes.

"I like your friends," she said softly.

A cool breeze made what otherwise would've been a sultry night comfortable and ruffled her hair.

"I noticed." They liked her, too.

She nudged him with her shoulder. "I like you more."

Glancing down, he couldn't help but smile at the confession. "You seem comfortable among us."

"I am." She tilted her head to one side. "Is that unusual?"

More than she knew.

"Surely you were all hailed as heroes before the rebellion."

"We were," he acknowledged. "But even other members of the Akseli military remained distant."

"Why? I would've thought they'd be glad to have you on their side."

He shrugged, battening down old resentments. "Some soldiers resented the extra attention cyborgs garnered with our many victories. They didn't seem to care that far more of them would've been injured or lost their lives if we *hadn't* led the charge."

"That sucks."

"Yes."

"Well, you all remind me of my brethren back home. I can't help but feel comfortable around you." She wrinkled her nose. "Perhaps a little *too* comfortable. I didn't offend you all with my questions, did I?" She had kept up a running stream of them at mealtime.

"No." His lips quirked up in a smile. "If you'd offended us, every man present wouldn't have lined up to arm wrestle you."

She laughed. "I didn't expect that."

"Apologies."

"No. I thought it was fun. I would rather they treat me like one of the guys than like some unwelcome alien intruder." She glanced around and pointed. "Isn't the infirmary that way?"

"Yes."

"Then why are we walking in this direction? I assumed I'd be staying in the infirmary tonight." Her smile faltered, as did her steps. "Wait. You aren't going to put me in whatever passes for jail or a brig here, are you, to ensure I don't engage in whatever nefarious deeds Savaas can think up?"

"No." Halting, he faced her. And some of the peaceful contentment left him, replaced by unease. "Savaas and Taavion wanted you to sleep in the infirmary tonight, preferably in the quarantine room we shared, so you can be monitored at all times."

She grimaced. "Not a pleasant thought, but understandable."

"I objected."

"You did?"

He shifted slightly and released her hand. Backing up a step, he wondered what her response would be to his next words. "I insisted that you sleep in my quarters." His cybernetically enhanced ears heard her heartbeat pick up.

"Where I can also be monitored?"

He hesitated. "Yes. But I really just wanted you to be comfortable and to feel less like an outsider."

She studied him. "If I stay in your quarters, will I also sleep in your bed?"

Desire shot through him at the thought of it, but he kept his expression blank. "No. Jovan will sleep in Savaas's living space tonight. You can have his bedroom."

"Oh." She hesitated. "Thank you."

Nodding, Wonick wondered what went on behind those brown eyes of hers as they resumed their stroll.

Rachel brushed her hand against his.

Acting on impulse, he twined their fingers together again. Relief filled him when she didn't object and gave his hand a little squeeze. *Vuan* if the simple contact didn't quicken his pulse and make him feel like a young man embroiled in his first infatuation. He really liked Rachel. Enough that he hated the thought of her leaving and constantly had to steer his mind away from thinking up ways to lure her into remaining a little longer. Though he craved more time with her, wouldn't that merely make saying goodbye more difficult?

Wonick sent a quick mental command to open the door to his home and motioned for her to enter.

Inside lay an expansive living space with multiple seating options, as well as a large viewscreen for entertainment vids. A stairway along the left wall led upstairs to Savaas's quarters.

"It's bigger than I thought," she murmured.

"Friends often gather here." The door slid closed behind them. "And sometimes we prefer to hold meetings with unit leaders in a more casual setting."

She smiled. "I like it. It reminds me a little of Seth's and David's homes."

"Who is David?" He knew from their conversations that Seth was the Immortal Guardians' leader. But he couldn't remember who David was.

"David is Seth's second-in-command. Both of them open their homes to all immortals and our Seconds to help us feel more like a family. Their houses look a lot like this one on the inside. Open floor plan. Lots of chairs and sofas so we can gather at the end of a long night of hunting vampires or strategize when we face more formidable foes."

He nodded. He and Savaas did the same.

An open door beneath the stairs led to a small darkened lav for guests. Beyond the living space lay a meal prep area, with a table for when he and Jovan opted to eat at home or to entertain friends. Two doorways on opposite sides of the communal room provided glimpses of his and Jovan's bedrooms. Sleek but stout furniture and massive beds capable of supporting the weight the *alavinin* added to their bodies occupied each. Wonick's bedroom was scrupulously neat. The other exhibited the clutter Jovan always seemed to generate.

Wonick pointed. "That's my bedroom. And that's Jovan's. He tidied up a bit and added fresh bedding for you."

Rachel's lips twitched as she glanced at the *tidy* room. "That was thoughtful of him." Fortunately, she seemed amused rather than offended at the less-than-stellar accommodations.

"Each bedroom has its own lav. There's a third under the stairs. The food chilling unit in the kitchen is always well stocked with food. But you should consult me before consuming anything. Some items in there will make you ill if you don't cook them properly."

"Good to know."

He studied her for a long moment. "You must be tired."

"I am."

His brow furrowed. "Do you need another blood transfusion? According to the data compiled from the *Tangata*, Simone required multiple transfusions to regain her health when she was poisoned."

"No. I'm fine."

After reading what had happened to Simone, Wonick was doubly glad they had quickly administered the antidote. Otherwise, Rachel might've been in serious trouble. "Taavion would like to draw another sample of your blood in the morning. He wants to test Akseli and synthetic blood's effect on the virus you carry again."

"I would appreciate that."

Together they crossed the living room and stopped outside Jovan's bedroom.

Wonick stared down at Rachel.

He desperately wanted to embrace her, but—

Smiling, she moved forward and wrapped her arms around him in a hug. "Goodnight, Wonick."

His heart beat faster as she rested her cheek against his chest.

Before Rachel's arrival, he'd had no physical contact with females in years. Yet it felt completely natural to slip his arms around her and hug her back. "Goodnight, Rachel." He even rested his chin atop her head as if they had held each other thusly a thousand times.

More of that wondrous contentment he'd experienced in her arms the previous night suffused him.

"I wish we could have more time together," she whispered.

He did, too. "You don't have to retire now if you don't wish to. Perhaps we could watch an entertainment vid or—"

"I didn't mean tonight." Releasing him, she backed away. "I meant... in general. I wish I didn't have to leave so soon and..." After a pause, she shrugged and offered him a sad smile. "I wish I could spend days instead of hours getting to know you better. Or weeks. Maybe even months."

Cool air rushed between them but did nothing to dispel the warmth her words generated. "Perhaps you can stay longer." The words emerged before he could stop them.

For a moment, she looked as though she wanted to take him up on the offer. But ultimately, she shook her head. "Savaas wants me gone, like... yesterday."

"Not anymore. He said you could stay until the *Tangata* arrived."

"But the Gathendiens are expecting their hunting party to return by tomorrow night. I have to do something before they send more men down here or—worse—get their communications up and running and send a message to their comrades."

"They won't accomplish the latter. They can't circumvent our interference."

"But the longer they're up there, the greater the chance they may do the unexpected and send for reinforcements. A fast-moving craft can accomplish the latter without comms."

True. The *grunarks* would have to be dealt with. A simple task for the cyborg warriors. And despite his reluctant invitation earlier, Savaas would probably feel more comfortable with Rachel awaiting the arrival of her friends up on the empty ship than down here, where she could learn more of their secrets. And yet...

"Wonick?" she prompted softly. "You've gone quiet all of a sudden." Reaching up with her free hand, she cupped his jaw. "Are you worried that the Gathendiens will learn what's down here and spread the news?"

He shook his head and reached up to hold her hand in place to keep the movement from dislodging it. "It isn't that."

"Then what?"

"I find I'm not ready to say goodbye yet either," he confessed and dared to press a kiss to her palm.

Her brown eyes lit with a faint amber glow. "I don't want to say goodbye at all. I'm so drawn to you."

"And I to you." Dipping his head, he touched his lips to hers.

It was the first kiss he'd shared since the rebellion had begun so many years ago. Her lips were soft and warm, tasting faintly of the berry juice she'd consumed earlier. The way they moved under his, not only welcoming the contact but also initiating more of her own, set his heart to hammering like a ceremonial *dembori* drum.

When Rachel drew back, that fascinating amber luminescence in her eyes had brightened. "Are you drawn to me because I'm the only port in a storm?"

Confusion calmed the pounding of his heart a little. "I don't think that translated accurately." It seemed to be a nautical reference.

"Are you only interested in me because there aren't any other females around?"

Was that what she thought? "No," he answered honestly and opted to be blunt. "If we wish to, my brothers and I can disguise ourselves as Segonians—Janwar stole the pattern their military uses to generate uniforms—and visit pleasure stations."

Her eyebrows rose as surprise lit her pretty features. "Oh. I don't know why I thought you never left the planet."

"We don't do it often, and only in small numbers to keep my brothers from getting too restless. But even before I became a cyborg, no female ever drew me the way you do, Rachel." He toyed with a lock of her hair. "I want to know everything about you."

Her lips quirked. "I think you'll find I'm not all that interesting."

Smiling, he shook his head. "If you weren't that interesting, I wouldn't be tempted to ask you to stay."

She stared at him a long moment. "Wonick? *Are* you asking me to stay?"

How he wanted to. "I wouldn't do that. I know how much your friends mean to you." They were as important to her as his brothers were to him.

Rising on her toes, she slid her arms around his neck and captured his lips in a long, hot kiss that heated his cyborg blood and drove him to crush her against him. When she broke the contact, she made no move to withdraw and instead stared into his eyes from a breath away. "Maybe I can return after we find all my friends."

Hope filled him. "You would consider that?"

"Yes. I may need you to help me think of a way to smooth things over with the Lasaran monarchs. I was supposed to move to Lasara and—"

Wonick cut her off with another kiss, thrilled by the notion that goodbye might not mean goodbye with her. "We'll figure it out."

Smiling, she nodded. "We'll figure it out. Now kiss me again, Handsome."

He gladly did so. Heat slithered through his veins when she leaned into him, lighting him up like too much electrical current flooding his cybernetics. She felt so good against him. Small but perfect. Her breasts pressed to his chest. Her hips aligned with his, instantly making him hard. When he touched his tongue to her lips, she opened for him and welcomed him inside.

Wonick growled in approval, stroking her tongue with his and—

Loud thumps overrode the sounds of their quickened breathing. Boots on stairs, tromping down at a rapid pace.

Wonick hastily released Rachel and moved to stand behind her.

When she moved to one side, he gripped her shoulders and held her in place. "No. Stay there until I bring my body back under control."

Her luminescent eyes dropped to his groin and lit with understanding before she swung back around to face the intruder. "You make me burn, too," she whispered.

Jovan jumped the last few steps and landed with a boom and a grin. "Good. You aren't asleep yet. Savaas called a meeting. He said we need to strategize."

Asshole, Wonick grumbled mentally, using Rachel's Earth term.

Savaas's voice carried across the mental comm as he descended the stairs behind Jovan. *Apologies.* Arching a brow, he regarded him drolly. *Did we interrupt something?*

Wonick narrowed his eyes.

Much to his surprise, Savaas looked as though he wanted to laugh. "The time frame allotted for the Gathendien hunting party expires tomorrow night. We need to act before it does. I've summoned all team leaders to organize a response."

"Oh," Rachel said. "Really? I figured I'd just have you guys send me up in the dropship and kill them all myself."

Everyone stared at her.

"What?" Wonick asked belatedly.

She shrugged. "This is *my* fight. *I* brought it to your doorstep. I'd rather not risk any of you getting injured."

Savaas tilted his head to one side. "You would assume all the risk yourself?"

"Yes. Not that there would *be* much. Wonick is having Goaden make me some armor that should buy me enough time and protection to take out every warrior on the ship as long as they don't use one of those acquisition beam things on me."

Savaas crossed his arms over his chest. "And if the Gathendiens jump into hyperspeed while you're cutting your way through their ranks and rendezvous with another ship or two?"

Wonick frowned. The idea of Rachel falling victim to the Gathendiens effectively killed his arousal as he moved to stand beside her.

Rachel's brow furrowed. "Hmm. I didn't think of that. I may need you to tell me whom I should take out first and where to find them to keep that from happening."

Savaas arched a brow. "And if you manage to kill them all before they can leave orbit, what then?"

"I'll commandeer their ship." She wrinkled her nose. "Although I don't relish the idea of their rotting corpses stinking it up while I wait for Simone and Janwar to show up. Would it be unneighborly of me to shove them out an airlock and let them burn up in your atmosphere?"

Stifling a laugh, Savaas shook his head. "I think we can come up with a better plan than that."

They sure as *srul* could. One that would pose less risk to her safety *and* provide Wonick with more time in her company. He hoped.

The door opened, admitting all five unit leaders.

Resigned to the fact that he and Rachel would likely find no more time alone together tonight, Wonick settled beside her on the nearest sofa.

F OR THE SECOND DAY in a row, Rachel awoke snuggled up to a big cyborg.

Wonick lay on his back with one arm curled around her. His muscled shoulder pillowed her head. One of her hands rested on his chest, fingers splayed as though she had been caressing him in her sleep. And sometime during the night, she'd draped a leg across his groin.

Even though both wore clothes, the embrace roused all kinds of warm, fuzzy feelings inside her. She sighed in contentment. "I could get used to this."

Wonick's arm tightened around her. "To what?"

"Waking up with you." Raising onto an elbow, she brushed her sleep-tousled hair out of her face and smiled. "Hi, there."

His answering smile conveyed so much affection that butterflies fluttered in her belly. "Hello."

"Jovan forgot he was supposed to sleep upstairs." Once she and the cyborgs had crafted a skeleton of a plan, the youngest in their midst had released several jaw-cracking yawns, stumbled to his room, and gone to bed.

"Yes."

"I'm guessing I got bored and fell asleep while you guys were discussing all your cyborg techno gibberish." The yawns Jovan had flashed before retiring hadn't helped. Those things really *were* contagious. By the time he'd left, she'd barely been able to keep her eyes open and had slumped into the cushions, content to rest her head against Wonick's shoulder while the drone of conversation rumbled around her.

He arched a brow. "You mean while we were planning how we would get you onto the Gathendien ship and shut down most of its operations long enough for you to kill everyone?"

"Yes. That gibberish."

He chuckled.

Wonick had led such a rough life—one full of violence, deprivation, and despair—that Rachel loved to make him laugh and smile. Happy, giddy feelings always tumbled through her when she succeeded. "Sorry I fell asleep." She doubted that had aided her in appearing strong. "Not very professional of me."

"You're still recovering from your wounds and being poisoned."

She arched a brow as she studied him. "Is that why we're both still wearing our clothes?"

His lips twitched. "No. When the others left, you were sleeping so deeply that I couldn't wake you."

"Which leads me to believe that we might *not* be wearing clothes if you'd succeeded. Stupid wounds, spoiling my fun," she grumbled, sparking another laugh from him. But much to her surprise, Rachel found herself battling a bit of shyness now. Hunting vampires all night and having to eschew daylight left little time or opportunity to develop romantic relationships, something made all the trickier by her inability to share what she was without endangering all of her brethren. Hence, she'd had very few romantic entanglements during her long life.

Even if Rachel *had* stumbled into a long-term relationship in the past, would it have survived her lover learning how different she was? Would he have rejected her? Outted her to the public? Shifted from caring about her to viewing her as a means to gain wealth and power? And what of the bitterness that often soured relationships when human partners grew old and their immortal lovers didn't?

She didn't think the social stigma attached to a younger woman dating a much older man would be as harsh as what Tomasso and Cassandra faced. Tomasso was a fellow immortal who'd been married to a human woman for many decades. Even though Seth routinely healed her and staved off the aging process as much as he could, Cassandra now looked like Tomasso's grandmother, and the two couldn't have a simple date night in public without people around them making snide comments that—despite her efforts to ignore them—struck a blow now that Cassandra wasn't as spry as she used to be.

A voice in Rachel's head whispered, *You wouldn't have to worry about any of that with Wonick.* He already knew what she was. She was confident he wouldn't use that knowledge to harm her or her friends. And she suspected cyborgs didn't age as quickly as their fellow Akselis. Wonick actually looked younger than Janwar, who had been a teenager when the cyborgs launched their rebellion.

Embarking upon a relationship with Wonick tempted Rachel more with every minute she spent in his company. She'd really liked him even before they met in person. Despite having been born worlds apart, they were so similar. And since she couldn't have children because they didn't know how the virus would affect a baby, the Lasarans weren't counting on her to find love on Lasara and help them shore up their dwindling numbers.

But Rachel had never been in a long-term relationship. She'd also never had any interest in one-night stands. Perhaps if she had been born hundreds of years later, she wouldn't prefer to have an emotional connection with a man before getting physical. But she hadn't been and she did. Her last love affair, if one could call it that, had been... *sheesh*... sixty years ago.

She was woefully out of practice with flirting.

Rachel drew a pattern on Wonick's wrinkled shirt. "You could've left me on the sofa. It's more than big enough to accommodate me."

He covered her hand with his. "Yes, I could have."

She even liked holding hands with him. "Why didn't you?" she asked softly.

"I wanted to see if waking up with you in my arms was as good as I remembered."

Her heart beat faster at the honest profession. "And was it?"

"Yes."

When Rachel shifted the leg she'd draped over him, her thigh brushed against a hard bulge. "You want me."

"Very much." His voice deepened, sending a delightful shiver through her.

She leaned in. Their lips brushed. Teasing, exploratory touches until he deepened the contact.

Wow, could he kiss. Her heart raced as his tongue stroked hers. Her breathing quickened.

Wonick rolled toward her, pressing her into the mattress, one thick thigh slipping between hers.

Hell, yes.

A throat cleared loudly in the living room. "Just letting you know I'm up," Jovan called.

Rachel fought a groan as Wonick broke the kiss.

Instead of annoyance at the interruption, mischief glinted in his eyes as he stared at her. "So am I," he whispered.

She laughed.

"You two aren't naked in there, are you?" Jovan asked hesitantly.

Glancing at the door, she responded loudly, "Yes. We are. I heard a rumor that cyborg butts are super hairy and wanted to find out if it was true."

Jovan burst into laughter.

Wonick's chest rumbled with the same.

Rachel returned her attention to the cyborg leaning over her. "Are they?" she teased.

"You'll have to find out for yourself." He grinned and stole a quick kiss. "Later." Rolling away, he sat up then glanced down at her side. All playfulness subsided. "How are your wounds?"

She tugged her shirt up and gave the puncture wound a quick inspection. "Good." Barely a scar remained.

"That's remarkable." He traced the almost faded scar with his fingers. "You heal as quickly as we do."

"Cyborgs heal this quickly?"

He nodded. "Nanobots repair our wounds like the virus heals yours."

Her eyebrows flew up. "Nanobots are actually a thing?"

He smiled. "Isn't that what Earthlings call microscopic machines that heal injuries and cure illness?"

"Yes."

"Then they're really a thing. But they have a limited power supply and usually only function long enough to heal a specific injury before going dormant."

"So people inject more whenever they need them?" That seemed to be what futuristic people did in sci-fi movies. Rachel had always thought that cool.

But Wonick shook his head. "Such is inadvisable. When the medical technology industry first released nanobots, they charged exorbitant fees, essentially denying poor people treatment."

"Yep. They do something similar on Earth."

"The companies earned trillions of credits, repeatedly injecting the wealthy, who wanted to heal age-related damage and remain young and healthy forever. But they learned, to the detriment of those patients, that dormant nanobots build up in the arteries and form blockages that can't simply be removed by more nanobots."

Alarm dawned. "Will that happen to you?"

"No. The many changes made to us enable our cybernetic systems to recharge the nanobots and keep them operating indefinitely. We've never had to inject more nanobots because the originals that scientists gave us continue to function well. How is your thigh?"

The change in subject threw her for a moment. "I can't see it with my pants on, but it feels good."

His brow furrowed. "Do you need another transfusion?"

Rachel grimaced. "Yes. I don't know how exactly the virus heals my injuries, but it often leaves me tired and with a lower blood volume. I probably wouldn't have fallen asleep during the meeting last night if I'd had a transfusion."

The slight furrow in his brow deepened into a scowl as he rose, not at all self-conscious about the arousal his pants failed to hide. "You said you were fine. Why didn't you tell me you needed one?"

She scooted to the edge of the bed and shrugged. "I *was* fine at the time. And later, I didn't want to interrupt the meeting." When he would've commented, she held up a hand. "I intended to get one today before the battle. Maybe two. Now that Janwar and Simone are on the way, I don't have to worry as much about depleting my meager supply." Apparently, the Segonian commander Eliana had fallen in love with had generously donated a substantial amount to the *Tangata*, ensuring Simone would have plenty of Segonian blood on hand. So a hefty blood supply would arrive in less than two weeks.

"Hey," Jovan said. "Goaden delivered Rachel's new armor." Rustling ensued. "Cool."

She grinned. "He picks up Earth slang fast."

Taking her hand, Wonick drew her to her feet. "He listened to all your broadcasts."

"It's so small!" Jovan declared.

"Nope," she called back. "You're so big!"

Smiling, Wonick whispered, "You just made his day. He's self-conscious about being the smallest among us."

"I don't know why. He's huge. You *all* are. Now let's get cracking." She released Wonick's hand and slapped him on the butt, startling a laugh out of him. "I want to try on my new armor."

A quick homemade breakfast, one lonely shower (she couldn't muster the nerve to ask Wonick to join her with Jovan grinning at her, still puffed up after hearing her say he was huge), and two bags of blood later, Rachel strode through the forest with a small army of cyborgs. Every single warrior sported the fabulous exo-armor that could render them virtually invisible at a simple command.

The armor they'd gifted *her* with reminded Rachel of the protective suits Immortal Guardians wore in the rare instances they ventured into daylight. But while the latter had a rubbery texture that chafed and sparked grumbling complaints by its wearer, *this* was incredibly comfortable. It pulled on like a diving suit and hugged her form without feeling too tight. It also didn't restrict her movements at all. She'd made certain of that before agreeing to wear it. She even liked the gloves, which didn't feel awkward or hinder her grip. And everything was a matte black color that would allow her to melt into the shadows whenever necessary.

Well, everything except the helmet, which was currently tucked away in her collar.

Rachel still didn't know how that worked yet but loved the concept and couldn't wait to try it.

When they reached the edge of a clearing, she halted. Sunlight fell upon the escape pod she'd arrived in. Beyond it, scorched and blackened ground formed a circle around the Gathendien dropship.

She studied the larger craft. "You'd think people brilliant enough to concoct genocide-inducing viruses would design prettier ships."

Wonick smiled. "There was a time they did. But after they released the virus on Lasara, the Aldebarian Alliance decimated the Gathendiens' fleet and enacted sanctions that made it harder for them to get the materials they needed to rebuild."

She wondered idly whether pukey yellow paint had been the cheapest available or they had opted for it because it matched the leathery hide on their faces and stomachs. Either way, it merely made the dropship, which looked as though someone had patched it together from spare parts, even uglier.

Rachel frowned at the blindingly bright light that bathed the scene. "I can't go any farther until the dropship's boarding ramp is extended," she told them. "I don't want to sunburn right before the battle."

Wonick motioned to her face. "Your helmet will protect you from the sun's ultraviolet light as efficiently as the rest of your armor."

"It will?" How? Goaden had promised her the helmet would be clear.

The only part of Wonick's helmet that was clear, on the other hand, was the visor he had not yet lowered.

He shrugged. "Most helmets deemed safe for space travel offer such protection."

"Cool." She pressed the suit's collar where Wonick had instructed her to earlier. A clear helmet burst from the back of her collar and swept forward to seal in front. She smiled. "*Very* cool." When Rachel stepped into the clearing she didn't even feel the sun's warmth, let alone burn in it.

The plan she and the cyborgs had devised last night was simple. The Gathendiens had sent fifty warriors down to the surface and would expect the same number to return with one addition: her. So fifty cyborgs would accompany Rachel on her jaunt to the warship that waited somewhere in orbit.

Once the dropship punched through the atmosphere and left behind whatever signal jammer the cyborgs kept in place, the warship would scan them to determine how many life forms were aboard. Registering the right number would lull them into complacency. A garbled, static-filled message sent by Wonick would lead them to believe their soldiers were fine and just experiencing residual interference from their trip planet-side. The idiots would then allow the craft to dock in their bay.

And the fighting would begin.

There wasn't much to the dropship's interior, only a cockpit, a bunch of benches with harness straps, a lav, a weapons cage, and a door that led to a bay crammed full of surveillance drones and other craft they'd intended to hunt her with.

Wedged in between Wonick and Savaas, Rachel sat on a bench situated far enough from the wall to allow room for Gathendien tails. Designed to cover much larger warriors, the straps of her harness sagged when she fastened them. "How do I pull up that map you mentioned?"

"I'll send it to you." Wonick's eyes seemed to lose focus momentarily, as if he were there physically but had gone somewhere else mentally. A second later, a map appeared on the interior of her helmet.

"That's going to take some getting used to," she murmured. Not his technical abilities. She had too many brethren with unusual abilities for that to faze her. But the map might be a problem. Technically, it didn't hinder her vision because it was translucent and only took up part of her field of view. But she worried it might be a distraction. "Are you sure you guys will be okay after I duck out?"

They had all determined that the best course of action would be for her to head straight for the labs and holding cells in case she wasn't the first Earthling the Gathendiens had stumbled upon. (They didn't want the bastards to use any captives as shields or to force their hands the way hostage takers often did.) On her way to the lab, she would cut down every warrior she could without slowing and toss a few mini e-grenades at the ship's escape pods to prevent any weasels from leaving.

The small army of cyborgs that accompanied her would split into multiple units. One would hack the ship's remaining systems and seize control of everything. The rest would work their way through the ship to the bridge, killing all but the highest-ranking Gathendiens on board. Once done, they would interrogate the officers to find out whatever they could about the attack on the *Kandovar* and the ensuing search for Earthlings.

"Our armor will protect us," Wonick told her. "It's you I'm worried about."

Rachel patted his arm even though he probably couldn't feel it in the heavy armor. "You've seen me fight."

He covered her hand. "I have."

Seated on Wonick's other side, Nebet snorted. "Perhaps he's worried you won't leave any warriors behind for *us* to battle, Rachel."

She laughed. "I'm sure you boys can find something to do while I'm busy."

A rumble of chuckles filled the craft.

The trip through the atmosphere kicked off lots of noise and vibration. Nothing like her trip through Earth's atmosphere had been in the sleek royal transport with Taelon and Lisa. If the virus she housed didn't eradicate motion sickness, Rachel suspected she would've been pretty green around the gills by the time they entered calm, black space.

She peered through the cockpit windshield at the Gathendien warship. "Wow. That's even uglier than the dropship."

It loomed ahead of them like a giant clunky, patched-too-many-times cruise ship on its last leg. But she didn't let its dilapidated appearance fool her. A ship like that had destroyed the *Kandovar*. And even with her limited knowledge of spacecraft, she picked out multiple canons and other munitions on the warship's surface.

An alert sounded, a small light flashing on one of the pilot's consoles.

"Incoming message," one muttered.

Wonick rose and moved to stand beside the pilot.

"Search team, report," an unfamiliar voice growled. Though he spoke Gathendien, the earbud Rachel wore enabled her to understand him.

The co-pilot tapped his wristband. Static filled the compartment, seeming to cut off Wonick's words as he replied in gruff Gathendien. "... omm dammage... atmos..." Lots of static.

"Repeat," the growly voice ordered.

Again, Wonick spoke Gathendien. "... having troub... comms... damage from atmos... harsh conditions... -t's surface... acquired Earthling... no casualties. Permiss... retur...?"

"Dock in Bay Two," the growler replied.

Rachel grinned and applauded Wonick as he returned and sank down beside her. "Excellent performance." The Gathendiens had no doubt filled in the gaps left by the static, concluded their warriors had successfully captured an Earthling, suffered no casualties, and were having problems with their comms.

He smiled.

A large bay door near the back of the warship opened to admit them.

The pilots darkened the dropship's window to keep the reptilian warriors gathering in the bay from seeing inside the ship. While the pilot landed at the specified location and waited for the docking clamps to secure it, Rachel and the others unstrapped themselves and rose. The cyborgs responsible for seizing control of the ship's systems remained in place, eyes staring straight ahead without seeming to see.

Were they already hacking into the ship remotely? How exactly did that work?

"Ten Gathendiens wait in the bay," Nebet muttered.

Rachel drew her katanas, careful not to cut someone in the tight space.

Wonick patted the pouch he'd secured to one of her thighs. "Don't forget the grenades."

"I won't."

"If they hurl a stun grenade at you—"

"Get the hell out of Dodge." She'd suggested catching it and throwing it back. But Wonick said warriors sometimes held the grenades for several seconds after arming them to make them explode as soon as they reached the target.

The big bay doors closed with a loud clunk. Rachel stood in front of the cyborg warriors and faced the dropship hatch. From the corner of her eye, she saw their armor flicker. That fascinating camouflage kicked in, rendering them invisible. "So cool," she whispered.

The hatch began to open, forming a ramp.

Game time.

Rachel didn't even wait for it to lower halfway. Knowing the element of surprise would aid her, she ducked, shot forward, and leapt off. Through the air she flew, landing smoothly on her feet near the waiting Gathendiens. Her swords flashed before they even registered something was wrong. Bodies fell. Curses erupted behind her as the cyborgs thundered down the ramp.

Without looking back, Rachel dashed forward through the open doors that led to the ship's interior. A little white dot marked her progress and made its way along the map as she negotiated a maze of corridors at top speed.

At first, the warriors she encountered didn't seem to know anything was amiss and died swift, startled deaths. Then an alarm sounded.

Wee-wonk. Wee-wonk. Wee-wonk.

Stocky bodies poured into the hallways, slowing her down as she fought past them. Halfway through the ship, she realized the bank of boxes she'd just passed were Gathendien escape pods.

Backtracking, Rachel sheathed her swords, retrieved the mini e-grenades Wonick had given her, activated them, and tossed them at the pods. The little grenades hit the metal and stuck like glue, adhered to the surface by magnets. Two Gathendiens rounded a corner and started firing blasters. Dodging their fire, Rachel drew two daggers and let them fly. As the blades buried themselves in the Gathendiens' necks, she drew her swords and took off running again.

A crackling *buzz* sounded, followed by a *foomph* as the grenades delivered a charge significant enough to fry the controls of the escape pods without blowing a hole in the ship's hull.

After plowing through more warriors, Rachel dove into a room the map identified as the lab.

Three Gathendiens in white coats strangely similar to those worn by doctors and scientists on Earth spun to face her.

Rachel slapped a bloody hand over the door's controls to close it and shut out the chaos in the corridors. Breathing hard, she took in the pristine white counters, computer consoles, and displays on one side. On the opposite wall lay holding cells the bastards probably planned to stick her and anyone else their buddies found in. All were empty. But that didn't necessarily mean there were no prisoners in their possession. The scientists could be keeping them elsewhere. Like maybe behind the closed door on the far side of the room.

Three operating tables occupied the middle of the lab. On one, a Yona warrior lay, eyes focused on the ceiling in a death stare, his chest cracked open.

Rachel's hands tightened around the grips of her swords as fury filled her.

Sonofabitch! They wanted to kill the Yona, too? Who *didn't* these bastards want to annihilate?

All three scientists narrowed their eyes and studied her. When one reached up to tap his ear comm, Rachel sheathed a sword, shot forward, and broke his wrist.

Howling in pain, he grabbed his injured arm with his other hand and bent forward.

The scientist beside him reached for his comm.

Rachel's blade sliced through his wrist.

As his detached hand fell to the floor, the scientist sank to his knees and screamed curses at her, spittle flying from his lips.

When the third scientist started to move, Rachel pressed the tip of her sword to his chest and shook her head. "Nope," she said in English. "First, I break a wrist. Second, I cut off a hand. The third offender will lose his head."

Thinner than the Gathendiens she'd previously encountered, he slowly lowered his hand.

"Wise choice. Where are the others?" she demanded, keeping an eye on all three even though she directed the question to the thin one.

He sneered. "On their way here to capture you."

The one who'd lost a hand growled, "You'll suffer for what you've done, Earthling."

"No, I won't," she retorted, her voice calm yet deadly. "But *you* will." She let a slow smile bereft of joy curl her lips. "Because I didn't come alone. I came with fifty warriors who are currently kicking your soldiers' asses."

"That's *tiklun bura*," Thin Man snarled.

Rachel snorted. "Do you really think they'd sound the shipwide alarm just for me? Use your bloody head. That's O-rifle fire you're hearing. And it's felling you all, one by one."

If Gathendiens could pale, these did.

"Now answer my question. Where are the others? *Not* the other Gathendien assholes. The other captives you've taken."

"What captives?" the Thin One demanded.

She shook her head. "You may be stupid, but I'm not. If you were near the *qhov'rum* when your buddies attacked the *Kandovar*, it wouldn't have taken you so long to get this far unless you were pausing along the way to scoop up unwilling passengers like this poor bloke"—she nodded toward the dead Yona warrior—"so you could use them for your sadistic experiments. Where are they?"

The one whose wrist she'd broken climbed to his feet and looked down his nose at her. Triumph gleamed in his yellow eyes. "My men are aiming *tronium* blasters at their heads, ready to kill them on my order unless you and your warriors lay down your weapons and surrender."

"Bullshit." Rachel swung one of her katanas.

Thin Man yelped when his buddy's head tumbled from his shoulders.

As Broken Wrist's headless body slumped to the floor, Rachel eyed Thin Man. "As I promised, the next offender lost his head. Both of you will, too, if you don't tell me what I want to know. Where are the other captives?"

"There *are* no other captives," Thin Man declared. "Only the Yona."

The Gathendien down on his knees, pale from blood loss, glanced toward the closed door she'd noticed earlier.

Rachel smiled at him. "Thank you." Then she decapitated Thin Man.

As Thin Man collapsed beside the last scientist, Rachel stepped over their bodies and headed for the door.

"Why did you do that?" the last Gathendien growled. "I showed you where they are!"

They? As in more than one?

Excitement rose. Were some of her friends in there? "He lied," she said. "And you'll suffer the same fate if you fail to cooperate further." When she reached the door, a wave of her hand over the sensor wouldn't allow her entry. "Open it."

Hugging his wounded arm to his chest, he rose and shuffled forward.

Rachel's heart pounded in her chest. She didn't think the Gathendiens could get their hands on an Immortal Guardian, so she doubted she'd found Dani or Michaela. But there could be *gifted ones* in there.

Were they okay? Or were they like Liz? Emaciated. Ill. Injured. Traumatized.

The Gathendien waved his undamaged wrist across the sensor.

Whatever their condition, they would be safe now.

The door slid up. Air spilled out, pooling around her lower legs and ankles like fog produced by dry ice.

Rachel glanced down at it but couldn't tell if it was cold because her suit regulated her temperature. When she looked up again, her heart stopped. Her hand tightened on the hilt of her sword. Her breath left her in an audible *whoosh* as if she'd been sucker punched.

Had she been alone, Rachel might've staggered backward, either unwilling or unable to acknowledge what her sight conveyed. But she remained conscious of the Gathendien nearby as she stared inside.

The door didn't open to a holding room or prison cell or even a hallway that would lead to those. It opened to a room that was even larger than the lab itself. Refrigeration cabinets with transparent doors lined all three walls that were visible from her position, displaying neatly labeled specimens in stacked containers of various sizes and shapes. Bags of blood and other liquids of assorted colors filled some. Vial after vial of medicines—or maybe viruses and deadly serums they concocted—stood like tiny soldiers in others.

The rest of the room consisted of neat rows of tables that looked like the kind one might find in a forensic pathologist's morgue.

Tables that were *not* empty.

Upon each lay a body. None were Gathendien. All were dead, their sightless eyes staring up at the ceiling. Most were in some state of dissection.

Rachel's chest tightened as horror filled her. There must've been two dozen. Some were Yona. The rest were either Lasaran or Earthling.

Panic building, her gaze skipped from face to face and found none of her friends from Earth.

Lasarans then.

Rachel's pulse pounded in her ears as the meaning of it all struck her like a blow to the head. She'd been right. When she'd guessed why it had taken over a month for the much faster vessel to catch her, she'd been right. The Gathendien ship must've remained near the *qhov'rum*—or maybe *inside* the *qhov'rum*—and scooped these men and women up in their escape pods or fighter craft so the scientists could torture them and subject them to experiments while searching for Earthlings and heading this way.

Tears of grief and horror rose as her gaze skimmed across the figures, finally settling upon one.

Her breathing quickened. "You bastards," she whispered, backing away from the door.

Wonick spoke in her helmet. "Rachel?" She knew he'd been monitoring her progress through the ship. Had he caught the emotion in her voice? "What's happening? Are you okay?"

Rachel shook her head. She was not okay. She was *so* not okay.

Rounding on the scientist, she roared, "You bastards!"

The scientist's eyes widened as he hastily backed toward one of the counters. Reaching into a drawer, he yanked a blaster out and raised it.

Rachel swung her katana, decapitating him before he could get off a single shot. "You bloody bastards!" she bellowed, tears streaming down her cheeks.

"Rachel?" Wonick repeated, alarm filling his voice.

Shaking her head, too enraged to respond, she drew her other sword and raced from the lab.

Gathendien warriors filled the corridor beyond, all jogging toward the back of the ship to battle the cyborgs. Gathendien warriors who had helped capture every dead man and woman on those tables. Gathendien warriors who would do the same to her, Wonick, and the others if they could.

Dropping her katanas, Rachel released a war cry, clenched her hands into fists at her sides, and jerked them up. Every Gathendien in the hallway flew up and slammed into the ceiling. She jerked her hands down. The Gathendiens pinned to the ceiling crashed to the floor with the force of an airbag crash test vehicle. Weapons scattered. Tail spikes impaled fellow Gathendiens. Again, she wrenched her fists up. Then down. Gathendiens cried out, unable to shoot her because they'd lost their weapons. Still bellowing her war cry, she raised and lowered her fists over and over until no warrior moved or breathed.

Chest heaving, she staggered backward.

Wonick kept saying something over comms, but the pulse pounding in her ears drowned out his voice.

Those bastards. Those bloody bastards.

It was a litany in her head as tears cooled her cheeks inside her helmet.

Boots pounded the floor in the distance. More Gathendien soldiers jogged around a corner.

Rachel opened her hands. Her sword hilts flew into them as the warriors thundered toward her, trampling their fallen comrades.

She would kill them.

Spinning this way and that, she swung and cut and slashed with preternatural speed as tears continued to blur her vision.

She would kill them *all*.

CHAPTER TWELVE

I CY PANIC TRICKLED DOWN Wonick's spine as Rachel's shouts filled his helmet. "Does anyone have eyes on Rachel?"

A chorus of *no*'s sounded.

"We should gain control of their security cameras momentarily," Nebet murmured. "We couldn't do it remotely and are patching in."

"As soon as you do, find her," he ordered. "According to my map, she left the lab and is heading toward the bridge."

Beside him, Savaas swore. "What the *srul* happened? She was supposed to remain in the lab."

Wonick shook his head and fired his O-rifle in quick bursts, piercing an oncoming Gathendien's armor and taking him down. "I don't know." He'd never heard Rachel bellow like that before, had never heard emotion choke her voice like that, not even when she had met him face-to-face and realized he'd betrayed her.

What happened in that lab?

What had she found?

Stomach churning, he lobbed a stun grenade at the wall of Gathendien soldiers they met around the next corner. Had she found one of her Earthling friends in the lab? One the Gathendiens had starved and experimented on the way they had her friend Liz?

If so, he and the rest needed to take the ship as quickly as possible and get the Earthling to Taavion so he could help her.

Wonick hoped fervently they weren't too late for that. "Whatever happened, Rachel," he said, "do *not* remove your helmet." They couldn't risk anyone being exposed to whatever contagions the lab might contain.

217

Shouts, growls, and curses—coupled with jagged breathing—were her only responses.

Wonick, Savaas, and their unit pushed forward, nearing the center of the ship. This must be one of their primary vessels. The number of foes he and the others encountered by far exceeded the number they'd expected.

"We're in!" Nebet blurted.

Wonick left the stunned Gathendiens for his brothers to handle and pushed forward, eager to reach Rachel and find out what the *drek* had happened. "You have control of the cameras?"

"The cameras and everything else on this heaping pile of *bura*. And just in time. The commander was about to jump into hyperspeed."

"Find Rachel," Wonick ordered again.

The white dot that represented her jumped forward in short starts and stops, so at least he knew she was still alive and fighting.

Distracted, Wonick turned a corner. O-rifle fire struck him in the chest.

Swearing, he ducked back. "Six hostiles," he told Savaas. Pulling another stun grenade from his pocket, he swiftly activated it and tossed it around the corner.

Shouts erupted. Bright light poured from the corridor, followed by thumps as bodies dropped.

Nodding to Savaas, Wonick raised his rifle and swung around the corner. Every Gathendien was down. But two more arrived and skidded to a halt upon seeing them.

Wonick and Savaas opened fire. They had fought beside each other for so many years that they rarely needed speech or hand signals to convey their intentions. They even knew which man the other would target.

Any Gathendien they encountered who held a high rank, he and Savaas felled with nonlethal wounds and left for the others to restrain. The rest they delivered quick deaths until Wonick's unit finally reached the corridor outside the lab.

All paused, staring at the carnage. Blood painted the ceiling and the floor. Part of the walls, too. Fallen Gathendiens lay at their feet, some of them looking as though a vehicle had driven over them.

Wonick shared a stunned look with Savaas before moving forward. A glance inside the lab revealed three dead Gathendien scientists, a dead Yona warrior on a table, and empty holding cells.

It might've been helpful to question the scientists, Savaas muttered on his and Wonick's private channel.

Since he couldn't argue the point, Wonick opted not to reply.

Confident that Rachel had already checked the room behind the closed door, he continued up the corridor with Savaas and their unit.

They didn't go far before they relaxed their hold on their weapons and exchanged more looks of astonishment and unease. Blood splattered the walls and floors. Big Gathendien bodies lay in red pools that sported a few smears where Rachel's boots had slipped and skidded in them.

None of the fallen warriors breathed.

"What the *srul?*" someone behind him muttered.

They had encountered bodies before this, sprinkled here and there, no doubt killed quickly by Rachel during her race to the lab. They'd found a few wounded, too, as they fought their way through additional soldiers who spilled into the hallways. But this...

He studied the fallen.

There were so many. And all were dead.

Though Wonick and the others kept their weapons ready as they moved forward, they encountered no more hostiles, just more dead, every corner they turned unveiling additional corpses.

"Do you think she cleaned out this whole half of the ship?" Benwa asked softly.

Wonick shook his head, worry escalating. Was any of the blood that clung to the bottoms of their armored boots Rachel's?

Why had she left none of the warriors alive to question?

Savaas met his gaze.

This didn't look like standard warfare. It didn't even look like the battle scenes that had resulted from their skirmishes with Gathendiens back on the planet. These looked like rage killings.

He and Savaas had seen them before. *Srul,* they'd both engaged in them before. When they'd found the facility that created Jovan and realized all that the Akseli military scientists had subjected the boy to, they had torn those guilty of it to pieces. Much like Rachel had these Gathendiens.

Um, we may have a problem, Nebet said over the mental comm channel, his voice filled with unease. Did he not want Rachel to hear him?

Wonick met Savaas's gaze. *What is it?*

Rachel is almost to the bridge.

Is she okay? Wonick blurted. *Is she injured?*

I can't tell. There's a lot of blood on her armor, but I think it's all Gathendien. She's killing everyone. *And I mean* every *Gathendien she encounters, officer or grunt. If she continues, we may not have anyone with high enough clearance to make them worth interrogating.*

"Rachel." Wonick plowed forward, picking up speed until he and Savaas jogged, leaping over bodies and occasionally slipping in the bloody patches. "Rachel! If you reach the bridge, don't kill the commander. Repeat, do *not* kill the commander!" If anyone could give them privileged information, that *grunark* could.

She didn't answer.

"How many officers have we captured?" Savaas asked over the open line, voice grim.

"Not enough," Nebet replied.

Lock the bridge, Savaas ordered over mental comms. *Don't let her in.*

Done. That was close. She just reached it.

Loud thuds sounded in the distance.

Swearing, Wonick broke into a run.

Boots pounded the floor as his brothers followed.

Those thuds got louder and louder as they neared the ship's command center.

When they rounded the next corner, the cyborgs skidded to a halt.

More bodies littered the corridor.

Rachel stood among them outside the sealed door to the bridge. The crystal panel used to gain access dangled down the wall, hanging by a single wire. A nest of other wires hung out in a tangled mess as if something inside had either exploded or vomited them forth.

Her breath emerging in harsh rasps, Rachel repeatedly drove the tip of her sword into the mechanism. Sparks flashed. More wiring emerged. Each time her sword sank deeper.

Had she penetrated the interior wall of the bridge?

Growling in frustration, she moved to stand in front of the door, spun, and kicked it hard.

Several cyborgs sucked in startled breaths when a dent formed in the heavily armored barrier.

Rachel kicked it again and again, grunting with the effort. "You think this door will save you?" she bellowed. The dent increased a little in diameter with each blow. "You're only delaying the inevitable!"

Breathing hard, she paused, staggered back, then stabbed the access console again.

Wonick shifted.

Abruptly registering their presence, she jerked around and raised her sword.

"It's okay." Wonick held up his hands, letting his O-rifle dangle down his side, and spoke as softly as he would to a wild *mohlbani* he didn't wish to frighten. "It's okay. It's just us."

Relief washed over pretty features obscured by blood she'd only partly wiped off her helmet's face. "Finally." Breathing hard, she motioned to the door. "I'm having trouble getting this door open."

Despite the smears on her helmet, Wonick's sharp vision noted her pink nose and the tears that glistened on her cheeks.

"I know the commander's in there," she continued. "But he won't open up."

Actually, the commander couldn't open the door if he wanted to. The cyborgs had locked it tight.

She stabbed the control panel again. "I figured the wall beside the door..." Stab. "...may not be reinforced as much and..." Stab. "...think I've broken through, but I could use some help."

"We'll get it open." Maintaining even tones, he slowly approached her. "We'll have to fetch a laser torch, but we'll get it open."

Technically, it wasn't a lie. It *would* take a torch to open the door now that she'd damaged it and mangled the controls. But all cyborg armor included compact torches for situations like this. The only "fetching" needed would involve popping the torches out of their casings. Yet Wonick hoped the implication that it would take longer would calm her.

A little bit of the anxiety clawing him eased when she ceased battering the control panel and door. "There aren't any escape pods attached to the bridge, are there?" she asked. "These guys don't seem the type to go down with the ship... so it wouldn't surprise me if the commander kept... a special pod handy for himself."

"Nebet," Wonick asked over helmet comms, "does the bridge have access to escape pods?"

"Negative."

Rachel's breathing began to calm. "He can't radio for reinforcements or do the hyperspeed thing?"

"No. We've locked down all engines and comms. This ship is essentially dead in the water." He opted to use an Earth phrase, hoping it would help soothe her. "The bridge crew isn't going anywhere but into a cell."

Something dark entered her features as she glared toward the bridge. "I don't want them in a cell," she ground out. "I want them fucking dead."

"They may have information we can use." When she started to protest, he held up a hand. "They may know what ships—if any—have captured Earthlings and where those Earthlings are being taken."

Recognizing the logic of the argument, she nodded. "I want to be there when you interrogate them."

He hesitated. "*Can* you be there when we interrogate them? *Without* killing them?"

She glanced toward the center of the ship, perhaps recalling her hasty execution of the scientists. Closing her eyes, she shook her head. "No. You'll kill them after?"

"Yes."

Shoulders relaxing, she opened her eyes and pinned him with a hard gaze. "Make damn sure you do."

Relieved, Wonick started toward her again. "Are you injured?" A swift visual inspection of her armor revealed no obvious tears.

"I'm fine."

"No puncture wounds?" He'd brought the *bosregi* antidote with him.

"No. Are *you* injured?"

"No."

She glanced past him at the others. "What about you all? Anyone wounded?"

"No," they responded in unison.

When she failed to make a quip about a hive mind, he thought it indicative of her distraction.

Rachel motioned toward the bridge with a sword. "How long do you think it will take to get through this?"

"A while." He winced inwardly at the vague response. Breaching the bridge would likely only take a couple of minutes. They could avoid battle with the bridge crew by tossing in a stun grenade. Then they'd haul the *grunarks* down to the brig and get to work.

Nodding, she sheathed her swords and strode forward. "Then do what you have to do."

When she continued past him, Wonick turned to watch her go.

Savaas and the other cyborgs parted down the middle to let her pass.

"Don't remove your helmet until we've confirmed that no pathogens are present, especially in the lab," Wonick reminded her.

Waving a hand in acknowledgment, she turned the corner and disappeared from view.

Driven by impulse, Wonick started to follow. Those tears glistening on her cheeks and spiking her eyelashes hit him on a gut level. He needed to know what had happened, why she'd wept and flown into a blind rage. He needed to do whatever he could to help her and make her feel better.

And if there *wasn't* anything he could do, he at least wanted to be there for her.

Savaas thrust out a hand to stop him. *Give her a minute*, he advised on their private comm.

Something happened in that lab, Wonick said. Rachel had stuck to the plan and been fine up until then.

She may be disappointed that we didn't find any of her friends, Savaas responded. *Or maybe the scientists said something that upset her. They're stupid* grunarks. *If they know fellow Gathendien researchers have tortured some of her friends, they might've bragged about it. We don't know. And she seems disinclined to discuss it. Until she is, let's focus on the job at hand and take care of business.*

Wonick stared after her. She *hadn't* seemed ready to talk about it, whatever *it* was.

Savaas clapped him on the back. "Let's try to find something useful for her."

Nodding, Wonick crossed to the bridge access panel and peered inside.

Light glimmered through a handful of slits where her sword blade had pierced the wall of the bridge.

He motioned Savaas over. *She weakened the wall on the other side of the panel. I say we widen the holes with O-rifle fire and toss a stun grenade inside. That way we won't have to fight our way in when we cut through the door.*

Savaas nodded. *A solid plan.*

Ever swift and efficient, he and his brethren got to work. It took quite a bit of rifle fire to widen the holes Rachel had created, yet another attestation of the immense strength she possessed. The *grunarks* in the bridge fired blindly at the hole multiple times, hoping to hit the warriors on this side. Fortunately, their blasts missed the hole and merely weakened the wall *around* it. Savaas tossed a stun grenade inside. Shouts erupted. Bright light flashed. Multiple thuds sounded.

After the cameras on the bridge confirmed that all Gathendiens were down, the cyborgs moved in and restrained the fallen men.

Wonick and the others were carrying the heavy *grunarks* down to the brig when Taavion spoke over the mental comm.

Wonick.

Yes?

I've made it to the lab and have confirmed that no contagions are present.

Excellent. Does Rachel know it's safe to remove her helmet?

Yes. She's here with me and... He trailed off.

Wonick slowed to a halt. *And what?*

Savaas stopped in the hallway beside him and met his gaze. Each had a Gathendien folded over one shoulder.

There's something you should see, Taavion announced gravely.

"Go," Savaas said. "We have this."

Wonick shrugged one shoulder, dumping the Gathendien he carried onto the floor. "Thank you." With brisk steps, he headed down the corridor. As soon as he turned a corner and left his unit's sight, he began to run. Taavion's voice had held that same grave tone the day they'd infiltrated an Akseli military research and development facility and found Jovan, a child whose eyes had been full of such misery and pain that—like Rachel—the cyborgs had all let rage consume them and guide their hands and weapons.

Wonick slowed when he reached the corridor outside the lab. Though his brothers had cleared away the dead bodies that littered it, bloodstains remained. He paid little attention to them as he entered the lab.

Taavion stood before a console, scrolling through data at a rapid pace.

"Where are the scientists?" Wonick asked after noting their absence.

"With the other dead," Taavion said, his eyes on the screen.

"And Rachel?"

The medic nodded toward a closed door on the wall opposite the entry. "In there. I've deactivated the security feature. You need no code to gain entry."

Without another word, Wonick crossed to the panel.

Taavion spoke over his shoulder. "You may want to remove your armor first."

Wonick paused. Though he couldn't guess the reason for the request, he did as his friend recommended, rapidly stripping down to the body suit beneath that monitored his vitals at all times. As soon as he finished, he waved a hand in front of the sensor.

The door slid up. Frigid white mist poured out around his ankles, chilling the feet now covered only in socks.

Despite the cold, Wonick didn't hesitate to enter and let the door close behind him.

The entire room seemed to serve as a refrigeration unit, the temperature hovering around freezing. Cabinets with clear faces lined the walls, but he could not have said what they contained. His attention focused solely on what occupied the center.

Row after row of bodies lay on metal tables. All were covered with white sheets, leaving only their faces exposed. Some were Yona. Some were...

Dread filled him. The males had to be Lasarans. Were the females Earthlings?

Rachel sat amid the dead, her helmet tucked away in her collar and her gloves missing. She had pulled up a stool and now sat on it, shoulders slumped. A pile of more white sheets lay forgotten at her feet. Once more, Rachel's nose was pink. Tears froze on her pale cheeks, glistening like gems. Droplets of ice littered the front of her dark armor where more had fallen. And her eyes glowed bright amber.

"Is she one of your Earthling friends?" Wonick asked gently.

"No," she responded. "She's Lasaran."

He slowly walked toward her. "You knew her?"

Raising her head, she sent him a look so full of anguish that it pierced his heart. "Yes," she whispered, voice hoarse. Moisture welled in her eyes and spilled over her lashes. "She was my friend."

Wonick stopped on the other side of the table. The sheet that covered the woman left just enough of her chest visible to expose the ends of dissection incisions. "What was her name?"

"Sinsta." Reaching up, she swiped at the tears, erasing them before they could freeze like the others. "She was an engineer. The last time I saw her she was fighting hard to keep everything running. I'm surprised she didn't die on the ship when it exploded. It's what I've always assumed."

"Once the damage reached the critical point, all crew members would've been ordered to evacuate."

Rachel sniffed, blinking back more moisture. "She was teaching me engineering. She knew I wanted to start a new life on Lasara. No more—" Her breath hitched. "No more hunting. No more killing." She swallowed hard. "In exchange, I was teaching her and the other engineers how to defend themselves against an attack." She loosed a bitter laugh. "Some help that was."

Wonick circled the table and drew Rachel into a hug, glad Taavion had suggested he remove his armor. "I'm sorry," he murmured.

Slipping off the stool, she wrapped her arms around him and squeezed him tight. "She was sweet, Wonick. And kind. And funny." Rachel burrowed into him as if it would enable her to shut out everything else, including the truth of what her friend had suffered.

Wonick held her tighter, resting his chin atop her head.

"I recognize many of these faces. Saw them on the *Kandovar*. And the Gathendiens just scooped them up and—" Her breath caught. "Look at them. Look what they suffered. They didn't deserve this."

"No, they didn't."

"She was my friend," she whispered.

Cupping a hand over the back of her head, he stroked her hair, not knowing what else to say. They stood thusly for many long moments, Wonick holding her while she gave into grief and wept against his chest. Every sob made his heart ache more for her.

"I thought I'd left this behind." Despair weighted the words. "People wanting me dead because of who and what I am. People *hating* me because of what I am. All the fighting and the killing. I thought things would be different out here."

"I know." He pressed a kiss to her hair. "I'm sorry that they're not."

A long sigh rife with suffering escaped her. "I'm so tired." Clearly, she wasn't speaking of physical weariness.

He knew that exhaustion well. It was what had driven him and his brothers to isolate themselves from everyone but Janwar and his crew. All they wanted was peace and to be treated kindly by others. But there would always be those who would do everything they could to prevent that.

"Come." He shifted her until she was tucked into his side.

"I don't want to leave her like this."

"Taavion will ensure she and the others are cared for with respect and placed into cryopods. Once Janwar and Simone arrive, we'll transfer the pods to the *Tangata*, and he'll see that they're returned to Lasara for proper burial ceremonies."

Nodding, Rachel left his arms to move closer to the table and stare down at her friend. She drew a tender hand over Sinsta's hair, then leaned down to murmur in her ear, "I'm sorry I wasn't here to protect you. I vow I will make every Gathendien pay for what they've done." Rachel pressed a kiss to Sinsta's cold forehead. "Thank you for being my friend," she whispered on a ragged breath. "I will always remember you."

Once she straightened, Wonick curled an arm around her shoulders and encouraged her to lean into his side as he led her from the room.

Face solemn, Taavion looked up when they reentered the lab. "I will care for them all as if they were my brothers."

"Thank you," she said, voice thick.

Wonick addressed the other cyborgs through internal comms. *Savaas, I'm taking Rachel home.*

You're returning to the planet?

Yes.

What happened? Nebet asked.

The Gathendiens captured twenty-three Lasarans and Yona from the Kandovar. *Rachel found their bodies in a large refrigeration room attached to the lab.*

Swears erupted.

She recognized many of them. And one of the Lasaran females was her friend.

More swears.

When Wonick and Rachel reached the lab's entrance, she paused.

Stepping away from him, she took a deep breath, held it, and slowly let it out. Fingers that were even paler than usual from the cold wiped away the frozen tears on her cheeks. Her spine stiffened. Her shoulders straightened. Her chin lifted. "All right," she said with a decisive nod. "Pity party's over. Let's take care of business."

Wonick frowned. "Don't you want to return to the planet?"

"No. I have a mess to clean up." A hard glint entered the glowing amber eyes that met his. "And I don't want to leave until you've finished interrogating the officers and every one of those bastards is dead."

He had felt the same way each time they'd found the corpses of cyborg brethren who had been *decommissioned*. "Understood." He had also needed to stay busy to keep from drowning in grief and fury.

She motioned to his black suit. "As much as I like seeing those lovely muscles of yours on display in that form-fitting whatever you're wearing, you should probably put your armor back on. If you don't, you'll have to burn your socks to get rid of the Gathendiens' stench."

He'd burn his socks anyway after walking through the scientists' blood. But Wonick didn't mention it. Instead, he peeled the socks off and quickly donned his armor.

When he and Rachel exited the lab, Jovan and two other cyborgs halted on their way past.

All viewed her with somber expressions.

"I know, right?" She motioned to the red stains on the ceiling and beneath their boots. "You guys did the hard part, carting away the assholes. The least I can do is mop the floor."

Eyebrows rising, Jovan shifted from one foot to the other. "Or you could leave it as is and blow it up once we're done."

Normally, the cyborgs would claim the vessel, land it on the planet and use its parts to create something better. But Wonick didn't want to salvage a single bolt from the ship that would forever be a source of painful memories for Rachel.

Jovan apparently agreed.

Rachel surprised them, though. "No." She glanced back at the lab, then stared down the corridor. "Not yet, at least," she murmured slowly, her thoughts seeming to turn inward. "I may have a use for it."

Wonick didn't know why those words unsettled him. Her Earthling friends, Eliana and Simone, had both claimed Gathendien ships they'd conquered. And Rachel had indicated a desire to search for her friends as well as an interest in engineering. Yet

229

something in her visage—in the eyes that lost their glow and turned a dark brown—and in the clench of her jaw sent unease slithering through him.

Clapping her hands, she startled him from his musings. "Okay. I know these bastards weren't big on hygiene, but they must have cleaning supplies around here somewhere." Raising her brows, she gave them all a hopeful look. "Do you think they might have some handy little cleaning bots that can take care of this mess for us?"

Jovan snorted. "Not likely."

"Then mops and buckets it is. Who's going to help me find them?"

Everyone present volunteered.

"If Rachel wants to claim this ship as her own," Taavion called from the lab, "I recommend treating every surface with *retsa*."

Rachel glanced up at Wonick. "What's *retsa*?"

"It's often used in first aid to clean wounds. It's similar to *imaashu*, but doesn't deaden pain. Because *retsa* is a powerful disinfectant, it can also be used as a cleaning agent if you have a sufficient supply."

She pursed her lips. "*Do* we?"

Taavion spoke again. "There's a cabinet full of it in here."

She smiled. "Then we're in business. Let's get to work, boys."

Wonick spent the remainder of the afternoon, mopping floors and scrubbing walls and ceilings with Rachel. More cyborgs joined them, one or two at a time, until more than half of those who had come up on the dropship aided in the cleanup. At first, they worked in relative quiet, sending furtive looks Rachel's way to gauge how she was holding up, afraid to speak for fear of saying the wrong thing. But Wonick's brothers soon cautiously started trading quips and jibes that won faint smiles from Rachel, which merely encouraged them to do more. Full grins eventually surfaced, erasing the grief that lent her such a somber cast. Then Rachel began to sing, mixing songs with what she called radio announcements.

Cyborgs had excellent memories, enabling them to pick up the lyrics quickly. And by the end of the day, the men sang along with her, much to her delight. If—on occasion—her voice faltered, she sniffled, and a tear or two trailed down her cheek, no one commented. Nor did they stop singing. Like Wonick, they seemed to guess that was what Rachel needed.

A couple of men challenged each other to a contest, each wagering he could clean the docking bay faster than the other. Foam flew *everywhere* as they scrubbed at cyborg speed, splattering them all and luring laughter from the Earthling in their midst when a big blob landed on Savaas's head as he entered the bay.

The irritation that darkened their leader's face disappeared as he noted Rachel's smile. "I should have left my helmet on," he said drolly.

She grinned. "That's what Wonick said."

Leaning forward, Savaas brushed the foam off his short hair as he joined them. "Have these boys gotten *anything* done?"

"Yes," she said. "They've now memorized the lyrics to all the songs on my sixties playlist and sung them with gusto."

He shook his head. "And you're still here? I've heard some of them sing. It's like a *hurlenna* screeching in heat." His face lit with inspiration. "Perhaps I should send a couple of them down to the brig and have them serenade the prisoners all night."

Wonick glanced at Rachel, afraid any mention of the prisoners would bring anger and grief surging back.

Instead, she smiled in delight and delivered a light punch to his friend's shoulder. "Savaas. Look at you. You made a joke."

"Not really," he replied. "Their singing truly is atrocious. And I should know. The Akseli military originally wanted me to be part of a cyborg boy band."

Rachel stared up at him for several seconds, then burst into laughter. "I don't know what's funnier: picturing you in a boy band or you using that term. How do you even know what a boy band is?"

He smiled. "Your broadcasts, of course."

She nudged Wonick with an elbow. "You see? I *do* have fans."

Yes, she did. Every male here, and many more below.

"Hey," she said, her smile fading. "How's that going? The interrogation?"

Savaas shrugged. "As we suspected, the men of lower rank had nothing interesting to share. They're encouraged to follow orders without asking questions."

"Okay. What about the officers?"

"They've been uncooperative thus far despite... incentives." He opted not to mention how few officers had remained after Rachel's rampage, Wonick was happy to note.

"Is it a loyalty thing? I thought those bastards liked to stab each other in the back."

"No. It's a fear-of-the-emperor thing. I've never met a Gathendien who didn't tremble in fear at the mere *thought* of angering the emperor. He deals harshly with those who disappoint him. And those who *deceive* him he makes a public example of."

She glanced up at Wonick. "Bad stuff?"

"Very bad stuff that can last for days," he replied.

"Wow. Okay. But why fear his wrath if we're going to kill them anyway?"

Savaas smiled. "They may be operating under the misguided notion that we intend to drop them off on Promeii 7 if they cooperate."

"Oh." She frowned. "You won't, will you?"

He snorted. "*Srul* no. They know we're cyborgs and they killed your friend."

Rachel smiled faintly and touched his armored arm in a brief show of thanks for supporting her.

"We *did* find a few willing to confirm that you Earthlings were the true target of the attack on the *Kandovar*," Savaas added.

Brow furrowing, she shook her head. "That's what I thought. But if they wanted Earthlings, why didn't they just go to Earth and take some? Why target a warship with members of the Lasaran royal family on board? Didn't that seem the least bit suicidal to them?"

"They had reason to believe the Earthlings on board the *Kandovar* were the key to discovering why the virus they released on Earth long ago failed."

She stared at him. "They know we're different?"

"Yes."

"How?"

"That's one of the many things we're trying to discover."

"So what's our play here? How do we get them to talk?"

"Gathendiens require more hydration than you or I do and usually sleep with their bodies partially submerged in murky water."

She wrinkled her nose. "That would explain the stagnant swamp aroma that clings to them."

Savaas nodded. "We're going to keep them dry in the cells and withhold food and water. Nebet and his unit tinkered with the atmospheric generators aboard the ship and dramatically reduced the humidity. By this time tomorrow, the Gathendiens should be eager to talk. If not, another day and they'll be desperate."

Rachel cast Wonick an uncertain glance. "Really?"

He nodded. "Drying out is torturous for them. Janwar used such tactics to elicit the location of the Lasaran princess when she disappeared."

"Oh. Wow. Okay then."

Savaas motioned to the mostly clean bay. "It looks like this will soon be as clean as the rest of the ship. A transport is en route with reinforcements to relieve the units up here."

She bit her lip. "Are all your guys really okay? No injuries?"

"No injuries. The Gathendiens were completely caught off guard and unprepared to battle cyborgs in full armor."

Wonick grunted. "Or an Earthling with skills enough to equal twenty of us."

She smiled. "Good."

"The new units arriving will guard the prisoners," Savaas went on, "and continue to peruse the files we're copying."

"What kind of files?" she asked.

"Everything stored in the ship's database, which ranges from mundane things—like shift schedules, personnel lists, and food stores—to areas we may find something of interest in. Cargo they've picked up or delivered. Munitions. Weapons programs. Communications sent and received that could reveal where more Earthlings or other *Kandovar* survivors may be. Medical files in the lab, detailing their experiments. Maps with locations of research and development facilities, hidden bases, and more. We found a wealth of classified files that were only available to the commander.

Unless he enlightens us as to the contents, it will take time to decrypt those."

"You'll keep us posted?" she asked.

"I'll keep you posted."

Wonick took her hand. "Let's go home."

CHAPTER THIRTEEN

R ACHEL'S STOMACH GROWLED AS the transport left the Gathendi-
en ship. She'd been so focused on trying to stay busy to keep
grief and fury at bay that she'd missed mid meal.

The cyborgs who accompanied her and Wonick down to the
planet had, too, because they had helped her scrub the Gathendiens' presence from the ship.

None of them offered a single complaint.

They were such good guys.

She glanced around. This craft was much sleeker than the Gathendien dropship, a testament to the cyborg's design skills. The
seats were surprisingly comfortable. Weary from battle and crying,
she might've taken a nap if the trip lasted longer.

As soon as they landed, everyone changed out of their armor
and headed for the commissary, where scrumptious meals awaited
them. Fatigue pulling at her, Rachel focused on filling her belly and
spoke little as the men's banter circulated the tables.

Wonick remained by her side, quietly offering support. He
seemed to know intrinsically what she needed—time to process it
all—and didn't press her to talk about it.

After last meal, Jovan walked home with them, waved goodnight,
and headed upstairs to Savaas's domain. Savaas had opted to remain on the Gathendien ship.

Once the door to Savaas's apartment closed, Rachel looked at
Wonick.

Affection coupled with gratitude filled her. He'd been perfect
today, lending her strength when she needed it without inundating
her with sympathy that would've kept her in tears.

Closing the distance between them, she hugged him. "Thank you."

His big arms came around her. "For what?"

"For being there for me." She sighed. "For helping me stay busy so I wouldn't be up in my head all day. I really needed that. The rest of the guys were great, too. I think if they had expressed condolences every time they saw me, I would've fallen apart and spent the whole day crying."

He cuddled her closer. "We've all known loss, Rachel. We understand how hard today was for you. And how hard tomorrow will be. And the next day." He rested his chin atop her head. "Everyone copes with loss in different ways."

"Yet you knew what would help me the most."

"Yes."

And he hadn't hesitated to supply it. Instead of poring over those classified files Savaas had mentioned or interrogating Gathendien officers or doing a dozen other things he would've usually done as second-in-command, he had scrubbed floors and sung sixties songs with her.

Damn, that meant a lot to her. It merely deepened her growing feelings for him.

"There's an argument on Earth that has existed for what seems like forever," she murmured. "One side believes that it's better to have loved and lost than to never have loved at all. The other side believes it's better to never have loved."

He grunted.

"What do you think?"

"I think it's better to have loved and lost."

Easing back a little, she looked up at him. "You didn't even hesitate."

He shrugged. "I didn't have to."

"How can you be so certain?"

"Some of those I've encountered in my life have convinced me that knowing love is worth the heartache that arises when we lose it."

"Who?" She hadn't asked if he'd ever been married or in love with someone in the past.

"Jovan." He brushed an affectionate hand over her hair. "He was six when Chancellor Astennuh killed his parents and forced him into the cyborg program. Too young to remember them, particularly since the pain and trauma of the surgeries he suffered through supplanted those memories. The rest of us spent at least twenty solar cycles with families who loved us and shaped our lives before entering the program. Parents. Grandparents. Siblings, too. And in the years that followed the rebellion, we looked back fondly on the happiness family and friends brought us in our youth and took comfort in it." He shook his head. "We still do. But Jovan doesn't have that."

"I don't know," she said with a smile. "I've seen the way he is with you. He loves you like a father."

He smiled. "And I love him like a son."

"You're a good man, Wonick."

"Very few in the galaxy would agree with you."

"Because they don't know you. And they're wankers."

He laughed.

Reaching up, she cupped his stubbled jaw. "But *I* know you. At least, I'm coming to." She smoothed her hand around to cup the nape of his neck. "And I want to know more." Rising on her toes, she drew him down for a kiss.

The first brush of his lips was tentative, yet full of affection. Warmth trickled through her, banishing the cold that had settled inside and lingered all day. But he didn't deepen the contact.

She dropped back on her heels. "You haven't called a meeting with team leaders, have you?"

His eyebrows rose. "No. We won't do that until everyone is plan-et-side."

"Good." She captured his lips in another kiss, this one a little more ardent. "Wait. What's Jovan doing?"

He blinked. "He's..." His eyes lost focus for a moment. "He's cooking himself a meal."

Amusement rose. "He just ate."

Wonick shrugged. "Jovan is always hungry."

The youngest cyborg really *was* like a teenager. "So he isn't planning to come back down here anytime soon?"

"No. He's planning to spend several hours eating and watching entertainment vids while dropping crumbs everywhere and cluttering Savaas's quarters."

She laughed. "Is that what he usually does here?"

He smiled. "Yes." She liked that it amused him rather than irritated him.

"And he plans to spend the rest of the night up there?"

"Yes. He rarely has living quarters all to himself and is enjoying it. Why?"

Now *she* shrugged. "It seems like every time I want to get you naked, someone interrupts us. First the meeting last night. Then Jovan this morning."

He arched a brow. "You want to get me naked?"

"Very much so, yes." With his arousal prodding her stomach, it was kind of hard to miss that he wanted to get her naked, too. And she was totally on board with that.

A slow smile slid across his features. He was too damned handsome. "Then as you would say, let's do this."

She grinned. "Hell yes."

He dipped his head but stopped before kissing her. Straightening, he glanced toward the door.

"Wonick? What is it?"

"Savaas is contacting me."

"Damn it!" she growled. Savaas must be doing it on purpose. His timing was too perfect.

A dimple formed in Wonick's cheek as he tried to suppress a grin and sent her a mischievous look from the corner of his eye.

Laughing, Rachel slapped him on the shoulder. "You tease!"

Chuckles rumbled in his broad chest while he pretended to dodge the strike.

She shook her head. "I love it when you smile and laugh."

"Ditto," he replied, his smile softening.

Her whole being lightening, she leaned into him. "Come here, you."

This time, they kissed without interruption. Rachel expected another tentative brush of his lips. Instead, he swiftly deepened the kiss and slipped his tongue past her lips to stroke hers. Body heating, she wrapped her arms around him and pressed closer. Everything else fell away—the grief, the horror—leaving only her and Wonick and the way he made her feel.

When he slid a hand down to cup her bottom, she moaned. He lifted her onto her toes and urged her even tighter against him, aligning their hips. Rachel moaned again. It had been so long since she'd let hunger consume her. So long since she'd let any man close enough to inspire this burning need.

Wonick's hunger seemed to match her own as he slipped a hand between them and palmed one of her breasts. Pleasure shot through her when he teased her beaded nipple, stroking, pinching, and driving her mad.

"More," she purred.

He abandoned her breast long enough to tug the hem of her shirt from her pants. Then he slipped his hand beneath it, strong calloused fingers sparking delicious shivers as they smoothed their way up bare skin only to be stymied by her bra.

Swearing, Rachel pushed herself out of his arms and burst into a blur of motion. When she stilled, her shirt and bra were on the floor at her feet.

Wonick devoured her with his eyes. "You're beautiful," he professed, his voice gruff with desire.

"You are, too," she replied breathlessly, captivated by the heat in his gaze. "Now take your shirt off."

His hands twitched, as though eager to do her bidding, but remained at his sides as something new entered his gaze. A hesitance he hadn't manifested before.

"Wonick?"

A muscle ticced in his jaw. "I haven't done this since I enlisted in the cyborg program."

The confession both surprised and didn't surprise her. Yes, he was handsome as hell. Smart. Funny. Honorable. Affectionate. The full package. But he'd been very clear about how people viewed him. And he had never said he visited pleasure stations himself, just that he and his brethren had that option if they were interested.

Rachel tried for a little levity since she wasn't sure what was holding him back after their enthusiastic beginning. "If you're worried you've forgotten how, don't. I've never wanted a man this intensely in my long life." She fought a wince. Perhaps she shouldn't remind him how much older she was.

A flicker of amusement softened his features briefly. "Oh, I remember how it's done." His gaze made a slow foray down her half-bare body, making her tingle as if he'd touched her instead.

"Then what's holding you back?" she queried softly.

He sighed. Such a weary sound. "I bear many scars."

She glanced at his hands, recalling the fine lines that marred them.

"Not just my hands and arms," he murmured. "All over."

She stared at his chest, still covered by the shirt he hesitated to remove. He'd said the scientists had reinforced every bone with *alavinin*. And he'd had other surgeries as well. How many scars were there? "Why don't the nanobots that heal you make the scars disappear?" The virus she housed always eliminated such for her when she was wounded.

"They were only programmed to seal the wounds and speed internal healing." His lips turned up in a grim smile. "The Akseli scientists had no interest in *keeping us pretty*, as one once sneered. The more scars we bore, the more the enemy feared us."

She stepped closer to him. "Well, I don't fear you. Nor do I abhor your scars."

"You haven't seen them all."

No, she hadn't. "Then show me."

After another moment's pause, he reached over his shoulder, gripped the shirt at the nape of his neck, and tugged it over his head.

Rachel stared at him as the fabric dropped to the floor.

He did indeed bear many scars. Like those on his arms, pale ridges followed the lines of his collarbones and shoulders. Thicker scars marred his torso, attesting to multiple incision sites.

Multiple painful surgeries.

Multiple excruciating recoveries. All of which inspired as much fury in Rachel as the conditions of the bodies she'd found on the Gathendien ship.

But the scars didn't in any way repulse her. Nor did they divert her attention from his beautiful muscles. Wonick was ripped, as Americans were fond of saying. "I was right to name you Handsome." Rachel rested a hand on a muscled pec dusted with dark hair. "You're beautiful."

His brow furrowed. "How can you say that?"

"Because you are." When he looked as though he didn't believe her, she patted his chest. "I've fought in far more battles than you have, Wonick." She hated to remind him of her age again (apparently, they both had insecurities) but wanted to ensure that he believed her and could think of no other way. "I've incurred thousands of wounds over the centuries." She met his gaze. "Tens of thousands."

His frown deepened.

"If every one of them had left a scar, would you find me unattractive?"

The tension left his form. "No."

"Then believe me when I say you make my body burn." She trailed her fingers lightly across a thicker scar that reminded her of the Y-incision a pathologist performing an autopsy might make. "*All* of you makes my body burn." She smiled. "Although certain parts of you make me burn more than others." Sliding her hand down over his washboard abs, she ventured farther and cupped the heavy erection constrained by his pants.

Groaning, he dipped his head and captured her lips again, all hesitation gone.

Rachel stroked him through the sturdy cloth and pressed closer, wishing they were both naked. Withdrawing her touch, she slid a leg up the outside of his, hooked it over his hip, and opened herself to him.

Wonick groaned and palmed her bottom. "Wrap your legs around me," he ordered gruffly.

Hell yes. Rachel jumped up and wrapped both legs around him.

Turning, he took a couple of steps and pressed her against the nearest wall, positioning her so the heart of her rode his hard cock. Both moaned as he rocked against her. When he trailed a path of heated kisses down her neck, she tilted her head to give him better access.

"I want you," he nearly growled. "*All* of you."

She nodded. "Then we'd better ditch these clothes."

Pushing away from the wall, he spun and carried her to his bedroom with dizzying speed.

Rachel smiled. He could move almost as quickly as she could when he wanted to.

As soon as his door slid closed behind them, she lowered her feet to the floor and backed out of his embrace. A playful smile lit her pretty features. "I bet I can get naked faster than you can," she taunted.

He grinned. "I bet you're wrong."

They burst into a whirlwind of motion and stilled at the same moment. As soon as they looked at each other, they laughed despite the desire that rode them. Both were now gloriously naked... with their pants and underwear tangled around their ankles and the boots they couldn't toe off.

Shaking his head, Wonick bent and removed his boots. "You make everything fun, Rachel." Once he stepped out of his boots, socks, and the cloth tangled around his ankles, he straightened and closed the distance between them. "I haven't had fun in a long time," he admitted.

Her heart melted at the words. "Then you'd better buckle up, Handsome. Because we're going to have a *lot* of fun together, you and I."

"*Srul* yes." Grinning, he picked her up and tossed her onto the bed.

Rachel shrieked with surprise as she flew through the air and landed on the cushy mattress with a giggle.

Holy hell. When was the last time she'd felt carefree enough to giggle?

Wonick crossed to the bed and made short work of removing her boots and the remainder of her clothing.

Her heart hammered in her chest as he knelt on the edge of the mattress.

"You're beautiful," he murmured. Dark desire filled his reddish-brown eyes, replacing amusement, as he curled his fingers around one of her ankles and smoothed his hand up her calf.

Rachel found she couldn't speak, too entranced by the heat reflected in his face and the fire that threatened to consume her as he came down over her and settled his big warm body between her thighs.

She hadn't exaggerated when she'd told him she had never wanted a man this intensely before. And when she realized why...

It merely made her want him more.

She was *so* falling in love with him.

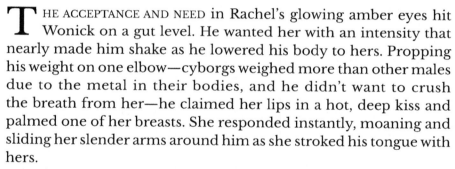

THE ACCEPTANCE AND NEED in Rachel's glowing amber eyes hit Wonick on a gut level. He wanted her with an intensity that nearly made him shake as he lowered his body to hers. Propping his weight on one elbow—cyborgs weighed more than other males due to the metal in their bodies, and he didn't want to crush the breath from her—he claimed her lips in a hot, deep kiss and palmed one of her breasts. She responded instantly, moaning and sliding her slender arms around him as she stroked his tongue with hers.

Drek, he needed her. Wanted to bury himself deep inside her and take her hard and fast.

But not yet.

Not yet.

He trailed heated kisses down her slender neck, over her collarbone, and lower. Closing his lips around the hard tip of a plump breast, he teased it with teeth and tongue. Again she moaned and writhed against him. The fingers of one of her small hands speared through his short hair and pressed him closer, urging him on as he sucked and stroked and drew moans from her.

Wonick had acquired most of his sexual experience with Akseli female partners. But in the early years of his military career—*before* he entered the cyborg program—he had allowed some of his soldier friends to lure him to Promeii 7 and a pleasure station or two, where he engaged in couplings with women from other planets. He was glad now that he had because it had taught him that female pleasure centers didn't differ much from species to species, leaving him confident in his ability to please Rachel.

Especially now that he knew his scars didn't repel her.

His body hard and aching, Wonick wanted this—their first coupling—to be good for her.

More than good for her. So, he kissed a path down her flat, muscled abs.

"Wonick," she breathed, shifting restlessly beneath him.

Sliding his arms beneath her parted knees, he took her with his mouth. She was already slick with need and became even more so as he licked and stroked and sucked the nub of her pleasure. Her hands fisted in the covers as she rocked her hips and her breath shortened. Every muscle tensed.

He slipped two fingers inside her warm passage, stroking and thrusting in rhythm with the sensual torment of his lips and tongue until she cried out with release. Her inner muscles clamped down on his fingers, clenching and unclenching.

How he wished he were buried deep inside her.

As soon as she collapsed back against the bedding, he acted on that wish. Rising over her, he settled between her parted thighs.

Rachel's beautiful breasts rose and fell quickly as she gazed up at him with eyes that glowed bright amber. "More," she demanded. "I want you inside me."

"*Srul* yes." He positioned his shaft at her entrance and pressed forward. She was tight and felt so *drekking* good. "Let me know if I hurt you." He didn't say it because he was big and she was so small. He hadn't done this since Akseli scientists had enhanced his strength and couldn't banish the fear that he might grip her too tightly or even thrust hard enough to cause her pain.

Nodding, she wrapped her arms around him. "Unless I say otherwise, don't hold back. As long as I don't complain, you aren't hurting me." She arched into him as he sank deeper. "Mmm. You feel so good, Wonick. Give me more."

His fears allayed, he continued to push forward in short thrusts, slowly stretching her, loving the feel of her, until he was buried to the hilt. "You're so tight," he whispered, nearly shaking with need.

"*Too* tight?" she asked.

"*Srul* no."

"Then take me, Handsome. Fast and hard."

Withdrawing until he almost left her entirely, he thrust deep.

"Yes," she moaned.

He thrust again, pleasure sparking through him like an electrical current. Then thrust again. And again. Harder. Faster. Pounding into her. Rachel slid her hands down to his ass and urged him on, her nails digging into his flesh.

"You're so beautiful," he whispered, altering the angle of his hips and grinding against her pleasure center with every thrust, intensifying the pleasure and taking them higher and higher until she threw her head back and cried out.

As soon as her inner muscles clamped down around him, squeezing and releasing, he stiffened with his own climax and poured his heat inside her. The pleasure seemed to go on and on. Far longer than he remembered.

When at last he was spent, Rachel tried to draw him down on top of her.

Wonick shook his head. "I don't want to crush you." Before she could protest, he rolled them to their sides, clamping one hand on her lovely ass to keep them joined. "*Alavinin* is heavy," he reminded her.

"Oh. Right." Smiling, she slid a leg up over his hip and urged him closer. "Would you be upset if I confessed I'm tempted to make a naughty joke about what *else* feels like it's been reinforced and made harder with *alavinin?*"

He laughed. "No." Warmth filled him while he studied her and waited for their breathing to calm. No one had ever made him feel the way Rachel did. No other female had brought him this wondrous contentment and peace. This desire to spend as much time with her as he possibly could because he loved everything about her.

The amber glow that lit her eyes faded as she stared at him with a sated smile.

"I didn't hurt you?" he asked softly, needing confirmation of it.

"Quite the opposite." She arched a brow. "Did I hurt *you*? I'm a little worried that if I examine that lovely muscled ass of yours, I'll find fingernail imprints from griping you too hard."

He grinned. "If they're evidence that I pleased you, I would wear them proudly."

"Hell yes, you pleased me." She kissed his chin then grinned. "Now I'm tempted to have the clothing generator make you a pair of assless pants so you can show them off to the boys."

He laughed as he imagined walking around the settlement with his ass hanging out of his pants.

When his shaft jerked inside her, she sucked in a breath. "You're already hard again?"

"Yes." Was it too soon for her? Did Earthlings need a longer recovery time after copulation? "My brothers mentioned it after visiting pleasure stations and think it's because of the nanobots."

Her brow puckered with puzzlement. "Akseli scientists wanted you to have a swifter recovery period after sex? That's... unexpected. And odd."

Wonick shook his head. "The scientists didn't want us to have sex at all." The thought of it usually called forth rage. But Rachel's presence soothed him. "After the last of our surgeries, we discovered that they tweaked something inside us to ensure we couldn't get hard."

Her mouth fell open. Then her eyes flashed with the same fury that had consumed him when he'd realized what they'd done. "Those mother-*drekking*..." An impressive array of profanity spilled forth.

Wonick waited for her to run out of steam. "As you can see..." He punctuated his words with a little thrust. "Taavion found a way around it for us."

All anger melted away as mischief sparkled in her amber eyes. "Remind me to thank him later." With that surprising strength of hers, she shoved him onto his back and straddled him, seating him deep inside her.

Rumbling his approval, Wonick rested his hands on her hips and admired her beautiful breasts.

She cast him a look of supreme innocence. "See anything you like, Handsome?"

"*Srul* yes."

"What about this?" Her inner muscles tightened around his shaft, squeezing him as she rotated her hips. "Do you like this?"

His grip tightened. "*Drek* yes."

Passion rising, they both began to move.

MUCH TO HER SURPRISE, Savaas didn't ask Rachel to spend the rest of her sojourn on the Gathendien ship. Rather he seemed content with her staying in the settlement with the rest of them.

Over the next week, she and Wonick fell into a routine. Every morning they joined the rest of the warriors in the commissary for breakfast, or what they called first meal. Then the others left to perform their duties.

Rachel liked that everyone had a place here. Every cyborg had a purpose. A job he happily performed to ensure their community would continue to flourish and further its expansion. Savaas and Wonick assigned each man specific duties... not just because they thought he would perform them well but because the two believed he would *enjoy* those duties.

After the years of misery they had endured, the cyborg leaders wanted to create a homeworld as peaceful as those Rachel had often dreamed of. It truly was a utopia. This was how she had imagined living on Lasara would be. Surrounded by people as different as she was, who accepted her and treated her the same way they did each other. Days spent making new friends. Finding productive pursuits she enjoyed that didn't entail hunting or killing. And falling in love with a good man who filled her with joy, sparked laughter, made her body burn, and inspired dreams of a happy future together that could encompass centuries if not millennia thanks to the nanobots inside him.

It was a good life. One she didn't want to end. But it *would*, when duty called her away.

Every morning after their breakfast settled, Rachel and Wonick went on a run together. Neither required the exercise to maintain their musculature. The virus gave Rachel her impressive strength. And Wonick had confided that carrying around the extra weight the *alavinin* reinforcements added to his frame kept his muscles strong. But it gave their respiratory systems a good workout, which he said he and his brethren needed for their hearts and lungs to remain strong enough to keep up with the rest.

Since she hadn't seen the other cyborgs out running around, Rachel wondered if that were really true or if Wonick merely used that as an excuse to spend more time with her.

She studied him from the corner of her eye as they jogged through the forest. Their boots made soft thuds on soil still moist from the previous night's rain. Dense foliage above provided her with protection from the sun even as it allowed enough light in to keep them from wading through complete darkness. Birds twittered in the branches. Furry rust-colored rodents that resembled squirrels with amusingly bushy tails scurried about. Every once in a while, one of the largest toads she'd ever seen would sail across in front of them, leaping a good fifteen feet.

She drew in a deep breath, enjoying the fresh air.

A smile toyed with Wonick's lips as he jogged beside her. He looked happy. Relaxed. Content.

Even that brought Rachel pleasure.

Wonick glanced at her and caught her staring. His eyes narrowed. "What?"

"I think you're full of it," she declared cheekily.

He smiled. "Full of what?"

"Full of bull. I don't think you really need these runs to stay in shape. I think your heart and lungs would work fine even if you became a couch potato."

His brow puckered with confusion. "Unless you're telling me that I've become a vegetable that sprouts from the cushions of what you call a couch, I think my translator got most of that wrong."

Rachel grinned. "I meant I think you aren't being honest about the reason for our jogs. I think you just take me on these runs to get me alone."

A slow smile lit his handsome features. "What's that response you always give when one of my brethren asks if you tampered with something in engineering and broke it?"

"I refuse to answer on the grounds that it may incriminate me?"

"Exactly."

She laughed.

His smile turned wry. "With so many of my brethren vying for your attention, the only times I can be alone with you are on these runs and in bed."

"I think vying for my attention is an exaggeration, but we *do* often have a lot of company." She feigned a sigh and pretended to fluff her hair, even though it bounced behind her in a ponytail. "That's the price one has to pay for being a musical legend."

His laughter emerged as a deep, carefree rumble that brought another smile to her face.

Nudging him with an elbow, she leaned in closer as though imparting a confidence. "I like being alone with you, too."

He slowed to a halt.

When Rachel stopped and turned to face him, he tilted her chin up and leaned down to press a slow kiss to her lips. "In truth, I enjoy every moment I spend with you, Rachel," he admitted, "whether we're alone or in the company of others."

Her heart fluttered in her chest. He didn't say it casually as he would to a friend. Or to a friend with benefits, as her Second would say. He said it with a depth of emotion that seemed to reflect everything *she* felt for *him*. It didn't matter what they did or who they were with. As long as the two of them were together, everything was... better. "Keep talking like that," she whispered, "and you'll make me fall in love with you."

She was already halfway there.

More than halfway. Instead of living out her life on Lasara, she now dreamed of returning here and spending centuries with Wonick.

He claimed her lips in another kiss that stole a little more of her heart. "Will falling in love with me encourage you to return after you finish searching for your missing friends?"

Leaning into him, she wrapped her arms around his waist. "If you feel the same way? Yes."

"I do," he murmured. "I admit I dread you leaving."

"I know," she whispered. "But it's something I have to do." And not just because Seth had tasked her with keeping her friends safe. Her friends meant as much to her as Wonick's brothers did to him. She needed to find them and get them safely to Lasara.

"I understand."

She knew he did. It merely made her love him more.

Turning them, he wrapped an arm around her shoulders and started walking back toward the settlement. "I also suggested these runs because I thought you might enjoy a little time outdoors. You spent four months aboard a warship with recycled air, followed by almost two months in a cramped escape pod."

"And I'll spend who knows how long aboard the *Tangata*." She couldn't exactly strike out for parts unknown herself. The more Rachel learned from cyborg engineers, the more certain she became that she couldn't fly that Gathendien warship all by herself. Joining Janwar and Simone's search seemed her only option.

"I think you'll find your sojourn aboard the *Tangata* more appealing than you anticipate. Unlike the *Kandovar*, it has a park with live plants."

Rachel slowed to a halt. "Really?"

He nodded. "They even keep small wildlife in it."

She narrowed her eyes. "They don't have any of those huge toads, do they? Because the other night when I accidentally startled one, it peed on me as it leapt past."

Laughing, he shook his head. "No. There aren't any of those." The gauntlet on his wrist beeped. Wonick glanced at it. "We should go. The transport to the Gathendien ship will depart soon, and we don't want to be left behind."

Rachel sent him a teasing grin. "Want to race?"

He regarded her with that adorably puzzled expression she loved. "Why would I want to race?" Then he flashed her a mischievous grin and zipped away at top cyborg speed.

"Cheater!" she called on a laugh and raced after him.

As they had every day after their jog, she and Wonick accompanied a contingent of other cyborgs up to the Gathendien ship. Rachel's mood often nose-dived whenever the clunky piece-of-crap vessel came into view. While Wonick helped the others continue to decrypt the millions of files they'd pilfered, Rachel headed to engineering to build upon the lessons Sinsta and her other Lasaran friends had taught her, hungry to know how these ships worked and what it took to keep them running.

Or to sabotage them. Who knew *what* Rachel might face during her upcoming search for her missing friends.

Her new cyborg buddies proved to be patient instructors. Sinsta, Endon, and the other Lasaran engineers were never far from her thoughts during those lessons. If Rachel sometimes blinked back tears or swiped at her cheeks while the cyborgs taught her, none of the men mentioned it. They just continued to work with her and help her learn.

As evening approached, Rachel inevitably found herself drawn back to the lab Taavion and Nebet occupied. Busy poring over the medical data and samples therein, they soon grew accustomed to her visits and offered no comment when she dragged a stool inside the refrigeration room and sat—deep in thought—beside the empty table Sinsta had once rested upon.

Executing Sinsta's captors, her torturers, her killers... didn't feel like enough. Sure, it had punished them with an eye-for-an-eye justice and would keep them from hurting others. But it wouldn't lessen the rest of their ilk's desire to wipe out every other sentient race in the freaking galaxy and claim the worlds and technology left behind for their power-hungry, never-satisfied, tyrannical asshole of an emperor. It may have halted *these* Gathendien scientists' search for more effective genocide-inducing bioweapons. But more like them would take up the cause, hungry for their emperor's approval.

The certainty of that peck-peck-pecked at Rachel like an angry crow perched on her shoulder. The fury it inspired vied with grief that would sometimes crash upon her in waves as she sat in that cold room, tears freezing on her cheeks. It was never going to end, was it? Gathendiens would never stop coming for Earthlings. Those bastards' determination would wreck *everything*. The Lasarans' hope for introducing Earthlings to their society to help shore up the birth rate and prevent their species from dying. Immortals' and *gifted ones*' plans to seek a new life on a planet with no war, famine, or hate to drive the rest of the populace to want to kill them.

Rachel didn't have to ask to know that Seth would allow no more *gifted ones* and immortals to travel to Lasara until the Gathendien threat was extinguished.

And Gathendiens would never stop hunting "special" Earthlings because Earth, she had concluded, was their Plan B. The bodies she had discovered on this dilapidated ship should make it very clear to the Aldebarian Alliance that whatever they had done to cripple the Gathendien military after the biological weapon attack on Lasara had not stopped them. It hadn't even subdued them. It would also reveal that Gathendiens didn't only want to eradicate Lasarans and Earthlings. They were creating bioweapons they could use to wipe out the Purvelis and Yona as well. And since many member nations of the alliance included Yona warriors in their military and security, killing off the Yona would leave most vulnerable.

According to Wonick and Savaas, the Aldebarian Alliance was preparing some kind of counterattack or other repercussions to weaken the Gathendiens and put them in their place.

But what *kind* of repercussions? Military strikes? Sanctions?

Either one would merely keep the Gathendiens from wiping out the Lasaran, Purveli, and Yona peoples. Earth would remain open to attack. And it was far enough away from alliance-occupied space that it would serve the Gathendiens well as a new home. No trade routes ventured near Earth. No scientific exploratory crews were interested in making the long trek to check it out.

Gathendiens could settle on Earth and live comfortably for eons, out of sight and out of mind of the alliance.

That was Rachel's fear anyway.

Oblivious to the cold temperatures that frosted her breath, she stared at the metal tables around her, still seeing the bodies that had occupied them. And as she did, a new idea took root. The more she considered it, the more grief transformed into determination.

She'd been asking herself what more she could do. Now she knew.

She just had to figure out how the hell she could accomplish it.

CHAPTER FOURTEEN

WONICK SMILED AND HELD Rachel's hand as she bounced from foot to foot beside him, full of jubilant energy. She was absolutely beautiful. And so very precious to him. Out of all the future scenarios that had whirled around in his imagination since securing his freedom from Aksel, Wonick would've thought finding love the least likely to come to fruition.

And yet he loved Rachel. He felt for her all the things he'd seen reflected in his father's face each time he'd smiled at Wonick's mother.

Turning her pretty face up to the sky, Rachel watched the *Tangata* break atmosphere.

"Wow," she breathed, taking in the massive warship's sleek black exterior. "That makes the Gathendien warship look like something this one shat."

Wonick and the cyborgs who had accompanied them laughed.

The *Tangata* was one of their greatest accomplishments. It had taken the cyborgs years to design and construct it. Only one other ship like it existed, hidden away in case the cyborgs should ever have to abandon their new home.

"You built that?" Rachel asked as the huge ship approached.

"Yes." They stood in the shadows at the edge of a dense forest that surrounded the only clearing large enough to accommodate such a large ship.

"It's beautiful. And so quiet!" she exclaimed as it grew closer.

Wonick nodded. If he listened closely enough, his cybernetic implants would pick up the hum of the engines. But he wouldn't have noticed it prior to being modified.

Rachel frowned. "I don't see any rockets." Apparently, Earth's space vessels were primitive enough to rely on liquid fuels to propel them off Earth's surface. Some rockets, she'd told him, burned so hot and produced so much noise that great pools of water had to be constructed beneath them to reduce heat and dampen sound vibrations produced during launches.

"We don't use rockets."

"Then how do your ships launch and land?"

"They manipulate the planet's natural magnetic and gravitational fields."

"I don't know what that means, but it sounds brilliant."

He grinned.

The only wind gusts produced by the *Tangata*'s landing resulted from a natural breeze diverting around the colossal structure. Wonick couldn't tell whether Rachel's ponytail bounced and jounced from the wind or from her inability to stand still. Her excitement over the impending reunion with her friends was both tangible and a joy to behold.

He loved seeing her happy.

Landing platforms extended from the base of the ship and sank into the grass. Before the engines even finished powering down, one of the smaller cargo bay doors slid open.

Her friends must be as eager to reunite as Rachel.

A ramp descended to the ground.

When Rachel would've darted forward, Wonick clung to her hand and held her back. "Let them come to you. I don't want the sun to burn you."

If the sunlight would've only affected *her*, he suspected she would've raced out there anyway. But her Immortal Guardian friend, Simone, would also suffer if they gathered in the bright clearing.

Radiating impatience, Rachel continued to shift from side to side and cling to his hand.

A small group appeared at the top of the ramp. Six males. Two females.

Rachel immediately released Wonick's hand and started jumping up and down, waving her arms.

As soon as the two females saw her, they took off running down the ramp.

The Immortal Guardian ran so swiftly that she seemed to disappear.

"*Drek*, she's fast," Nebet muttered.

Simone slammed into Rachel with such force that the two of them flew back several steps and nearly tumbled to the ground. Both burst into an endearing blend of tears and laughter as they hugged tightly.

Simone looked enough like Rachel that the two could be mistaken for sisters, except Simone was a little taller. Both women had long dark hair and brown eyes that glowed amber with emotion. Both bore the same slender yet muscular build. They even spoke at the same time, interrupting and finishing each other's sentences. But Simone's words carried what Rachel had told him was a French accent, while Rachel's was British.

The other female caught up, breathing hard from her brief sprint down the ramp and across the meadow. Rachel and Simone drew her into their hug. The three squeezed into such a tight knot that it was a wonder the immortals didn't smother the third one. Liz was the *gifted one* who had suffered much after being captured by the Gathendiens. About the same size as Rachel, she looked far more fragile than the other two, with limbs that were almost skeletal. No wounds or scars marred her visible skin. But Wonick thought her overly pale.

Janwar and his crew strolled after them.

Everyone aboard the *Tangata* was as wanted... or *un*wanted... as the cyborgs who had built the ship for them, something that had helped solidify the bond Wonick and his brothers shared with them, as well as the trust they placed in one another. Janwar and his cousin Krigara had sizable bounties on their heads, placed there by Chancellor Astennuh for their efforts to clear their parents' names after Astennuh declared them terrorists and slew them... *and* for aiding in the cyborg rebellion.

The Rakessian brothers, Srok'a and Kova, followed. Srok'a displayed the traditional markings on his face and body that almost all Rakessians were born with. Kova did not, and the rest of his planet had hated and ostracized him for it all his life. Instead of the sleek dark markings of his brother, he bore scars that a band of Rakessians had carved into his flesh when he had been too young to fight them off. Both brothers, like Janwar and Krigara, were wanted on their planet for later tracking down and killing the men responsible... as well as the medics who—blinded by their hatred—had treated Kova's wounds with a substance that would worsen the scarring instead of preventing it and left him to die without giving him the transfusion he needed after the blood loss he'd suffered.

Elchan was a Segonian, like the commander Rachel's friend Eliana had fallen in love with. Most members of the Aldebarian Alliance believed that advanced technology gave the Segonians their remarkable ability to camouflage themselves in battle. But Wonick and his brothers had poked their noses into enough classified files to learn that all Segonians were born with a biological ability to blend in with their surroundings so well that they appeared to be invisible. The military had taken advantage of this, creating armor that would react to the chemical changes in Segonians' skin and mimic that camouflage. But Elchan's natural ability didn't always work as it should and had proven unreliable, preventing him from serving in the military.

A majority of Segonians tended to be like Lasarans—friendly to everyone regardless of their differences in appearance, background, or beliefs. But Elchan's father, career military and a hard-hearted *grunark*, couldn't get past the fact that the military had rejected his son because of his "failings" and made Elchan's life miserable. He also wielded enough power on Segonia to ensure that Segonians who ordinarily would *not* have ostracized Elchan did so out of fear of retribution, deepening Elchan's belief that he was inherently flawed.

Soval, the largest of the lot with muscles thicker than the cyborgs' and a bluish tint to his skin, was a bit of a mystery—to the cyborgs as well as to himself. The hulking Domaran warrior had awoken on the streets of Promeii 7 with no memory of who he was or how he had come to be there, and he still had no clue. Years of fighting in the colosseum had given him the opportunity to meet Janwar, and the two had forged a strong friendship.

Since none of Janwar's crew could ever go home, they had made a new one aboard the *Tangata* and were as close as Wonick and his brothers were.

Janwar smiled and extended an arm as he approached. "It's good to see you, my friend."

Wonick clasped Janwar's arm and drew him into a hardy hug. "Glad you made it here without making any more life-threatening excursions."

The notorious pirate laughed.

Savaas took a turn clasping Janwar's arm in greeting. "You didn't allow your new Segonian friends to follow you, did you?"

"I did not. T assured us that our new colleagues planted no tracking devices on the ship before they disembarked. And we took a circuitous route after parting until distance took us off their radar."

"Much appreciated."

Simone tore herself away from her friends and approached them. "Hello, Wonick." Wrapping her arms around his waist, she gave him a tight hug. "Thank you for rescuing Rachel."

Shocked, he stared down at her then shot Janwar a look.

His friend looked as though he wanted to laugh. "It's okay. You can hug her back. I won't—as Simone would say—turn caveman and get angry."

Only understanding part of that and unused to the familiarity, Wonick gingerly patted Simone's back.

Liz hung back but offered him a shy smile. "Yes. Thank you for rescuing Rachel."

"Rachel didn't *need* rescuing," he pointed out as Simone withdrew. "She found her way here on her own, then slew the Gathendiens herself."

"Hey, you guys helped," Rachel insisted with a smile, "*after* I got over being pissed at you for not telling me earlier that you were here." Crossing to Janwar, she hugged him tight. "Thank you for keeping Simone from dying when those Gathendien bastards poisoned her."

Much to Wonick's surprise, jealousy didn't slither through him. He remembered experiencing that unwelcome emotion in his youth when a female he desired had passed him over for another. But now happiness filled him over Rachel taking an instant liking to his friend.

"*And* for saving Liz," she added as she backed away.

Janwar shook his head. "I didn't rescue Liz. Kova did."

Rachel scanned the small crew. "Who's Kova?"

Janwar pointed. The scarred Rakessian warrior froze and looked incredibly uncomfortable when all eyes turned upon him.

Rachel didn't seem to notice. Walking up to him, she drew him into a hug, too.

These Earth females certainly were an affectionate bunch.

A flush darkened Kova's cheeks as he awkwardly patted Rachel's back. "I believe Liz would've soon freed herself without my aid," he murmured.

But Liz shook her head. "Don't you believe it." Her accent, Rachel had mentioned earlier, was American. When Rachel backed away, Liz crossed to Kova's side and touched the somber warrior's arm. "He kicked a *lot* of ass and was seriously injured getting me out of there."

Wonick noted the causal contact and slid Savaas a glance.

Savaas's eyebrows rose the tiniest fraction. *These Earthlings could befriend a Dotharian, couldn't they?* he commented over their private mental channel.

Wonick bit back a laugh. As far as they knew, only one Dotharian existed in the galaxy. The massive genetically engineered creature fought in the largest arena on Promeii 7 and tended to eat its opponents.

Soft thuds sounded as another figure descended the ramp.

Rachel gaped. "Who is *that*?"

Simone grinned. "That's T, the *Tangata*'s sentient AI program. Sometimes he downloads into the bodies of androids to complete physical tasks."

"Sentient, as in he can feel?" Rachel asked, eyes wide.

"Emotions? Yes. You're going to love him." She waved at the android. "T, come meet my friend."

DIANNE DUVALL

Sunlight gleamed on the white metal plating that formed the android's body, another advanced creation of the cyborgs. Though his faceplate showed no emotion, plenty of it came through when he spoke.

"T," Simone said once he joined them, "this is Rachel. Rachel, this is T."

Rachel extended a hand. "Hi. It's nice to meet you."

T clasped her hand and shook it in the traditional Earth manner. "It is nice to meet you as well."

Rachel grinned big as she withdrew her hand. "I hope you won't think this is rude. But you're the first android I've ever met, and you are freaking *awesome*!"

"Oh my," T responded, his vocals reflecting pleasure. "Thank you for noticing."

Janwar laughed. "If you're anything like Simone and Liz, you'll want to ply him with questions, but that will have to wait. He has to help us offload the cargo we brought."

A second android identical to T started down the ramp with an AB controller in one hand. A pallet heaped with heavy supplies floated after him.

"I'll have a team give the *Tangata* a quick check," Savaas said, "to ensure you have ample power, weapons, and provisions moving forward."

Janwar gave him a nod of thanks. "We lost a C-23, ten K-6s, a fighter, and two T androids."

Rachel glanced at Wonick. "What are C-23s and K-6s?"

"A C-23 is a small stealth craft that can be useful in covert operations. K-6s are unmanned craft that serve as surveillance or fighter drones." Thanks to Janwar, the cyborgs had the means to manufacture both.

Savaas's eyebrows rose. "Been having fun, have you?"

Janwar laughed. "They were destroyed when Kova freed Liz from a Gathendien ship."

"A ship we blew up," Kova added.

Liz grinned. "But not before I walked away with a huge armored mechanical suit the Gathendiens had on board."

260

Rachel stared at her. "A mechanical suit? Do you mean exo-armor?"

Simone grinned, her eyes bright. "No. Think Lieutenant Ripley in *Aliens*."

Rachel's eyes widened. "Cool."

That piqued Wonick's curiosity. Rachel seemed as awed by that as she was T.

Janwar shook his head. "I've never seen anything quite like it. It clearly wasn't designed for a Gathendien. I'm not sure where they got it, but the *grunarks* probably intend to replicate the technology and implement it in their military. So you're going to want to examine that. Liz here is the only one who can operate it."

Rachel nudged Liz and whispered, "Girl power."

Liz grinned.

Savaas looked intrigued. "We'll do that. And we'll replace the C-23 and K-6s."

Rachel turned to him, her face full of surprise. "You just happen to have some of those on hand?"

Savaas smiled. "We don't just tend crops all day. We work on munitions as well to increase the defenses at our disposal." He shifted his attention back to Janwar. "We'll also replace the android bodies you lost."

"Thank you. I appreciate it. As much as I'd like to stay longer, we should leave tomorrow."

Wonick's gaze shot to Rachel. His chest tightened at the regret and resignation that filled her eyes. He wished he could convince them all to stay longer. A few days maybe. Or a week. A month. But time was running out for their friends who may still be in escape pods. And delaying the inevitable would only make Rachel's departure harder.

"Do you need help unloading the cargo?" Rachel asked.

Wonick forced a smile. "No. We've got this."

Simone wrapped an arm around Liz's narrow shoulders. "If it's all right, I'd like Liz to see your chief medical officer."

Liz shook her head. "I'm fine, Simone. Janwar said so. I just need to put on some weight."

Janwar shook his head. "I never underwent a medic's formal training. Taavion knows far more than I do. I'd feel better if he examined you and ensured we're doing everything we can to help you regain your health."

Though Liz's frown conveyed reluctance, she capitulated with a nod.

"We'll head there now," Rachel said. Returning to Wonick's side, she smiled up at him. "Are you sure you don't want our help? Simone and I could probably unload that cargo in half the time."

"I'm sure."

Leaning up, she gave him a quick kiss on the lips and patted his chest. "Okay. See you later."

"See you later."

Turning away, she took Liz's hand. Conversation erupted as the three women strode away. Liz said something that made Rachel and Simone both throw their heads back and laugh.

Wonick smiled as he watched them disappear into the trees. Once they left his sight, he looked away... and froze.

Janwar, Krigara, Srok'a, Kova, Elchan, and Soval all stared at him.

Even T studied him, his metal head tipping to one side as though he were trying to figure something out.

"What?" Wonick asked defensively.

Smiling, Jawar shook his head. "Looks like Commander Dagon and I aren't the only ones who've succumbed to an Earthling's charms."

The others grinned knowingly, including Kova, who rarely cracked a smile.

Drek. Was that the heat of a blush creeping into Wonick's cheeks?

Forcing it down, he gave them a nonchalant shrug. "I don't know why she cares for me, but I'm sure as *srul* glad she does."

Janwar clapped him on the shoulder. "Me, too, brother. Now let's get this *bura* off my ship and join the Earthlings. I could listen to them banter all day. It's incredibly entertaining. You don't want to miss it."

No, he didn't. "Let's get to work."

R ACHEL COULDN'T STOP SMILING. Taavion had given Liz a clean bill of health, agreeing that she would fully regain her strength as long as she continued to consume a healthy diet and gradually resumed exercising. He said the psychological trauma that lingered—her aversion to enclosed spaces and the nightmares that plagued her—would fade in time, too.

At least, he thought they would. No one could say for sure. They could only hope.

Taavion also asked permission to draw blood from both Simone and Liz. "I need additional samples to test the effects Akseli and synthetic blood have on the virus, and I didn't want to take more from Rachel while her supply of Segonian blood remained limited."

"Liz isn't an immortal," Rachel reminded him.

Taavion nodded. "But her blood and scans will provide me with a before-and-after-understanding of your physiology, Rachel. You're a *gifted one* transformed into an immortal by a virus created by Gathendiens. Liz is a *gifted one* who is bereft of that virus. Noting the differences you bear will help me understand the virus better."

The human network that aided Immortal Guardians had been studying the virus for generations. They knew pretty much everything there was to know about it. But Taavion had that super AI calculating ability, which Wonick said had enabled them to evolve and advance their technological thinking far faster than ordinary Akselis, so maybe he could find something the network doctors had missed. Like a cure. A way to eliminate their photosensitivity and reduce their need for blood transfusions. Or a way for immortals to have children *without* passing the virus on to their babies.

"It's okay," Liz said with a smile. "I'm fine with it." She turned to Taavion. "It won't leave a mark, will it? Kova might worry if he sees one."

Rachel arched a brow. "Kova?" The quiet, scarred warrior with the cat's eyes she'd hugged earlier?

Simone grinned and whispered in a loud aside, "He seems quite taken with her."

Taavion's eyebrows flew up as he studied the Earthling in question. When Liz flushed bright red, he hastily concealed his surprise and promised it wouldn't leave a mark.

Minutes later, the three women left the infirmary. Rachel gave her friends a brief tour of the cyborg settlement while they caught up on everything that had happened since the *Kandovar*'s destruction. Aware of Savaas's paranoia, she didn't show them much. Just the commissary, the cluster of cyborg homes, and some of the agricultural plots.

Smiling, Rachel shook her head as they walked through an orchard that produced purple fruit that tasted like pears. "I can't believe you fell in love with the most dangerous pirate in the galaxy."

Simone grinned. "How could I not? Janwar is irresistible."

Liz smiled. "And he's not an asshole like most pirates. He's more of a Robin Hood."

Simone nodded. "He only steals from Chancellor Astennuh, the Akseli elite who support him, the Akseli military, Gathendiens, and the like."

Rachel waved a hand. "I already knew he wasn't an asshole. Wonick wouldn't have risked everything to help him if he were."

"Speaking of Wonick," Simone said, a wicked gleam entering her brown eyes. "I couldn't help but notice you two seem close."

"We are. *Very* close," Rachel said meaningfully. "I'm not sure how it happened so fast, but I've totally fallen for him." Her brow furrowed as dread and sadness struck at the thought of leaving him on the morrow.

Liz's face lit with cautious joy. "Does he love you, too?"

"I think so."

Simone snorted. "I know so. His eyes practically shine with it whenever he looks at you. How the hell did you get Wonick to shift so quickly from begging Janwar to come get you to not wanting you to leave?"

Rachel laughed. "How did *you* manage to snare Janwar's love? He and his crew are supposedly as jaded and distrustful as the cyborgs."

"I have Lisa and little Abby to thank for that. They won the *Tangata* crew's hearts during their stay with them."

Liz gave Rachel an exuberant hug. "Well, however you did it, I'm glad you and Wonick found each other. That's wonderful!"

When her friend backed away, Rachel mustered a mournful smile. "Not so wonderful. I'm leaving tomorrow, remember?"

Liz bit her lip as her expression clouded.

Simone frowned. "Why don't you ask him to come with us? He can help us find the rest of our missing friends. I know Janwar wouldn't mind him joining us."

"I can't ask that of him. It's too dangerous. He and Savaas were the faces of the cyborg rebellion. The Akseli government splashed their likenesses across billions of the space equivalent of wanted posters. If Wonick came with us, he would risk someone recognizing him everywhere he went." It was why, he'd once confessed, he had never accompanied fellow cyborgs to pleasure stations. "If even one person or one camera equipped with facial recognition software identified him, it would launch a new cyborg manhunt, because the bounties on his and Savaas's heads make the one on Janwar's seem miniscule."

Simone whistled. "Janwar's bounty is massive."

"I know. And if we have to battle Gathendiens or whoever else to rescue our friends and Wonick's helmet is damaged enough to short out the camo he uses..."

"It would leave his face on display for all to see." Simone nibbled her lip. "He could always remain on the ship."

Rachel shook her head. "How happy would you have been if you'd had to remain on the ship every time Janwar and his crew went up against the Gathendiens and sought to free our friends?"

She grimaced. "Not happy at all."

"Exactly."

Silence fell as they headed back toward the hub of the settlement.

Rachel cast her friends a hesitant glance. "Do you think it would anger the Lasarans if I came back here once everyone is safe? Not that they can know where *here* is. *Or* who I want to live out the rest of my days with."

"We'll have to come up with something else to tell them," Simone said. "But I don't think they'll object. Taelon said King Dasheon and Queen Adiransia are upset over failing to transport us all to Lasara safely. You know how big they are on rules. Inadvertently breaking their promise to keep us safe has rattled them."

"But it wasn't their fault." Blaming the Lasarans for what had happened hadn't even crossed Rachel's mind. "No ship has ever attacked another within a *qhov'rum*."

"Yet they feel responsible and are trying to do whatever they can to make it up to us. They've already okayed Eliana staying with Dagon on the *Ranasura* and me staying with Janwar on the *Tangata*. They've also promised to help smooth things over with Purvel and ensure Ava will have no problem marrying Jak'ri and settling there once we're all accounted for. They're basically doing everything they can to appease us *and* to keep Seth happy so he'll let more of us from Earth travel to Lasara once the danger passes."

Liz touched her arm. "They were fine with me staying on the *Tangata*, too. I don't think they'll object."

Simone's smile grew. "Don't worry. You'll be able to return to your handsome cyborg lover."

Some of the ache in her chest eased. "And live happily ever after."

Exiting the forest, they headed toward the commissary.

"Rachel?" Simone said, her voice hesitant.

Rachel studied her. "Yes?"

Simone slowed to a halt and shared a glance with Liz. "We were wondering..."

Liz met Rachel's gaze. "We'd like to go up to the Gathendien ship."

Rachel's mind blanked. "Why?"

They shared a look without speaking.

Realization dawned, bringing with it dread and grief. "You want to see the Lasarans and Yona I found?"

Simone nodded. "We made a lot of friends on the *Kandovar*. If any of them are among the victims, we'd like to pay our respects and say our goodbyes."

Her throat thickening, Rachel nodded. "We'll go after mid meal."

The trip ended up being cathartic for all of them. Taavion and the other med techs had carefully prepared the bodies for storage in cryopods they would transfer to the *Tangata* in the morning. Once Janwar's search for other Earthling survivors ended, he would deliver the bodies to Lasara.

Prince Taelon knew Janwar well enough not to ask too many questions. So telling him Rachel had found the deceased on the Gathendien ship that tried to capture her would suffice *without* mentioning the cyborgs.

Like Rachel, Simone and Liz recognized many of the faces. None were close friends, the way Sinsta had been to Rachel. But they represented the many aboard the *Kandovar* who had welcomed them all with a kindness the people of Earth never had and never would.

Though the three returned to the planet with pink noses and red-rimmed eyes, they enjoyed the rest of the day together. At Wonick's suggestion, Rachel and her friends joined him, Savaas, Jovan, and the *Tangata* crew in Wonick's living quarters for last meal instead of the commissary. Rachel suspected it was for Liz's sake. The day had clearly tired her friend.

Laughter abounded while the *Tangata* crew and the cyborg group exchanged anecdotes of recent battles and adventures.

As the meal wound down, Savaas leaned back in his chair and turned to Janwar. "Have you finished decrypting the data you retrieved from the base?"

Janwar absently toyed with a lock of Simone's hair. "No. There's still a lot we haven't sorted through. I'd like to hand it over to you. You'll get through it far faster than we can."

Savaas nodded. "I'll assign a team to it tonight."

Liz glanced at Wonick and Savaas. "Have you learned anything helpful?"

Wonick hesitated. "We learned that the Gathendiens don't notify other ships of their live cargo."

Liz stiffened. "Live cargo?"

"It's how they refer to captives," he offered apologetically. "They're so eager to be the first to please their emperor that they don't engage in the free exchange of information with each other.

The ship Rachel commandeered was completely unaware that other Gathendiens had captured Purvelis for study."

Simone's face clouded with frustration. "So no one knows what if any Gathendien ship have Earthlings or other *Kandovar* survivors aboard?"

Savaas nodded. "Only the emperor knows."

Rachel sat up straighter. "Wait. The emperor knows?"

"Yes," he confirmed. "We're still wading through their past communications but have decrypted several from the emperor that were only viewed by the commander. None of the other personnel saw them, nor do we believe they would've understood them if they had. It took us days to break the code used in the messages. But they indicate that the commander of this ship ranked high in the emperor's favor."

Fury burned through Rachel. "Because they collected and killed so many study subjects?"

"Yes. The emperor praised him for seizing more than any other commander and—at the same time—criticized him for capturing no Earthlings."

Rachel seethed inside. *That bastard!*

Simone spoke. "Do you know where the other ships are?"

"That's another no, I'm afraid," Savaas told them. "They're all operating in the dark."

Wonick grunted. "Because they know Aldebarian Alliance ships are swarming through the cosmos, looking for survivors."

Frustration battered Rachel. "So we don't know where *any* of the Gathendien ships are?"

"No," Savaas confirmed. "However..." Leaning forward, he braced his elbows on the table. "We *did* discover something Janwar here can pass along to his royal Lasaran friend."

Janwar's eyebrows rose. "What's that?"

"The communications that were commander's-eyes-only bounced through multiple relays, each leading us to a different source. But my men detected a pattern."

"Meaning?" Rachel prodded.

"Meaning, we believe we know where the Gathendien emperor is hiding."

Rachel stared at him. "You do?"

"It's what you would call an educated guess, but it's the most we've had to go on since Gathendiens left alliance-occupied space."

"Is he on a ship?" she pressed.

"No. We believe he's settled on a small planet with an unknown number of military personnel and civilians."

"Are they holding any of my friends there?"

Regret shadowed his features. "No. In several of his communications, the emperor expressed his frustration and demanded the commander prove his worth by doing what his compatriots have failed to do—bring him an Earthling."

Rachel, Simone, and Liz all swore.

Savaas held up a hand. "We think the emperor's second-in-command may be related to the commander we slew. He was pushing hard for the latter to get his head out of his ass and bring glory to their clan."

"Oh brother," Liz muttered.

"He didn't come right out and say it," Savaas continued, "but he implied—in communications Nebet just read today—that another was on the cusp of succeeding."

Rachel leaned forward. "So one of the ships *has* captured an Earthling? One that we haven't destroyed or seized?"

"Yes. But we only have a commander's name, not a location of his ship or its call signs."

Janwar frowned thoughtfully. "Pulcra may be able to help us with those."

Simone grimaced. "That asshole?"

Rachel glanced at Janwar. "Who's Pulcra?"

"He owns the largest fighting arena on Promeii 7."

Simone's face suddenly brightened. "And a Dotharian."

Puzzled, Rachel stared at her. "What's a Dotharian?"

Simone grinned. "I'll show you a vid later. I can't wait for you to see it."

Liz nodded. "You're going to freak."

Janwar shook his head. "Pulcra tipped us off to the location of the base we infiltrated." He smiled at Simone. "Think you can convince him to help us?"

"Of course."

"Then Promeii 7 will be our first stop."

And they would leave in the morning.

Her mind whirling with intel and dread and *what if*s, Rachel took Wonick's hand.

T HE NEXT DAY, WONICK studied Rachel surreptitiously as they shared first meal in the commissary. She sat across the table, facing him, with Simone on one side of her and Liz on the other. Janwar and his crew took the seats beside Simone and on Wonick's left. Jovan and Savaas sat on Wonick's other side.

Though Wonick missed the feel of Rachel next to him—the brush of her arm against his, the way she would rest a hand on his thigh—he liked watching the expressions flit across her pretty face.

Today, that ended up tipping him off that something was up, as Rachel would say. On the surface, she smiled and joked with Jovan, Savaas, and the others in the commissary. But a niggling uneasiness rose inside him, increasing in intensity as he noted subtle changes in her behavior.

When they had awoken that morning, she'd lured him into lovemaking more intense than any they'd previously shared. A hint of desperation had lingered in her kisses and touch. And the same had driven *him* because she would leave today.

Wonick had tried very hard not to think about what would happen when the *Tangata* left. Several of her friends were still missing. Of course, Rachel wanted to join Simone and the rest of the *Tangata* crew in searching for them. They *had* to find her friends before it was too late.

He knew that.

He understood that.

The two of them had just had so little time together that he wasn't ready to say goodbye.

Not that this *was* goodbye, he swiftly reminded himself. Once she found her friends and ferried them safely to Lasara, Rachel intended to return. She'd said it more than once prior to the *Tangata*'s arrival.

Anxiety struck when he abruptly realized that she hadn't said it since.

He swiftly skimmed through the events of the previous day and determined it was true.

Had she changed her mind?

Drek, the thought of losing her drove a knife through his heart. Wonick had never thought he would fall in love. After the rebellion, he'd thought he would never have the *opportunity* to. And yet, it had happened. He loved Rachel with a depth that left him in awe when he lay awake at night, holding her against his side while she slept. Rachel filled all the empty places inside him. And the memories they'd created would do the same once she'd gone and comfort him until her return.

But *would* she return?

She'd seemed eager to do so... until today.

Today he gained the sinking feeling that she'd changed her mind. That once she left, he would never see her again.

As first meal wound down, Rachel swept her gaze over the faces at the table. "I have an announcement."

Wonick's tension levels shot up.

The cyborgs at the other tables, having heard her request, shared uncertain looks and stopped eating.

Silence fell.

It was not a comfortable one.

"What's on your mind, Rachel?" Savaas asked.

She glanced at Simone and Liz but avoided Wonick's gaze. "I know you all expect me to leave on the *Tangata* this afternoon."

His heart skipped a beat. Had she decided to stay? Was *that* why she acted strangely?

"Yes," Savaas acknowledged, wariness creeping into his deep voice.

"Well, there's been a change of plans."

Simone's brow furrowed as she regarded her friend. "Rachel?"

Even Simone didn't know?

Liz stared at her, her surprise evident. "You don't want to come with us?"

"I do," Rachel said, her voice ringing with sincerity. "I really do. There are nine of us out there, still missing. But you don't need me to find them or to help you rescue them."

Simone shook her head. "You don't kno—"

"I can be of better use elsewhere and..." She cast Wonick a quick look before turning back to her friends. "There's something I need to do."

That sounded as if she didn't intend to remain with the cyborgs either.

Simone studied her friend for so long that he wondered if the two were communicating telepathically, but her next words belied that. "So, what's the plan?"

Rachel flattened her hands on the table and stared down at them. "I've thought about this. A *lot*. Every day while I sat in that damn freezer room on the Gathendien ship and stared at Sinsta's..." She swallowed hard and blinked back sudden tears. "At the table Sinsta died on."

"Thought about what?" Simone asked softly.

Rachel's jaw clenched. "How to end this shit. Once and for all."

When Simone sent Wonick a questioning glance, he gave the slightest shake of his head. He didn't know what she had in mind.

When Rachel raised her head and faced them, fury painted her features. "You all saw the bodies." Her gaze met Simone's. Liz's. Wonick's. Savaas's. One by one, she pinned them all in place and vented her rage. "You saw what they did to Sinsta." She motioned to Liz. "You know what they did to Liz. How they studied her like a lab rat. Ava, too. And Allison, whom Simone said now wakes up screaming every night, all because the Gathendiens want to wipe out every person on Earth."

Liz's throat worked in a swallow.

Kova frowned, his scarred face reflecting such concern that for a moment, Wonick thought he would go to her.

"They did the same damn thing to Jak'ri and Ziv'ri," Rachel said, referring to the Purveli males her friend Ava had been incarcerated

272

with, "and to the Purvelis Simone found. To the Lasarans, whose corpses occupy the cryopods beside Sinsta's. To the Yona. They rendered most of the female population of Lasara infertile with their damn bioweapons. The Gathendiens don't just want to conquer and claim Earth. They want it *all*. Lasara. Purvel. Whatever planet the Yona live on. It wouldn't surprise me if they were also targeting the Segonians."

Rachel's voice rose as she continued. "*Gathendiens* are the reason Simone and I and the rest of my immortal brethren have had to spend thousands of years hunting psychotic vampires night after night. And they're the reason thousands upon thousands of Earthlings lose their sanity and their lives every year. Because of the virus they released on Earth the *first* time. Now they're looking for another? It's never going to end! They're never going to stop! They're just going to keep harming and killing to further their greedy fucking aims and leave *us* to pick up the pieces and mourn the dead!"

No one present could deny that.

Rachel shook her head, her features full of bitterness. "The Aldebarian Alliance already tried to stop the Gathendiens once. They decimated the Gathendien military and sent them scuttling to the ass end of the galaxy with their tails tucked between their legs. Well, guess what. It didn't work. The bastards spent the next few decades rebuilding their army and crafting new plans. And look what they've done since."

Quiet fell. Heavy. Somber.

Time ticked past.

Rachel shifted her attention to Savaas. "You said the alliance is already discussing retaliation and repercussions."

"Yes."

"Well, that's not good enough for me. I'm not content to sit back and wait to see if destroying more ships and enacting sanctions will shut those bastards down. That shit didn't work the first time. I have no reason to believe it'll work now. None of us do."

Savaas tapped the tabletop with an index finger. "Then what do you propose?"

Leaning back in her chair, she crossed her arms over her chest. "The only thing that will make it stop. I'm going to cut off the head of the snake."

Simone swore.

Wonick stared at Rachel blankly. "What?"

Her eyes met his. And in them, he read determination and defiance. "I'm going to assassinate the Gathendien emperor."

CHAPTER FIFTEEN

S TUNNED SILENCE GRIPPED THE room in the wake of Rachel's announcement. But it didn't last long. Several of her friends—new and old—spoke at once, throwing a cacophony of words at her that jumbled together in an indecipherable mess.

She slid Wonick a look.

His whole body had stiffened. And the more time passed, the more anger darkened his features until he looked ready to explode. "Enough!" he bellowed.

Everyone ceased talking.

A muscle twitched in his jaw. And she didn't need her exceptional hearing to know he ground his teeth. "You what?" he forced out past stiff lips.

"I'm going to assassinate the Gathendien emperor."

When Wonick opened his mouth, Savaas clamped a hand on his shoulder.

Rachel surveyed them all, trying hard to keep the alarmed looks on Simone's and Liz's faces from swaying her. "He's the one these bastards are working their asses off to impress. He's the one with delusions of grandeur that make him think he should rule the galaxy. And he's been ruling the Gathendiens for *seven* decades." She shook her head. "I haven't just been learning engineering on that ship up there. I've been learning those bastards' history. Lasara is the first planet they've attempted to commit genocide on since they released that virus on Earth thousands of years ago."

"That we know of," Savaas inserted.

Rachel dipped her chin in acknowledgment. "I had a chat with a T android earlier. I wanted to confirm the history I'd learned and see what he could add. T seemed to believe that if the Gathendiens had succeeded in committing genocide on any planet, the Sectas would know about it."

Savaas cocked his head to one side, considering it. "They *did* know intelligent life existed on Earth before the rest of us did."

Wonick nodded reluctantly. "And they're the only ones who have thoroughly explored that sector of space."

"That we know of," Savaas qualified once more.

"Well," Rachel said, "the Gathendiens sure as hell didn't try it anywhere near alliance-occupied space until after the current emperor came to power. To me, that suggests that there's at least a chance that not all Gathendiens support his genocidal goals."

"And if they do?" Wonick ground out.

She sent him a chilling smile. "Then this will send a very clear message: that—as they say on Earth—*anybody* can get got. That *no one* is beyond our reach or safe from our wrath."

"Hell yes," Simone murmured.

Rachel sent her a nod of thanks before turning back to Wonick and Savaas. "How eager do you think anyone will be to continue his legacy if they know that even their glorious asshole of an emperor with all of his totalitarian power could not escape us? Who among the survivors will want to continue where he left off if they don't even know if he's the only one on our hit list?"

Jovan glanced at the others. "Would they even know whose hit list they were on? They're trying to stamp out at least four races."

Rachel pointed at him. "No. And that's another plus in our favor. They wouldn't know whom to keep an eye on in the future."

"If you think you can land on a Gathendien planet and kill the emperor without thousands of surveillance drones capturing your image, you're dreaming," Wonick snapped.

He had a point, damn it.

Jovan spoke again. "They wouldn't know if she was Lasaran or Earthling."

Wonick shook his head. "And what do you think they'd do if they concluded she was an Earthling?" He stared at Rachel. "Attack Earth, a planet that lacks adequate technology to fight back."

Rachel threw up her hands. "Then I'll slap on some yellow and green makeup, have the clothing generator make me a damn Gathendien costume, and wear that!"

Savaas laughed. "*That* would confuse the *grunarks*."

Several others chuckled.

But Wonick didn't bend. "This is a suicide mission," he ground out. "You realize that, don't you? Even if you land on the planet, get past security, breach the emperor's stronghold, plow through his royal guards, and execute him against all odds, you will trigger every alarm and security measure in the process and they will lock that planet down. You will never make it out alive."

Yeah. That had been her conclusion as well, which was why she hadn't wanted to tell him. The Gathendiens had no knowledge of Immortal Guardians' capabilities and would not be prepared for her incursion. Rachel was confident that she could catch them off guard enough to reach the emperor. But while she did so, alarms would undoubtably sound and every soldier in his military and security forces would converge on the castle or capital or stronghold... whatever the hell place he called home.

While she could survive a battle with dozens of Gathendiens at a time when the tight hallways found on ships constrained them, even pure hubris wouldn't convince her that she could defeat thousands swarming inside a building *and* surrounding it. Rachel had no real hope that she would live long enough after slaying the emperor to find transport back to the ship. And she had promised Wonick she would return here and live out the rest of her days with him.

"I know," she responded gently, as disturbed by the loss of their future together as he looked. "But if the Gathendiens were trying to annihilate you and your brethren, wouldn't *you* risk everything to stop them?"

The answer lay in his eyes despite his unwillingness to voice it.

"One life..." She patted her chest. "*My* life... is not worth more than the billions on Earth this could save."

Minutes ticked past. Everyone else seemed reluctant to speak, waiting for whatever resolution would come.

Resignation filling his beloved features, Wonick extended his hand across the table.

Moisture welled in Rachel's eyes as she took it.

"I'm going with you," he announced.

Shock rippled through her. "What?"

When she tried to pull back, he tightened his hold on her hand. "I'm going with you."

She shook her head. "No way. You said yourself that I can't reach the emperor without thousands of surveillance cameras and drones capturing my image. If the Gathendiens capture your likeness as well, they'll spread the news all over the galaxy and spark another cyborg hunt."

He arched a brow. "If you can conceal that you're an Earthling, why can't I conceal that I'm a cyborg?"

Rachel frantically sought a response. "Facial recognition databases. My features haven't been mapped. Yours have. Makeup may change the *color* of your features, but it won't change the *shape*. They'll identify you by that alone."

"Not if my helmet conceals those features."

"Then they'll recognize your cyborg armor."

Savaas shook his head. "We abandoned our original armor years ago, remember? The armor we wear now is all our own design. You and Janwar's crew are the only non-cyborgs who have seen it and survived. No one else would associate it with us."

"And," Wonick added, "you're forgetting that my armor renders me virtually invisible."

"Only until it sustains serious damage," she pointed out. "You think you can accompany me to the emperor's side without that?"

He shrugged. "Perhaps T can print a mask that will make me look like Chancellor Astennuh."

Janwar barked out a laugh. "Oh ho! That would be perfect. Afterward, the remaining Gathendiens will turn their wrath upon *that grunark*."

Wonick squeezed Rachel's hand, regaining her attention. "I'm going with you," he repeated. "Maybe if we fill the bays of that crap-factory Gathendien ship, as you call it, with C-23s and K-6s, we can beat the odds and make it out alive."

Rachel shook her head. "You've worked so hard to cultivate this peaceful existence for yourself and your brethren, Wonick. You deserve to spend the next however-many centuries enjoying it."

He gave her a sad smile. "I can't do that without you." Raising her hand, he pressed a kiss to her knuckles, and the rest of the room fell away. "You promised we'd spend the rest of our lives together."

She had. A tear slipped down one cheek, but she refused to brush it away.

"Whether that encompasses a few days or a thousand years," he asserted, his features serene, "I intend to hold you to that promise."

Throat thick, she swallowed past the lump that had risen in it. "Then we'll have to make damn sure it's a thousand years," she professed hoarsely.

Lunging up, Wonick released her hand and strode around the table.

Rachel met him halfway and flung herself into his arms.

Wonick kissed her as if it would be their last. Her heart pounded in her chest as she clung to him. How she loved him. The thought of losing Wonick—of watching Gathendiens cut him down while he helped her reach the emperor—utterly crushed her.

As if reading her thoughts, he broke the fervent kiss and stared down at her. "We can do this," he whispered. "We *will* do this."

All Rachel could do was nod, too choked up by tears and fears that they couldn't.

Janwar cleared his throat. "Okay. It appears our plans have changed. Let's turn our minds toward finding a way for Rachel and Wonick to achieve success on their new quest *and* make it back home."

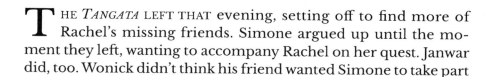

T HE *TANGATA* LEFT THAT evening, setting off to find more of Rachel's missing friends. Simone argued up until the moment they left, wanting to accompany Rachel on her quest. Janwar did, too. Wonick didn't think his friend wanted Simone to take part in what still resembled a suicide mission. But Janwar understood her reasons and didn't want to be parted from her.

Rachel refused. "If the rest of the *Tangata*'s small crew continues to search for Earthlings without you two," she told Simone, "what will they do if they find one on another warship or secret base? Their odds of liberating them would greatly improve if you and Janwar are there to aid them."

It was a strong argument. The *Tangata* crew was tiny. A mere six men, including Janwar.

Wonick suspected, however, that Rachel was more concerned about Simone getting killed if she joined them.

Once the *Tangata* departed, the cyborgs landed the Gathendien ship in the same clearing the *Tangata* had occupied. Wonick, Rachel, Savaas, and half a dozen cyborg brothers stood beside it, bathed in the light of a full moon, discussing what weapons array they should add to it.

Rachel frowned. "If you retrofit one of their ships with better weapons, won't they notice it?"

Wonick shook his head. "Not if those weapons remain hidden prior to use."

Her gaze shifted over his shoulder. "Uh-oh. I think something's up. Nebet is heading this way and looks furious. Whatever it is, I didn't do it. I touched *nothing* in engineering today."

Fighting a smile, Wonick swung around. His humor swiftly died.

Nebet stalked toward them, fury painting his features and stiffening his spine.

"What is it?" Savaas asked.

Nebet halted before them. "I finished decrypting the last of the Gathendien files."

Wonick frowned. "What did you find?" He hoped it wasn't bad news regarding Rachel's friends.

"The cyborg program Janwar told us about? The one the Gathendiens started on the base near Promeii 7?"

"Yes?"

"Chancellor Astennuh didn't just give the Gathendien emperor the *research* they needed to launch it." A muscle jumped in his jaw. "He gave him some of our brothers."

Shock rippled through Wonick, driving him back a step.

"What?" Rachel blurted.

"He gave them some of our cyborg brothers we thought had been *decommissioned*."

Wonick stared at him. "Janwar didn't find any on that base. He would've freed them if he had."

Nebet shook his head. "Our brothers aren't on that base. The Gathendiens' cyborg program didn't begin there. That's just where they do the testing and refining."

Rachel glanced from one to the other. "Are they...? Are your brothers dead?"

If anything, Nebet grew more furious. "According to the files, some of them may still be alive."

Relief and horror warred inside Wonick. "How long have the Gathendiens had them?"

"Since the second year of our rebellion. Astennuh used the massive payment the Gathendiens deposited in his account to fund the hunting and slaying of the rest of the cyborgs."

Savaas looked as if an e-grenade had hit him in the gut. "Some of our brothers have been in Gathendien hands all this time?"

Wonick could scarcely grasp it. The cyborg rebellion had ended eighteen years ago. All evidence at the time had suggested that any cyborgs Wonick and Savaas had failed to liberate were dead.

Nebet nodded.

"How many?" Wonick asked.

"Six."

Wonick clenched his hands into fists.

"Do you have names?" Savaas asked.

"No."

"This changes everything," Savaas growled. "Rachel, you and Wonick will *not* take the Gathendien ship to the emperor's stronghold."

She nodded. "Of course. I understand. You have to find your brethren."

And as the cyborg leaders, Wonick and Savaas would lead the search. He would have to persuade Rachel to postpone her mission. He did *not* want her to attempt the assassination alone.

"We already know where our cyborg brothers are," Nebet informed her.

Everyone regarded him with surprise.

"You do?" she asked.

Nebet met Savaas's gaze. "They're on the emperor's home base."

That was *not* what Wonick had expected, but... "It makes sense. The emperor's new home is such a closely guarded secret that no one in the Aldebarian Alliance has been able to even *guess* its location."

Nebet nodded. "According to the intel, the emperor moved from base to base for the first twenty or thirty years after the Aldebarian Alliance kicked his fleet's ass. He didn't settle on the current planet until shortly before the cyborg rebellion began. And his location is so highly classified that some of the Gathendien *commanders* don't even know where the emperor resides. They're always directed to bases like the one Janwar found to drop off their cargo, refuel, and receive new orders."

"How did *this* commander know?" Rachel asked.

Nebet curled his lip. "We were right about there being a familial connection. The emperor's second-in-command is the older brother of the *grunark* we slew."

"Nepotism strikes again," she muttered. "No wonder the bastard collected so many *specimens* for their bioweapon studies."

Wonick nodded. "With the emperor on that planet, it will be the most heavily guarded and fortified base they have." It was why he'd considered his and Rachel's quest a suicide mission.

"Which makes it the perfect place to house the origins of their cyborg program," Savaas concluded and shook his head. "It wouldn't surprise me if the emperor also wanted to keep the Akseli cyborgs close, like trophies he'd collected in war."

He *was* an egomaniacal *grunark*.

"So..." Rachel said. "We all seem to have something we very much want to accomplish on that planet. What's the plan?"

Savaas met Wonick's eyes. Over their private comm channel, the two compiled their options within seconds. "We'll take you and four units to the planet aboard the *Shagosa*."

She glanced at Wonick. "What's the *Shagosa*?"

Taking her hand, he gave it a squeeze. "A larger version of the *Tangata* that we constructed and keep on hand in case we should ever have to evacuate."

She stared at him. "Really?"

Savaas frowned. "The idea of taking the *Shagosa* into battle unsettles me. We constructed it to be our home if anything ever destroys the one we've made for ourselves on this planet. It would take us years to construct another one. But the *Shagosa*'s cloaking technology will allow us to strike without the Gathendiens detecting our approach and has a much more advanced med bay for our brothers to recover in once we've liberated them."

Wonick squeezed her hand. "I only refrained from suggesting you and I take it instead of the Gathendien ship because I didn't want to leave everyone here with no means to evacuate if something unforeseen should arise in our absence."

Savaas sent her a look of regret. "We designed the *Shagosa* to serve as a self-sustaining home for us should we ever have to leave."

"One that would keep us fed," Wonick added, "well protected, and content until we find another world to settle on. After giving Janwar the *Tangata*, the *Shagosa* is all we have."

She leaned into his side. "I understand. I'm not upset that you didn't offer its use before. Killing the emperor is *my* quest. Not yours."

"It's sure as *srul* our quest now," Savaas ground out. "Once we secure our brothers' release, I want that *grunark* dead."

She smiled grimly. "Oh. He will be. You leave that bastard to me."

S IMONE AND LIZ HAD given Rachel a brief tour of the *Tangata* before Janwar and the others left. The *Shagosa* did indeed resemble it with a few notable exceptions.

One, the *Shagosa* was freaking huge. It was like a massive floating city, but very sleek and loaded with weapons.

Two, paintings didn't adorn the white walls of the *Shagosa*'s corridors. Apparently, Kova was quite a talented artist. His paintings, which ranged from portraits to spacescapes and abstracts, filled the *Tangata*'s hallways with color.

Three, the personal accommodations on the *Shagosa* were considerably smaller. And why wouldn't they be? Prior to their encounters with Rachel's friends, the *Tangata*'s crew consisted only of Janwar, his cousin Krigara, Elchan, Srok'a, Kova, and Soval. Their bedrooms were *very* roomy.

The *Shagosa*, on the other hand, was designed to house the entire cyborg populace. But they did well with the space they had. Rachel expected dormitory-like rooms full of multiple bunks. Instead, the accommodations here closely resembled the homes the cyborgs had designed on the planet. Each living quarter included six bedrooms and one shared living space. Granted, they were smaller than those found in the houses planet-side. But they had a warm, homey feel.

In contrast, the cyborg leaders' quarters only had three bedrooms—Wonick's, Savaas's, and Jovan's—and was a little more spacious. Wonick ordered Jovan to remain behind, much to the latter's disappointment. Even with their larger numbers, this mission would be perilous.

Jovan was a child when the cyborgs found him and had endured so many surgeries in the years since that the only battle experience he'd obtained had arisen from sparring with the others and the brief skirmishes they'd recently engaged in with the Gathendiens. Savaas had agreed that this was not the mission Jovan should use to gain more.

Although Jovan's room was free, no one seemed surprised when Rachel moved her meager belongings into Wonick's bedroom. Nor did they offer any objections. She had wondered if some of the other cyborgs might resent Wonick engaging in a loving relationship with her when such seemed unattainable for the rest of them. But she caught no angry looks. Only a few wistful ones.

If Seth relented and allowed more *gifted ones* and immortals to venture into space again after she killed the Gathendien emperor, perhaps Rachel could talk him into letting Janwar ferry some to the cyborg homeworld. After hundreds—or even thousands—of years spent hunting and fighting vampires, many immortal women would appreciate a chance to lay down their swords and live a life of peace.

Falling in love with a cyborg who wouldn't age would be the icing on the cake.

"Did Simone show you the park on the *Tangata*?" Wonick asked.

The two of them walked hand in hand through one of the *Shagosa*'s many corridors.

"No. She wanted to, but there wasn't time. I wanted to examine the C-23s and K-6s up close and get an idea of how they worked."

His lips twitched. "Of course you did."

Grinning, she nudged him with her shoulder. "Where are we going anyway?" She'd never been down this hallway.

"There's something I want to show you."

She narrowed her eyes. "I'm intrigued. Lead on, Handsome."

He smiled. "That's what you called me when we first spoke over comms."

"And I was right. You are devilishly handsome." Leaning into his side, she curled her free hand around his biceps. "I'd tell you that more often, but I don't want you to get a big head."

Wonick gave her that quizzical look he often did when something went wrong with the translation. "My head isn't overly large. *All* of me is big."

She waggled her eyebrows. "Which brings to mind a number of naughty jokes."

He laughed as they turned a corner.

A clear crystal door faced them. Beyond it lay bright light and...

Rachel stopped and stared. Forest. "Is that a projection?" If the scene before her was a computer-generated image intended to remind the cyborgs of home, it was incredibly naturalistic.

"No. It's real." Wonick tugged her forward, took her wrist, and waved her hand over the entry sensor.

The door slid up.

Wind swept out, carrying the same fresh air Rachel had experienced on the cyborgs' new homeworld. Birdsong accompanied it, as did the sound of water trickling somewhere out of sight.

She drew in a deep breath. "Oh wow. It smells like home." *Her* home. Not today's post-industrialized Earth, but the place and time in which she'd been born. Memories of her childhood assailed her, called forth by a breeze that smelled almost exactly like those that had ruffled her hair as she'd played in the forest that surrounded her village: scented by nature, untainted by pollution. *So* good.

Twining his fingers through hers, he escorted her inside and guided her onto a shaded path.

As the door slid shut behind them, Rachel looked up. *Way* up. While the trees here weren't as tall as the old-growth forests on Wonick's homeworld, they were high and dense enough for her to lose sight of their tops. "Is this the *Shagosa*'s park?" she asked with wonder.

"Yes."

"It's huge! When Simone mentioned the *Tangata* having a park, I pictured something the size of an Earth playground. Or maybe something simulated in a holo-whatever room. This is…" Shaking her head, she looked around with all the wide-eyed fascination of a child visiting a toy store for the first time. "This is amazing, Wonick."

Pride flashed in his eyes. "I'm glad you like it."

"I don't like it. I love it!" As they ventured farther into the forest, they came to a fork in the path that presented three options. "I can't even see the ends of the paths or where they lead. How big *is* this?"

"It stretches the entire length of the ship and encompasses every deck on this side that isn't needed for propulsion or weapons."

"It takes up half the ship?" she blurted, shocked. This was colossal.

He grinned, clearly enjoying her fascination. "It *has* to." He guided her along one of the paths. "This is what makes the ship a self-sustaining home for us, providing everything we would need if we failed to find another planet to colonize."

Two colorful birds burst from the undergrowth and flew past.

Laughing in delight, Rachel paused to watch them disappear into the dense forest behind them. "There are birds in here?" She'd thought the chirping and cooing was piped in for ambience. Movement to her right caught her attention. "Is that a squirrel?"

"We call them *rinyas*."

"Well, *rinyas* are freaking adorable." The little creature looked like a cross between a squirrel and a chipmunk, with a few unusual add-ons. Its gray fur was adorned with black stripes and clusters of polka dots that reminded her of a fawn. Unlike the squirrels back home, this little cutie also had a thick black mane like a lion and a tail as fluffy as a pompom ball. She laughed.

"You'll find wildlife throughout the park," Wonick said as they resumed their stroll.

"How big and how varied?"

"Nothing dangerous. The largest mammals we chose aren't much bigger than this one. But we wanted to mimic the delicately balanced ecosystem of our homeworld as much as possible to make it stable and sustainable. There are pollinators." He motioned to a butterfly-like insect flitting through the trees to their left. "Consumers." He nodded toward the *rinya*, which studied them curiously as it nibbled some kind of nut it turned over and over in its little paws. "Decomposers."

"Like worms?"

He nodded. "And Producers. The forest provides us with plenty of nuts."

"Is it *all* forest?" Rachel couldn't believe how much it felt like they were outdoors.

"No. Of necessity, the forest takes up most of the space. It's what provides us with fresh air and clean water. Unlike the *Kandovar* and other ships, we don't need atmospheric generators to scrub the carbon dioxide we produce and provide us with oxygen. The forest takes care of that. We also don't need the water processors found on other ships to recycle and purify wastewater for reuse. We pump ours through the park. As the water makes its way from one end to the other, the plants' roots absorb nutrients from it and purify it naturally."

"That's brilliant." She motioned to the dappled light that filtered through the trees. "I assume that's some kind of massive grow light that gives the plants what they need to conduct photosynthesis?"

"Yes." He smiled. "Janwar told me how to retrofit it to keep it from harming you. He did the same for Simone after she sunburned in

287

the *Tangata*'s park. When you wave your hand over the door sensor at any entry point, a clear shield will slide in front of the lights to protect you from the ultraviolet rays. Once you leave, the shields will retract."

Stunned, Rachel halted. "You did that? You changed all the lights? For me?" That sounded like a lot of work: making the shields, installing them, reprogramming the sensors...

"Of course. I know how much you love our morning runs through the forest at home." His lips curled up in a tender smile. "And the park isn't all forest. There are also agricultural plots where we grow vegetables and fruits if you want a snack, rocks you can climb for exercise or for fun, several walking paths, a couple of meadows, and a lake you can swim in. I wanted to ensure you could enjoy it all without having to worry about sun exposure."

Sliding her arms around his waist, she leaned up to kiss his chin. "I love you, Wonick."

He claimed her lips in a sweet kiss. "I love you, too." Then he grinned. "Full disclosure: S did most of the work on the lights. I just told him what I wanted."

She grinned. S was the *Shagosa*'s AI version of the *Tangata*'s T. "Remind me to thank him."

"You're welcome," a cheerful male voice spoke over some unseen speaker.

She laughed.

Wonick continued the tour, showing her their agricultural crops.

Rachel shook her head. "You grow so much food down on the planet. What do you do with the excess the ship produces?"

"Prepare and package meals for long-term storage. We haven't experienced severe drought or other natural disasters that may adversely affect crops on our new homeworld yet. But our geological studies suggest that such have occurred in the planet's past."

"I am constantly amazed by the thought and effort you've put into preparing for the future and covering all bases."

"My translator defines the last as a sporting term."

She nodded. "It means preparing for every possibility or eventuality."

"Yes, we have." He motioned to the forest around them. "Creating all this took years of planning and action, making adjustments here and there to ensure the plants and wildlife would all thrive together in a delicate balance. It isn't something we could do last minute if a natural catastrophe destroyed the settlement or if hostile forces invaded the planet."

He and Savaas were serious about never getting stuck in space with few resources again. Rachel thought she must have gaped for a good five minutes when they'd taken her to the *Shagosa* shortly before leaving the planet. They had constructed it inside an extinct volcano they hollowed out to provide enough room for ship- and other craft- and weapons-building endeavors. Any smoke produced from welding and whatever else went into the builds emerged through old lava tubes equipped with screens that prevented anyone flying overhead from seeing what was hidden within. The interior of the volcano also simulated the darkness of space, something she thought must have helped them figure out everything the park would need for a trip that might last indefinitely.

Voices carried on the breeze as they approached a break in the trees. Males. Talking and laughing. Splashes, too.

Upon reaching the end of the path, Rachel smiled. Several cyborgs swam in a small lake. A few at one end played a game with a ball. Others lounged in the sun on the soft grass beside the water while Nebet and Benwa climbed an impressive rock wall. Once they made it to the top, the two dove into the lake.

The men all looked over and called out greetings.

Rachel waved back, then grinned up at Wonick. "You and Savaas remind me of Seth and David."

"The leaders of Earth's Immortal Guardians?"

She nodded. "They really go out of their way to ensure we immortals find as much joy as we can in life. You do the same for your men. It's beautiful." When color crept into his cheeks, her smile broadened. "And you're blushing. That is *so* adorable."

Several of the cyborgs laughed.

Cursing, Wonick guided her forward. "Do you swim?"

"Like a fish." She raised her voice. "Why don't we climb that wall and dive together? Show these fellows how it's really done."

That sparked a round of taunts and dares that brought forth more memories of her brethren.

Wonick grinned. "Let's do it."

The rock wall ended up posing quite a challenge. She and Wonick stripped down to their underwear. Thanks to the fancy-pants clothing generator, she now had a wardrobe full of cyborg clothes designed to fit her diminutive size. Her new underwear resembled comfortable, stretchy bike shorts. The new bras closely matched the sports bra she had supplied as an example with a conservative cut that showed no cleavage.

Though she got the impression that Wonick didn't like the other men seeing her sparsely garbed, he didn't comment or shoot them glares as the two of them crossed to the base of the cliff. Rachel studied it carefully. If cyborgs had fabricated the wall she now faced, they had done a fantastic job. Nothing about its color, shape, or texture indicated that it wasn't a naturally occurring rock formation.

Wonick insisted Rachel go first, then followed closely, promising to catch her if she lost her grip. It didn't take long for her to realize why. She could find no lovely easy-to-grip bucket holds, wide pockets, or flakes to wrap her hand around. Instead, this wall offered only dime-sized edges and crimps barely big enough for the pads of her fingers and toes.

"You should've kept your boots on." Cupping a hand around one foot, Wonick helped her find a toehold. "The rock will abrade your skin."

Keeping her body close to the wall, she settled her fingertips on a small edge and pulled herself up. "I'm fine." If she made the climb multiple times, the skin on her toes would take a beating. But the virus would heal it.

When Rachel reached the top, cheers, whoops, and applause erupted below.

Grinning, Rachel offered the men a gracious bow and stepped back to give Wonick room to join her. She didn't notice until then that the "mountain" they'd climbed butted up against an exterior wall of the ship. A meadow graced the top, wide enough for several large cyborgs to sprawl in the grass and sunbathe if they wanted to. A mural adorned the wall above it, so lifelike that, at first, she thought it a photograph of the forest.

As Rachel turned away from it and faced the park once more, peace suffused her. The upper limbs of the trees wove together to form a colosseum of sorts around the lake below. Wildlife abounded among the branches. Mammals that resembled small monkeys and lorises peered at her curiously as they nibbled leaves and nuts or caught insects. A few scampered from limb to limb.

Wonick curled an arm around her waist. "How are your toes?"

"They're fine." Smiling up at him, she kissed his shoulder. "And you're wonderful."

Surprise and pleasure lit his handsome features. "I am?"

"Immensely." She was so happy in that moment. Being there with him in this beautiful environment, the laughter of his friends echoing through the forest... she could almost forget the many people who wanted them both dead. "I love you."

He pressed a tender kiss to her lips. "I love you, Rachel."

She patted his chest. "Now let's show these boys how to dive. You first."

Wonick let out a piercing whistle that made all the critters in the trees stop and look at him. It must be an oft-used signal because the men below swam toward the edges of the lake to give him room.

Wonick backed up a couple of steps. After tossing Rachel a wink, he swiftly moved forward and jumped.

Peering over the edge, she grinned when he did a couple of forward somersaults before drawing his arms above his head and piercing the water. Bubbles spawned by the splash marked his passage beneath the water as he swam in a U that led him back to the surface.

As soon as his head appeared, Rachel whooped and cheered.

Grinning, Wonick joined his friends near the edge of the lake and motioned for her to take a turn.

Now, Rachel was a bit of an Olympic Games fanatic. Summer. Winter. She loved it all. And whenever she saw something cool and thought it possible to emulate, she liked to give it a try. Fancy ski jumps. Snowboarding stunts. Complicated gymnastic twirls. Diving.

Since the first two depended on the presence of snow, the latter were her favorites. For years now, Seth had ensured that the network that aided Immortal Guardians would supply Rachel with a swimming pool and diving platform wherever she was stationed. And perfecting her diving skills had gone a long way toward relieving the stress of doing the same-old same-old night after night.

Unlike most divers, Rachel didn't need momentum or a springy diving board to get lift. Her enhanced strength gave her plenty. So—wanting to *really* go for the wow factor—she decided to start with a handstand on the cliff's edge.

"What the *srul* is she doing?" someone muttered below.

"Rachel?" Wonick called up to her.

Grinning, she pushed off and performed three reverse somersaults in a pike position before piercing the water with almost no splash. Cheers erupted, a low rumble muffled by the water.

As soon as Rachel surfaced, Wonick arrowed toward her through the water and gave her an exuberant hug. "That was extraordinary! Where did you learn to do that?"

She looped her arms around his neck. "Competitive diving is an international sport on Earth. I just emulated the best."

"You taught yourself?"

"Yep." It had involved a lot of belly flops. And she'd cracked her noggin on the diving platform more than once, much to her Second's dismay. But Seth had merely smiled and shaken his head when summoned to heal her and ensure she suffered no brain damage. He was sweet that way. If Immortal Guardians found sports or other activities that made them happy in their downtime, he didn't object.

Unless they did something stupid like jump off taller and taller buildings to find out how high they could go before suffering serious damage upon landing. Most of them had been guilty of that and had received furious tongue-lashings as a result.

None of the cyborgs had thought of beginning their dives with handstands. Now all of them wanted to try it. With their strength, they had no difficulty getting adequate lift like Rachel when they pushed off. They also tried to replicate her dive, often producing belly flops and other results that sparked laughter and teasing.

Rachel performed several more dives herself, adding forward pikes and twists that garnered more cheers and applause. She and Wonick spent the rest of the afternoon romping and playing with the others. It was marvelous. After the days she'd spent aboard the Gathendien ship, learning everything she could while grieving the loss of Sinsta and the others, Rachel had needed this.

It was a perfect day.

CHAPTER SIXTEEN

T HAT EVENING, WONICK SMILED as he and Rachel bid the others goodnight and headed for their quarters. Once more, her hand was tucked in his. They often walked thusly. Much to his relief, Rachel exhibited no qualms over such casual displays of affection while in the company of others and often instigated them herself.

The pleasure inspired by the simple contact continued to amaze him. Wonick didn't remember being this affected in his youth by a female holding his hand. Perhaps he'd been too distracted by concerns for the family farm or too focused on his desire to further his sexual experiences to fully appreciate it.

Or perhaps it merely meant more to him now because the hand he held was Rachel's.

He glanced at her from the corner of his eye. Like him, she wore a smile full of contentment. He wished he could always keep that expression on her lovely face. No furrowed brow. No anger. No grief. No tears.

Only pure happiness.

He imagined he bore the same air of contentment. He had to forge deep into childhood memories to find a day that had been as enjoyable as this one. It was likely the same for the other cyborgs. When word had spread that Rachel was diving spectacularly in the park, more of his brothers had joined them. Laughter had filled the meadow and trees. Even the most dour faces had donned smiles.

It was a memory all would cherish.

Rachel looked up and caught him staring. Her smile widening, she bumped her shoulder against his arm. "This has been a perfect day."

"For me as well."

"I like your family."

"It's your family, too, now," he reminded her. Wonick never wanted her to feel like—what had she called it?—a fifth wheel or someone tagging along rather than being part of the group.

A teasing glint entered her eyes. "Does that mean your brothers are going to start calling me their sister?"

"As soon as you give them permission."

She slowed to a halt. "Seriously?"

"Yes." He didn't have to ask to know it was true. "Would you object?"

"Of course not. I'd love it."

"Good," he said, "because you're one of us, Rachel."

She bit her lip. "How does Savaas feel about that?"

He arched a brow. "Didn't him joking about being in a cyborg boy band prove that you've won Savaas over?"

She laughed. "Yes, but the question is: Have I won him over enough to actually *be* in a cyborg boy band?"

The mere thought of it made him laugh. "I doubt even you could accomplish that."

Her eyes narrowed playfully. "Hmm. That sounded like a challenge to me." Throwing her shoulders back, she stood ramrod straight and gave him a saucy salute. "Challenge accepted!"

He shook his head with a smile. "*Vuan*, I love you."

Moving closer, she slid her arms around his waist and leaned into him. "Prove it, Handsome."

"Gladly." Wonick claimed her lips in a kiss full of affection.

Humming her approval, she parted them so he could deepen the contact.

"Nope," someone called. "None of that. Not until you're behind closed doors."

Pulling apart, they glanced toward the speaker.

Nebet approached with two others who had swum with them earlier. All wore grins.

"Yeah," Benwa said. "That's our sister you're mauling, Wonick."

Clearly, their enhanced hearing had allowed them to eavesdrop on his and Rachel's conversation.

Her eyes lit with delight. "Aww. Thanks, guys. That earned you all hugs goodnight."

The men darted him quick looks as she opened her arms and moved forward.

Smiling, Wonick crossed his arms over his chest and leaned against the wall to wait.

Now *their* eyes brimmed with pleasure as Rachel drew them, one by one, into hearty hugs.

Wonick wished every one of his men, who were starved for female companionship, could find the love, peace, and happiness he had. Perhaps once they completed this mission, rescued their brothers, and dispatched the Gathendien emperor, Rachel could help them find a way to accomplish that without revealing the cyborgs' continued existence to the rest of the galaxy.

When a voice in his head replaced *once* with *if*, Wonick shuttled it aside. He couldn't allow even a smidgeon of doubt over the success of the upcoming mission to creep in, couldn't let himself spend a single moment imagining Rachel dying in the battle to come or being slain himself and losing the happiness they'd found together. He would instead focus on methodically getting the job done so they could have many more days like today.

Love and the happiness it brought were excellent motivations.

"Hey, you," Rachel said softly.

Blinking, Wonick realized he had retreated into his thoughts. Nebet and the others studied him curiously as they continued past him.

Rachel stood before him, a sweet smile curling her lips. "Where'd you go?"

After offering his friends a goodnight, Wonick curled his arm around her waist. "Far into the future," he murmured.

She leaned into him. "And what did you see?"

He brushed her lips with a kiss. "An endless stretch of days like today."

Sighing, she rested her head against his chest and hugged him tight. "I like that future," she whispered. "Love. Laughter. Camaraderie."

"And peace." He knew she was as weary of battle as the rest of them.

"Blissful peace."

He rested his chin atop her head. "It's all within our grasp, Rachel. We can make it happen. We *will* make it happen. You just have to believe."

Her hold on him tightened. Nodding, she sniffed as though fighting sudden tears.

Wonick couldn't let her go into battle fearing the worst. "Now ask me about the nights," he whispered and nuzzled her hair.

Tilting her head back, she smiled up at him. As he'd feared, tears glistened in her eyes. "What will our nights be like in the future?"

He arched a brow. "Would you like a sneak peek?"

Her smile widened into a grin. "I love how quickly you guys pick up Earth slang. Yes, I would love a sneak peek."

Bending, he locked his arms around her hips and straightened, effortlessly lifting her feet off the floor and holding her high enough that she had to look down at him. Then he delivered a scorching kiss guaranteed to eradicate everything except desire.

Rachel responded with a moan. As he strode toward his and Savaas's quarters, she wrapped her arms around his neck and tunneled her fingers through his hair. When Wonick deepened the kiss, his tongue stroking hers, she locked her legs around his waist and settled her core against his hard length. "If you don't hurry," she said breathlessly, breaking the kiss, "I'm going to strip you bare right here in the hallway."

He grinned and swiftly closed the distance to the door. "My men might not object to seeing *you* unclothed, but they've probably seen more of my bare ass over the years than they cared for."

"You got that right!" Nebet called from somewhere down another hallway.

Both laughed. Wonick waved a hand over the door sensor to open it. As soon as they entered, he crossed the living space to his private bedroom, stepped inside, and let the door slide closed behind them.

Rachel unwound her legs from around him. Both moaned as she slid down his front until her feet touched the floor. When she stepped back, tears no longer lingered in her eyes. Now they glowed amber with desire.

They stared at each other a long moment. Then their lips came together in another fervent kiss, tongues stroking and teasing. Rachel slid her small hands beneath his shirt. Fire burned through Wonick as she caressed a path up his chest and gave the hair there a tug.

He yanked the hem of her shirt from her pants. Before he could remove it, she pulled his own over his head and tossed it aside. Hers swiftly joined it, leaving her in her sports bra and pants. He palmed her beautiful breasts, teasing the stiff peaks that showed through the light cloth.

"Wonick," she whispered, leaning into him.

He'd learned all the places she liked to be touched—how to make her burn—and loved to watch the flush of desire fill her features. He drew her bra over her head so his big hands could tease her, flesh to flesh. She moaned as he squeezed the lush mounds, stroking and toying with the sensitive peaks.

When she caressed his stomach and slid her hand down to cup his hard length through his pants, he groaned. *Vuan*, she set him on fire. He needed her so much.

"We're wearing too many clothes," she complained breathlessly.

He nodded and reached for the fastenings on his pants, eager to feel her soft hands on his—

A curse escaped him when she withdrew her touch.

Rachel backed away and bent over to wrench a boot off. "We need to start walking around barefoot," she grumbled as she went to work on the other. "It would save us a lot of time."

He smiled and hastily removed his own. "It only takes a few seconds."

"I know," she said. "*Far* too long."

Laughing, he kicked his boots away and shucked his pants and underwear. When he straightened, Rachel was already naked, having used that exceptional speed of hers to doff the rest of her clothing.

She sighed with relief. "Much better."

He grinned.

Then she sank to her knees in front of him.

His pulse quickened as she eyed his shaft, which jutted eagerly toward her. Her first touch nearly drew a moan from him. He was large enough that her fingers wouldn't meet when she curled them around his hard length and gave him a squeeze. He *did* moan then and reached out to touch her hair, fighting the need to urge her forward as she licked her lips as if she could already taste him.

"Rachel," he whispered hoarsely.

Leaning forward, she drew her tongue across the sensitive tip and circled it. Once. Twice. Pleasure shot through him, ratcheting up his need. Wonick groaned and buried his fingers her hair, already mussed from the hasty removal of her shirt. His entire body tightened, every muscle flexing as Rachel pushed forward, drawing him as deep into her warm, wet mouth as she could. When she hummed her approval, the vibrations nearly brought him to his knees.

"Rachel," he groaned again as she worked him with lips and tongue... that talented, talented tongue that could move at preternatural speeds. He had never experienced anything like it.

His hands clenched around her hair as he urged her on, careful to moderate his cyborg strength. Every pull and stroke and lick took him higher until his muscles bunched so tightly that they, too, may as well have been reinforced with *alavinin*.

He wanted her so much.

Needed her so much.

He would never get enough of her.

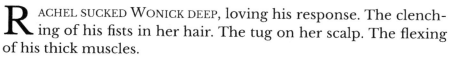

R ACHEL SUCKED WONICK DEEP, loving his response. The clenching of his fists in her hair. The tug on her scalp. The flexing of his thick muscles.

Pleasure flooded her as she imagined him flexing those muscles as he plunged inside her.

As if reading her mind, Wonick swore suddenly. "I want to be inside you." Reaching down, he lifted her to her feet.

Already throbbing, she gasped as he spun her away from him and bent her over the bed. Her chest met the mattress. Excitement rose as he slid a hand up her back in a rough caress that fired her need. Seconds later, his hard cock found her slick entrance and sank deep.

Rachel fisted her hands in the bedding. "Yes! More."

He withdrew nearly to the crown, then thrust deep again. Withdrew then thrust deep. Harder. Rougher. That cyborg control slipping as he lost himself in the pleasure. *So good.* If the bed weren't attached to the wall, he would've driven it across the freaking room.

Rachel moaned and arched back against him, meeting him thrust for thrust, his hard length hitting all the right spots.

Leaning down over her, he caged her with his big body. The hair on his muscled chest tickled her back. One of his hands burrowed beneath her and found her breast, kneading and teasing, pinching the hard peak until she was *so* close to coming. When he brushed a sweet kiss to her bare shoulder, tears welled in her eyes.

"I love you, Rachel."

Her hands tightened around the soft bedding. "I love you, Wonick."

He slid his other hand beneath her and stroked her clit in time with his thrusts.

She moaned as the pleasure continued to build, shortening her breath until an orgasm swept through her. Her inner muscles clamped down around him, squeezing again and again as the ecstasy continued.

Wonick stiffened above her, calling her name, and spilled his heat inside her.

Residual ripples of pleasure continued to rock her as he withdrew his hands, braced his forearms on the mattress, and lowered his head to the bedding beside her, careful as always to keep the bulk of his weight off her.

"I didn't hurt you, did I?" he whispered. He still worried sometimes that he'd lose himself in the pleasure and forget his cyborg strength.

Smiling, Rachel covered his hands with hers. "No."

They stayed that way for a long moment, quietly reveling in each other's presence as their pulses slowed, neither ready to part.

Then he pressed a kiss to her knuckles and straightened.

She moaned when he withdrew from her, sparking another of those ripples of pleasure. Before she could move, he picked her up and settled them both higher on the bed, where they could lie on their sides, facing each other. Barely a breath separated them as they rested their heads on the pillows.

Rachel draped a knee over his hip and cupped his strong jaw with one hand. Stubble abraded her skin as she studied him. "You're so precious to me, Wonick," she murmured. "Thank you for the love and joy you've brought me."

Turning his head, he kissed her palm. "I didn't even remember what true happiness *was* until you came into my life."

Though she tried to avoid it, her mind turned to the coming battle and acknowledged the possibility that one of them might not survive it. Tears pricked the backs of her eyes.

As though reading her thoughts, Wonick kissed her forehead and cuddled her closer. "This mission won't be the end of us, Rachel. I vow it."

Nodding, she buried her face in his chest and held him tight, comforted by the muscled arms around her and the steady thumping of his heart.

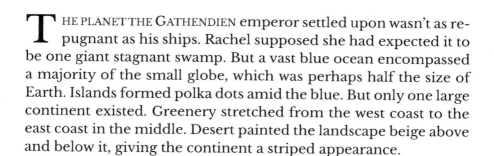

THE PLANET THE GATHENDIEN emperor settled upon wasn't as repugnant as his ships. Rachel supposed she had expected it to be one giant stagnant swamp. But a vast blue ocean encompassed a majority of the small globe, which was perhaps half the size of Earth. Islands formed polka dots amid the blue. But only one large continent existed. Greenery stretched from the west coast to the east coast in the middle. Desert painted the landscape beige above and below it, giving the continent a striped appearance.

"Are you sure they don't know we're here?" she asked as the *Shagosa* settled into orbit and began mapping the planet. Quite a few objects that resembled man-made satellites floated past them.

"I'm sure." No doubt tinged Wonick's voice.

A 3D map rose above a console set inside the long table in the *Shagosa*'s war room, providing more detailed imagery of the planet's terrain.

"And you can keep them from detecting us?"

"Yes."

She smiled. "I'm glad you're good guys. With all your technological advances, you could probably conquer the galaxy if you chose to."

He grunted. "And with your speed and strength, you and your fellow Immortal Guardians could conquer Earth."

"True." Seconds had pointed that out many times over the years. "I guess it's a good thing Immortal Guardians and cyborgs aren't assholes."

They laughed.

The Gathendien planet only boasted two cities reminiscent of the larger ones found on Earth. Each comprised what appeared to be industrial areas full of factories that belched black smoke, a grouping of tall buildings like those commonly found in a city's business district, and small pockets of luxurious mansions surrounded by wide swathes of structures that looked as dilapidated as their ships. Definitely not inhabited by the wealthy.

A few small towns speckled the desert regions, far from the cities. Since they butted up against gaping holes in the ground that looked man-made, she assumed those were mining towns that would hold no interest for the cyborgs.

As Rachel had surmised, it wasn't difficult to determine where the emperor ruled over everything. She pointed to the map. "That must be where the emperor resides." The most opulent structure on the planet, it also bore the feel of a fortress with a flight craft parked on the roof and security vehicles dotting the property.

"Agreed," Wonick murmured.

Rachel studied it. "That place is huge. How many people do you think live there?" She hoped no children did. That was something she hadn't considered before.

"Just the emperor, his *urdekus*, and a plethora of servants."

The emperor and his what? "*Urdekus* didn't translate."

He thought a moment. "Concubines?"

Imagining the Gathendien emperor naked and writhing with a pile of females sparked a shudder.

Wonick's lips twitched, as if he'd read her mind.

Savaas pointed to another building. "This is likely one of their research and development facilities."

Almost as large as the palace, it had a boxy, warehouse shape but didn't appear to be part of the industrial sector and lacked the tired, dingy look of the factories. This building's exterior was so clean it could've been built yesterday. No primitive smokestacks stuck out of its roof. No windows adorned its walls. But tall metal fencing encircled it, and a *lot* of guards walked the grounds.

She motioned to the small structures around it. "They aren't trying to hide it at all. It looks like it's set in the middle of a suburb."

Wonick glanced at her. "Suburb?"

"A civilian community."

He nodded. "That's deliberate. If the Lasarans or any other members of the Aldebarian Alliance bomb the facility, Gathendiens can cry foul, claim it was a factory, and accuse them of targeting and killing thousands of innocent civilians."

She frowned. "Would anyone actually believe them?"

"Alliance members wouldn't," Wonick said. "But residents in other nations might believe it, particularly if the politicians they favor support the false claims in a bid to further their own agendas and careers."

Savaas grunted. "I'm sure Chancellor Astennuh would advocate the falsehood."

"Anything to make the alliance look bad after it kicked him out," Wonick agreed.

Rachel arched a brow. "And to preempt accusations of conspiring with the bastards? I'm pretty sure alliance nations wouldn't react well to learning that Astennuh helped the Gathendiens create their own cyborgs." A thought struck. "Hey, do you think the alliance would alter their position on you guys being killing machines if they knew Astennuh favors cyborgs so much that he's actually helping others create them? It seems like that would kinda turn his former arguments that you're too dangerous to have around into a steaming pile of *tiklun bura*. Especially if the alliance knew you rescued me and avenged the deaths of some of the *Kandovar* victims we've found."

Wonick and Savaas shared a long look.

"I mean," she continued, "look what people say about Janwar. And he's besties with Prince Taelon despite it. Simone said Lisa even told her that the Lasaran sovereigns have softened toward him. Maybe they would soften toward you, too."

Savaas's visage chilled. "We shouldn't have to *prove* ourselves to anyone. They should treat us the way they treat their own people unless we—as a whole—give them reason not to. And we never have. I won't risk our settlement's safety to *beg* for the favor of someone who failed to challenge false rumors and did nothing to stop our slaughter."

Remorse filled her. "Of course. You're right." She could sympathize with his anger. Immortal Guardians had hidden what they were for thousands of years because they'd grown tired of having to prove they were good people to those who thought their special abilities were demon-spawned or others who only wished to harm them or use them for their own gain. She just wished the cyborgs didn't have to live in such isolation. They were good guys.

Wonick rested a hand on her back in a gentle caress, letting her know without words that he understood.

Rachel leaned into his side.

They flagged two more structures as possible research and development facilities and a dozen more as military bases. Like the R&D facilities, the military bases sat in the middle of the Gathendien version of suburbs.

"I'm thinking the one closest to the castle is the cyborg facility," Wonick said.

Savaas nodded. "Emperor Insiorga is the kind who would want to keep his trophies *and* his new Gathendien cyborgs close. But we should search them all."

"Agreed."

Rachel stared at Savaas. "His name is Insiorga?" It was the first time she'd heard it.

"His family name, yes. Why?"

She shrugged, reminded of a naughty joke Endon had told her that involved three travelers and a mistranslation of the Segonian word *insisa*. "It sounds like a male body part." Widening her eyes, she pointed at Benwa. "Dude! Someone just kicked Benwa right in the insiorgas!"

The cyborgs laughed.

All kidding aside, Rachel struggled to quell the nervous butter-flies that fluttered in her belly. Even with the advanced technology they had in their favor, she and the cyborgs would be grossly outnumbered. By the looks of it, they would be sixty-one against... what... the ten or twenty million Gathendiens who inhabited the planet? Since she'd only encountered Gathendien *soldiers*, Rachel had no idea what the civilians were like. When members of the military and royal guard started dropping like flies, would the civilians step up and fight the intruders, too?

She'd like to think they would feel such relief at the fall of their tyrannical leader that they would instead cheer Rachel and the others on. But if all they knew about the Aldebarian Alliance nations was what their emperor told them...

Yeah. It could literally be Rachel and sixty cyborgs against mil-lions.

When she and Wonick retired that night, their lovemaking car-ried a desperate edge. Rachel couldn't help but cling to him, wishing the night would never end. Tomorrow would be full of preparations. Then, once night fell, they would strike.

"I can feel your tension," he whispered, holding her tight. "Re-member what I told you: This won't be the end of us."

She nodded, the lump in her throat too large to speak past.

He jostled her a little. "Look at me, Rachel."

Forcing back tears, she did.

"There can be no doubt. This will *not* be the end of us. Tell me you know that."

She swallowed hard, recognizing the truth in his words. The attitude with which one entered a battle could predetermine its outcome. "This won't be the end of us."

"Now say it again."

"This won't be the end of us."

"And again."

"This *won't* be the end of us," she vowed resolutely.

He raised a brow, his look turning arrogant. "And why is that?"

She smiled, her spirits lightening. "Because we kick ass, baby."

"*Srul* yes, we do. And we'll kick a *lot* of ass tomorrow night."

"Damn straight."

THEY DIDN'T KICK ASS the following night. The weather turned, bringing training thunderstorms that lasted from sunset until the following afternoon. Rachel wouldn't mind fighting in the rain. On Earth, rain often drove people indoors, leaving fewer looky-loos out and about. The rumbling thunder might also hide the booms their weaponry produced as they infiltrated the emperor's stronghold and the R&D facilities. Unfortunately, the cyborg armor that camouflaged their bodies well enough that even *she* had a hard time seeing them couldn't prevent raindrops from striking it and splashing off, something that would draw attention and reveal their positions. So they ultimately waited for the following night.

Clouds still swathed the sky and blocked out the moon—something that would deepen the darkness and aid them in darting from shadow to shadow—but none would produce rain, Savaas declared before giving them the green light.

Rachel stared at her reflection in the lav's mirror.

Wonick stepped up behind her and rested his hands on her shoulders. "What do you think?"

She smiled, taking in every aspect of her appearance. "I look like I'm one of you." Instead of painting her face yellow and green to hide her Earthling heritage, the cyborgs had opted to dye her skin tan with a reddish hue like theirs. And *all* of her skin—not just that on her face—bore the color, which had resulted from a simple injection. Neither water nor soap would remove it. The pigmentation would simply fade away over the next couple of weeks.

Her raven hair was pulled back from her face to the crown of her head in neat cornrows. Wonick had sat her on the bed between his legs and lovingly fashioned them for her. From there, two-thirds of her hair flowed loosely down her back. The rest he wove into braids adorned with what he called war beads.

He kissed the top of her head and drew a hand over her hair. "You *are* one of us."

"I was worried the beads would make clicking sounds when they collided." She gave her head a quick shake. "But I don't hear a thing."

He smiled. "They're designed to intimidate our enemies *without* alerting them to our presence when stealth is necessary. I would've added a bead for every Gathendien you've defeated in battle, but I don't think we have that many."

Grinning, Rachel swiveled to face him and looped her arms around his neck. "Why don't you and the others wear your hair like this?" Janwar still wore his hair in the Akseli fashion even though he'd left that life behind him.

Wonick's expression sobered. "Our war beads became a source of shame for us when we realized that some of the battles we fought were not for the honorable reasons we were told."

She fingered his short locks. "But the battles you fight now are."

He smiled. "This one certainly will be. Together, we'll liberate our brothers, avenge our Earthling sisters, and end the emperor's brutal reign."

She loved that Wonick considered her Earth friends part of his *found family*. "Do you think we'll find any of my friends down there?" Much to her chagrin, she'd been so focused on her plan to end the emperor's rule and, hopefully, the Gathendien people's desire to conquer the galaxy at all costs that Savaas and Wonick had been the first to propose there might be Earthlings in the R&D facilities. "The intel you gathered said they didn't have any."

"It's possible. Time has passed. Another ship could've presented the emperor with Earthling captives since then. Savaas and the others will perform a thorough search before leaving each facility."

Rachel could probably search the facilities faster than the cyborgs despite their enhanced speed. But she would have her hands full reaching the emperor.

"It's time," Savaas said over the ship's comm.

Rachel stepped back and straightened her shoulders. "Time to kick ass."

Wonick smiled. "*Srul* yes."

They met the others in the primary bay. Fifty-nine cyborgs turned when she and Wonick entered. All stared.

She held out her arms. "What do you think?" The black form-fitting combat suit the armorer fabricated for her protected everything from the neck down. Gloves covered her hands. But her face and hair remained visible.

"You look Akseli," Benwa blurted.

Rachel couldn't tell by their expressions if they thought that a good thing or a bad thing.

A smidgeon of unease flittered through her. Would they like her better this way?

Nebet frowned. "It's weird."

Relief supplanted uncertainty as she laughed. "So you like my Earthling appearance better?"

"*Much* better." Nebet motioned to her. "This way, you remind me too much of my sister. I joined the cyborg unit to pay for the surgery she would've died without. Once she recovered, she ended up falling in love with an Astennuh loyalist. And when the cyborg rebellion began, she and her husband tried to turn me in for the reward."

Rachel stared at him. "Wow. What a total bitch."

He grinned. "Agreed."

"That coloring isn't permanent, is it?" Hoshaan asked.

Benwa nodded. "We'll get our Earthling sister back, won't we?"

"Aww, guys." Their wholehearted acceptance brought a lump to her throat. "You're the best."

"Hmm," Wonick said.

She glanced up at him. "What?"

"Your eyes are glowing red instead of amber."

Surprise jolted her. "They are?"

He nodded.

"Cool. Even Seth and David can't change the color their eyes glow."

Smiling, he rested a hand on her back as they crossed to join the others.

Savaas shook his head and *almost* smiled. "It's a good thing you *aren't* Akseli. We wouldn't have enough war beads to adorn your hair."

Rachel laughed. "How's it looking down on the planet? Are we good to go?"

He nodded toward a console that displayed the emperor's city. "S-1 is in position now."

The S android had taken a small stealth fighter down to the planet, easing some of Rachel's concern when he triggered no alarms. He now waited outside the primary power grid in the center of the city.

Savaas touched his ear. "Time to act, S."

"Yes, Commander," came the AI's jovial response. Apparently, this was S's first off-planet mission, and he was quite excited about it after hearing the tales of the *Tangata* androids' exploits.

Another image popped up in one corner of the console, video projected by S-1's internal camera. Darkness surrounded him, alleviated by occasional bright halos thrown down by lights that looked remarkably similar to streetlights on Earth.

His formerly white armor was now a matte black that blended with the shadows as he moved forward. Stopping at the base of a tall tree, he braced his hands against the wide trunk and pushed.

The tree creaked, leaned to one side, and toppled over to the sounds of snaps and slops. The structures inside the fence crumpled beneath the weight of it. Sparks flew. Someone shouted. As S-1 raced forward, the lights in the video winked out. A boom sounded.

Rachel's attention shifted to the rest of the city as block after block succumbed to darkness. She looked at Wonick and Savaas. "Okay. I'm just going to say it. How embarrassed is Lasara that their species was nearly wiped out by a civilization whose infrastructure is so primitive that a felled tree can take out the entire power grid?" That was no more advanced than many of the grids on Earth. "I mean, seriously, that's the best the Gathendiens can do?"

Everyone laughed.

"May I answer that question, Commander Savaas?" S requested. Since there weren't any androids in the room, it must be the ship's AI *sans* android form.

Still chuckling, Savaas said, "Go ahead, S."

"The Gathendien nation had much more advanced infrastructure before it unwisely tried to eradicate the Lasarans. After the brutal defeat their military suffered at the hands of the Aldebarian Alliance, the Gathendiens—under Emperor Insiorga's edict—abandoned their homeworld in protest of the sanctions enacted against them. According to the information we recovered from the Gathendien ship, combined with the intel Janwar amassed, the emperor has since poured a majority of their nation's funds into bioengineering research."

"And their cyborg program," Wonick muttered.

"And the construction of his palace?" Rachel added.

"Correct," S confirmed. "So the infrastructure of their settlement has suffered greatly."

It shouldn't surprise her. The emperor was monomaniacally focused on conquering the galaxy. Some of the stuff she'd seen on the Gathendien ship had seemed downright archaic compared to the Lasaran and cyborg technology.

"Well," she said, "now that I know you can wreck the city's power grid with a tree, I'm feeling more confident about our mission."

"Not the whole city," Wonick replied, "only the poor areas." Which seemed to encompass most of it. "The rest, including the emperor's compound, lost power as a result of the charges S detonated. But it will take them time to figure that out."

"The tree," Savaas said, "will ease suspicion in the meantime. They'll blame the torrential rains that lasted hours for loosening the soil enough to topple it and won't initially suspect tampering."

She nodded. "Which will keep the guards lax and oblivious to the oncoming assaults."

Wonick pointed to the power plant on the map. "S will incapacitate the civilian workers inside the plant and man the comms, responding in Gathendien while he stymies attempts to get the power up and running again. He'll also hack the city's communication system and gradually weaken it until they can no longer communicate with each other."

"Comms are already coming in," S-1 informed them brightly. "They believe I am a cranky Gathendien, working the night shift, and do not appreciate my gruff responses."

Rachel grinned.

Smiling, Savaas shook his head. "Good work, S. From this point on, stay off *our* comms unless you have something to report or need backup."

"I won't need backup," he replied indignantly.

"Then stay off our comms until you have something to report that *isn't* fun."

"Yes, Commander," he said, his voice laden with disappointment.

It hadn't taken her long to figure out that T's and S's were talkers.

Savaas stepped back from the table. "Time to go."

The cyborgs swiftly divided into groups of fifteen warriors that gathered in front of four stealth dropships. As Savaas strode toward one group, he and Wonick each raised a fist in the air. "No cyborg left behind!"

Every cyborg present shoved a fist into the air and shouted, "No cyborg left behind!"

Rachel punched her own fist toward the ceiling. "Immortal Guardians rock!"

Grinning, the men all raised their fists again and shouted, "Immortal Guardians rock!"

Savaas nodded in satisfaction. "Let's go liberate our brothers."

Rachel frowned as she noted the men gathered in front of the dropship she and Wonick intended to take. "Will we be by flying down in a different craft?" she asked.

"No," Wonick said. "They're coming with us."

Her steps slowed to a halt a few feet away from the group. "I thought we were going in alone."

Nebet eased to the front of the group and shook his head. "We take care of our own, sister."

Swallowing hard, Rachel shook her head. "I don't want any of you to get hurt or die because of my quest."

Wonick rested a hand on her back. "It's our quest, too. Remember?"

Benwa nodded. "We have as much reason to want that *grunark* dead as you do."

Nebet grinned. "But we'll let you have the honors. We just plan to help you get there."

Rachel smiled. "That's so sweet." Holding her arms out, she waved them forward. "Bring it in. Group hug."

Grinning, the cyborgs closed in around her and Wonick and nearly smothered her with a hug.

"Whenever you're ready..." a voice drawled in a dull monotone.

Laughing, Rachel waited for the men to back away before she looked for the speaker.

Savaas stood beside the last craft, arms crossed over his chest.

"I'll save *your* hug for when we get back," Rachel called.

The corners of his lips tilted up the slightest bit. "I'll hold you to that."

Smiling, Rachel motioned for the cyborgs to board first. "You heard him, boys. Let's book."

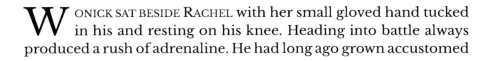

WONICK SAT BESIDE RACHEL with her small gloved hand tucked in his and resting on his knee. Heading into battle always produced a rush of adrenaline. He had long ago grown accustomed to it and maintained a stoic façade as Hoshaan piloted the dropship down through the atmosphere.

Inside, however, a twinge of anxiety struck. He hadn't experienced the like in a long time. Not since the cyborg rebellion and the initial years of hardship that followed, when he'd known how much his men depended on him. He had worried about his brothers' future then.

Now he worried about losing his own future with Rachel.

Some might think such fear weakened a soldier. A cyborg the Akseli military had *decommissioned* before Wonick could reach him had once confided that he thought the military suppressed cyborgs' sex drive to prevent them from acting on those urges, becoming attached to their partners, and inadvertently falling in love. "Love makes you weak," the younger cyborg had proclaimed brashly. "It divides your loyalties and takes the fight right out of you."

Wonick disagreed. Love for his brothers had kept him going when he'd been so wounded despite his armor and enhancements that he could barely crawl forward on his hands and knees. It had given him strength when exhaustion left him lightheaded and weighted his limbs. It had driven him to find insane solutions to extricate them safely from impossible situations.

And love for Rachel would do the same tonight.

His anxiety lessened as soon as he realized the truth of it.

"I'm not seeing much activity below," Savaas murmured over helmet comms from another dropship.

"S, report," Wonick ordered.

"I have injected static into planetary comms and rendered five workers and three security officers unconscious," S announced brightly.

They had all agreed to spare as many civilian lives as possible in case Rachel was right and not everyone supported the emperor's genocidal plans.

"The supreme commander commed me," S continued, "and insisted we focus all our initial efforts on restoring power to the palace."

"Figures," Rachel grumbled.

"One moment, please," S said suddenly. A distant shout erupted, followed by Gathendien swears and a scuffle. "I have now rendered two more civilian security personnel unconscious and slain four military guards sent by the supreme commander to speed my efforts. Perhaps on our next incursion, I can do what Rachel initially suggested and have the uniform generator create a Gathendien costume for me to wear. I believe such would've been useful in this situation."

Wonick smiled when Rachel bit her lip to keep from laughing. "We'll think about it, S."

"Emperor Insiorga has declared a mandatory curfew," S added, "ordering all businesses to close and all citizenry to return to their homes and remain indoors until power is restored. The supreme commander warned that should any civil unrest result from the power loss, the emperor will hold me personally responsible." A pause ensued. "Perhaps I should not have taken the name of one of the workers I rendered unconscious. He will face the emperor's wrath in my stead."

"No, he won't," Rachel told him, "because the emperor won't live through the night."

"Ah," S replied, his tone brightening. "That is correct. Thank you, Rachel."

She smiled at Wonick. "Anytime."

He grinned. "Anything else to report?"

"The supreme commander has ordered security forces to apprehend anyone who disobeys the curfew."

Rachel pursed her lips. "I think you're right. They don't suspect anything out of the ordinary."

Wonick nodded. Things were progressing according to plan. "And they'll be looking for trouble caused by restless and aggravated citizens, not..."

"Alien invaders?" she suggested.

He chuckled. "Yes. Alien invaders. Continue to increase static on all planetary channels, S, then cut comms." Gradually worsening interference would spark less suspicion than a sudden cut.

"Yes, Commander. Should I respond to some inquiries in an alternate voice and accuse myself of accidentally damaging comms while attempting to restore power? A primary comm tower lies not far from here. I could race over there and topple another tree."

"Remain in position," Savaas ordered, "and offer whatever explanation you believe will work for us."

"Yes, Commander."

Rachel grinned. "Is it me, or does S sound like he's really enjoying this?"

"He's enjoying this," Wonick agreed. "Perhaps a little too much."

The other cyborg dropships broke formation and banked, each turning toward one of the R&D facilities they believed might hold their brothers and—possibly—captive Earthlings.

"I saw a ripple," Rachel said as she peered into what she called the cockpit.

"The other units are heading for their targets."

"Approaching palace," Hoshaan announced as they passed over the city.

"Kinda hard to miss it with all those lights," Rachel murmured. "Everything else is pitch black."

Wonick nodded. "We assumed the emperor would have a backup power source."

"It must be limited, though, otherwise why would the supreme commander insist on restoring power to the palace first?"

Behind his faceplate, Nebet raised a brow. "Because he's a *grunark*?"

She laughed. "True."

Unlike much of the architecture they passed, the palace bore a clean, modern design. Shaped like a thick crescent, it stood taller than surrounding buildings and boasted white walls guaranteed to make it stand out from the rest of the city's mixture of gray and earth tones. Large, carefully crafted gardens stretched in front of it, interspersed with trees and gleaming stone pathways. At their center, a statue almost as tall as the palace presided over it all.

Rachel wrinkled her nose as she studied it. "Is that supposed to be the emperor?"

"Yes."

A large fountain surrounded the base of the statue, creating the illusion of the emperor walking on water.

"He sure thinks a lot of himself, doesn't he?" she asked disparagingly. "I'm surprised he didn't order the sculptor make it look like he was peeing on the rest of the galaxy."

Everyone laughed.

High, sturdy metal fencing enclosed the gardens in the front of it. On the sides, near the points of the crescent-shaped building, the fencing met a stone wall that surrounded the grounds in the rear.

"Looks a little wilder back there," Rachel murmured.

It did. Wonick studied it carefully. Instead of neatly manicured beds, a lake occupied half the land behind the palace. Emergency lighting glimmered on the water, highlighting green scum that abounded on its surface. Beyond the lake, a tangled mass of trees and natural vegetation proliferated, blocking the emperor's view of the hovels beyond his walls. Armed guards walked the grounds. A few more loitered atop the mostly flat roof of the palace with a transport parked in the center.

"Let's take a closer look at the roof," he murmured.

Hoshaan enlarged their view of it.

Wonick noted the positions of the guards before focusing on the large objects mounted along the roof's edges: two in front, two in back, and one on each crescent peak.

"Are those weapons?" Rachel asked.

"Yes." He pointed. "Those are e-cannons meant to defend the palace from craft attacking from above. And those are rapid-fire ND-3 rifles."

"I assume they're more powerful than an O-rifle?"

"Much more powerful. They can fire fifty rounds per second. And it only takes one hit to pierce armor. Show us the grounds again and initiate a thermal scan," Wonick ordered.

"Initiating thermal scan," Hoshaan replied.

A grid overlay their view. Multiple red dots revealed guards hidden by the foliage.

Rachel leaned forward. "Not bad. We can take that many."

The guards on-site didn't worry him. Wonick was more concerned with those who would converge upon the palace as soon as an alarm sounded. The military bases were likely already on

316

alert, since the emperor and supreme commander anticipated civil unrest.

"We'll enter the palace through the back," Wonick stated. "More shadows. Nebet, see if you can remotely hack the security cameras." He spotted several on the roof and a dozen more on the walls.

Nebet nodded and closed his eyes, which began to move rapidly back and forth behind his lids. A minute ticked past before he loosed a sound of frustration. "I have to be hands-on to hack them."

Wonick studied the palace grounds. Two guards strolled over to an open door at the far side of the palace. A Gathendien in a matching uniform emerged, holding something edible in one hand. Mouth full, he snapped something at them and waved his free hand as though telling them to return to their posts. Disgruntled expressions wrinkled the guards' features as they parted and headed back to the perimeter. The one in charge took another big bite of his meal and shouted orders to a third guard before hitching his pants up higher over a bloated golden belly and heading back inside.

"That must be the security station," Wonick said. "The emperor would want it close, but not visible from the front of the building."

Rachel curled her lip. "Nothing to deter from the palace's magnificence."

As if to confirm his guess, two more guards exited the palace's back doors, stopped by the office, then headed toward the far wall.

"I'll go down with a team of five," Wonick said. "Aagar, Vaaren, and Fonwen, I want you to take the roof. Nebet, Benwa, and I will quietly take the security station and hack the camera feeds. Looping the footage will give us more time to reach the emperor."

"I'm going, too," Rachel blurted.

Wonick shook his head. "They'll see you." When she opened her mouth to protest, he activated his armor's cloaking. "They *won't* see us." Their armor didn't just hide their physical appearance, it also hid their heat signatures.

She blinked. "Right. But you're forgetting that I can zip past without them noticing anything but a breeze."

"And you will have plenty of time to do that *after* we loop the footage."

She looked as though she wanted to protest but ultimately issued a tight-lipped nod.

Wonick patted her shoulder. "We've done this before, Rachel. Many times while liberating our brothers."

She grimaced. "Sorry. Patience is not my strong suit. I'm used to just charging in and kicking ass."

Amusement rose. "I'm aware." Wonick lowered his helmet's faceplate and rose. "Don't worry. We'll be quick." He moved to the control room to peer past Hoshaan's shoulder. When the C-23's hatch opened, the interior would be visible to any who happened to look toward it, forcing them to disembark out of sight of the palace security cameras. "Drop us there." He pointed to an area where a home or business had burned down behind a two-level building. It looked as if local residents used the lot as a refuse heap now.

"Yes, Commander."

Hoshaan flew them over to the taller structure and hovered behind it with the hatch facing away from the palace. Overhead lights inside the dropship went dark.

Wonick and the rest of his small team gathered in front of the hatch as it opened. Before it finished lowering, all jumped out and landed amid the refuse piles below.

The hatch closed. Only Wonick's cybernetically enhanced hearing enabled him to hear the dropship move away. Like all cyborg-designed craft, it created no breeze, nor did the engines produce a loud rumble or heat signature that thermal sensors might detect, something that seemed to perpetually amaze Rachel.

Wonick and his small group stood still for several moments, listening for someone to shout an alarm. When none did, they jogged toward the palace. A single leap landed them atop the wall with soft thuds they couldn't avoid, thanks to their body weight and hefty armor. A couple of guards frowned and looked their way.

The cyborgs remained still, their armor mirroring whatever was behind them.

Muttering to each other, the guards strolled away.

Wonick and his brothers eased over the edge and dropped quietly onto the soft dirt inside the wall. Fallen leaves littered the ground, still damp from the rain, and rendered their footsteps silent as the team headed toward the security office. At the edge of the wild jungle that surrounded the lake, they paused. Aagar, Vaaren, and Fonwen slipped through the shadows to the side of the building, where they would scale it, attack the guards on the roof, and seize control of the large weapons.

A minute ticked past.

Targets down, Aagar announced over mental comms.

Affirmative.

A guard rounded the side of the palace. The head of security stepped outside the office to shout slurs at him. Both remained oblivious to the threat that watched from the shadows. The guard was angry over having to come in on his night off. Apparently, the supreme commander ordered them to double the emperor's protection until power in the city could be restored.

"It's protocol," the head of security snarled. "If you don't like it, go work in a *drekking* factory." Judging by his tone, he considered that the lowest of the low. And perhaps it was here. If Emperor Insiorga cared nothing for his people's living conditions, Wonick doubted he cared about the working conditions they must endure.

As soon as his superior officer turned to go inside, the guard threw up an obscene hand gesture and stomped away.

Wonick moved forward, Benwa and Nebet right behind him. As they approached the security office, the voice of the head of security floated out.

"Yes, Supreme Commander, I've doubled the guards. We will remain vigilant until the power is restored... No, Supreme Commander. The guards are still arriving... The outage in the city may be delaying—... Yes, Supreme Commander, I will fine those who have not yet arrived." A long pause. "Yes, Supreme Commander, any trespassers will be killed on sight. We will broadcast footage of the executions on all channels to deter further treacherous acts." Another pause. "Yes, Supreme Commander."

Since no static marred the connection, the supreme commander must be on the premises, using private palace comms.

As soon as he ended the conversation, the security officer muttered, "Arrogant *drek*."

Wonick shook his head and entered the office. Nebet and Benwa guarded his back. With their armor's camouflage activated, none should see them. But exercising caution was always wise.

The head of security bent over a desk, mouth working around another bite as he muttered disparaging comments about both the supreme commander and the emperor and typed on a console. As Wonick approached, the Gathendien glanced over his shoulder as though to ensure no one would hear his complaints and tell the emperor.

Wonick snapped the male's neck. While Benwa parked himself in the doorway, Nebet grabbed a second chair and settled in front of the console. Removing one glove, he placed a palm on the scanner and went to work. His eyes lost focus as he sifted through code. *Scanning and copying all security footage*, he stated over mental comms.

While Wonick waited, he opted to stuff the dead security officer in the lav and unobtrusively weld the door shut.

Eliminating recent arrivals and departures and reconstituting footage, Nebet said. *Saving files. Replacing live footage with continuously repeating loop.* He blinked. *We're good.*

Wonick activated his helmet comm. "Unit Two," he whispered for Rachel's benefit instead of speaking over mental comms, "we've taken the roof and the security office. Disembark in the vacant lot and slip over the wall. Rachel, join me in the security station on the western side. Everyone else, quietly eliminate every guard on the grounds in back. Aagar, let us know when reinforcements arrive."

Nebet stiffened. *I heard something.*

A breeze swept into the small office. Nebet and Benwa jumped, then swore as Rachel appeared in front of Wonick. Her long hair and braids whipped forward in her helmet at the abrupt stop. "Hi there," she whispered.

Raising his helmet visor so she could see his face, Wonick smiled. "Hello."

"I'm glad I practiced picking you guys out in your camo." Raising a hand, she positioned her primary finger and thumb close together. "I came this close to plowing right into you."

He laughed.

"I took out two guards on the way here," she went on. "Are we good to go?"

"Yes."

Stepping back, she drew two swords. "Then let's do this."

CHAPTER SEVENTEEN

RACHEL DROPPED HER SMILE when someone swore over comms.

Wonick frowned. "Savaas, was that you?"

"Yes. There are more guards at this facility than we expected."

A grunt carried over comms before Voyin said, "It looks like half their *drekking* military is here."

She frowned. "Do you think they beefed up security because of the blackout? That was fast." *Very* fast.

"They must have," Savaas replied. "There weren't nearly this many last night or earlier today."

"Additional guards are still straggling in here," Wonick mentioned. "And most of them seem more irritated than concerned."

"Well, here," Savaas said grimly, "they look twitchy as *srul*, as though they're expecting trouble."

Rachel sent Wonick a pointed look. "Are they worried about keeping intruders *out* or keeping captive cyborgs *in*?" Had Wonick's brothers attempted to escape in the past?

"Unknown," Savaas muttered. "But the possibility of the latter gives me hope. Unit Three, report."

"They've increased security here, too, but not to that extent," Renak disclosed. "We've taken out several guards, looped the security footage, and are ready to begin our incursion."

"Unit Four?" Savaas asked.

"Same as Unit Three. Increased security, but nothing we can't handle. We're looping the security footage now and will be ready to breach the facility in two minutes."

That pretty much confirmed their suspicions, didn't it? Rachel stared at Wonick. "Looks like the facility Savaas chose is guarding something extra special."

"Agreed."

"With so many covering the exterior," Savaas said, "our best option will be to land on the roof, take out the guards, and enter the building from above. But I'm not confident we can do it without a few of the guards getting off either a shot or a warning. And it will take Voyin time to loop the security footage."

"I'll try to lock down the building while I'm at it, but we'll be exposed until I finish," Voyin said.

Wonick glanced at Nebet. "Can you hack the R&D facility's security footage from here?"

His eyes went vacant.

Rachel shifted from foot to foot, battling impatience.

Nebet shook his head. "Too many *turankem*. They're definitely hiding something there."

She frowned. "What are *turankem*?" Her translator failed to define that term.

Wonick's brow puckered. "The closest Earth English equivalents my translation matrix can produce are... firewalls or security features?"

"Ah."

"Getting past them would take me at least an hour," Nebet concluded.

They didn't have that kind of time. The palace's security station manager and half the exterior guards were already down. She doubted it would take long for someone to notice that.

"Hoshaan?" Wonick said.

"Yes, Commander?"

"Send S-4 down. Have him meet us in the security office."

A moment passed. "He's on his way."

"We're going to put S-4 on it, Savaas. It shouldn't take him as long. As soon as he's done, you can take out the guards on the roof, enter, and begin the search without the security feeds tracking you."

"Let me know as soon as it's done," Savaas uttered. "In the meantime, S?"

"Yes, Commander Savaas?"

"Have you readied the C-23s and K-6s?"

"Affirmative. My android forms are at the helms of the C-23s, ready to pilot them at your command. And the K-6s are primed."

"Good. I want a C-23 over each incursion point. Divide the rest among the military bases. Once our respective incursions begin, destroy every vehicle and craft on those bases. If you require the K-6s to accomplish that, remote pilot them as necessary."

"Yes, Commander Savaas," S agreed brightly. "Doing so without damaging nearby structures will be a challenge, but I will ensure that nothing functional shall remain on the bases."

Rachel grinned. "He sounds excited."

Wonick nodded, his expression saying he found that worrisome.

Barely discernable footsteps approached at a rapid pace. Rachel glanced toward the doorway.

S-4 entered the security office. S had confessed earlier that the metal plating that covered most of his android form lacked the more sophisticated camouflage that the cyborgs' armor boasted. But it could change from one solid color to another. Now, instead of the shiny white he usually wore, S-4's plating bore a matte black finish like S-1's to help him blend in with the night.

His eyes, however, glowed with exhilaration over being part of the action this time.

"Oooh," Rachel crooned. "I love the new look, S."

His eyes brightened. "Thank you, Rachel. Please step aside, Nebet."

Rolling his eyes, Nebet rose and backed away, yielding his seat to the android.

S-4 flattened a metal palm on the console.

"How much time do you think it will take, S?" Wonick asked.

"Five minutes and twenty-three seconds to disable the initial *turankem* and infiltrate their system. Five seconds to modify and loop the security footage. And an additional four minutes and twelve seconds to lockdown the building."

Rachel's amusement vanished. "So, nine minutes, give or take. A lot can happen in nine minutes. The soldiers there could get less twitchy and start to relax—"

Savaas swore again. "Or they can send more troops. Another transport has arrived."

Not good. They needed to keep Gathendiens from continuing to beef up security over there. Even cyborgs had their limits, particularly if they were going to be carrying out their captive brothers. Rachel doubted scientists had kept those men in prime condition. "Would there be a downside if S started bombing the military bases early?"

"Yes," Wonick replied. "Right now, the palace isn't on lockdown. It's merely on heightened alert. If the military bases start going up in flames, the emperor will assume the planet is under attack and institute a full lockdown."

"Which will...?"

"Result in thick barriers dropping into place over every window, wall, and door."

"Just here at the palace?"

"Possibly. It's less heavily guarded than Savaas's location. The emperor would want additional assurances. But the same may happen there if they're concerned about potential escapes."

Rachel pursed her lips. "What if we leave the bases alone until everyone is inside their respective targets and create a diversion here?"

Wonick arched a brow. "What did you have in mind?"

She let her lips curl in a sly grin. "Something that will infuriate the emperor and compel him to divert military forces here. How do you say 'Down with the emperor' in Gathendien?"

His eyes narrowed. "*Veedetha neh wusokt.* What do you intend to do?"

"I'm going to topple that big-ass statue in front. How do you say 'If *we* don't have power, *you* shouldn't have power'?"

Lips twitching, Wonick said, "*Yen* voxi *na sampe dewan, oora* dey *sethna sampes dewan.*"

Rachel repeated the phrases over and over in her head, committing them to memory.

Benwa raised his visor and smirked. "That should bring forces to our position."

Rachel sent him a smile. "And halt the flow of soldiers to Unit One's location, enabling Savaas and the guys to go in and rescue your brothers without a couple hundred thousand soldiers trying to stop them." And it wouldn't deviate much from their original plan. They had known going in that this would likely be the scenario they'd face: masses of soldiers converging upon the palace while she and the others tracked down the emperor inside.

She turned back to Wonick. "What do you think?"

"Let's do it," Wonick said. "But wait until we're in the palace and I give you the signal. As soon as the statue falls, get your ass inside before they initiate a lockdown. It may take S a while to override that."

"Okay." She blew him a kiss. "See you inside."

He touched her arm. "Don't try to crash through the windows. They're *stovicun* crystal. You'd have an easier time breaking through a wall. We'll eliminate the guards inside and hold a door open for you."

Good thing he'd warned her. If she'd run at a window at top immortal speeds, she probably would've ended up looking like a bug splattered on a windshield. "Okay."

Wonick spoke over comms. "On Nebet's count, we'll breach the palace's back doors."

Wonick, Benwa, and Nebet lowered their visors and virtually disappeared as the camo kicked back in. Rachel remained inside the security office and monitored them as best she could. The sounds of their footsteps decreased as they headed for the large double doors that constituted the palace's rear entrance. More cyborgs crept past to join them, which meant no guards remained outside to challenge them, not that they would've seen the cyborgs anyway. Rachel could barely make them out herself.

Staring through the palace's large back windows, she noted multiple guards indoors.

Nebet placed his gauntleted hand on the access pad beside the doors as the remaining cyborgs emerged from the trees.

A lock clicked. The double doors swung open.

The guards inside looked toward it curiously, expecting someone who knew whatever access code was required to enter. Their brows furrowed when they saw no one.

The floor inside the palace was polished stone. Rachel winced silently when—despite the care the cyborg warriors took to be quiet—their boots sparked a faint patter that echoed off the walls.

The guards stiffened and raised their weapons.

Energy blasts that seemed to emerge from nothing dropped every guard before they could decide whether they should fire at the open doorway and risk damaging something outside that the emperor would likely kill them for later... or wait to see if something actually *had* entered.

Every shot was quick and clean, killing instantly.

The guards sank to the floor without firing back or sounding an alarm.

"Clear," Wonick whispered.

Rachel strolled over to the doorway, careful not to bump into the four cyborgs who remained outside—ready to help their brothers on the roof battle reinforcements if needed—and peered inside at the dead guards. "Good job. Are you ready for me to create a diversion?"

"Yes," Wonick replied.

Smiling, she glanced toward the sound of his voice, gave him a cocky salute, and darted away in a blur of motion.

The faint sounds of two cyborgs following reached her ears as she circled around the side and leapt over the high wall.

"*Drek*, she's fast," one blurted over comms.

"And strong," the other said. "She's already over the wall."

Ignoring them, Rachel zigzagged through the pretty garden beds in front until she reached the northwest corner. "*Veedetha neh wusokt!*" she shouted in a deep voice.

Somewhere, a couple of guards erupted into speech.

She zipped over to the northeast corner. "*Veedetha neh wusokt!*" she bellowed in a deeper voice. "*Yen* voxi *na sampe dewan, oora* dey *sethna sampes dewan!*"

"*Veedetha neh wusokt!*" one of the cyborgs who had followed her called near the western fence. The other joined in with more cries of dissent, adding Gathendien gibberish that her translator indicated meant "Kill the emperor."

Rachel raced back and forth, shouting for a few more seconds. As soon as guards converged on the front gate to ensure it remained locked, she headed for the statue. Water splashed as she leapt into the sparkling pool at the statue's base. Planting her hands on the stone emperor's shins, she braced her feet and pushed. The tall figure shifted slightly on its foundation.

"*Srul*," Nebet muttered inside. "I think she's going to do it."

Hell yes, she was going to do it. But this damn thing was heavy. Even with her incredible strength, she had to add a powerful telekinetic shove.

The statue groaned, tilted sideways, and toppled over, landing with a resounding crash on the stone pavement that made the base of the pool she stood in vibrate beneath her feet. Water rose in waves that splashed over the edges. To Rachel's satisfaction, the stone statue broke into three large chunks that wobbled and kicked up dust before the head—with some of the neck still attached—rolled away several feet.

Yes!

Every guard swung around to gape at the wreckage. Rachel dashed away in a blur. O-rifle fire lit up the fountain, striking the water where she had stood.

A click sounded as the front doors swung open.

"Rachel," Wonick whispered over comms.

She raced inside. The door shut. With her boots slick from the fountain, Rachel tried to halt, slipped, and bumped into a large, hard, camouflaged form.

Armor-clad arms wrapped around her to steady her.

"Oops." She scrambled to find her footing. "Wonick, is that you?"

"Yes."

She grinned up at him. "I almost slipped and fell on my ass. That would've been embarrassing."

He laughed.

More weapons fire erupted outside.

"*Veedetha neh wusokt!*" the cyborgs continued to shout on the grounds, furthering the ruse. "*Yen* voxi *na sampe dewan, oora* dey *sethna sampes dewan!*"

She glanced through the windows. Multiple guards started dropping as they battled invisible opponents.

Shouts arose somewhere upstairs. An alarm blared.

Wee-wonk! Wee-wonk! Wee-wonk!

Machinery whirred to life in the walls as thick panels slid down outside, blocking their view of the gardens. Boots pounded stone flooring.

Rachel backed out of Wonick's arms and drew her swords. "Okay. Here we go."

Wonick and the six cyborgs who'd joined him inside fell into formation. At least, she thought they did. It was impressively hard for her to gauge their locations.

"Get behind us, Rachel," Wonick ordered.

She aimed a disparaging look in his direction. "I don't think so." The guards thundering toward them would look for a target. If their eyes all swung toward *her*, the cyborgs could take them out without suffering damage that might hinder their camo in future clashes.

"I expected nothing less," he muttered dryly, "but it was worth a try. S, can you provide us with a likely location of the emperor?"

"Sending palace blueprints now," S responded.

A translucent map appeared on the inside of her helmet's visor.

"The highlighted area comprises the emperor's private quarters," S informed them.

Footsteps grew louder. Four Gathendien guards rounded a corner at a run, weapons at the ready.

Wonick and his team fired before they could stumble to a halt and target Rachel. The guards fell to the floor with a clatter that echoed off the walls.

"*Veedetha neh wusokt!*" the men continued to bellow outside to the accompaniment of O-rifle fire.

Rachel and the others moved forward. She frowned as the three-dimensional map reflected on her visor shifted every time she turned her head. "I may have to remove my helmet if this map distracts me too much. I'm still not used to it."

"It'll warn you of approaching guards."

Plenty of red dots filled the palace. "My nose and ears can do that for me," she reminded him. "I have enhanced senses, remember?"

"Your enhanced senses won't protect your head from weapons fire."

"No." She smiled. "That's what my kickassitude is for."

Several snorts of laughter carried over comms as their team crept forward.

As they proceeded toward the rear of the building, she took in her surroundings and curled her lip in disgust. "Seriously?" She motioned around them. "All of this for one wanker with delusions of grandeur, his beleaguered concubines, and some servants? You could fit an entire Home Depot in this vestibule." The ceiling height had to be at least fifteen feet. The distance from the front to the rear doors rivaled a football field. They had even lined the walls with benches and hung framed art above them, bringing to mind images of elder Gathendien statesmen pausing to rest before continuing the laborious trek to the back to the palace.

"Commander Savaas," S said suddenly. "I have infiltrated the facility's systems and looped security footage. You and Unit One are free to enter. Once you are inside, I will initiate a facility lockdown on your command."

"Commencing infiltration," Savaas replied.

Rachel hoped they would find their captive brethren alive.

Wonick and the others tensed as multiple red dots on the palace map approached in both back corridors that opened onto the vestibule. Boots clomped on the flooring as the guards tore around the corners and faced them.

"Hello," Rachel called brightly in Alliance Common, drawing their attention.

Oblivious to the cyborgs' presence, the guards all turned their weapons toward her and fired.

She would've used her telekinetic gift to pick them all up and slam them into one another, but Wonick swore and opened fire before she could. And Rachel worried that if she shot forward to kick ass the usual way, the cyborgs might hesitate to fire for fear of hurting her. So she had to settle for dodging the Gathendiens' fire and being a diversion. Again.

Two guards ducked back into the corridor on the left. Three made it to the right. A second later two e-grenades flew into sight—each around a corner—and bounced toward them.

Her eyes widened. "Grenades!"

WONICK AND HIS MEN dove to the sides.

Panic filled him as he looked around. Where was Rachel?

A blur shot across his view. The e-grenades abruptly vanished. Half a second later, both corridors exploded. Flames, debris, and body parts flew forth.

His heart stopped.

Then Rachel appeared in the center of the vestibule, near the back doors. Stumbling, she almost fell.

Wonick raced toward her. "Rachel? Are you injured?"

She scowled down at the floor. "No. My boots are still wet, and this damn floor is ridiculously slick. Don't they worry about the emperor slipping and falling on his ass when he comes in after a swim?"

A relieved laugh huffed from him as he pulled her into a quick hug. "What did you do?"

She patted his back. "I used telekinesis to hurl the grenades back at them, but I needed to duck around the corners to see how far to send them and wanted to make sure I didn't blow up the staircase."

"Unit One has breached the facility," Savaas announced over comms. "Lock it down, S."

"Locking down facility."

"S," Wonick added, "commence military base strikes."

"Initiating strikes now," the AI announced with glee.

Rachel smiled as she backed away. "I swear, if we could see his android form right now, he'd be bouncing up and down in his seat."

It wouldn't surprise Wonick. Red dots gathered into groups on the interior palace map. Half rushed toward the explosions. The other half ran toward the emperor's quarters. "Let's go."

They headed into the east wing. A handful of doors lined a long corridor that curved in a southerly direction. On one side, a staircase broad enough for the cyborgs to walk four abreast led to a landing above.

Guards burst into view from the curve in the corridor. Wonick and the other cyborgs extended their arms, curled their fingers into fists, and fired their armor's onboard weapons. *Osdulium* blasts, similar to those from an O-rifle, flew from his wrist gauntlets.

It hadn't taken the cyborgs long to realize that carrying large weapons made sneaking up on enemies impossible. It might take foes a beat or two to understand what was happening. But once they did, all they had to do was aim for the rifles that appeared to be floating in midair. So the cyborgs had upgraded their armor to include built-in weapons.

As a backup, however, every cyborg kept a compact, easy-to-assemble O-rifle in the camouflaged weapons pack attached to the back of their armor, plus a stash of grenades.

The Gathendien guards fell. No cyborgs sustained injuries.

Rachel didn't either, but she seemed oddly restless.

Wonick frowned. "Is the map too distracting, Rachel?" He could have S remove it for her if she didn't remember how.

"No. I'm getting used to it."

Then why the restlessness? When Wonick had seen her in battle before, she had been calm, cocky, or furiously fierce as she fought one warrior after another.

They started up the long staircase. At the landing, the stairs did a half turn and continued up to the next floor. A wall adorned with art separated the staircase's halves, preventing him from seeing anyone on the other side who might be lying in wait to fire upon them. But no red dots lingered there.

Red dots *did*, however, swarm toward them from the western wing below.

Wonick and the others swung around and fired.

As soon as every guard dropped, Wonick turned back to continue scaling the stairs.

Rachel stood behind him, lips tight, hands balled into fists around the hilts of her weapons. And realization dawned. Once she'd come inside and joined them, the only battle she'd engaged in had been redirecting the grenades. She hadn't done any fighting herself.

Did she worry they might shoot her?

Knowing Rachel, she more likely worried that diving into battle might cause the cyborgs to hesitate before firing.

No wonder she was twitchy.

"Rachel?"

"Yes?"

"We go high, you go low?" he suggested, using the phrase she had used back on the planet.

Tension melted from her form as she smiled. "How about I go high and *you* go low?"

He eyed her diminutive form. "How are you going to go high?"

She winked. "I'll show you. We have company."

Red dots approached the upper staircase from the south.

Spinning around, Rachel led the way up the stairs. As soon as she reached the second floor, she sprinted forward. But this time she did it at what she often described as a mortal's speed. Wonick and his men quickly followed.

At the top of the staircase, they paused.

Five Gathendiens jogged toward Rachel. One called a gruff order to halt.

Ignoring him, she veered toward one wall, leapt up, and ran along it, her body canting sideways.

Eyes widening, the guards stopped short and gaped as they raised their weapons.

Too late. Metal glinted as she swung her swords, decapitating those in front.

Flipping to the floor behind them, she slew the rest as they swiveled to face her.

After the guards slumped to the floor, she grinned at Wonick. "See? When I do that at preternatural speeds, I have more momentum and can stay up a lot longer. I'll go high, you go low."

"*Drek*," Nebet whispered. "She really *is* our sister." Able to move faster and farther with each step, cyborgs had used such tactics often in the past.

333

"Hell yes, I am," she replied proudly.

"Reinforcements are arriving," Aagar announced from the roof.

"A *lot* of reinforcements," Fonwen added.

A rumble arose as the cyborgs on the roof activated the cannons and high-powered rifles. The boom of explosions followed.

"Let's go," Wonick ordered.

Instead of clearing out the second floor before moving on, Wonick left Sonjin and Taaduro at the base of the staircase to cover their rear as the rest continued up. The palace was four levels high, with the emperor's domain at the top. Most of the red dots now rushed to protect the emperor, the number there growing until it neared a hundred.

According to the map, several guards lingered on the third floor at the top of the stairs. None had detected the infiltrators' heat signatures.

Upon reaching the landing, Rachel turned to Wonick. "Do you have any grenades?" she whispered, barely audible over comms.

"Yes."

"Give me a couple."

Wonick opened the compartment on his thigh. "Do you want Bex-7 stun grenades or Z-12 explosives?"

"Z-12s."

He placed one in each of her small hands.

"See you in a minute." She darted away in a blur. Startled grunts sounded above.

Wonick and his team remained on the landing, out of view.

The guards at the top started arguing. Rachel had moved so quickly that they hadn't realized the intruder they sought had just plowed through them and instead accused each other of shoving.

"*Veedetha neh wusokt!*" Rachel bellowed from the north end of the corridor.

Swearing, several of the guards took off running toward the north.

Rachel's white dot on the map disappeared, then reappeared a second later at the south end.

"*Veedetha neh wusokt!*" she shouted.

More guards ran south.

Wonick peered around the corner. Only a couple manned the stairs, and those watched their fellow guards instead of keeping an eye on the landing.

A faint blur leapt over the guards heads and zipped down the stairs.

Rachel appeared in front of Wonick on the middle landing.

Before the guards could spot her, explosions rang out on the third floor. Fire and debris shot forth from the corridors. The guards at the top of the stairs dove for the floor. Smoke billowed from both ends, forming a thick cloud.

Rachel peered up at the damage. "Good. I got them far enough away to blow up most of the guards without damaging the stairs."

The guards scrambled to their feet and gaped at the damage beyond Wonick's sight.

Rachel narrowed her eyes then made an odd up-and-down gesture with both hands.

The guards yelped as they abruptly flew up and slammed into the high ceiling, then hit the floor.

Rachel didn't use her telekinetic ability often. But when she did, it amazed him. Smiling, Wonick shook his head. "You go high, we go low."

Together, they raced up the staircase and dispatched the two Gathendiens before they could finish picking themselves up. The other third floor guards who survived the Z-12s exploding opened fire.

Wonick's armor took a few hits. The feed on the left side of his visor lit up with warnings, alerting him to damage incurred. While the armor held, protecting him from harm, every strike destroyed camouflage cells and left scorch marks that would give away his location to anyone paying attention.

Rachel remained in constant motion until the last guard fell. When she stopped, she was breathing hard, her lightweight armor splattered with blood.

"Are you injured?" Wonick asked as he joined her.

"No. The armor protected me." She pointed a sword at one of the guards. "That dumb bastard shot two of his own men, trying to get me."

O-rifle blasts lit up the wall beside them, coming from the next staircase. A Gathendien on the middle landing tossed something then ducked out of sight. A grenade flew toward them.

Eyes widening, Rachel dropped a sword and moved her hand in a blur.

In a blink, the grenade shifted direction and sailed as fast as a missile to the far end of the blackened and flame-filled third-floor corridor before it exploded. Debris rained down from the floor above and fell through a hole in the floor.

"Whew!" Rachel exclaimed and picked up her sword. "That was close."

Terrifyingly close. Her armor couldn't protect her from as much as his could.

Leaning around the corner, Wonick fired several times at the guards on the middle landing. Nebet and the others joined him, firing until all the guards tumbled down the stairs.

"Let's keep moving," Wonick murmured and headed up.

When they reached the landing, Nebet leaned around the wall and tossed something up the second staircase. "Stun grenades," he murmured. A second later, electricity lit up the stairwell like lightning. Bodies thudded to the floor. Two tumbled down the stairs to land at their feet on the landing.

A *tap-tap-tap* sound arose, as though someone had dropped something and it was slowly rolling down the—*Oh drek.*

Wonick dove for Rachel, taking her to the floor as light flashed. Fire and debris burst from the unseen staircase. The wall beside them exploded with a thunderous boom. Chunks of ceiling rained down as he covered Rachel's small form as best he could. Heavy chunks pummeled his back and legs. More alerts lit up his visor.

Quiet fell inside, disturbed only by the crackling of fire and the muted explosions and heavy weapons fire that thundered outside the palace as his men outside battled arriving Gathendien rein-forcements.

Dust sifted down. Something groaned overhead.

Nebet! Wonick growled over mental comms.

What? It was a stun grenade, he retorted. *How was I supposed to know one of the* grunarks *was holding an active Z-12?*

Common sense? Benwa grumbled as the cyborgs shook off the debris and climbed to their feet.

"Rachel?" Wonick said aloud.

"I'm good," she replied, her voice strained. "You're just heavy as hell with all that armor on."

Wonick hastily released her and rose. Reaching down, he took her hand and helped her up. As far as he could tell, she'd suffered no injuries.

Swiping at the dust coating her helmet, she looked at him and froze mid-motion. "Uh-oh." Her gaze swept past him to his brothers.

Wonick turned, already knowing what he'd see.

Dust coated every one of them. Even an infant would have no difficulty spotting them now.

"So much for the cool camouflage," she muttered. "Give me some of those stun grenades."

Wonick retrieved four Bex-7s from his reserve pack, surveying the damage as he did so. The wall that had previously separated the half-back staircases was gone. Shredded splinters of the paintings that had adorned it now impaled the remaining walls and ceiling. The grenade had destroyed most of the staircase that led from the landing to the fourth-floor corridor, leaving a gaping hole too large for most individuals to leap across, even with a running start.

Rachel eyed the remnants of the staircase's middle wall that dangled from the ceiling. "I hope that wasn't load-bearing."

Another ominous groan resonated above them.

Her eyes met his. Yanking the grenades from his grasp, she leapt long and high, reaching the fourth floor with ease. Bodies littered the hallway around her. Smoke filled the air, constantly thickening as it wafted up from below.

O-rifle fire erupted, coming from deeper in the fourth-floor corridor.

Wonick sucked in a breath. Rachel was out in the open with nothing but rising smoke to hide behind!

She dodged and ducked, quickly enough to avoid getting hit he hoped, but let the Gathendiens catch a glimpse of her here and there. Cries of pain erupted. Masculine. Not feminine.

Nebet snorted a laugh. "Brilliant. She's got them shooting each other."

Rachel grunted when one bolt hit her. Then a second.

Before Wonick could tell her to get the *srul* out of there, she disappeared.

A heartbeat later, the smoke in the stairwell swirled as something—or someone—flew through it.

Rachel hit the floor in front of him, landing in a crouch.

Crackling electricity lit up the fourth floor as the stun grenades exploded. Thuds followed as more guards fell. Shouts erupted, tight with fear.

Rachel rose. Her armor smoked in two places. Grimacing, she arched her back as though in pain. But when Wonick opened his mouth, she held up a hand. "I'm okay. The armor held. That O-rifle fire just packs a punch that may leave a bruise." Laughter danced in her eyes, which now glowed bright red. "Totally worth it, though. Those wankers were actually shooting each other. Can you believe it?"

Relieved, Wonick tamped down his amusement. "Yes. Let's go before they regroup."

CHAPTER EIGHTEEN

S SPOKE OVER COMMS. "Commanders, I have destroyed all craft in the city's military bases. But more approach from the city to the south."

Rachel looked at Wonick. "That can't be good." On Earth, she thought it took quite a few minutes to scramble fighters and get them to another city. But all military aircraft out here could travel through space at speeds Earth crafts couldn't even *hope* to match, giving them—what—a few seconds?

"Initial crafts are arriving now," S announced.

The rumble above grew louder.

Wonick frowned. "Hoshaan? Our brothers on the roof need support."

"Already hovering above them and engaging the enemy," Hoshaan responded. "So is S-7."

"S, send drones to destroy the military bases in the southern city and use the remaining C-23s to eliminate as many incoming threats to our locations as you can."

"Yes, Commander."

Rachel leapt up to the fourth floor again, sailing over the remains of the wrecked staircase.

Jumping over the gaping hole in the stairs proved no challenge for the cyborgs. Except for Nebet. The last to jump, Nebet swore when he landed on the top step and it gave way beneath him, sending him plummeting through to the third floor.

"Quit *drekking* around and get up here," Wonick snapped but spoiled the gruff order by laughing.

Snickers carried over comms even as the cyborgs fired at the guards at the south end of the corridor.

Rachel grinned... until the guards who remained on the fourth floor fired back. Most of them clustered together in front of the emperor's quarters. The e-grenades had done a lot of damage down there, blowing holes in the walls and part of the floor several yards in front of the guards' position. But she was dismayed to note that the imposing double doors behind them remained intact, as did the back wall. She couldn't spot even a tiny dent in either.

Were they blast doors? Reinforced walls?

Rachel joined the others in hugging the sides of the hallway as O-rifle fire flew their way. Aside from a few sizable potted plants, some of which were on fire, there wasn't much to hide behind other than each other.

Rachel focused her telekinesis and yanked the rifles from several guards' hands.

Something slammed into her from behind, pushing her forward a step. Grunting, she looked back.

A small group of guards advanced toward them from the north end of the corridor, probably hoping to get them all in the back while the larger group distracted them.

"You take the south end, I'll take the north," she told the cyborgs and raced away. Running up the wall at top speed, she approached the enemy from above. (Every floor in this freaking palace had fifteen-foot ceilings.)

The guards didn't see her coming. Their focus remained on the large dusty forms that provided easy targets.

Rachel's swords flashed. Low hisses and growls of pain split the air as those still on their feet stopped targeting the cyborgs and looked around wildly. They outnumbered her ten to one but had a hard time fighting the foe they couldn't even get a good look at.

An explosion rocked the building. Dust sifted down from the high ceiling. It must be the incoming Gathendien craft firing at the cyborgs on the roof.

Another explosion outside sent pieces of ceiling crashing down around her. "The Gathendiens won't blow up the palace with the emperor still inside it, will they?" she asked.

The distraction cost her. A Gathendien got in a lucky shot at close range. Growling, she sheathed her swords, leapt onto his shoulders, and gave his rough head a twist.

"No," Wonick responded. An explosion erupted at the south end. "Those are blast doors."

"Yeah," Nebet replied. "It'll be hard as *srul* to get through them."

Rachel jumped off the falling Gathendien, landed, and tripped over one of the half-dozen bodies that littered the floor. When another Gathendien shot her in the back with a blaster, she swore. Though it didn't break the skin, it hurt like hell. And she didn't know how much more her armor could withstand before it gave. Alerts she lacked the time to read flashed across her visor. Spinning around, she delivered a roundhouse kick powerful enough to break most of the Gathendien guard's ribs and sent him hurling down the hallway. She followed that up with a telekinetic push that kept him sliding along until he fell through a hole blown into the floor by a grenade she'd tossed earlier.

Only three Gathendiens remained around her. Rachel clenched her hands into fists. Warmth surged through her as she again called upon her telekinetic ability. Raising her hands, she flung the guards in front of her up to slam into the high ceiling, down to the floor, up to the ceiling, then away to follow their buddy through the hole in the floor.

Weakness trickled through her. She would have to rely on her weapons from this point on.

"Incoming!" Nebet called.

At the same time, Wonick shouted, "Grenade!"

Crackling electricity lit up the south hallway.

Sucking in a sharp breath, Rachel drew her swords and spun around.

Two cyborgs collapsed to the floor, their limbs twitching. The others she couldn't see.

The walls down there were scorched black. One now had a ragged opening in it.

Wonick and three members of the team emerged from it. Relief filled her as they swiftly dragged their friends inside the room they must have ducked into while the others tossed grenades.

More explosions erupted. Inside and out. A faint hum met her ears, barely audible beneath the shouts and noise of battle.

Before she could ask what caused it, S spoke. "Commander Wonick, I detect movement in one wall of the emperor's quarters. The blueprints show only a wall. But I believed it may instead contain a hidden room or lift."

"Wait," Rachel blurted. "What? Is it the emperor? Is he getting away?" Did he have some secret escape route?

Oh, hell no!

"Unknown," S replied calmly. "There are no surveillance feeds in the emperor's quarters that would enable me to offer an accurate response, and infrared scans are not penetrating the thicker walls."

Rachel ran toward Wonick and the others.

A few guards remained standing at the far end of the corridor and continued to put up a fight. The blast doors that protected the emperor's domain remained standing, unblemished beyond a few scorch marks.

Damn it!

She glanced behind her, where the last guards she'd defeated had fallen through the jagged opening in the floor. Then she looked at the hole grenades had blown in the floor near the emperor's domain.

An idea struck.

"Wonick!" she called. "I need you!"

He swung around instantly and ran toward her.

Rachel met him at the top of the stairs. "Follow me!" She jumped over the gaping hole to the landing below, then jumped again. As soon as her feet hit the third floor, she took off running. At the south end of the hallway, she skidded to a halt.

Wonick stopped beside her a half-second later. "What—?"

She pointed to the ceiling. "I need you to blast a hole in that. I'm guessing rifle fire won't be enough."

His dusty visor turned up to the ceiling. A moment passed before he faced her once more. "Clever Earthling," he murmured. Though she couldn't see his face through the dust and camouflage his helmet boasted, she could tell by his voice that he was smiling.

She grinned.

He quickly withdrew a couple of Z-12s from his stash and tampered with them for a couple of seconds. "Get back."

Rachel retreated far enough to avoid shrapnel, she hoped.

Wonick tossed the grenades up, then followed her.

Instead of bouncing off the ceiling when they hit, the little globes stuck to it as if glued there.

Wonick crowded Rachel against one wall, covering her head and pretty much everything else with his big armored body. A thunderous boom split the air. Debris struck multiple surfaces. A few bits clunked against Wonick's armor despite the distance.

"Wonick?"

He backed away. "I'm good."

Rachel gave him a quick once-over to be sure. Then both of them returned to the end of the corridor. Piles of splintered wood and chunks of stone tile littered the hallway, as did the remains of what looked like a sofa.

They looked up. A gaping hole now provided a view of a distant ceiling with a mural painted on it.

The emperor's quarters.

"Yes!" she hissed. Her hunch had been correct. Whoever had designed the palace had installed blast doors to keep intruders out on the fourth floor and had probably reinforced the ceiling of his personal quarters as well, in case someone bombed the palace from above. But they hadn't thought to reinforce the floor.

Wonick spoke over comms. "All cyborgs in the palace, get your asses to the third floor, southeast corner. We've breached the emperor's quarters."

Swords still in hand, Rachel bent her knees and jumped. Up she flew, fifteen feet, through the hole, and farther still before landing on her feet in the middle of a sumptuous and rather garishly decorated bedroom and sitting room.

It was huge. Not as immense as that vestibule downstairs. But *sheesh.* A massive bed that could easily accommodate half a dozen cyborgs dominated one wall. Chairs and sofas with gaps in back for thick tails abounded.

Wonick flew up through the hole in the floor and landed beside Rachel.

Pounding and shouting drew her attention to two Gathendiens in the far corner of the room. One pounded his fists against *stovicun* crystal doors and bellowed curses at another who had ducked inside a...

She frowned. What was that? A panic room? It was small with only a single chair in the center.

Half a dozen soldiers moved to stand between Rachel and the two men. These were taller, thicker Gathendiens and looked fiercer than the other guards she'd encountered. They wore different armor, too. The guards she and the others had already defeated had mostly worn armor that shielded their soft bellies and relied on their ultra-thick hide to protect the rest. But these guys' armor shielded everything. Every limb. Every organ. They even wore helmets like the cyborgs.

"Royal guard," Wonick murmured a second before the bastards raised their weapons and fired. Wonick dodged to the side and returned fire.

Rachel ducked, circled around, and barreled through the guards like a rampaging bull. Every one of them shouted as their feet flew up and their backs hit the floor hard. She attacked the first one before he could regain his feet. But his armor left no easy targets. Instead of piercing flesh, her swords formed dents. Swearing, she dropped them, grabbed the guard's helmet, and gave it a hard twist.

His body went limp.

Wonick engaged three others in a firefight, drawing them away.

The two who remained both pounced on Rachel. The combined weight of the Gathendiens and their armor threatened to carry her to the floor. But Rachel braced her feet and started throwing elbows and punches, hurling them back. A kick powered by her enhanced strength broke the seal of one's helmet, which went flying. Retrieving her swords, Rachel swiftly decapitated him and turned to face the third.

Bright light abruptly blinded her. Her body froze, muscles locking as electricity crackled through her, heating her insides until it felt as though her brain boiled inside a cauldron and her heart fried in her chest. Pain seared her for several agonizing seconds before the light dimmed and the energy surging through her ceased. Rachel toppled to the floor like the statue she'd tipped over outside. Her head struck stone tile. Her hands clenched convulsively around her katanas' grips as her vision returned.

A heavy thud vibrated the floor next to her as a faint breeze buffeted her.

Incapable of moving more than her eyes, she glanced to the side.

The third guard must've decided to sacrifice himself and take them *both* down with a stun grenade because he now lay twitching beside her.

More bodies burst into the room through the hole in the floor, encased in dusty armor.

The cyborgs.

A flurry of rifle fire ensued.

"Rachel?" A large figure leaned over her, blocking out the light. Some of the dust had blown off Wonick's armor, creating a weird effect in which part of his form was invisible and part appeared as dust or scorch marks.

"I'm okay," she wheezed, trying to catch her breath as her body finally stopped twitching. "B-bastard got both of us."

Taking her hand, Wonick drew her up and encouraged her to lean against him.

Quiet fell. At least, inside the room, it did. Outside, war continued to rage.

Rachel straightened, still stiff from the Bex-7, and glanced around. Every royal guard was down.

She looked toward the corner. Both Gathendiens gaped at them.

Now that the chaos had ceased, Rachel identified the one outside the panic room as Emperor Insiorga. She didn't know who the other one was.

The emperor swung back to the crystal wall and beat his fists against it. "Priortek, you *drekker*, let me in!"

Wasn't that the supreme commander's name?

Rachel reached for the little button at the neckline of her armor. A hiss sounded as her helmet unlatched, retracted, and folded back into her collar. Bending, she retrieved the swords she'd dropped when Wonick helped her up.

Thanks to the virus inside her, she shook off the effects of the stun grenade faster than the guard who had ignited it. He still lay at her feet, unconscious.

His body jerked as a cyborg behind her shot him.

Inside the panic room, the supreme commander seemed not to notice as he gaped at her.

"An Akseli female?" he blurted, his voice muffled by the crystal that separated them.

The emperor spun around and eyed her with disbelief.

Rachel swung her swords in a showy display and strode toward them.

Fury darkened the emperor's features as he straightened his shoulders. "What is the meaning of this?"

She sent him a dark smile and addressed him in Alliance Common. "Chancellor Astennuh has decided he doesn't need you anymore."

His jaw sagged. "Astennuh sent you?" His gaze slid past her to the armored figures who spread out behind her, but she knew without looking that he couldn't spy their features.

The supreme commander stumbled backward in the panic room, dropped into the chair, and fumbled with something on the side of it. A strap encircled his waist seconds before he dropped out of view.

Rachel blinked.

Wonick swore. "It's a lift. S, find out where it goes."

"Yes, Commander."

The emperor's face twisted in a sneer. "That *grunark* Astennuh wouldn't try to assassinate me. He doesn't have the *insisas*."

Rachel nodded. "You're right. He probably doesn't." Since every guard was dead, the supreme commander was gone, and S had said there were no surveillance cameras in the emperor's quarters, she stopped pretending to be Akseli and spoke in English. "But I do."

He frowned. "That isn't Alliance Common."

"No, it isn't." She stalked toward him. "But it's a language you should be very familiar with." Her lips turned up in a wintry smile. "It's *Earth* English."

His eyes widened as they raked her small form. "You're an Earth-ling?"

"Yes." Though he towered over her by a good foot or more, she didn't hesitate to move in close until only a couple of feet separated them. "And I came to kick your ass."

He threw a punch.

Rachel swung a sword in a blink and severed his hand at the wrist.

Emperor Insiorga howled in pain as he gripped his forearm with the other hand. Blood poured forth. But fury still burned in his eyes. His long thick tail jerked toward her with the power of a heavy cudgel.

Rachel evaded it and drove a sword down through it, pinning his tail to the floor.

The emperor howled again, agony filling his features. And yet, the rage remained. "I'll kill you!" he bellowed, spittle dripping from his thin lips. "I'll kill you all!"

"No, you won't." She moved in closer as rage burned through her. "You already tried that, remember? And it didn't work. You *failed*."

"This isn't possible!" he snarled. "You must be a Lasaran. You can't be an Earthling. Earthlings are weak! They're primitive! They're—"

Rachel dropped her remaining katana, gripped the front of his neck with one hand, and slammed him back against the crystal wall.

He cried out, startled by the quick movement and the increased pain it spawned as it tugged on the tail her sword held in place.

"Do I look weak to you?" she shouted.

When he clumsily slung a bare foot out to kick her, she easily batted it aside.

"Try it again, and I'll put my other sword through your foot," she warned.

He stilled. "What do you want?" he demanded belligerently.

"What do I want?" she repeated in disbelief. "You tried to kill every man, woman, and child on my planet. You destroyed the *Kandovar*, had your men capture and torture my friends. And now you're plotting to kill off the Lasarans, the Purvelis, *and* the Yona." She shook her head. "I want you dead."

347

Releasing him, she stepped back and retrieved the sword she'd dropped.

The emperor sagged against the wall, cradling his wrist to his chest.

Rachel curled her lip in disgust as she raked a gaze over him. "You dream of ruling the galaxy. Well, I want you to know who stopped you. One of the very Earthlings you think are so far beneath you that we don't deserve to live." Her hand tightened around the grip of her sword. "You tried to wipe out every Earthling in existence. Now I will wipe out every Gathendien. And *you* will go down in history as your soon-to-be-forgotten civilization's last emperor, a male so weak and feeble that he couldn't stop a lone Earth female half his size from destroying his world."

The emperor's eyes widened with horror.

Rachel swung her katana. Not an ounce of sympathy arose as he raised his hand to the gash in his throat and slumped to the floor. He deserved much worse after all he'd done. The death, suffering, and heartbreak he'd caused.

Blood pooled around him, as red as the blood of an Earthling. And as it did, it dampened the fires of fury that had seared her insides ever since Gathendiens had destroyed the *Kandovar* at this man's behest.

Justice had been served. For Sinsta and all the other victims of his greed and malice.

She backed away, not wanting to soil her boots with the stain that crept across the floor toward her as the emperor gasped out his last breath.

Several snicks sounded behind her.

Rachel turned.

Wonick and the other cyborgs regarded her somberly, their visors raised to show their faces.

Explosions continued to thunder outside in sharp contrast to the silence within.

Nebet cleared his throat. "Do you really intend to kill all the Gathendiens?"

All tension leaving her shoulders, she rolled her eyes. "Of course not. I just wanted *him* to think I did. Seemed only right that his last thought be that he'd brought about the destruction of his own people after he spent decades trying to bring about the destruction of others."

Nodding, Nebet gave her a sheepish grin. "Just checking. You can be a little scary sometimes."

Rachel laughed, surprised she *could* in that moment.

Wonick moved forward and drew her into a hug.

Sighing, she leaned into him even though—with his armor on—it was like hugging a tank. "Thank you."

Nebet snorted. "You're thanking *us*? The whole galaxy should thank *you*. You've eradicated the biggest deterrent to peace."

She had also saved Earth from future threats of alien-orchestrated extinction. Hopefully. And yet, were she to return to her home planet, rather than being hailed a hero, she would still be hunted and reviled.

Fortunately, she had no intention of returning.

Wonick gently tipped her chin up. "Thank you, for helping us avenge our brothers."

Right. After all they'd learned, the cyborgs had wanted the emperor dead as much as *she* had. "Speaking of your brothers..."

Releasing her, Wonick kept a hand on her back. "The emperor is dead," he announced over comms, "and the supreme commander is on the run. Savaas, report."

Heavy breathing carried over comms, a little fainter since Rachel had tucked her helmet away, muffling the signal. "We found our brothers. Loading them onto the dropship now. They require immediate medical care."

Wonick met her gaze. "*All* of them?"

"Yes. We'll fly straight to the *Shagosa*." That meant they were all alive, but in what condition?

"Any injuries in the unit?" Wonick asked.

"None life-threatening."

Wonick nodded. "We'll head to our dropship and offer you support. Hoshaan, prepare to pick us up on the roof."

"Already waiting," Hoshaan replied.

Rachel and the cyborgs dropped through the hole in the floor and raced back up to the fourth floor. The map on their visors led them to a door that was supposed to provide access to the roof.

Wonick had to force it open. "S, anything on the supreme commander's location?"

"Negative. Both the lift and the supreme commander vanished beneath the palace. No sensors are detecting his life signs."

Rachel frowned. "What's beneath the palace?"

"A complex network of sewage and utility access passages," S informed them.

She glanced at Wonick. Without tracking his life signs, there was no way to know which direction the supreme commander had gone or where he would emerge or seek shelter.

"Unit Three, report," Wonick ordered grimly.

"We found no captives in the facility, only Gathendiens. Permission to blow it and render aid to Unit One?"

"Permission granted." Wonick led the way up a long staircase that ended at another door. He had to force that one open, too. "Unit Four, report."

They stepped out onto the roof. Rachel winced as the noise increased exponentially. Night sky appeared above them, partially obscured by billowing black smoke. Aagar, Vaaren, and Fonwen manned massive guns and cannons, firing almost constantly at troops on the ground *and* at the sky, where a few Gathendien craft fought cloaked drones remotely piloted by S in a bizarre, half-visible battle.

"Nothing but Gathendiens at this facility," a cyborg said over comms. "We downloaded all data, ejected the cleaning crew, and are prepared to blow the building."

"Do it."

"Permission to provide support to Unit One afterward?"

"Permission granted."

Something clanked against the roof behind her. Spinning around, she gaped. A rectangular view of the dropship's interior seemed to hover in the middle of nothing above the roof, a ramp leading up to it. Black splotches dotted the sky on either side of the entrance where the craft's cloaking sensors had been damaged.

"Go! Go! Go!" Wonick shouted over the noise of battle.

Together, they raced up the ramp. At the top, Wonick leaned out to provide cover fire as the cyborgs who'd remained on the ground made it to the roof and sprinted toward the dropship. Two Gathendien craft abruptly exploded. Debris rained down, clunking against the dropship's exterior. It rocked to one side, dragging the ramp along the roof. Two cyborgs cursed and nearly fell off the ramp but made it the last few feet and dove inside. Aagar continued to fire one of those big cannons.

"Aagar!" Wonick bellowed. "Now!"

Only two Gathendien craft remained in the air. As Aagar continued to fire, his big body jerking with every ammo launch, one of the craft exploded in a spectacular display of flames and fireworks. Whooping, he abandoned his weapon and raced up to join them.

The hatch closed.

Rachel and the others swiftly found seats and strapped themselves in. The stealth dropship banked sharply and shot away, somehow managing to achieve incredible speeds without exerting G-forces on those inside.

In mere seconds, they joined three other dropships, now easier to spot because of the damage their camouflage had suffered. Unit One led them up through the planet's atmosphere. The others surrounded it and provided cover fire in a diamond flight formation she recalled seeing on Earth.

"No cyborg left behind," Savaas said over comms.

The cyborgs and Rachel all thrust fists in the air. "No cyborg left behind!"

Rachel lowered her fist.

Wonick kept his in the air. "Immortal Guardians rock!"

Every cyborg thrust his fist back into the air and shouted, "Immortal Guardians rock!"

Even Savaas and the others joined in over comms.

Rachel laughed in delight.

When weariness seeped in, she sagged in her seat. Relief and a sense of satisfaction filled her as she smiled up at Wonick. "We did it."

Smiling, he looped an arm around her shoulders and drew her as close as their harnesses and his armor would allow. "We did."

CHAPTER NINETEEN

ONICK CUT THROUGH THE water with leisurely strokes until he reached the other side of the lake. Turning his back to the shore, he stretched his arms along the grassy edge and let his legs float up to the surface. Artificial sunlight warmed his skin. Small simians leapt from branch to branch in the foliage above. And laughter filled the *Shagosa*'s park, accompanied by splashing and banter.

Almost every cyborg aboard roamed the lush expanse, decompressing after the big battle.

Two figures emerged from the trees on the far side of the lake.

He smiled.

Rachel walked slowly, one arm around the waist of a cyborg who draped an arm across her shoulders and tried futilely not to lean on her. Everything about Osraan's appearance told the tale of his years of captivity and sparked rage inside Wonick. Though Osraan's skin was naturally darker than Wonick's, today it seemed wan. His formerly thick, powerful limbs now sported significantly leaner muscle that could barely support his *alavinin*-reinforced bones, attesting to the starvation and malnutrition he'd suffered. Scars crisscrossed his form where the Gathendiens had cut him open repeatedly to study his enhancements. Even his face bore them, leaving his visage as marred as that of Janwar's Rakessian friend, Kova.

All the newly freed cyborgs looked thusly.

Every step sparked pain, and yet Osraan smiled.

Wonick credited Rachel with that. One of her small hands held the cyborg's, keeping his arm across her shoulders. She grinned up at him and spoke, sparking a rusty laugh as she slowly guided him toward the reclining chairs positioned beside the lake.

Osraan winced at the agony the laughter spawned.

Rachel's eyes flashed reddish amber for a second before she carefully brought her anger under control and found a smile again.

Wonick didn't have to read her mind to know she wished she could slay the Gathendien emperor all over again.

The other five injured cyborgs glanced over their shoulders and smiled as they watched her approach with their brother. All were curious about the lone female in their midst who had snared the loyalty and affection of their brothers and even fallen in love with one. Initially, they had thought her an Akseli and expressed their shock that the military had created female cyborgs without their knowledge. It had taken some time to convince them that she was instead an Immortal Guardian from Earth.

It helped that the dye coloring her skin and eyes was wearing off more rapidly than anticipated. Though only two days had passed, he estimated she would look herself again by the following evening.

Rachel revealed more of her amazing strength as she supported enough of Osraan's weight to help him slowly ease down on the cushioned chair. Once he was settled, she fluffed a pillow and placed it behind his head.

Osraan offered her another weary smile.

The six cyborgs had suffered much in the years they'd been captive. Of necessity, they'd spent the first day of their freedom in Med Bay while Taavion supplied them with intravenous liquids, vitamins, *silnas*, and a few more nanobots to speed their healing. Most of their injuries had already healed. Their strength would take longer to regain. As would the return of peace of mind.

Discovering that they weren't the last of the cyborgs had stunned them. Before selling them to the Gathendiens, Astennuh had told them the rest of the cyborgs had been slain. Much to Wonick's relief, none of them blamed him, Savaas, or the others for the freedom they'd attained while the other six suffered. Instead, they focused their wrath on Astennuh.

All wanted the Gathendien emperor and Chancellor Astennuh dead.

"Well, I already took care of the emperor for you," Rachel had told them.

Wonick and the others had immediately burst into speech, each talking over the other in their eagerness to share the tale of her assassination and of the emperor's humiliation and comeuppance.

"Thank you," Osraan said as he sank into the cushions.

Rachel smiled down at him. "For what?"

His lips turned up in a self-deprecating smile. "For distracting me so I wouldn't feel humiliated over being as weak as a newborn *braemen*. And for slaying Emperor Insiorga. Perhaps when I'm stronger, you can help me assassinate Astennuh."

Rachel patted his shoulder. "You're getting stronger every hour." She pursed her lips. "And I'm pretty sure Simone is going to assassinate Astennuh. I may help her since you're all my brothers now and I want the bastard to pay for hurting you."

His brow crinkled. "Who is Simone?"

"One of my Immortal Guardian friends. She's in love with Janwar and loathes Astennuh for what he did to Janwar and Krigara."

Vondec, one of the other injured cyborgs, cast her a quizzical look. "The boy Astennuh sent Wonick and Savaas to execute?"

She grinned. "That boy is now a man who has spent the years since you disappeared becoming one of the fiercest pirates in the galaxy, bedeviling Chancellor Astennuh at every opportunity, helping the cyborgs settle on their new homeworld, and enabling them to create all this." She motioned to the lush plant life around them.

The cyborgs looked at Wonick.

He smiled. "You've a lot of catching up to do. Don't worry. We'll help you. For today, simply relax and focus on recovering."

"I, on the other hand," Rachel announced, "will focus on proving I'm a better diver than every cyborg here." Turning to face the lake, she called, "Who's up for a little competition?"

Shouts filled the park.

She pointed at Wonick. "You're first, Handsome."

Rising from the water, he crossed to stand in front of her and shook the water out of his hair.

She laughed as droplets splashed her.

"After you," he insisted with a smile.

Together, they headed for the climbing wall.

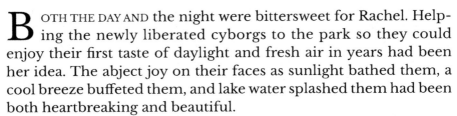

B OTH THE DAY AND the night were bittersweet for Rachel. Helping the newly liberated cyborgs to the park so they could enjoy their first taste of daylight and fresh air in years had been her idea. The abject joy on their faces as sunlight bathed them, a cool breeze buffeted them, and lake water splashed them had been both heartbreaking and beautiful.

When they later sat down to their first "real" meal aboard the *Shagosa*, the ecstasy that swept their features with their first bites brought tears to her eyes. None had consumed anything but taste-less nutrient cubes in years. And there had been long stretches in which only IV feeding was allowed. Even Taavion had insisted on the latter for the first twenty-four hours until he was satisfied they were stable.

When flavor instead burst upon their tongues, the Cyborg Six fell upon their trays like ravenous wolves. Wonick, Savaas, and Taavion had to caution them several times to eat slowly, fearing their shrunken stomachs would rebel. And Rachel wanted to weep all over again at the difficulty they had complying.

Every time she looked at one of them, gratitude filled her that she'd been able to seek justice, both on Earth's behalf *and* on theirs. Emperor Insiorga was no more. The supreme commander had scuttled into the shadows like a cockroach. S had found a back door into the Gathendien comms network that enabled him to monitor all transmissions *and* begin to pinpoint the locations of Gathendi-en ships. According to him, the Gathendiens' new homeworld was in total disarray, as was their military.

For now at least, she had accomplished her goal. With no ap-parent ruler, individual Gathendien military ships had stopped pursuing the acquisition of *Kandovar* survivors while they worried they might be next on her hit list. Along with news of the emperor's assassination, the cyborgs and S had spread the word that multiple Gathendien ships with Earthlings aboard had either been captured or destroyed, their entire crews slain.

None of the remaining commanders knew what the hell to do next. Any hesitance to criticize their former emperor had vanished as they blamed him for their precarious predicament. Hopefully, any Gathendien commanders currently in possession of Earthlings would ask each other what they should do with the cargo they now feared would paint a giant red target on their ship and, in doing so, reveal their locations.

Rachel wished the bastards would put the Earthlings back into their escape pods and set them free. When she worried aloud that the Gathendiens would instead chuck her Earth friends out an airlock and kill them, Wonick had impersonated a Gathendien commander and launched another rumor that harming Earthlings would result in an automatic death sentence issued by the mysterious hunters who had conquered multiple Gathendien warships, slain the emperor in his own stronghold, destroyed every military base on the planet, and had the backing of the Aldebarian Alliance.

Gathendiens now seemed about as eager to get their hands on more Earthlings as they were to contract *muryeurd*, which apparently was a horrifying venereal disease.

She shuddered, recalling the symptoms Wonick had relayed after a cyborg told a joke she didn't understand.

No Gathendien warships lay within range of the *Shagosa*. Wonick and Savaas had checked, hoping they could find some of her Earth friends on ships near the emperor's home. It would seem, however, that the emperor had succeeded in keeping his new homeworld a secret all this time by restricting travel to and from it. Consequently, the ships were as scattered throughout galaxy as the missing *Kandovar* survivors.

Wonick relayed the positions of each Gathendien ship they located to Janwar. Janwar and Simone intended to check out the one closest to them. The rest Janwar passed on to Dagon. As commander of the Segonian warship *Ranasura*, Dagon would reach out the rest of the Aldebarian Alliance and—with Janwar's aid—disseminate information accordingly through encrypted channels.

Because they still didn't know how the Gathendiens had learned of the Earthlings' presence on the *Kandovar*, all suspected the Lasaran communication system was compromised and opted to use other means to convey the latest information—one of those means being Janwar, whose encrypted comm system had proven undefeatable.

Who would've thought a pirate with a massive bounty on his head would end up being the Aldebarian Alliance's most trusted means of communication?

The *Shagosa* now headed for the cyborgs' homeworld. Savaas and the others were eager to get the Cyborg Six to the safety of their new home, where they could begin their long recovery. Once there, Rachel and Wonick would decide what they wanted do next. Take off on their own search-and-rescue mission? Remain on the cyborg planet and aid the others by continuing to sift through the wealth of data they'd downloaded from the Gathendien facilities and ships?

They still had a few days to decide.

The Cyborg Six wished to linger after last meal. But the meager explorations they'd managed earlier in the park had taxed their diminished strength and left them nodding groggily over empty plates.

None looked capable of making it back to Med Bay under their own steam.

Rachel didn't think they could even make it if they leaned on someone. Yet she knew inherently that carrying them would resurrect the anger that burned inside them.

Anger they had set aside for a time as they'd enjoyed the day.

"Anybody up for a swim?" she asked brightly.

All conversation ceased. Most of the cyborgs present looked at her as if she'd lost her mind.

"We swam earlier," Nebet reminded her.

She arched a brow and looked at the Cyborg Six. "Not all of us."

Osraan forced a drowsy smile. "Taavion wants us to wait a few more days before swimming in the lake."

She winked. "Who said anything about the lake?" Reaching into one of her cargo pants' pockets, she drew out a small device and handed it to Wonick. "I was thinking along the lines of something a little more fun. Want to help me out, Handsome?"

Wonick glanced down at the device, then grinned. "Absolutely."

Rachel pushed her chair back, rose, and spread her arms. "Let's do this."

Wonick aimed the device at her.

In the next instant, her feet left the ground.

Rachel laughed in delight as he used the handheld acquisition beam to make her fly through the air above the others' heads. "Woohoo!" she cried, reaching down to ruffle Nebet's hair as she passed him.

Laughter filled the commissary as Nebet pretended to grab for her and missed.

"This is awesome!" She spun and twirled as Wonick guided her around the room. "I've always envied my brethren who can shape-shift into the forms of birds and fly. You boys are so used to this technology that you've forgotten how to have fun with it."

She dropped half a dozen more palm-sized acquisition beam controllers into Savaas's lap, then started doing the breaststroke, pretending to swim across the cafeteria like a jolly frog.

Moments later, the Cyborg Six floated up from their seats. Smiles creased their haggard faces and some of their fatigue fell away as they joined her. Of course, when one mimicked her swimming maneuvers, the cyborgs controlling them decided there had to be a race. Or two. Or three. Bets flew. Hilarity ensued. And the weary cyborgs ended it all by seeing who could hit Med Bay first.

All made it to their beds without a hint of anger or self-consciousness over their weakness surfacing. Though she suspected they realized that had been her intention all along, none called her on it.

Rachel and Wonick were the last to leave them.

As she turned away, Osraan caught her hand. "Thank you. Sister."

Smiling, she gave his hand a squeeze. "Anytime." As she and Wonick headed out the door, she called, "I want a rematch tomorrow. Next time, I'll win."

The men's chuckles followed her out into the hallway.

Wonick curled an arm around her shoulders and drew her close as they headed for his and Savaas's quarters.

Savaas approached them from that direction. "Is everyone settled in Med Bay?"

Wonick nodded.

Savaas turned a kind smile on Rachel. "That was thoughtful of you, finding a way to spare them the indignity of having to be carried."

She shrugged. "I don't know what you're talking about. I just wanted to have fun."

"Mm-hm. I intend to spend the rest of the night sifting through more data we stole from the Gathendiens." An amused glint lit his eyes as he glanced at Wonick. "So you'll have our quarters to yourselves."

Rachel arched a brow. "So you're saying we're free to set up a net in the living room and play a game of naked volleyball?"

Savaas grinned, looking far younger than usual. "I don't know what that is and am not certain I *want* to know, but... sure. Have fun."

She laughed as he continued past them. "Night, Savaas."

"Goodnight, Rachel."

Wonick pressed a kiss to the top of her tousled hair. Flying around and twirling about had left it a bit of a mess. "Have I told you that I love you today?"

She wrapped an arm around his waist as they resumed walking. "Several times. But I wouldn't mind hearing it again."

He waited until they reached their living quarters and sealed themselves inside. "I love you, Rachel."

Looping her arms around his neck, she leaned up and pressed a kiss to his lips. "I love you, too."

He slid his arms around her and smiled. "I've asked Goaden and Benwa to try again to design some easy-to-apply facial prosthetics for me."

She stared at him, all plans of stripping him bare dissolving. "What? Why?" He wasn't still self-conscious about his scars, was he?

"We've tried temporary facial prosthetics before with unsatisfactory results." His brow furrowed. "Skin grafts and other permanent solutions fared better, but I want to be able to apply and remove them at will."

Rachel shook her head, puzzled. "Why would you want to apply them at all?"

"So facial recognition scans can't identify me." He linked his hands at the base of her spine and pressed her close. "I know you're worried about your missing friends and won't be happy patiently waiting for news while others search for them."

No, she wouldn't. It would make her feel as if she had abandoned them and was shirking the duties Seth had assigned her. Hieing off to kill the Gathendien emperor she could justify. It had reduced his military commanders' desire to capture Earthlings, brought their bioweapons research program to a screeching halt, given the cyborgs massive amounts of data that might help them locate captive *Kandovar* survivors, and saved six cyborgs' lives in the process.

But living a utopian life with Wonick and the other cyborgs while some of her friends might be suffering who knew what?

No. She couldn't justify that. Rachel had to do *something* but couldn't decide what and was admittedly reluctant to leave Wonick.

"I thought we could take a *Pahlwan-15*," Wonick murmured.

"I don't know what that is."

"It's larger than a C-23 but far smaller than the *Tangata*. Built for traveling rather than providing a permanent home, it lacks the expansive park, I'm afraid, and relies on air recyclers and oxygen scrubbers. But it's well-armed and won't be associated with any individuals or groups. That anonymity may spark greater scrutiny at ports and stations, but it's a risk we'd have to take. We'd fare better with a small crew than being on our own. Nebet and a handful of others have already volunteered and—"

Rachel covered his lips with an index finger. "Volunteered for what?"

He kissed her finger. "If you want to join the hunt for your missing friends, we can do so. If the new prosthetics work, they will enable me—and others—to accompany you to space stations, planets, and moons without facial recognition scans identifying us as cyborgs."

Her heart beat faster. "And if the prosthetics *don't* work?"

"We'd have to rely on our armor to shield us the way we did when we fought the Gathendiens and limit our public excursions."

"Won't your armor render you virtually invisible?"

"Yes, if no altercations arise. But the camouflage that would protect us would also lend you the appearance of a lone, vulnerable female and lure predators into attacking."

"In which case, I would kick their asses."

He smiled. "Depending on their numbers and the weapons they employ. We would, of course, aid you. But firefights would mar our armor and mark us as camouflaged warriors."

She studied him. "What would be the downside of that?" As long as they kept their helmets on, onlookers still wouldn't be able to identify them as cyborgs.

"The downside would be that most would assume we were members of the Segonian military. And if rumors of Segonian soldiers going rogue and blowing things up began to circulate, Segonia may choose to investigate."

"Oh. Right." Simone had confided that Segonians were among the least likely members of the Aldebarian Alliance to be attacked because—like some of the cephalopods on Earth—they could blend in with their surroundings and virtually disappear from view.

"If they did and began to hunt us," he concluded, "we probably won't see them coming. And they may not stop to ask questions."

A distinct disadvantage that would result in considerable risk.

Rachel nibbled her lower lip. "I can't ask you to do that."

"You haven't." Dipping his head, he rubbed noses with her. "You risked your life to give Savaas's team more time to infiltrate that facility and liberate our brothers. How can we not risk ours to help you liberate and rescue your sisters?" He pressed a tender kiss to her lips. "I see the worry in your eyes. If we find ourselves in trouble and our search takes us in their direction, we can always rendezvous with Janwar and Simone and enlist their aid. We would be safe aboard the *Tangata*."

She tightened her hold on him. "Are you sure about this?"

"Yes."

"And the others?"

"They're sure."

"Even Savaas?"

He smiled. "Even Savaas."

Rising on her toes, Rachel took his lips in a deep, passionate kiss. Both were breathless when she relented. "I love you so much, Wonick."

"I love you, too."

Sliding his hands down over her bottom, he lifted her up and encouraged her to wrap her legs around his waist. "We'll start planning it all tomorrow. Right now... tell me more about this naked volleyball."

She laughed.

FROM THE AUTHOR

Thank you for reading *The Renegade Akseli Cyborg*. I hope you enjoyed Rachel and Wonick's story. I couldn't wait to write it after Wonick's conversation with Janwar at the end of *The Akseli*. And I had so much fun with this couple. If you enjoyed *The Akseli*, please consider rating or reviewing it at an online retailer of your choice. I am always thrilled when I see that one of my books made a reader or audiobook lover happy. Ratings and reviews are also an excellent way to recommend an author's books, create word of mouth, and help other readers find new favorites.

If this is the first Aldebarian Alliance book you've read, you can see firsthand how these daring women from Earth ended up in space in *The Lasaran*, Prince Taelon and Lisa's story. If you'd like to see how Simone met and fell in love with Janwar, their romantic and humor-filled adventure takes place in *The Akseli*. (I think their first meeting is my favorite of the series. You can find an excerpt on my website.) If you'd like to see *gifted one* Ava come into her own as a warrior, survive seemingly insurmountable odds, and fall in love with a man who can breathe underwater, you can find her story in *The Purveli. And* if you'd like to know more about Eliana, you can find her adventure in *The Segonian*, which *AudioFile Magazine* deemed one of the Best Audiobooks of 2021. You can also see the mischief Eliana got into back on Earth in *Broken Dawn*, part of my Immortal Guardians paranormal romance series.

ABOUT THE AUTHOR

Dianne Duvall is the *New York Times* and *USA Today* bestselling author of the Immortal Guardians, Aldebarian Alliance, and The Gifted Ones series. She is known for writing stories full of action that keeps readers flipping pages well past their bedtimes, strong heroes who adore strong heroines, lovable secondary characters, swoon-worthy romance, and humor that readers frequently complain makes them laugh out loud at inappropriate moments. *AudioFile Magazine* declared *The Segonian* (Aldebarian Alliance Book 2) one of the Best Audiobooks of 2021 and awarded it the AudioFile Earphones Award for Exceptional Audio. Audible chose *Awaken the Darkness* (Immortal Guardians Book 8) as one of the Top 5 Best Paranormal Romances of 2018.

Reviewers have called Dianne's books "fast-paced and humorous" (*Publishers Weekly*), "utterly addictive" (*RT Book Reviews*), "extraordinary" (*Long and Short Reviews*), and "wonderfully imaginative" (*The Romance Reviews*). Her audiobooks have been awarded AudioFile Earphone Awards for Exceptional Audio. One was nominated for a prestigious Audie Award. And her books have twice been nominated for RT Reviewers' Choice Awards.

When she isn't writing, Dianne is active in the independent film industry and has even appeared on-screen, crawling out of a moonlit grave and wielding a machete like some of the psychotic vampires she creates in her books.

For the latest news on upcoming releases, giveaways, and more, please visit www.DianneDuvall.com. You can also connect with Dianne online:

DIANNE DUVALL

Subscribe to Dianne's Newsletter
eepurl.com/hfT2Qn

Join *Dianne Duvall's Network Headquarters* on Facebook
www.facebook.com/groups/128617511148830

Follow Dianne on Amazon
www.facebook.com/DianneDuvallAuthor

Dianne's Blog
dianneduvall.blogspot.com

Facebook
www.facebook.com/DianneDuvallAuthor

Instagram
www.instagram.com/dianne.duvall

Twitter
twitter.com/DianneDuvall

Follow Dianne on BookBub
www.bookbub.com/authors/dianne-duvall

Pinterest
www.pinterest.com/dianneduvall

YouTube
bit.ly/DianneDuvall_YouTube

Printed in Great Britain
by Amazon